Hits & Mrs.

Hits & Mrs.

A NOVEL

Karen Stollznow

This is a work of fiction. All of the characters, organizations, and events portrayed in this novel are either products of the author's imagination or are used fictitiously.

Copyright © Karen Stollznow 2016

All rights reserved. No part of this publication may be reproduced, stored in a retrieval system, or transmitted, in any form or by any means, electronic, mechanical, photocopying, recording or otherwise, without the prior permission of the author.

Cover art by Matthew Baxter.

For Blade

"The manipulator knows that his mark will be inclined to try to make sense out of whatever he is told, no matter how farfetched or improbable. He knows, too, that people are generally self-centered, that we tend to have unrealistic views of ourselves, and that we will generally accept claims about ourselves that reflect not how we are or even how we really think we are but how we wish we were or think we should be. He also knows that for every several claims he makes about you that you reject as being inaccurate, he will make one that meets with your approval; and he knows that you are likely to remember the hits he makes and forget the misses."

The Skeptic's Dictionary

Contents

Chapter 1	11
Chapter 2	21
Chapter 3	31
Chapter 4	39
Chapter 5	50
Chapter 6	58
Chapter 7	68
Chapter 8	78
Chapter 9	84
Chapter 10	93
Chapter 11	101
Chapter 12	109
Chapter 13	118
Chapter 14	127
Chapter 15	137
Chapter 16	144
Chapter 17	148
Chapter 18	158
Chapter 19	168
Chapter 20	173
Chapter 21	181
Chapter 22	193
Chapter 23	202
Chapter 24	213
Chapter 25	222

Chapter 26	**234**
Chapter 27	**239**
Chapter 28	**244**
Chapter 29	**251**
Chapter 30	**259**
Chapter 31	**267**
Chapter 32	**278**
Chapter 33	**288**
Chapter 34	**296**
Chapter 35	**301**
Chapter 36	**304**
Chapter 37	**312**
Chapter 38	**321**

Chapter 1

"Your husband is here with us now," announced Gil Godsend in his deep, smooth voice. He opened his piercing blue eyes slowly and gazed across the table at his client. The curtains were drawn and the room was dark, but through the soft yellow light of the flickering candle he noticed tears welling up in the widow's sad brown eyes. He also noticed that from this angle he had a view of her firm cleavage peeking through the plunging neckline of her silken wrap dress.

"Mrs. Thompson, I validate my psychic readings for my clients by sharing information I couldn't possibly know if I wasn't in communication with their deceased loved ones," he said. He stared off into the distance as he tried to see across worlds. "I'm getting the name Al, Alan, or Alex..."

Kate Thompson's heart rate sped up at the mention of her husband's name.

"His name was Alex," she confirmed.

"That's right. Short for Alexander."

"Yes. But I only ever called him by his full name when we were having sex," she blurted out before she could stop herself. "He liked that," she explained as a hot blush crept up her neck. Gil looked at her kindly, as if to say that this was a safe place and there was no need for embarrassment.

"Alex tells me he's pleased to see you're wearing the diamond earrings he gave you for your third wedding anniversary," he said. In shock, Kate's hands rose instinctively to touch the chandelier earrings that glimmered as they dangled from her ears. "He was also honored when you wore them to his funeral."

She gasped. "How do you know all of these things?"

Gil grinned. "Aren't you here to see the world's best psychic medium?" he bragged with a charm that would have reeked of arrogance from anyone else. "I can hear and see your husband, Mrs. Thompson. He's here in the room with us," he said, waving his hand through the air.

"We psychics don't use crystal balls anymore."

Gil didn't use tarot cards, pendulums, or other psychic paraphernalia.

"Props are unnecessary bullshit. Real psychics don't need gimmicks," he liked to say. His house was filled with antiques and objets d'art rather than wind chimes, Himalayan salt lamps, and other new age knickknacks, with the exception of an enormous amethyst cluster. The magnificent natural crystal was proudly on display in the reading room where he received his clients. During a spiritual trip to Sri Lanka a Buddhist monk gave it to Gil as a gift and he cherished it. A jagged mass of vibrant violet crystals, it had an imposing phallic-shaped point thrusting out from the middle of the cluster. Gil found that his female clients always commented on his bulging purple crystal, and he saw Kate eyeing it at that moment. She looked a little embarrassed that she had been caught.

"I'm wearing one of your amethyst pendants," she said, directing his attention to the lilac-colored stone around her neck. The necklace was an item from Gil's popular line of Celestial Jewelry. He hadn't failed to see the pendant resting on her chest, rising and falling slowly as she breathed in and out.

"I see that," he nodded approvingly. "Did you know that amethyst is a variety of purple quartz that was once believed to be as precious as diamonds? That is, until large deposits were discovered in Brazil. The word *amethyst* comes from the Greek word *amethystos* that meant, "not intoxicated". In Ancient Greece, the gemstone was worn as an amulet to protect its wearer from drunkenness and people drank wine from amethyst cups in the belief that this would prevent intoxication. Today, amethyst is believed to be a healing crystal that can cure addiction. Placing it under your pillow at night is said to ward off insomnia and induce prophetic dreams." He fixed his eyes on her. "Amethyst is a 7 on the mohs scale of mineral hardness," he added.

How did Gil know all of this weird stuff? Kate wondered if he'd memorized this information from Wikipedia.

"No. I didn't know that," she said with a confused blink. "That's… very interesting."

"Let's get on with the reading," Gil said, as though she was the one who had interrupted the session. "Alex shows me that he passed about three years ago."

Kate nodded.

"He was just a young man when he died. I feel that he was in his early thirties."

"That's right. He was only 33-years-old."

Gil frowned and began massaging his forehead.

"I'm starting to get a headache." He squinted, closed his eyes and turned his head away. "My vision is blurred and my eyes are sensitive to light." His hands dropped to his stomach. "I'm not feeling so good." He took a few deep, calming breaths until the episode passed. Then he opened his eyes and looked straight at her. "Mrs. Thompson, I'm sensing that your husband died of a stroke or maybe an aneurysm?"

"Yes," Kate replied as she shut her eyes tightly in pain. "He died of a ruptured cerebral aneurysm." She couldn't hold back her grief any longer. Tears began streaming down her face as she recalled the day that changed her life. "It was sudden and I raced to see him as soon as I found out he was in the hospital…but it was too late. I…I never had the chance to say goodbye to him."

"But you *did*," Gil assured her. "Alex heard you say goodbye before he crossed over. He also felt your final kiss on his lips."

Kate remembered the last kiss she planted on Alex's cold, blue-tinged lips as she held his cool, clammy hands. She began sobbing uncontrollably.

Gil nudged a box of tissues across the table towards her and gave her this time to grieve. In his clients' eyes, Gil was a psychic medium who communicated with the dead, but he was also a spiritual counselor who offered comfort and peace of mind to the living. They saw him as a confidant and friend, albeit one who charges $1,000 an hour. Gil's psychic reading room became a confessional for sins, secrets, and skeletons in the closet. He had heard more personal stories and gossip than any psychologist, priest, or hairdresser. Crimes and affairs were common confessions, while one client even revealed she was an accomplice to a murder. She'd convinced her young lover to kill her husband for his insurance money so the two could run off to Fiji together.

Gil's clients feel like they can tell him anything, because he already knows.

With a final sniff, Kate collected herself and Gil continued.

"Alex wants you to know that he's okay now. There's no more pain. He doesn't want you to worry about him but he worries about *you*, being all alone by yourself in that big old house." Gil paused and then chuckled. "He's getting bossy! He has many chores for you to do around the home. You're to get the furnace and chimney inspected professionally. He wants you to test the smoke detectors and clean the leaves out of the gutters this fall. He also warns you of a possible problem with one of the toilets."

What she once saw as her husband's incessant nagging now cheered Kate up considerably. She'd happily put up with his whining now if it meant he was still alive.

"He thinks the garden needs some attention too, especially the plum trees he planted."

She pictured all of the fallen, rotting plums scattered across her backyard and resolved to rake them up as soon as she got home. Presented with all of these specific details about his personality, there was no doubt in Kate's mind that Gil was in contact with her dead husband.

"You're talking with Alex alright!" she said. "He was always such a practical man."

"Yes, he was practical," agreed Gil, "but he had his romantic side too. He's telling me right now that he likes the way you're wearing your hair today. He says this is the style you used to wear when the two of you went to a party."

Kate raised a hand to her upswept hair and wistfully ran a finger through one of her honey brown-colored ringlets, the way he used to do. The appointment with her hair stylist that morning had been worth the money. She wanted to look good for her husband, wherever he was.

"Mrs. Thompson," said Gil, "I hope I'm not overstepping any boundaries by saying this, but I agree with him."

She smiled shyly as that annoying blush crept up her neck again.

"Please, call me Kate."

She was still in mourning for her husband, but she was uncomfortably aware of the handsome man in the stylish navy blue suit sitting across from her.

Gil didn't have the appearance of a stereotypical psychic. There weren't any turbans, tie-dyed t-shirts, or capes in his closet. He wore suits, but he hated baggy, boxy, ill-fitting off-the-rack ones. Gil preferred the sartorial splendor of bespoke suits custom-made by tailors on London's Savile Row. He dressed more like a stockbroker or a fashion model than a mystic. He didn't carry an evil eye, wear chunky crystal rings on his fingers, or dangle a cheesy pentagram pendant around his neck, but he wore a limited edition platinum oyster perpetual Rolex watch on his left wrist. He didn't grow his hair long or sport a Merlin the wizard-like beard; his thick, chestnut brown hair was styled perfectly and he treated himself to a straight razor shave twice a week. Gil didn't smell of patchouli incense and sage smudge sticks like the psychics at the metaphysical fair. As he walked by he left a trail of expensive cologne lingering in the air.

"You know, I often think I'm smelling his cologne." Kate murmured as she inhaled the air deeply. "I swear, I can smell you right now Alex!" she called out to him.

"He enjoys it when you're alone and you talk to him," Gil said.

"Sometimes I think he talks back to me. I hear him whispering my name." She closed her eyes and shook her head. What's wrong with me? I think I'm going crazy!"

"You're not crazy," Gil insisted. "This is your intuition alerting you to the presence of your husband's spirit. Whenever you smell his scent, whenever you hear his voice, whenever you see him out of the corner of your eye, and all of those nights when you cry and think you can feel his touch on your skin...*he is there with you.*"

Kate stared into the mesmerizing glow of the candle flame. She thought about how lonely she felt every day as she wandered around the cold, empty house and jumped at shadows. There were constant reminders of him everywhere, his clothes, photographs of the two of them, and her memories. Most nights she dreamed he was still alive only to wake up with a start in a pool of sweat and remember that he was gone. She didn't know how much more she could take. Sometimes she wished she were gone too.

"I miss him so much. I don't think I'll ever be happy again until I'm reunited with him," she thought to herself but realized she'd said it out loud.

"He misses you too."

"Tell him I miss him every day!" she cried. "Tell him I've been faithful to him since he died! Tell him I ache for his touch! Tell him I need him!"

"He hears you, Kate," said Gil sympathetically. "He sees your pain. He wishes there was some way he could be here to comfort you." Gil fell silent. His expression went blank and he stared past her into nothingness. "No. I can't do that!" he yelled suddenly, seemingly talking to someone invisible. He shook his head. "No... I will NOT do that!" He locked eyes with Kate and said sternly, "I'm sorry, but we must end this session immediately."

She wasn't ready to be torn from her husband yet.

"Why?" she asked in a panic. "What's going on?"

"Your husband...he is a very persistent and passionate man, but what he's asked me to do goes beyond my job description," he said sternly.

"W-what's he saying to you?" she stammered. "Please tell me!"

Gil exhaled deeply.

"Your husband wants to use my body to be able to touch you again. But I simply can't put you in that...position," he said as he reached over and touched her hand gently.

Kate's eyes widened. "Really? You can do that?"

"Yes, I can," he replied. "I'm not only a psychic medium but I'm also a trance channeler. Channelers manifest spirits of the dead, but most can only allow spirit beings to speak through them. Spirits can not only speak through me, but also have full control over my body for short periods of time."

Then that meant...she could be with him one last time...

"Please, bring my husband back to me," she asked with a steely look in her eyes.

"No," he replied. "I won't do that."

"Why not?"

"I don't like to channel spirits because I can't control what happens when they take over my body," he explained. "I develop what's known as "psychic amnesia" and I won't have any memory of what takes place," he said with a frown. The idea of privacy appealed to the shy woman even more.

"Please," she pleaded as her body shook. "I *need* this..."

"It's a kind of possession. It could even be dangerous for you," Gil warned her.

"I can trust my husband!"

"I'm sorry but I just can't do it," he said firmly. "It's unethical."

"But I'm desperate!" she begged him with tears in her eyes.

"...I don't normally perform this service..."

"I'll pay more!"

Gil paused.

"I see how much this means to you..." He looked down at the floor. "Okay. I'll do it."

"Thank you! Thank you! Thank you!" Kate gushed in relief.

"I hope you don't regret this."

"I promise I won't!" she vowed. "How do we do this?"

Gil leaned in towards her and covered her hands with his.

"Here's how it works. I will create a psychic protection field to shield us from negative energy during the channeling. Then I'll grant permission to your husband's spirit and he will be able to use my body as a vessel. This means that he'll be able to see you, talk to you, and touch you through my body, just as if he were living. This is only a temporary state that usually lasts about an hour, and then he will have to cross over again. When he departs my body I'll be left feeling drained and depleted and will probably require a short nap. This time with him will be your own because I won't have any recollection of what transpired. Now...are you ready?"

"Yes..." she whispered nervously.

"Imagine a bright white light in front of you," Gil instructed. "Focus your mind on it. Imagine the light surrounding your whole body like a bubble. Now say to yourself, this light will protect me against psychic attacks and banish all negative energy. I am blessed with love and light. I am ready."

Kate mouthed the words to herself.

Gil closed his eyes and began breathing slowly and deeply. His rhythmic breaths made the candle flicker every time he breathed out until one powerful exhale blew out the flame. There was complete darkness and silence. Kate could only smell the smoke rising from the freshly snuffed candle. She sat there in the pitch-dark room for what seemed like minutes, her body trembling with excitement and terror at the same time. She had no idea what to expect.

She felt a gentle caress on her hand and she jumped. The hand moved teasingly up her arm to her shoulder. Then she felt her hair being softly stroked and a finger ran through one of her ringlets, *the way he used to do*. Two strong hands cupped her face.

"Alex?"

There was silence.

"Alex...is that you?"

"Yes, Sugarplum. It's me..."

It was *his* voice! This was *his* nickname for her! He pulled her towards him and she felt his soft lips on hers. They were warm, not cold like the last time. "I've missed you so much, Alexander!" she managed to gasp between feverish kisses.

"I've missed your body, baby," he said hungrily as he kissed away her tears of joy. She had so many questions to ask him. There were so many things she wanted to say, but there was no time for small talk about life and death; it was time to make love. He picked her up with ease and carried her off into the darkness. They reached a dimly lit bedroom and as they entered the door it felt just like it did when he carried her across the threshold on their wedding night. He laid her down gently on the enormous bed and slowly began unraveling her wrap dress. "I remember when I bought this dress for you to wear to that work Christmas party. I enjoyed taking it off you then too..."

She helped him undress and he climbed onto her, their bodies melting into each other. After three years of grief-imposed celibacy, it felt incredibly sexy to have a man on top of her again, his weight and size holding her down. She nuzzled her face into his neck as she breathed in his cologne. She'd never smelled his distinctive, spicy scent on any other man.

"Mmm. You smell so good, Alexander." His touch sent electricity through her entire body. "You feel so good too. I need you..."

"There's nothing more important to me than being able to touch you in this way again," he whispered in her ear.

They made love tenderly, like it was their first time together, although knowing it was their last. She soon felt her orgasm building up and she began screaming, "Alexander!" just like she'd always done in bed with him. She sang his name again and again as she came hard and fast, propelling him to join her.

"Katherine... I love you," he groaned as he drained himself deep inside of her. He wrapped his arms around her tightly and they fell into a deep sleep as their time together slowly ran out.

When Kate awoke she was naked in the bed between blue satin sheets, but alone. She quickly threw on her crumpled clothes and did her best to fix her tangled bed hair. She grabbed her high heels by their straps and navigated the maze of halls and rooms until she finally stumbled across the reading room. The mood was now completely different. The curtains were open and the room was brightly lit by sunshine, although Kate could see outside that the trees were swaying and their colored leaves were falling to the ground. She found Gil sitting at the table drinking a cup of coffee and leafing through the latest issue of *GQ*. She stood there in her wrinkled dress with her unruly hair, mascara stained cheeks and smeared red lipstick, while Gil looked as poised and polished as he did during the psychic session; just like a fashion model out of the magazine he was reading. She tiptoed into the room but he looked up instantly when her feet stepped on a creaky floorboard.

"Ah, Mrs. Thompson!" he greeted her enthusiastically but formally. "I hope my reading gave you a sense of comfort and closure."

"I-it d-did," she spluttered, unable to make eye contact with him. She kept reminding herself that he couldn't possibly know what had just happened. "I can't tell you how much it meant to me. Thank you for bringing my husband back to me."

"The pleasure was all mine," Gil said with a grin. He stood up from his seat and approached her. "I have another client who'll be coming here soon, so please allow me to show you out." He placed his hand on the small of her back and ushered her towards the door.

As they walked together she said, "Mr. Godsend, my husband died three years ago and I've spent that entire time on your waiting list for a private reading."

"I apologize," he said. "I'm glad I could finally fit you in. My waiting list is long, but I always make time for urgent readings such as this. Here's my business card with my direct phone number."

She exchanged this with her payment for the session. Gil took the check from her shaking hand and as she threw on her shoes his eyes flickered down momentarily to ensure that the amount was correct. He typically requested a "donation" of $1,000 per hour for his private readings. Kate had written a check for double this amount.

"Thank you and goodbye, Mrs. Thompson. Call me."

"Goodbye, Mr. Godsend."

As she stepped outside an icy cold gust of air hit her face and the afterglow flush disappeared from her cheeks. She suddenly felt alone, like she'd lost Alex all over again. Then a jolt of realization struck her. In five years of marriage, her husband had *never* called her "Katherine".

Chapter 2

Author Gem Forrest was invited to spend three weeks with Gil Godsend to experience his lifestyle and mission. Gil had been somewhat of an enigma to the public, so he welcomed Forrest into his home in San Rafael, California, where she had the opportunity to observe his psychic readings with clients, meditate with him, and take long walks with Gil to discuss his philosophies about life and death, and the beyond. During their time together, he shared his life story with Gem, which she retells in the authorized biography *21 Days with Gil Godsend*.

According to the book, Gil Faulkner grew up in Sebastopol, California, a city known as The Gravenstein Apple Capital of the World. His parents owned a large farm where they grew apples, cherries, and berries. The family had a roll-up-your-sleeves, old-fashioned work ethic and the young Gil picked raspberries from the field and helped his mother make jams and bake pies for their roadside farm store. Year after year, Mrs. Faulkner was the winner of the Best Apple Pie award at the Sebastopol Apple Fair. Her secret was to poach the apples in spiced orange juice before baking the pie.

Gil became aware of his psychic gift at an early age. Even as a young boy he didn't see eye to eye with his parents, but he was very close to his father's sister, Tillie, who had a deep interest in the supernatural. When he was 10-years-old, Aunt Tillie introduced Gil to the occult. One day his mother discovered him playing with a Ouija board when he should have been canning blackberries. He was sent to bed without dinner, although later that night his mother sneaked into his room with a slice of strawberry rhubarb pie.

A year later, Aunt Tillie was diagnosed with a rare and aggressive form of thyroid cancer. She was dying. Gil and his aunt began holding lengthy conversations about spirituality and the after life. She promised him that after she died she would return to enlighten him about the other side. Merely months after her diagnosis, Aunt Tillie died. She passed at home in her sleep at 2am so Gil wasn't there to say his final farewell. Instead, she appeared to him by his bedside and said, "Goodbye Gil, but just for now. I will return."

And she did return. Aunt Tillie started reappearing to Gil daily to continue schooling him in the supernatural and to bring him revelations from the other side. One morning, his mother was distraught because her antique string of pearls had vanished. She tore the house apart searching for them, but to no avail. The family had a maid who cleaned the house on Wednesdays, and she accused the woman of stealing them. She was about to report the necklace as missing to the police when Aunt Tillie's ghost appeared to Gil and revealed their whereabouts. "The string of pearls is in a box of tissues underneath the passenger seat in your car," he told his mother. Gil was accused of hiding them as a prank and he was grounded for two weeks.

Gil continued to make predictions based on the information his Aunt Tillie shared with him from beyond the grave. At first, these seemed like good guesses to his parents, but they became concerned when his visions became too specific, and too accurate. One night his parents were watching television when there was breaking news about a 6-year-old girl who had gone missing from her home in San Francisco. The girl's disappearance was a complete mystery. Gil wandered into the room as they were discussing the incident and he assured them, "Don't worry, in two days she'll be found alive in an abandoned building near her home." Sure enough, the little girl was discovered two days later in a derelict factory, right near her home.

One evening during dinner, Gil and his parents were eating in their usual uncomfortable silence. All that could be heard was the scraping sound of silverware grating on crockery. In order to avoid eating his Brussels sprouts, Gil decided it was the right time to ask about a family secret, and not his mother's secret to baking winning apple pies.

"Why didn't you ever tell me that I had a twin brother named Will?" he blurted out. His father choked on his lamb shank while his mother began crying. It was true. Will died of pneumonia at six months of age and they never talked about him again.

When he'd dislodged the offending chunk of lamb from his throat his father demanded, "How did you know about that? While we're at it, how did you know that Uncle Jim was adopted, that your cousin Michael is gay, and that Grandpa has Alzheimer's? How did you know these things before they did? How do you know everything about everybody before anyone else?"

"Aunt Tillie told me," Gil said to their astonishment.

Gil began having encounters with other spirits too. Attending a school excursion to Alcatraz, he was startled by the spirit of a prisoner who asked him for a cigarette through the bars of his cell. During a trip to the hospital to see Grandpa, in the next room Gil saw the spirit of an elderly man who had just died and was gazing sadly at his own corpse. When he was at the cemetery visiting Aunt Tillie, he saw the spirit of a strange woman staring at him as she stood over her freshly covered grave. At first, he thought that everyone could see these spirits. Then he realized that he had a special gift that few others had. Soon, Gil began seeing spirits everywhere he went. He discovered that if he paid attention they could communicate with him using pictures, words, sounds, and smells. Then he discovered that he could talk back to them…

Knowing that they had a link back to the earthly realm through Gil, these spirits begged him to deliver messages to their loves ones. And he did. He startled a widower in a supermarket by telling him that his deceased wife was angry he was buying that bottle of whiskey. He embarrassed his schoolteacher by revealing that her Catholic mother was disappointed with her for taking birth control pills, and for having sex with a Jewish man. He horrified Reverend Jones by divulging to the congregation that the clergyman had a crush on Mrs. Faulkner. Now everyone knew why Mrs. Faulkner kept winning those awards for her pies because the Reverend was the judge of the competition each year.

Gil was popular with his school friends for telling their fortunes, but unpopular with their parents for exposing their embarrassing secrets. At Tommy Cook's birthday party, Mr. Cook was furious when Gil informed Mrs. Cook that her husband was having an affair with his large-breasted secretary. Mrs. Cook was furious when Gil then informed Mr. Cook that Tommy wasn't his biological son.

The biography says that Gil sees spirits wherever he goes, but he also has a number of spirit guides to help him through life and assist him in his readings. Aunt Tillie is his chief guide and she introduced him to his guides from the other side, his twin brother Will, and a man named Oleg.

Oleg had lived in the town of Voskresensk, Russia, during the

19th century. Raised in poverty and living as a vagrant, he became a pickpocket as a child. Over his lifetime he was guilty of poaching, burglary, and many other crimes. When Oleg passed, his spirit lingered in the void because of the pain he caused other people during his lifetime. When he learned to experience remorse he finally crossed over to the light, and his spirit became dedicated to atoning for his wrongdoings. After a life spent in making people lose things, through Gil, Oleg can now help people find things they'd lost. At least, this is the story that Gil told his parents.

Initially, his parents referred to the spirits as Gil's "imaginary friends". They were staunch Christians and didn't believe that Gil's gift was of God. They feared Satan was deceiving him. They quoted the Bible at him, and warned him against wizardry and necromancy. Then, a framed tapestry of Leviticus 19:31 was hung over the mantelpiece: "Do not turn to mediums or spiritists; do not seek them out to be defiled by them. I am the LORD your God."

Gil began reading the Bible, much to his parent's delight, until he discovered Revelation 1:3: "Blessed is he who reads and those who hear the words of the prophecy." In defiance, he took a pencil and scrawled this verse on a piece of paper and taped it over the tapestry. When Gil was 16, his mother found him in her bed with the maid one Wednesday afternoon. Pre-marital sex was even worse than conjuring the dead, and it was then that his parents became convinced that Gil was possessed by a demon. They dragged him to church and insisted that he be exorcised. Reverend Jones was only too happy to oblige, although during the exorcism he got a black eye from Gil's "demon". The exorcism didn't seem successful. Mrs. Faulkner didn't win the award for Best Apple Pie that year and Gil continued to communicate with spirits, and sleep with the maid.

It was at this time that Gil started to have trouble in high school. He was always an extremely intelligent boy who had a remarkable encyclopedic knowledge of many topics, but he was easily bored. He stopped doing his homework and then he stopped going to school. The principal called Mr. and Mrs. Faulkner into school one day for a serious talk. They learned that Gil wasn't turning up to school for anything other than art class, and that was only because he was having an affair with his art teacher, Mrs. Grant. He had also beaten up his history teacher, Mr. Grant. Gil was expelled.

Teenagers are too old to have imaginary friends, and non-Catholic psychiatrists don't believe in demons, so at the age of 18 his parents decided Gil's gift was a mental disorder. During a mental health evaluation he was diagnosed with schizophrenia and shuffled off to a psychiatric institution for six months. He soon learned to tell his doctors exactly what they wanted to hear; he was no longer seeing spirits or hearing voices. Those were just hallucinations and delusions. He was cured. But he was furtively disposing of his antipsychotic medication and mood-stabilizers using a slight-of-hand trick. When the doctors were off-duty for the night, Gil was still giving psychic readings to the nurses who smuggled alcohol into his room and dragged him off to the padded cell to have sex with him.

When Gil was released from the hospital he didn't return home. Now that they were getting older, his parents had expected him to come back to the farm to take over the family business. He refused, saying that he didn't care about jam and pies; he wanted to become a professional psychic medium. His mother and father were inconsolable. First they had lost Will, and now Gil. To this day, he is estranged from his parents.

Without the spiritual oppression of his parents, Gil was now free to pursue his psychic destiny. But his career had inauspicious beginnings. He traveled to Berkeley, California, where he became just another psychic reader on Telegraph Avenue. He read palms, tarot cards, and rune stones. His penniless clientele consisted mostly of students asking, "Will I pass my exams this semester?" instead of studying, and hippies asking, "When will we have world peace, man?" One regular was a stoner who always asked Gil to perform divination using the loose marijuana he'd just bought on the street. No longer a cheap refuge for starving artists, Gil ended up joining Berkeley's burgeoning homeless population, where he often worked in exchange for food, beer, or a couch to crash on for the night. Gil considered his time living down and out as his homage to the poverty experienced by his spirit guide Oleg.

When he was 22, Gil worked for a telephone psychic hotline in Los Angeles. He spent a year finding lost pets, advising people how to find a new job, and telling women when they'll meet Mr. Right. Answering questions about relationships, career, and money was his bread and butter, although that sandwich amounted to cents on the dollar. Gil often worked the graveyard shift when the psychic infomercials ran on television, which would invariably bring an influx of gamblers demanding, "What are these week's lotto numbers?" or potheads asking esoteric questions such as, "What's the meaning of life?"

It was usually after 1am when drunken women would call and ask through their tears, "How do I win back my ex?" or "Is he cheating on me?" These same women then told Gil he had a sexy sounding voice and propositioned him for phone sex. He later discovered that many telephone psychics were former phone sex operators or doing both jobs at the same time to make ends meet. Worse still, the company's other psychics were simply reading from scripts. These experiences left him feeling bitter and disillusioned with the commercial psychic industry. He even considered going home to face the music and take over the family farm. However, Aunt Tillie appeared in a dream and told him to hang in there. One day very soon he would become world famous for his psychic abilities.

"It's always darkest before the dawn," she said.

With few options left, Gil decided to join the psychic fair circuit at age 23. He traveled across California with a troop of psychics attending a different fair each weekend. He enjoyed the travel, and the attention of the throngs of hot hippie women, but he didn't like the image enforced by the event organizers. His female colleagues wore gypsy clothes, headscarves, and hoop earrings, while he was expected to wear a puffy satin shirt and a turban, complete with a feather and a fake jewel like he was something out of a Zoltar fortuneteller machine.

"Why can't I do my job without wearing a tacky outfit?" he asked his boss.

"Because your clients expect you to dress like a psychic," came the reply. Gil learned that appearances were more important than talent. Many of the people he worked with looked the part, but they didn't have psychic abilities at all. They simply had the gift of the gab and concealed their lack of talent with costumes, crystal balls and other gimmicks. Gil resolved to reject the stereotypical image of psychics. He stumbled across a second-hand Armani suit in a thrift store and this became his uniform.

He was fired.

Aunt Tillie convinced him to take a job doing psychic readings for customers at a coffee shop in Santa Barbara. He worked there for a year although it didn't seem like much of a job until one morning when Gil was honored to give a reading to television psychic Celeste Stone. She was impressed with his accuracy and said, "You're good. If you want to be the best, call me." He called her that afternoon. That night he demonstrated his talents to her, and the next day he moved into her beachside home. Celeste became his mentor and nurtured his psychic gifts. Some 35 years older than him, she also became his sugar mama. She indulged his taste for haute couture clothing, good food, and fine wine, and he indulged her taste for younger men.

Under Celeste's tutelage, with the help of his spirit guides, and unfettered by psychic trappings, Gil was able to hone his natural abilities. He discovered that he had many metaphysical skills. As a psychic medium he could communicate with spirits, and as a channeler he could actually manifest the dead in physical form. Spirits could talk through him. As a psychic he had the gift of past, present, and future sight. As a spiritual counselor and teacher he could educate people about the paranormal and counsel them in their crises. As an empath and medical intuitive he could diagnose disease in people. He doesn't like to call himself a spiritual healer; genuine healers never do, although people reported experiencing healings, miracles, and life transformations in his presence. At this time he left Celeste, when he realized he was more spiritually advanced than she was, but it suited her because she realized she wanted to upgrade to a newer model.

Taking advantage of the contacts he made through Celeste, Gil landed a late night gig with radio station KNOW in Santa Barbara. On *Insight* he talked about a variety of self-help paranormal subjects, including psychic development, exploring past lives, and dream interpretation. A favorite segment of listeners was when he predicted the news for the following day. He always did a better job than the weatherman. The show had a steady stream of callers hoping to hear from their deceased loved ones. One night a widow called into the show. Her husband had an urgent message for her; she needed to visit a doctor immediately. He wanted to see her again, but it wasn't her time yet and she was sick. The woman called back the following week. She'd seen a specialist who diagnosed her with heart disease, but her condition had been detected just days before it became life threatening.

"Gil is a godsend!" she praised him. From that moment on, Gil Faulkner became known as Gil Godsend.

Gil got his big break when he gave an impromptu psychic reading to a producer who recognized him in a Los Angeles bar. The man asked about the success of his next reality TV series *Booobs!*, a paranormal show in which ghost hunters investigate haunted places in the nude. Yes, the show was going to have a successful run on Spike TV, but during the reading a relative kept butting in with an important message from beyond.

"Uncle Larry is sorry for molesting you all of those years," Gil revealed.

The producer didn't say a single word, but handed Gil his business card. Three months later he became the star of his own TV show, *Between Heaven and Earth with Gil Godsend*.

The show was filmed in front of a live studio audience and Gil gave readings to members of the crowd. On other TV shows, psychic mediums play a game of charades and make the audience do all of the work by asking, "Who is 'K'?" or "Who likes surfing?" Their messages from the dead are vague and ambiguous. But Gil was known for his astonishing accuracy. He provided incredible detail in his readings, which people validated in interviews afterwards. The show also followed him outside of the studio as he gave spontaneous readings to strangers in the supermarket, in restaurants, and on the street. After one year, Gil became producer of the show, which was aired across the United States, and in Canada, the U.K., Australia, and New Zealand.

Between Heaven and Earth propelled Gil to stardom. He became a personal psychic to celebrities, politicians, and other high-profile clients. He earned the reputation of being a psychic to his fellow psychics; he was a psychic's psychic. Gil was a frequent guest on numerous radio and television shows and was invited to lecture at universities and for Fortune 500 corporations. The Texas Rangers and other law enforcement agencies enlisted his help as a psychic detective for his expertise in cracking cold cases, although he keeps his involvement in these confidential.

As *21 Days With Gil Godsend* shows, Gil's is a true rags to riches story of a man who went from a modest family upbringing to living on the streets, to fame and fortune. He moved back to NorCal where he bought a palatial six-bedroom home in the lush green hills of San Rafael complete with a library, sauna, and an air-conditioned wine cellar. By the tender age of 30 Gil had already enjoyed a distinguished career. But he realized that his loyal fans, people who desperately needed psychic readings with him, faced a long five-year wait. After six seasons, Gil quit his show so that he could focus on private readings and writing. He penned the books *Peeking Through the Veil*, *Psychic Confessions*, and the *New York Times* bestseller *Between Heaven and Earth*. His latest title is *Messages From The Other Side*, which he's currently promoting on a nationwide tour.

Psychics are always under attack from nonbelievers and Gil has his share of rabid critics. Over the years, many skeptics have tried to debunk and discredit him. He's been branded a con artist, a charlatan, and a fraud that preys on people's vulnerability and grief. In particular, professional skeptic Claudia Cox is his long-term nemesis who has tried and failed to expose him on numerous occasions. She argues that Gil uses magic tricks in his readings and only pretends to have psychic abilities. Gil staunchly denies these claims. It's important to mention that Claudia and Gil were once lovers, and she only started attacking him after he broke up with her. Hell hath no fury like a woman scorned…

Skeptics say, "Extraordinary claims require extraordinary proof" and Gil provides that extraordinary proof with his validation. Through him, the spirits validate readings for his clients with highly specific details, to prove that he is in communication with their deceased loved ones. He boasts 99% accuracy in his readings and his psychic skills have been confirmed by numerous laboratory studies.

Gil insists, "I'm not here to prove to the skeptics that psychics are real". He always invites his audience to make up their own minds about the paranormal with his catch phrase, "Do psychic powers exist? It's up to *you* to decide…"

Rather than wasting his time arguing with skeptics, Gil focuses his energy on those who truly need him. There are many people who are in mourning and craving closure and reassurance that their friends and family are doing well on the spirit side. Gil is a bridge from the physical world to those on other planes of life, and he helps both the dead and the living to find peace. He also advises people who are searching for guidance and support in their daily lives.

Gil Godsend has touched the lives of millions of people around the world, and inspired them with his wisdom, joy, and love.

Chapter 3

As she slept, Claudia Cox dreamed she was the host of a tacky television game show. The stage looked like a newscast set in drag with its sequined gold curtains, plastic palm trees, and flashing neon lights. The contestants were male "celebrities" from the previous decade who were greedily demanding their second fifteen minutes of fame. They knew that any appearance on television offered them the possibility of a role on a reality TV show. The contestants were all drunk, and in trying to outdo each other for attention they used cheesy pick up lines on her as they pounded their buzzers incessantly. Claudia gradually began to wake up and in her grogginess she realized that the "buzzer" was actually her cell phone buzzing with text messages. Then she remembered the events of the night before.

She was drinking a glass of red wine in a fashionable bar in the mid-Market area of San Francisco. Wearing a figure-hugging black sheath dress with peep toe pumps and showing a bit of leg, it wasn't long before an inebriated businessman approached and hit on her. He bought her another cabernet sauvignon, which also bought him time to bore her with stories about his new Lamborghini. She thought he was sleazy, egotistical, and obnoxious, and that he suffered a rampant case of halitosis, but when he asked for her phone number she gave it to him eagerly and accompanied by a charming smile. It was her job. No, she wasn't an escort or a prostitute. Claudia was the owner of *Suspicious Minds*, a private detective agency that specializes in spouse surveillance. That is, catching cheating partners. This guy was her target.

Distrustful wives and husbands rifle through their significant other's phones, emails, credit card statements and bank accounts looking for telltale signs of marital infidelity. Claudia's clients make a pre-emptive strike against adultery instead. Her agency spies on spouses and puts them to the test. If given the opportunity, would they cheat? Her clientele consisted mostly of women who suspected that their men were cheating, or were at least capable of having an affair. These were wives and girlfriends, and even competitive mistresses who feared the men they were cheating with were also cheating on them. Most often, their suspicions were correct. Claudia had a stunning stable of decoys to appease the taste of every type of cheater; gorgeous blondes, brunettes, redheads, and raven-haired ladies of all different shapes, sizes, and ethnicities. The chosen decoy would have a "chance" encounter with the target, flirt shamelessly with him, and then offer her phone number. If the guy accepted her number, or worse still, called or texted her, he failed the fidelity test.

Claudia had already received nine text messages from last night's creep. It must have been some kind of record.

10:09 PM Hey baby. It was great meeting you tonight.
10:34 PM You looked so fucking hot in that little black dress, baby.
11:12 PM I should be fucking that tight little pussy of yours right now.
11:56 PM Good night, baby.
2:32 AM Are you awake, baby? Call me if you want some phone fun.
5:47 AM Good morning, baby.
6:28 AM Hey baby. It was great meeting you last night.
7:03 AM Are you free for breakfast this morning, baby?
8:38 AM Hey baby. Are you free for lunch?

Claudia needed to eat breakfast and then call the guy's wife to reveal that her husband had come onto her and sent her dirty text messages all night long. Unlike most other clients, this woman wouldn't be devastated by the news of his attempted infidelity. In fact, he'd cheated on her before with an intern at work. His wife caught him red-handed. She'd stopped by his office to bring him his lunch but found a naked woman spread-eagled across his desk. He was down on his knees already eating something else... Surprising their friends and family, the couple reconciled and formed a pact that if he was unfaithful just one more time, it was over. She knew he would cheat again but she didn't want to wait for that to happen. She wanted a divorce immediately, and she wanted her husband's money. Now she was going to get it.

Claudia's phone buzzed with a tenth text from the asshole.

9:11 AM "Baby?"

"Oh, for fuck's sake," Claudia huffed. So, she needed to eat breakfast, call the guy's wife, and then buy a new burner phone so he couldn't text her anymore.

Claudia had a full day of investigative work across the San Francisco Bay Area. Her morning would be spent flirting with a personal trainer at a gym in Novato to see if he became too personal during their chest pull stretches. Her afternoon would be spent viewing a house in Sausalito and asking playfully if real estate brokers ever have sex in empty properties. Her evening would be spent luring an architect in a Sunnyvale sushi restaurant to see if he would take the bait. Her night would be spent "accidentally" bumping into a doctor at a pub in Emeryville to see if he was wearing his wedding ring or if he'd "misplaced" it again.

Claudia was an attractive woman with long, wavy auburn hair and hazel eyes that captivated people. They changed color depending on what she was wearing, as hazel eyes do, but most of the time they were a fiery amber color with flecks of gold. As a professional prick teaser, she needed to stay in shape. She worked out at the gym six days a week and maintained a strict diet. As part of her beauty routine she had a blowout twice a week, and she enjoyed weekly manicures, bi-weekly pedicures, and monthly facials. She had regular massages and tried all of the latest, craziest spa treatments, whether it was a bee venom facial or one of those pedicures where the tiny fish nibble the dead skin off your feet.

Claudia spent most of her income on clothing, shoes, jewelry, and other accessories. Most of her targets were high net worth individuals who worked in banking and finance, so she had to look the part of a successful businesswoman, although she was often mistaken for a model or a high-class escort. She didn't like the fact that her job was often likened to that of a prostitute, without the sex part, although that was a crucial distinction in her eyes.

Claudia made herself a hearty breakfast of steel cut oats topped with sliced almonds and drizzled with honey, and she sat down at her laptop to check her emails. She opened her inbox and immediately deleted a discount offer for Viagra and a business proposition from a Bolivian

Prince. As she looked at the few remaining legitimate emails, one stood out like the flashing neon lights in her dream.

The subject title said: Gil Godsend.

"Oh, for fuck's sake..." she said as she closed her eyes and shook her head. There was a blast from the past she'd rather forget. She opened the email reluctantly.

Dear Ms. Cox,
A week ago I had a private reading with psychic medium Gil Godsend. Something strange happened during that session. Since that time, I've been reading your articles and I think you might be able to help me.
Can we meet?

Yours Sincerely,

Kate Thompson.

Before she became a private detective, Claudia had been what the media like to call a "professional skeptic", whatever that is. She was a journalist who wrote about the paranormal, but there wasn't a qualification or any training for what she did. She investigated all kinds of strange phenomena; haunted houses, UFOs, Bigfoot, and psychics. Claudia got her start in the game when she finished college and started an internship with a science magazine. After covering boring science fairs for a few weeks, one day her editor asked her to become a paranormal spy. Like a kind of modern-day Mata Hari, without the exotic dancing, she went undercover and infiltrated cults, psychic hotlines, and other shady operations to expose their scams. As a result, she became deeply involved in a movement known as skepticism, although she wasn't a cynic like the bald fat old men you see on TV who debunk everything. She was truly fascinated by the supernatural. She wished that ghosts, aliens, and psychic powers were real, but to her, there just wasn't any convincing evidence to say they do exist.

It was during this time that Claudia met Gil at a metaphysical fair in Monterey. She noticed the handsome young man as they were both browsing a shop that sold crystal ornaments and jewelry. She admired a pretty amethyst crystal pendant, and admired Gil's ass, before she walked away. A few minutes later Gil caught up with her. He had bought her the amethyst pendant. They began talking and walked around the fair together, laughing at the women psychics in their gypsy clothes and the men in their puffy satin shirts and turbans, who looked like something out of a Zoltar fortuneteller machine. Then he invited her to a coffee shop. Over a latte she discovered that Gil was clever, funny, and a psychic medium. It was lust at first sight and the two of them went back to his place.

Sure, Gil was a psychic medium, but she wasn't prejudiced against those with different beliefs to her, especially if they were good looking. If anything, their differences in opinion led to some intense discussions, and when they argued, which was often, some hot make-up sex afterwards. There was even the occasional moment when she wondered if he might be truly psychic, such as the time she modeled her new leather jacket for him and he asked, "Why did you buy that jacket today? It goes on sale next Tuesday."

She never quite knew if that was true psychic insight, or if he had fashion insider information about the sale because he was such a metrosexual.

Claudia and Gil dated for about a year. After months of territory marking, where he left his ties and cufflinks at her place and she left lipsticks and mascara at his place, they moved into an apartment together in Santa Barbara. They were blissfully happy for a while, although their dinner parties were known for catastrophic, alcohol-fueled fights between skeptics and believers. For a few months they were even engaged. Gil proposed to her with an engagement plant instead of a ring. The potted plant was a white peace lily that they kept on a tabletop in their kitchen. As Gil put it romantically, the plant was to "watch their love grow", but instead it withered and died. Claudia tried not to see this as a sign. She realized they had such opposing beliefs that the relationship wasn't ever going to work out, despite the fact that Gil believed they had been married in a previous life and Aunt Tillie had told him that Claudia was crucial to his success and happiness.

Claudia broke up with him.

Gil was a nice guy and she would have stayed with him if only he'd been a teacher or a nurse, instead of a psychic medium. He begged Claudia to come back to him, and she almost gave in because she still loved him. In the end, she made the decision to move on with her life and she consoled herself with a hunky firefighter from Fresno. Gil distracted himself with an endless string of married women and widows.

Little did Claudia know that Gil was on the cusp of success. Suddenly he was calling himself Gil Godsend, and he had his own television show, *Between Heaven and Earth with Gil Godsend*. His face was plastered everywhere. He was interviewed on radio and television chat shows. His books were on the bestsellers lists and piles of them were stacked high in stores where he did signings for lines of giggling women. Claudia soon found herself in the uncomfortable position where she was assigned to investigate Gil's psychic abilities. She pleaded to be relieved of the duty because her former connection to him was an obvious conflict of interest, but she was pressured into the work. They wanted her on the job because she had the lowdown on him. She hated having to read her ex-boyfriend's books, watch hours of footage from his psychic readings, and wear silly disguises to hide from him when she was forced to attend his public performances.

Claudia wrote dozens of articles exposing Gil as a charlatan. She showed how he used simple parlor tricks that can be replicated by magicians, who do them better... She pointed out that there was a disclaimer at the end of Gil's TV shows that admitted his psychic readings were "for entertainment purposes only". She revealed that his inaccurate readings were spliced together to make them seem accurate or they were edited out entirely. She explained that people only pay attention to the times he seemed to be accurate in his readings - the hits, but they tend to ignore his mistakes - the misses.

On many occasions, she caught Gil when he made embarrassing errors in his readings. There was the time he told a woman she would be pregnant within six months, but she divulged that she had just undergone a hysterectomy. Another time he spoke about a man's cravings for seafood, but the guy said that he suffered a severe shellfish allergy. His worst gaffe was when he predicted that a teenage girl was dead, but she was soon found to be alive and well. She was hiding from her parents and had taken a job as a stripper at a nightclub in Las Vegas.

Gil tried to weasel out of his error by saying that her parents were so embarrassed by her behavior that she was "dead" to them.

Claudia was seen as an expert on Gil Godsend by the media. She was invited to do radio and television interviews to talk about why she didn't believe he was psychic although most interviewers didn't care to hear what she had to say. "Skeptic" is a dirty word, and she was accused of being negative, closed-minded, and cynical. She tried to talk about how much damage Gil did to people who were grieving for their dead loved ones, but most audiences just wanted to know the juicy gossip about Gil. When she was dating Gil did he always predict what she was about to say? What was he like in bed? *He* dumped *her*, right? Surely it wasn't the other way around...

Claudia didn't have sour grapes over a relationship that went bad. It was her job to be skeptical about the paranormal, and Gil Godsend's claims in particular, although she was accused of being a biased bitch by his followers. It didn't matter how many "gotchas" Claudia uncovered about Gil, his zealous fans made excuses for him and attacked her. They set up hate websites that mocked her and she received hate mail daily. One psycho fan sent her handwritten death threats in sympathy cards mailed from all around the country and she had to report the matter to the police.

By this time she was seriously over skepticism. The movement was a viper's den of malicious factions. The few leaders of the movement considered themselves to be celebrities. These were the geeks who were picked on by bullies in high school. Now they were big fish in a small pond but they didn't know how to play well with others. As a token female in the community, Claudia found some skeptical men to be sleazier than her client's husbands. They delighted in accusing famous psychics, evangelists, and self-help gurus of abuses, but they were hypocrites who were oblivious to their own failings. The skeptical movement suffered many scandals of misogyny, harassment, and financial mishandlings. There were some good people around, but they drifted away from all of the drama. Feeling bitter and disillusioned, Claudia broke up with skepticism too.

She quit her job and moved to San Francisco where she found herself a nice little apartment in Hayes Valley, with the emphasis on *little*.
Claudia discovered that her investigative journalism skills

translated well to private investigation, and she got herself a job working as a decoy in spouse surveillance for a detective agency. She eventually founded her own business that became quite successful. Claudia was happy and fulfilled, for the most part. She was still looking for a man, but who wasn't looking for a man in San Francisco?

Seeing Gil's name after all of these years felt like a poison seeping throughout her body. Claudia felt sorry for this Kate Thompson but she didn't want to get involved. She ignored the woman's email. Gil was her past. Skepticism was her past. And she didn't want to revisit either again. Gil even emailed her a few years ago. She was surprised to find that this wasn't to criticize her for what she did to him, but just to say "hello" and to see how she was doing.

She never replied.

Claudia dressed in a pair of low-rise capri pants and a revealing sports bra and left for her "date" with the personal trainer at the gym.

Chapter 4

Rainbow Woods didn't want to host one of those boring Tupperware parties or a lingerie party, she wanted a psychic party instead. She sprang for a group reading with psychic medium Gil Godsend at her place. It cost her a small fortune. She wanted to make the most of it, so all of her friends were going to be there, and her sisters Sunshine and Breeze. Yes, their parents were flower children during the 1960s. Their mother Daisy was one of Ken Kesey's Merry Pranksters, the group who traveled around the country introducing people to LSD at their infamous Acid Tests. Daisy was such an expert in free love that the three sisters each had a different father. Their hippy names seemed groovy at the time, but today they made the three middle-aged women feel silly. The saying goes, don't trust anyone over 30, but you had to trust people over 30 when you were in your 50s. And if Rainbow's father didn't stop shaking the cage and start working for the man she wouldn't be living in a nice house in Tiburon. The place was no commune. It had six bedrooms and panoramic views of the Golden Gate Bridge and the San Francisco Bay.

The doorbell rang but Rainbow wasn't expecting her guests for at least another hour. She opened the door thinking she'd find those damn Mormon missionaries again, but instead Gil Godsend stood on her doorstep. He was even more strikingly handsome than he appeared on television. He towered over Rainbow who looked him up and down until she realized that she'd been caught in the act. She also realized she was only wearing makeup and a bathrobe. She looked like she was straight out of a scene in a bad British comedy where the bored housewife has sex with the milkman while he's on his rounds of the neighborhood.

"Hello, Mrs. Woods," Gil said in his deep, smooth voice.

A fantasy flashed through her mind in which Gil pushed her up against the wall, pressed his body against hers, and kissed her passionately. Her husband passed away eight years ago and it had been far too long since she'd been with a man.

"Mr. Godsend, I didn't expect to see you standing there!" she managed to splutter as a blush spread across her face. He was psychic. He could probably read her dirty mind.

"Well, I have a magnificent view from here, Mrs. Woods."

Did he just say what she thought he said? He must have meant the view from the house. Then she noticed that she was flashing a thigh through her parted robe.

"Thank you!" she said, still gawking at him as he stood waiting on the porch.

"Um…May I come inside?" Gil asked.

Rainbow looked at him lustfully as she contemplated that possibility. Then she finally snapped out of her daydream.

"Oh, of course! The guests haven't arrived yet. Let me give you a tour of the place."

She grabbed him by the arm and showed him the lagoon-shaped swimming pool and inbuilt spa that overlooked the Bay. "Clothing optional", she said cheekily. She took Gil into her library where she had a shelf full of his books. She led him down into the basement to the bar room where he broke free from her grasp and made a beeline for the snooker table.

"That's a Burroughs and Watts billiard table!" he gasped as he ran his hands over the green baize. "Such exquisite craftsmanship." He inspected the table closely. "You know, I think this particular model was once owned by Queen Victoria at Osborne House on the Isle of Wight."

"That's right!" Rainbow confirmed.

Wow! This guy sure knew his antiques.

"Prince Albert was a keen player," said Gil who hadn't taken his eyes off the table.

"Are you a player too?" she asked with mock innocence.

Gil looked up at her and grinned.

"I've played a few rounds in my time," he said as he picked up a red pool ball and held it up to the light. "These handmade ivory balls are superb!" he enthused. "They're the perfect shape, color, and weight, without any cracks or chips."

Rainbow liked a man who knew his balls. She picked up a cue and began caressing it mindlessly.

"How handy are you with your stick?" she asked with a flick of her hair.

"I'm pretty good at aiming for the pocket," he boasted. He took the cue from her and marveled at the hand-spliced ebony butt. "I can see that you polish your hardwood shafts," he said.

"I like the feel of a silky smooth glide," she said with a wink. "Perhaps I can show you my skills right now?"

Gil stepped back with a playful look of shock.

"Mrs. Woods, are you flirting with me?"

"Would that be so wrong?" she asked coyly and then bit her lip.

"I'm very flattered," he said. "You're a beautiful woman."

Rainbow took him by the arm, skipped the tour of the five guest bedrooms and led him straight to hers.

"This is my bedroom...and this is my bed," she said pointedly as she plopped down on it with a bounce. She smoothed the red satin comforter with her hands. "Why don't you come join me?" she asked with a sultry smile.

Gil cleared his throat. "I can't take advantage of a client, Mrs. Woods," he said.

"Perhaps it's me taking advantage of *you*," she replied.

"I'm here for business, not pleasure," he said firmly.

"I'm happy to pay you for services rendered," she said, surprised at herself for being so forward.

"Perhaps if we'd met under different circumstances..."

"Well, okay then," she pouted. "For a minute there your looks reminded me of my asshole husband anyway." She hopped off the bed and aimed for the door.

"Yes, he's been here with us the whole time," said Gil mysteriously. He grabbed her by her arm and spun her back towards him. With his eyes locked on hers he pushed her up against the wall, pressed his body against hers, and kissed her passionately. "This is what you were thinking, wasn't it?" he breathed in her ear.

"Oh... God yes," she moaned. It was exactly as she'd imagined in her fantasy. Was he reading her mind? She was already wet and she could feel his hardness pressed against her. "What am I thinking now?" she asked.

Gil tore off her bathrobe and threw her down on the bed. He slipped off his belt, slid off his pants and climbed on top of her.

"You're thinking about this," he said as he slipped inside of her.

She closed her eyes and groaned. "Mmm... you're right...I'm glad you came early."

"No, I didn't," he said with a grin.

An hour later, Rainbow emerged from the bedroom, looking slightly disheveled. Using her pinkie finger she fixed her lipstick in the corners of her mouth and patted down her hair. Most of her guests had already arrived and were wondering where she was.

"I was just showing Mr. Godsend around my...um, house..." she explained to the living room full of women.

She had transformed the room into an ashram, just like the one at the base of the Velliangiri Mountains in Tamil Nadu, India, to which she made an annual pilgrimage. The lights were switched off and candles burned around the room. Flowers were strewn across the floor. Brass statues of the Hindu deities sat on the mantelpiece and an Om flag flew above. The air was thick with the scent of sandalwood and musk wafting from incense sticks that competed with the smell of expensive perfume. Her guests looked out of place wearing haute couture and sipping glasses of champagne as they sat in the lotus position on meditation cushions. There was a tall wooden stool in the middle of the room for Gil. Everyone was anxiously awaiting the reading.

"Where is Mr. Godsend?" asked Rainbow. "And where is Sunshine?"

As if on cue, Gil made his entrance. He looked impeccable in a teal blue three-piece suit, mint-colored shirt, and emerald silk tie.

"Good evening, ladies," he said to a ripple of nervous giggles across the room. This was the sexy voice they all knew from his TV show! "My name is Gil Godsend and I'm a psychic medium. This means that I communicate with the dead." He sat down on the wooden stool. "I need to state upfront that I don't know *anything* about *anybody* here. I've never met *any* of you ladies before today." He looked around the room at them all, his piercing blue eyes taking on an eerie quality in the candlelit room. "I love these small gatherings... They're so much more...intimate," he said as he shot a look at Rainbow. "You all have loved ones who've passed and it's my job to reconnect you with them. I can see them, I can feel them, and I can hear them." He stood up and walked among the cushions dotted on the floor. "I'll validate my readings by sharing information I couldn't possibly know if I wasn't in communication with your friends and family who've crossed over."

Sunshine entered the room at that moment, looking slightly disheveled. She tugged on her skirt and patted down her hair. "Don't mind me," she said as she sat down cross-legged on a purple meditation cushion.

"If everyone is here then let's begin," said Gil as he closed his eyes and took several deep breaths. Then he opened his eyes slowly and looked around the room.

"I have a husband energy," he said. "I'm getting an "A" name, like Adrian or Adam. Who is this, please?"

"Adam was my husband," replied Rainbow with a frown.

"Then this is for you," said Gil. "He says to tell you the date March 15. Do you understand what that means?"

"Yes," she said. "That was our wedding anniversary, but he never remembered it when he was alive," she sneered.

Gil's body was suddenly seized by a fit of shaking.

"I feel very weak and unsteady," he said. "My heart is pounding… I feel so hot but my hands are cold." He turned pale and beads of sweat appeared on his brow. "I'm craving sugar…I'm *so* hungry…" He snapped out of his trance. "Can you explain this?"

"I can," replied Rainbow. "Adam had Type 1 diabetes. He had a severe attack of hypoglycemia, fell into a coma and died two days later," she said with a blank expression on her face.

Gil paused.

"I get the impression that you and Adam weren't close at the time of his death," he said. She nodded. "Adam… betrayed you somehow…"

"That's right," she said.

"He was unfaithful to you…"

"Yes…" she replied as she shot a dirty look at Breeze and Sunshine.

"With your sisters…"

"Yes," she said with tears in her eyes. Thinking about his death didn't make her cry, but thinking about the day she fell out of love with him did. That was when she discovered that he'd had a long-standing affair with Breeze and a one-night stand with Sunshine.

"Adam says he's sorry… but he's glad you had that time together earlier today," said Gil.

What did he mean by that?

"Adam begs for your forgiveness," added Gil.

"I've heard that one before," she said impassively.

"He also tells you to stop holding grudges," said Gil.

How dare Adam say that to her from beyond the grave? After all of these years she *still* wasn't over it. How does anyone get over that kind of betrayal? In some ways, she was glad when he died. She had hoped to hear from her mother or her aunt today, not her womanizing asshole of a husband.

"I'm getting pulled in a different direction," said Gil. "I'm sensing the presence of a young woman…She has a very strong energy… She's standing here beside me and holding a beautiful bouquet of flowers… I'm getting that she has a flower name that begins with "D", like Dahlia or Daisy."

"Daisy is our mother!" cried Rainbow excitedly.

"Your mother has just come through… She's been waiting patiently here all day for this reading… She's so excited that you're all here," said Gil. He paused. "She's named after a flower and she was also a flower child… She has long blonde hair and grey doe eyes that she outlines with thick black eyeliner." Rainbow and her sisters nodded. This was definitely their mother. This guy was good. The psychic they invited last year guessed that their mother was still alive.

"She's wearing a short crochet dress in an ivory color," said Gil. "And she has a headband of daisies."

Rainbow and her sisters looked at each other with wide eyes.

"That was the dress she was buried in," whispered Rainbow with tears in her eyes again. She could still remember her mother's funeral when she was just 8-years-old. Her aunt Indigo lifted her up so she could peer into the coffin and see her mother one last time. Her mother's beautiful, peaceful face still haunted her dreams.

"I'm getting a December connection," said Gil.

"Mom passed in December," said Rainbow.

"She wasn't ready to die… It wasn't her time yet… She's saying, 'I didn't want to go'."

"She was only 32," said Sunshine.

Gil looked around the room like he could hear something the others couldn't.

"I hear music," he said. "It sounds like a live band… There are people everywhere and bright lights… I feel like I'm at a rock concert."

"Mom died at a Peter Frampton concert," explained Breeze.

Gil shivered.

"I'm so cold." The color drained from his lips. "I'm feeling nauseous like I'm going to vomit," he said as he held his stomach. "My head is spinning… I'm so dizzy." Gil lurched like he was going to topple over. "I'm finding it very difficult to stay awake." He gasped. All of a sudden the trance was broken. "…I sense that Daisy died of a drug overdose," he said.

"That's right," confirmed Rainbow.

"She'd taken a fatal cocktail of barbiturates, amphetamines and alcohol," explained Sunshine.

"Her trip sitter abandoned her in the restroom to go hear Frampton perform *Show Me The Way*," added Breeze.

"She says she's sorry she left you," said Gil, as the three sisters started crying softly. "But she's never really left you. She's with you always in spirit." He looked around the room. "Another relative has joined the family reunion," Gil announced. "It's a young woman…She's showing me an "I" name." The three sisters looked at each other in suspense. "I think her name is…India or Indigo…"

"Indigo is our aunt!" Rainbow confirmed.

"Good." He paused. "…I feel like I'm moving at high speed," said Gil. "I'm very cold…I see blinding whiteness everywhere… It's snow…" He made an expression like he'd been struck in the face. "I just hit something very hard… What does this mean to you?"

"Indigo died in a skiing accident in Tahoe," Rainbow explained.

"She hit a tree," Sunshine said.

"And died on impact," added Breeze.

"She's coming in with a warm, caring energy… I'm getting that she cared for you after your mother passed," said Gil. The women nodded. Indigo became their mother figure. "I also feel that she kept you three sisters from feuding with each other," he said. It was constant war of rivalry and jealousy between the siblings. Now that Indigo was gone they were at each other's throats constantly. "The way they were in this world is the way they are in spirit on the other side," said Gil. "She wants you to stop your bickering. Love each other. She keeps saying, 'We are family'."

Rainbow, Sunshine and Breeze all screamed in unison, "*I got all my sisters with me!*"

Gil jumped back in surprise.

"You know, the song by Sister Sledge," explained Rainbow. "Indigo always sang this to us when we'd fight. It was her way of bringing us back together again."

A confused expression spread across Gil's face.

"Your mother keeps saying something…'*But it's the truth, even if it didn't happen*'." He paused. "Something isn't making sense here." His eyes widened. "Indigo wasn't your aunt…she was your *sister*," he revealed.

"What?" Rainbow cried.

"Um, no…" said Sunshine.

"You're probably just thinking that because we each had a different father," said Breeze.

"No, your mother is *very* clear about this," insisted Gil. "She gave birth to Indigo when she was only 14-years-old."

"Hmm…there *was* a 14 year difference between Mom and Indigo," Rainbow realized.

"Your grandmother raised Indigo as though she was her daughter," said Gil. "It was a family secret that your mother took to the grave. She says you need to check her real birth certificate to verify what I'm saying."

"Why didn't mom tell us?" asked Rainbow.

"She was ashamed," Gil explained.

"Did Indigo know?" asked Sunshine.

"No."

"How could mom lie to us all of those years?" asked Breeze.

"She said she's sorry that she hid the truth from you," replied Gil. "But she did what she thought was best at the time. She hopes that you will eventually forgive her, and that you will heal and learn from this experience."

Rainbow, Sunshine, and Breeze were stunned. They sat quietly throughout the rest of the group reading, thinking about this revelation.

When the session was over, Rainbow offered Gil a glass of champagne and invited him to stay but he declined politely.

"Thank you, Mrs. Woods, but I must go home," he said. "I have a client who'll be coming soon," he explained. Before Rainbow could say anything else, she'd wanted to ask him out on a date sometime, Breeze grabbed Gil by the arm.

"I'll show you the door, Mr. Godsend," she said as she dragged him from the room.

Just because Gil left didn't mean that the party was over. It went well into the night. After drinking ice cream cocktails the girls went skinny-dipping in the pool. They ended the night with cups of coffee, pot brownies, and a few rounds of snooker. As she chalked her cue, Rainbow thought of her secret tryst with Gil and smiled to herself.

When all her friends had gone, Rainbow dragged a heavy wooden trunk across the carpet into the living room. It was made from mahogany and covered with large brass studs. The trunk had belonged to their mother.

"Let's see if we can find Indigo's birth certificate," said Rainbow.

"But where's Breeze?" asked Sunshine. "We need to wait for her."

Breeze entered the room at that moment.

"Here I am!" she cried. She looked slightly disheveled. The top buttons of her blouse were undone, and she patted down her hair.

Rainbow grasped the small brass handle and opened the trunk. A musty old smell wafted out of it. The three sisters rifled through the contents. The trunk contained a treasure trove of memories. They found faded photographs, letters, and drawings the sisters had done when they were kids. It was like a time capsule. There was a vintage silver vanity set and a collection of 1960's jewelry, including a rhinestone brooch, orange Lucite clip-on earrings, and a chunky turquoise necklace that was so retro it was fashionable again. Breeze snatched it up for herself. Finally, they found a folder that contained the family's important papers. With trembling hands, Rainbow flicked through them until she found Indigo's birth certificate. She held her breath as her eyes scanned the document.

    She let out a noisy sigh of relief.

"Her birth certificate says that *grandma* was Indigo's mother," she confirmed.

"Indigo was our *aunt*!" exclaimed Sunshine.

"Gil was wrong," said Breeze.

"But he was right about everything else," said Rainbow. "Including the fact that my lovely sisters are cheaters," she said with a scowl.

"*And* he was right that you hold grudges," added Sunshine.

"Well," said Breeze as she poured herself another glass of champagne. "That's the end of that…"

Rainbow continued to search through the trunk. She found a stack of dog-eared books that were Daisy's favorites. She could still see her mother flopped on the couch at night, a glass of wine in one hand and a book in the other. She picked up a copy of *One Flew Over The Cuckoo's Nest*, the 1960s cult classic written by Ken Kesey who was a personal friend of her mother's.

"Hmm… Gil said, *But it's the truth even if it didn't happen*… Isn't that a quote from *One Flew Over The Cuckoo's Nest*?" she asked.

"I dunno. I never read it," replied Sunshine as she popped another pot brownie in her mouth.

As Rainbow flicked through the pages of the book a folded piece of yellowed paper fell out. She unfolded it and read it, her eyes scanning back and forth in disbelief.

"Oh my God!" she gasped. "I've found *another* birth certificate for Indigo, but this one says that *mom* was Indigo's mother!" She was in such shock she felt like she was about to faint. She took a few deep breaths. "Gil did say something about a 'real birth certificate'. The first one must have been a fake!"

Sunshine snatched the document from her.

"Indigo was our *sister*!" she screamed. "This explains a lot. I knew it!"

"Oh, you did *not* know that!" argued Breeze. "None of us did. Mom lied to us all those years…and she lied to Indigo…She never knew the truth while she was alive."

Rainbow sighed.

"Gil was right. He was right about *everything*."

"Well, he read me like a book," said Sunshine with a sly smile.

"Me too," said Breeze with a giggle. "He really knew how to turn my pages…"

The sisters looked at each other in confusion. Then the penny dropped.

"*You* slept with Gil too?" Rainbow asked them in dismay.

"What do you mean 'too'?" Sunshine demanded to know. "If I'd known you both had sex with him I *never* would have…"

"That didn't stop you before," hissed Rainbow.

"You *both* fucked him?" cried Breeze. "You filthy sluts!" She threw *One Flew Over the Cuckoo's Nest* at Rainbow who threw the chunky turquoise necklace back at her.

"You traitors!" screamed Rainbow. "First my husband and now Gil?"

"Gil was never yours…nor was Adam!" Breeze yelled at her. "He didn't love you. He was going to leave you for me."

"You fucking bitch!" sobbed Rainbow.

"Stop it!" Sunshine pleaded. "Stop it! Indigo wouldn't have wanted this! She would have wanted us to get along… *We are family*!" she sang. "*I got all my sisters with*…"

"Oh, shut the fuck up," spat Breeze as she picked up her chunky turquoise necklace and stormed out of the house.

Chapter 5

As she stumbled towards the espresso machine in her kitchen, Claudia thought about her "date" with a pilot from Denver the night before. She was hired to track the guy because his wife was convinced he had a woman in every port, or airport, as the case may be, and she was suspicious that he was getting laid on his layovers. He arrived at the location where his wife guessed he'd be, which was a bar where the two of them had met only a year before. He made quite an entrance wearing his pilot's uniform, flanked by a gaggle of giggly flight attendants. Claudia sat right near the group and, after joining in with a few well-placed giggles herself, she was invited to their little party. Over Blue Hawaiians that turned their lips a neon blue color, the guy told her predictable jokes about his cockpit and how everyone in the Mile High City is a member of the Mile High Club. He wasted no time in inviting Claudia to fly with him to Hawaii the following weekend because the weather is beautiful there at this time of year. He knew of a charming little cottage on the Kohala coast, which Claudia later discovered was where he and his wife had spent their recent honeymoon.

With bleary eyes, Claudia fixed herself a double espresso and gulped it down like it was medicine. She looked at the grandfather clock in her living room and it read 2:03 am. Her cell phone argued that it was 7:10 am instead. The old clock had clearly stopped again. It had defective gears and she'd have to be a clockmaker to keep it running smoothly. For her, it was a great-grandfather clock; it had once belonged to her great-grandfather and was passed down to her by her father just before he died. It was a strange and sad coincidence to her that the clock always stopped at this same time, which was the exact moment of her father's death.

"There are *no* coincidences," interrupted a familiar voice from the television. "That's a sign from your loved one." It was Gil Godsend on the *Sunrise* morning show.

"Oh, for fuck's sake," Claudia groaned. What was he doing on TV? She dropped down on the couch to watch him reluctantly. It was too early to fix a stiff drink, right?

"The dead are always trying to get our attention," he added.

Claudia felt as though Gil was a ghost from her past trying to get her attention. After laying low for several years he was obviously returning to the public eye for some reason, but she didn't know why. She hadn't seen him during that whole time and she had to admit he still looked good. Gil was a handsome guy, even if he was a big fat fraud. He hadn't aged a single day, although his suits kept getting more expensive.

Bella and Jack, the show's hosts, were interviewing Gil about some new book of his called *Messages From The Other Side*. Okay, so he was laying low to write a book and now he was back in the limelight again to promote this...ahem...work of fiction. Claudia cast a frown at the pile of Gil Godsend books in her library. Great. Here was yet another one that she needed to add to her collection. For someone who didn't believe in psychics at all, she had visited more psychics and bought more books about the paranormal than *any* believer.

"There's an invisible world of spirits who are trying to make contact with us from beyond the grave," said Bella with a flip of her bottle-blonde hair. "A few talented people, such as psychic medium Gil Godsend, can help us to communicate with them. Gil, how do we receive messages from the other side?"

Claudia thought she saw Bella fluttering her fake eyelashes at Gil.

"I have many clients who ask me to ask their deceased loved ones to send messages to them so they know they're okay," said Gil. "I've found that many spirits are doing this already, but you don't always need to see a psychic to receive them. Not everyone has the ability to tap into intuition to talk to spirits for others, like I do, but we all have the ability to tap into intuition for ourselves. You see... we *all* have psychic abilities."

"I'm a bit psychic," agreed Bella. "I often think about *someone* and then they call," she said pointedly, as though she was hinting that Gil should call *her*.

"That's an excellent example of an everyday psychic ability," praised Gil. Bella beamed like a teacher's pet. "Other psychic experiences include those moments when we say the same thing at the same time as someone else, when we wake up just before the alarm goes off, when we experience déjà vu, or we meet a person for the first time but feel as though we've known them in a previous life. Have you ever turned on the radio or walked into a store and heard song lyrics that speak to you personally?"

"That happens to me *all* the time," replied Jack as Bella nodded vigorously in agreement.

Claudia rolled her eyes.

"A spirit compelled you to turn on the radio or walk into that store at that exact moment to hear that message," Gil explained. "I wrote *Messages From The Other Side* to teach people how to pay attention to these messages. The spirits have a lot to say, to those who know how to listen."

Claudia noticed that Bella had shifted closer towards Gil on the couch, her knees pointing towards him. Her tight little skirt also seemed to be rising higher too.

"Can you tell us how our loved ones send us these messages?" Bella asked him in a way that made her sound like she was asking him out.

"Sure, Bella," Gil replied in a way that made him sound like he was saying "yes". "One of the easiest ways spirits communicate with us is via our dreams. Visitation dreams are common. Our loved ones appear in our dreams to offer us advice, warn us of possible dangers, or when they have unfinished business and can't rest until they've communicated something important. They often come to us in our dreams to say their final goodbyes soon after their passing."

"I have a friend who had a really vivid dream that her father was sitting on her bed," said Jack. "He'd been sick for years but he suddenly looked younger and healthier. He said he'd found peace and that he loved her. Later that day, she received news that her father had passed in the early hours of that morning."

Gil nodded wisely.

"We often receive these kinds of messages from our mothers and fathers who have just crossed over but still have a parental impulse to comfort us and reassure us that everything is alright," he explained. "We wake up from these visitation dreams feeling peaceful, happy, and loved. But some spirits do more than just visit us in our dreams; they actually visit us on this plane. It's common for the living to sense the presence of a recently deceased loved one, to hear that person's voice, or even see their apparition. Science hasn't been able to explain this phenomenon."

"Bullshit," said Claudia to the television. "It's a common reaction to grief. It's called a bereavement hallucination."

"But it *isn't* an hallucination," Gil added, as if he'd heard her explanation. "In these cases the loved ones weren't made aware of the death by ordinary means. It's a supernatural sign."

"Last night a framed photograph of my parents fell off the mantelpiece," said Bella. "It hit the floor so violently that the glass smashed! Mom and dad are both deceased. Was that a sign?" She asked as she twirled a lock of her hair playfully.

"Yeah… It was a sign that there was an earthquake last night…" replied Claudia. The minor quake knocked over bottles of perfume on a shelf in her apartment.

"If you've ever had something happen that makes you stop and ask yourself, 'Was that a sign?' Then that is your answer," Gil explained. "The very fact you asked that question is confirmation that it was a sign. Spirits send them to us all the time. A sign might be something like a clock that stops dead at the exact time of a loved one's passing."

"Or maybe it's just a defect in the gears!" Claudia yelled at him.

Gil ignored her this time.

"Spirits send us meaningful numbers or words that we see on license plates, bumper stickers, billboards, and in books and emails."

"That reminds me of the time I resolved to lose weight because my mother died of heart disease," said Jack. "One day I was tempted to buy a chocolate chip cookie until I read a license plate with the word FITNESS on it. I haven't eaten a cookie since that day!"

"That was definitely your mother's spirit reminding you to stay on track with your diet," Gil assured him.

Claudia was so annoyed that she went into her kitchen and got herself a cookie in defiance.

"There are numerous signs of spirit but it can be like learning a new language to identify them because they're often cryptic," Gil continued. "Our loved ones are trying to communicate with us when lights flicker, when appliances turn on and off, when we smell perfume, a favorite flower, cigarette smoke, or some other smell we associate with them, when a pet behaves strangely, when feathers, rocks, keys, or coins appear out of nowhere, when an object goes missing or is moved, when a lost item resurfaces, when broken equipment suddenly starts working again, when we feel a breeze or a cold chill, when we get goosebumps, when we see butterflies, dragonflies, and rainbows, when a stranger smiles at us, when we have a sense of being watched, when a thought just pops into our minds, or when a phone rings and we answer, but no one is there…"

"The pimple on my ass is a sign then too," Claudia mocked.

"We can even ask our loved ones to send a sign that they're okay," said Gil. "Invite them to come to you in a dream, or as an animal, and when you spot a sign, be sure to acknowledge it and thank your loved one. Encourage them to continue to communicate with you. If the dead think they're being ignored they usually give up…"

"I wish *you'd* give up," Claudia said to him.

"Gil, I've always wanted a psychic reading from you, but I know there's a three year waiting list," Jack said. "Can you give me a reading now to let everyone at home know what they're waiting for?"

"Yes, Gil. Give us a taste of what you can do," said Bella as she shot him a saucy side-glance and plucked invisible fluff off his blazer. Gil *never* had fluff on his clothes.

"Of course," obliged Gil as he returned Bella's look.

"Oh, go get a room," said Claudia.

"Your energy has been very powerful for me this morning," Gil remarked, leaving Claudia to wonder if it was a comment made to Jack or Bella. He closed his eyes for a few moments. "Hmm… You had a lot of anger as a child. You didn't feel a sense of being wanted when you were a little boy and you never felt like you belonged." Jack nodded emphatically. "I'm getting the impression you have two families… How interesting." Gil paused. "…Were you adopted?"

"Wow, Gil! Yes, I was," Jack replied, impressed that Gil could know that. He'd only just found out a few years ago himself and he was still getting to know his biological parents.

"There's a woman standing next to me… Has your adoptive mother passed?" Gil asked. Jack nodded. She was the only member of his adopted family that he felt close to, and he had been a mommy's boy. She died suddenly two years ago and he still missed her every day. "Mom is sending thoughts to me that are very strong," said Gil. "I feel that she died of some sort of cardiovascular disease."

"That's right!" Jack said in amazement.

"You just told Gil that your mother died of heart disease!" Claudia screamed at Jack.

Gil continued. "She's telling me that her name begins with an 'R'." Is it Ruth? Wait... her hands are full of sparkling red-colored gemstones...they're rubies. Her name was Ruby..."

"Yes!" confirmed Jack.

No wonder people waited three years to see this guy. He was good.

"Mom says that she loves you and wants you to know that she's still a part of you. She helps in your decision making every day," said Gil. "...Now she's showing me a baby. You have a young daughter?"

"I do!" Jack brightened at the mention of his gorgeous baby girl.

"Mom is still showing me rubies again... Was your daughter named after her mother?" asked Gil. "Was her name also Ruby?"

"Yes!" Jack confirmed. "That's incredible!"

"I feel that she was born soon after mom died."

"Yes," Jack whispered. Gone was his plastic smile and the mindless small talk he usually reserved for the woman with tips for lunch box treats. This was clearly a moving experience for him and he was still in mourning.

"Mom has to go now, but she has one final message," Gil said. He paused dramatically. "She wants to validate this reading by sharing something that I couldn't possibly know if I wasn't in contact with her... She's showing me a bookmark with a quote written on it... It says, "There comes a time when you have to choose between turning the page and closing the book". Do you understand that?" asked Gil.

"Oh, God. Yes, I do," replied Jack quietly. This had been his mother's advice to him several years ago when he and his wife were considering a divorce. They had grown apart due to their busy work schedules, and Jack's philandering. He'd gone off the rails when he learned he had been adopted. With the help of some counseling, Jack turned over a new leaf and the couple chose to "turn the page" instead of parting ways. Nine months later their baby girl was born. This was the best decision Jack had ever made.

"Mom says that she loves you, and love lives forever," Gil added.

The reading hit a raw nerve with Jack. He got all choked up and was unable to speak. This was an uncomfortable silence for a live show, so Bella flashed her professionally whitened teeth at the camera and swiftly took over the reins.

"Thanks to Gil Godsend for his remarkable psychic insight!" she said. "Do go out and buy yourself a copy of his amazing new book, *Messages From The Other Side*." She touched Gil's thigh. "Do you have any final words for our viewers?" she asked him.

"I want to remind everyone to pay attention to those signs," Gil said with a grin.

"I'm paying attention," Claudia replied. "This is a sign that I need to watch you, Gil…"

Jack was still visibly shaken so Bella continued.

"Coming up later on *Sunrise*, we'll be doing makeovers for women who want chic looks for the office, while our next guest will be sharing some fun ideas for quick and easy lunch box treats!"

Theme music began playing as the producer quickly cut to an advertisement. Gil was ushered off-stage by an assistant and Bella followed, tripping in her red high heels in her efforts to get to him.

"That was an incredible reading you just gave!" she cooed.

Gil fixed his eyes on her and raised an eyebrow.

"Just wait until I give one to you…"

She smiled.

"It just so happens that I'm on a short break now. Is there any chance I could have a quickie with you right now?" she giggled. "…A palm reading or something?"

"Absolutely," he said. "I always have time to fit you in, Bella."

She dragged him off to her dressing room. She didn't emerge for the rest of the show, leaving poor, emotional Jack to manage the makeover segment alone. Bella always disappeared on him like this when Gil was a guest on the show.

While Gil was presumably reading something other than Bella's palms in her dressing room, Claudia was busy doing some digging into TV host and former football player Jack Summers. Jack revealed that his mother died of heart disease and Gil fed this back to him blatantly, but

Claudia suspected there was some information available online about Jack that Gil may have used during his reading. Gil's game was too good. In the course of her research she came across many articles about Jack doing whacky and zany things for his morning show, including the time he fed a lettuce leaf to an iguana and it bit off the top of his pinkie finger, and a photo of him riding a unicycle, just seconds before he fell and broke his ankle.

Claudia also uncovered lots of personal information about Jack, including an interview in which he revealed that he had been adopted and that he grew up feeling like he didn't belong. Tabloids gossiped about Jack's flings with various actresses. There were also reports that Jack and Bella had engaged in a brief but torrid affair. Another article revealed that Jack's long-suffering wife had taken him back after some counseling, and that their reunion resulted in the birth of their baby girl, Ruby, who was named in memory of his beloved mother.

Chapter 6

"Your husband is here with us now," announced Gil as he opened his eyes slowly and gazed across the table at his client. The widow swept her long black hair out of her heavily lined brown eyes and fixed her gaze back at him.

"You're good," she praised. "My last psychic said he was in contact with my grandmother, but she wasn't dead!"

Gil shook his head in disgust.

"You need to be careful," he warned her. "There are many unscrupulous psychics out there…"

"Well, you're not one of them," she said, her leather jacket crinkling as she leaned in towards him. "I'm a little bit psychic myself and I can tell…"

"We're all a little bit psychic," he told her. "Now, Mrs. Cooper, I'm getting an "M" name that stands for either Mike or Mark…"

"Yes, his name was Mark!" she confirmed as she hugged a cup of coffee with both hands, revealing fingers that were covered with silver rings and fingernails painted with black polish. Her skin was a very pale white. "But you should call me Abby. Mrs. Cooper sounds way too formal and makes me feel soooo old," she said, her Celtic cross earrings jangling whenever she spoke.

"Abby it is then," he said with a grin. "Now, I'm going to validate my psychic reading for you by providing a specific description of your husband's character and appearance, along with some personal information that no one else could possibly know. This is evidence to prove to you, and to me, that I'm in communication with him."

Okay," she replied a little nervously. She was there to receive an answer from her husband to a specific question.

"I see a man with a short, rough beard," said Gil. "He has medium-length wavy brown hair that he hasn't cut in months."

That was her Mark!

"He wouldn't wash it for months either," she said with a shake of her head.

"He was a tall and muscular man," said Gil. "He liked to work out at the gym frequently."

"Yes. He had your height and build," Abby said, although he wasn't a sharp dresser like you, she thought. Gil was resplendent in a grey pinstriped suit, a lavender-colored shirt and a purple tie that day. He was cute, and a little older than her, just the way she liked her men.

"Mark didn't like wearing suits, he was a jeans and t-shirt man," Gil said.

It seemed like Gil was replying to her thought. She needed to be careful around him. After all, he was a mind reader!

"Mark always wore a black leather jacket," said Gil. "You wear it to bed at night."

"I do," she said as she closed her eyes and pictured the jacket laid across her pillow. Sometimes she wore little else. "It's the closest I can get to having his arms around me as I sleep," she said sadly. The jacket used to smell like a heady mix of Mark's deodorant and his skin, but it had faded over the years. Nowadays she had to breathe in deeply to catch a faint memory of the scent.

"He had several distinguishing features about his body," said Gil. "I see a small mark just below his lip. It appears to be a scar from a piercing of some kind."

"That's right!" she said. "He had a lip piercing. His boss forced him to take it out when he met with clients. One day, he got fed up and just took it out and left it out."

"I also see a tattoo of a girl's name on his ankle," said Gil. "But it's not your name. It begins with "P"."

"Um, noooo. I don't think so," Abby said with a frown. She'd kissed every inch of Mark's body, but she'd never seen a tattoo, much less one with another girl's name on it.

Gil was insistent.

"Speak to his relatives about this. You'll find out that I'm right," he said confidently. "He's also showing me that he had a large red birthmark or scar on his right hand, that's shaped like a crescent moon."

"Now I know that's right," Abby agreed. "That was a scar from a motorcycle accident."

"And it was such an accident that took his life one day."

She looked out the window, lost in thought.

"Yes. It was..."

Gil closed his eyes.

"Abby, I'm receiving a very clear vision... I'm there the day that Mark passed... I hear the roaring engine of the motorcycle... I'm feeling the sun on my face and the wind in my hair, and an incredible sense of freedom... The road twists and winds as it clings to a coastline of sheer, rocky cliffs... I see the waves are beaten into white froth against the jagged rocks below... I think I'm riding on Highway 1 along the central California coast."

"Yes," she confirmed. "He was driving on Devil's Slide. It's a very dangerous road."

"It's narrow and treacherous with many sharp drop-offs into the ocean," said Gil. "I'm starting to sense impending danger so I'm staying alert... *Fuck*... I see another car coming from the opposite direction but it's on *my* side of the road... It looks like it's full of teenagers trying to pass a slower vehicle... I'm feeling angry, not scared at all. *Fucking little punks*. I swerve to avoid the oncoming car..."

He drew a sharp intake of breath.

"I hit something! *Oh, shit*! ...I feel like I'm falling... I'm thrown onto something hard and sharp and everything turns black..."

Gil opened his eyes. There were tears in them.

Abby nodded furiously.

"That's *exactly* what happened. Mark swerved and hit another car parked by the side of the road. The impact catapulted him off his bike and straight into a cliff face."

Tears welled up in her eyes.

"Don't worry," Gil said kindly. "He didn't suffer. It's well known that people who die in car accidents leave their bodies before impact."

"Is he still seeing this blackness?" she asked in fear. "Is he in limbo or the void?"

"No, he chose the light and has crossed over," Gil assured her. "Mark survives in the world of spirit. He watches over you and protects you. He says you haven't always done a good job of taking care of yourself."

She sighed. "Boy, is that the truth!"

Gil appeared confused.

"Mark tells me that you were once known by another name, but not a maiden name or nickname. I think he's talking about an alias of some kind. I see a pair of beautiful brown eyes, just like yours, and some sort of black-colored gemstone that looks like onyx or jet…"

"Jet Brown…" she whispered in disbelief.

How could he possibly know this?

"That's it!" he said. "But this isn't your real name."

"No," she said, looking at the floor. "It was my pseudonym. I, um…I… worked in the sex industry," she admitted with a cringe. "But I wasn't a stripper or a phone sex worker. Jet Brown was my screen name. I was an adult actress. A porn star," she blathered. "My first producer came up with the name for me because my hair is jet black and my eyes are brown. Maybe you've seen a film I've starred in?"

Gil sat back in his chair and scoffed a little.

"No offense, but with my lifestyle I don't have much of a need for that kind of entertainment," he said.

Abby was relieved. She didn't like the kind of guy who watched those kinds of movies, even though she appeared in them.

"I get recognized on the street all the time," she said. "Guys don't say anything to me though because they're with their wives or girlfriends. They just stare at me. They know who I am and they know that I know they know."

Gil shifted in his chair, looking uncomfortable.

"Forgive me for this. Mark insists I validate the reading by saying something to you that's… quite explicit."

She wondered what could be more explicit than the fact that she'd been a porn star.

"Well, I want to hear *everything* Mark has to say," she said.

Gil paused.

"He says that you and he were into…kinky sex."

"That's right," she said as a light blush crept over her face.

"But we're not talking fluffy pink handcuffs and feather play. You two were into the hardcore stuff, like BDSM, and rough play…"

She smiled to herself. Only Mark would want to talk about sex from beyond the grave.

"You're definitely in contact with my husband!" she said.

"He says that since his death, you haven't been able to find a lover who can please you," said Gil. "You like a man to be...aggressive. He says you have..." Gil cleared his throat. "...He says you have a rape fetish."

She nodded. This personal information definitely validated the reading for her.

"I, um...still want to try that sometime," she admitted. "But as Mark used to say, acting out a rape fantasy is just roleplaying. It's still consensual. It's not rape. We never knew how to make it real while keeping it safe."

"Abby, you need to be careful what you wish for," Gil said in a fatherly way that turned her on a little bit. "Now, Mark says you're now out of the...movie industry," he said, changing the topic.

"Yes," she said. "I'm working in an office for an accounting firm. It's not as "exciting" as the porn industry, but it pays the bills and allows me to save some money."

"And you're trying to save enough to attend nursing school."

"That's right!"

"I see you working with small children."

"I hope so," she said with a sigh. "I really want to work in pediatrics. I just love kids."

"I see you finding the money to be able to afford college very soon."

"That's why I'm here," she said as she ran her fingers through her hair nervously. "I made a bit of cash shooting pornos, but that's running out fast. Just before he died, Mark told me that if anything ever happened to him, I'd be taken care of. What did he mean by that?"

"He had a premonition. He knew he was going to die," Gil explained. "Mark wants me to say that you have money owed to you that you don't know about. He had an insurance policy you need to claim," Gil revealed.

She clasped her hands to her face in shock.

"Oh my God! Thank you, Mark!" she said as she began to cry into the sleeves of her leather jacket.

Gil slid a box of tissues towards her.

He was silent as he let her cry for a while.

"Abby...I'm starting to lose my connection to your husband," he said as his eyes darted around the room. "Mark says goodbye, for now, and that he loves you... Our session has come to an end," Gil announced gently as he reached across the table and placed his hand on hers. "I hope my reading gave you some comfort and closure."

"It sure did," Abby said as she handed him her donation for the reading. "By the way, I heard that some psychics can channel the dead. Is that true?" she asked.

"Absolutely," replied Gil. "But I try to avoid doing that because it means I no longer have control over myself."

Abby frowned. "What do you mean?"

"When I channel spirits they speak through me, but they can also take over my body for short periods of time."

She raised her eyebrow and gave a slight smile.

"Do you mean they can possess you?"

"Yes," he replied. "Sometimes they do it without my permission. On occasion a very determined spirit has taken me by surprise," said Gil.

Abby thought that if anyone could take him by surprise it would be her husband. He'd always had a very…determined libido.

"It can happen at *any* time," Gil said with a strange smile as he directed her towards the door. "Goodbye Abby, and I predict that you'll finally get what you've been wanting…"

"Thank you, Mr. Godsend!"

Abby felt emotional, but she was in good spirits. She'd just received confirmation that her husband was watching over her from the spirit world. She was eager to explore this financial lead and hopeful that Gil Godsend was right. He'd certainly been accurate about nearly everything else he'd said. This psychic guy was the real deal…

She opened the door to leave but jumped in surprise when it was slammed shut.

She felt Gil standing behind her.

"You're not going anywhere," he growled, his hot breath blowing her hair about her ear. He pinned her firmly to the door with his chest, grabbed her wrists and raised them above her head. "Don't fucking move," he ordered. With one sweeping move of his foot he forced her legs apart, making her vulnerable to him. She felt his hardness against the small of her back and heard him unbuckle his belt and unzip his fly. Her heart thumped in her chest, she was shaking uncontrollably, and her mouth went dry.

      She wasn't sure if she was feeling excitement or fear.

Then she realized… this was her husband! She recognized his voice and his forceful touch. He had taken over Gil's body so they could fulfill their fantasy together.

It was Mark!

"Oh God, yes…" she whispered between gritted teeth.

He hiked up her short plaid skirt and gently massaged her taut ass. Then he slapped her hard.

"You dirty whore, wearing this slutty skirt," he laughed menacingly as he slipped a finger inside of her. "You knew you were gonna get fucked today, didn't you?"

"Stop!" she shrieked as she played along. "Please don't!"

Her bad acting skills were definitely those of a porn star.

"Shut the fuck up and take my cock!" he yelled. With one thrust he forced himself all the way inside of her and she squealed in shock at his size. "Many other guys have been here before me, but you still have a tight little pussy," he grunted. He pushed her face harder against the door until she could smell the lacquer on the wood.

"No!"

"No means *yes* with you," he panted. "*This* is what you wanted. To be helpless and overpowered by a stranger."

Abby gave into him. This *was* what she wanted. This was the real thing, and not roleplaying. But at the same time it was safe. It was another man but it was her husband.

He pressed her against the door and said all kinds of dirty things to her as he pounded her hard. She could barely think straight. This was so exciting. She soon felt him throbbing as he started to come and she joined him in an orgasm that pulsed through her entire body. He pulled out, leaving a thick trail of semen oozing out of her, and propelled her back into the room.

He glared at her with his piercing blue eyes.

"I'm not finished with you yet," he snarled. He edged closer to her like he was stalking his prey. She backed away from him towards the table and knocked over a Tiffany lamp that shattered into little pieces.

"What a naughty girl you are, trying to get away from me, and breaking Gil's expensive lamp," he said as he wagged his finger at her. "You'll pay for that… with your pussy."

He charged at her and threw her on the table with a thud. Her mug slid off the table and smashed onto the polished wooden floor, spilling coffee across his Persian rug. He pushed her down, tearing her leather jacket as she pretended to resist him.

"You're gonna make me come again before I let you go," he demanded as he spread her legs apart and drove himself back into her, making her feel like she was going to split into two pieces. That hurt a bit. Then he tugged on her hair. Hard. She liked lots of things that others would find violent, but if there was one thing she didn't like it was having her hair pulled. Her scalp was sensitive. Suddenly this wasn't so much fun.

"Ow!" she cried. "Don't pull my fucking hair!"

"At least your acting is improving," he said as he slapped her face.

Mark *never* hit her face.

"You're hurting me, Mark!"

"But you like it rough, don't you?" he bellowed as he held her down by her shoulders and fucked her hard and fast. "You want me to hurt you."

There was real fear in her eyes.

"Chocolate!" she suddenly screamed.

This was the safe word she shared with Mark.

But he kept pounding away at her. Why wouldn't he stop?

"Chocolate!" she screamed again. "Chocolate!"

"You're hungry, are you? The only thing you're going to eat right now is my cock," he taunted. He pulled out of her and thrust himself into her mouth where he shot his cum deep inside of her throat.

He was done.

Abby lay back on the table and tried to catch her breath. What just happened? Did she just have sex with her husband, or with a stranger?

A trickle of sweat ran down his face. He bent over her, planted a tender kiss on her forehead and said, "Goodbye, Angel." He started staring into the distance weirdly, then he collapsed on the floor and his body began shaking.

Abby's mind raced. Did Gil lose consciousness? Was he dying? Was he having a seizure? Was he faking? Maybe she should call for an ambulance. Or should she call the police? She didn't really want to involve the authorities. The whole scene looked very suspicious. Would they think she attacked him? Or had he attacked her? What would he do to her if he woke up? Should she just get out of there while she still could? She stood frozen in panic but before she could make a decision, Gil came to.

He seemed very disoriented as he clutched his head and grimaced in pain.

"Are you okay?" she asked him, even though she wasn't sure if *she* was okay.

"I think so," Gil groaned. "I feel a little woozy."

With bleary eyes he saw her standing there. She looked disheveled and wide-eyed, her pale white skin even more pallid than before. Her jacket was torn and her skirt was askew.

"…But are *you* okay?" he asked her.

She shrugged her shoulders. "I guess so," she said as she straightened her skirt.

Gil groggily surveyed the disorder in the reading room. He saw that his precious Tiffany lamp was destroyed. He spotted the broken mug and the coffee stains all over the 19th Century Persian rug he'd just bought from auction at Sotheby's. It appeared as though a thief had broken into the house and trashed the place. Then he looked down and noticed that his tie was loosened, his shirt was partially unbuttoned, and his pants were undone.

"What the fuck happened here?" he cried in alarm.

He sincerely seemed to have no recollection of what had taken place.

Abby filled him in…but left out a lot.

"Well…you finished my reading. I was about to leave and then you… passed out on the floor and went into convulsions," she said.

But not before my husband, or you, or something, fucked me… she thought.

Gil looked down at his pants questioningly.

"Oh, and I was worried you couldn't breathe, so…I loosened your clothes a little," she said unconvincingly.

Gil rubbed his temples. Abby noticed that his eyes looked red.

"I must have had a psychic seizure," he concluded. "Sometimes this happens when I'm overwhelmed by the psychic energy in the room, or when a spirit leaves my body," he explained.

She offered her hand to help him stand up.

"I don't remember what happened at all, but I'm lucky you were here to ensure my needs were met," he said with a thankful smile as he took her hand and squeezed it tightly. He stood up but his legs were wobbly. "I'm going to rest for awhile. I have another client coming here soon."

"Then I'd better leave," she said as he led her to the door slowly.

"Goodbye, Abby, and thank you," he said, shaking her hand formally.

"Goodbye again, Mr. Godsend."

She half expected him to block her exit again. Instead, he flung the door open wide and she was free to run out into the warm afternoon sun. But her mind wasn't free. She was confused by what had just happened and she tried to rationalize it. Did Gil really suffer a "psychic seizure"? Could it be that his body was taken over by her husband's spirit? He did refer to himself in third person during the episode, which was creepy. Then she recalled Gil's cryptic words; *I predict that you'll finally get what you've been wanting.* This was what he meant by that, right? He also kissed her forehead and said, "Goodbye, Angel", just like Mark used to do before he left for work each morning.

But if that was her husband, why didn't he stop when she used the safe word?

Abby had many conflicting thoughts. She was angry with Gil for taking advantage of her, if indeed he did, and she was angry with herself for enjoying it. That was the best sex of her entire life, but was it... rape? Wasn't that what she wanted anyway? She felt dirty and violated, ashamed and abused, but exhilarated.

Chapter 7

It was Friday and Claudia was scheduled to have a massage that afternoon. This wasn't for therapeutic reasons though, or for pleasure; this was strictly business. The manager of a spa in Larkspur contacted Claudia because she was concerned that her male massage therapist was acting less than professionally. She wasn't accusing him of offering "happy endings" or "full body massage" to his clients like the seedy late-night massage parlors with flashing neon "open" signs, but there had been complaints from female clients that his massages were sexually suggestive, that he made inappropriate remarks about their bodies, or he invited them out for a post-massage drink, and we're not talking Gatorade. Claudia's mission was to ensure that the therapist respected his client's boundaries, and avoided going near her lady bits.

Claudia checked her emails before leaving for her appointment but she immediately regretted doing so. She received a flurry of hate mail that morning. Gil's return to the limelight brought his obsessive fans out of the woodwork and they were on the warpath again. These women were brazen behind the safety of their keyboards, but they were also cowards who were anonymous online. They composed vicious messages but then signed off with pseudonyms that were cutesy or sexually charged. The emails appeared to be written by illiterate halfwits because they were peppered with bad spelling and grammar and missing punctuation. Didn't these idiots see the red and green squiggly lines before they hit the send button?

I think u r mean to Gil G cos he dumped u he deserves better then a bitch like u Gil if u r reading tgis I LUV U! lol

psychichottie94

your malicious attacks on gil godsend are wrong i don't think youve ever even seen him at work ive read many of your articles and while some of them are good you you are completely off the mark when it comes to gil you did no real research with him and let your sinical nature get the best of you i pray that you find a way to open your heart to the amazing gifts that gil brings nobody wants to be around your kind of bitterness

Geminibabe

Did you go too a bad psychic once?? It would explain youre negative attitude. TRUE psychics know exact detaild information WITOUT having to fish for it.. Their NOT tricks. Have you ever spoken with a ghost? Its not easy. I recently spoke to a dead male relative of a women that gave me the pet name that he used to call her when he was a little child when he was was alive. I said it in ONE word, no jerking around!! That peice of information was something SHE only know. Your stereotyping ALL psychics as fruds when some are good ones!. NOT cool.

Karmachick13

Hi. I need to contact my dead husband urgently. Please tell me the name of a good pyschic.

SxxyShadowSpirit

You say Gils a fake but i think your fake, you should kill yourself!!

dreamgrrl

    Years ago these insulting messages would hurt Claudia. She responded politely and respectfully to these people as she tried to reason with them. Then they came back with even more abuse and insults so the conversations spiraled into slinging matches. She found herself arguing back and forth late into the night with true believers. She wondered why the hell she bothered trying to save these nasty people from wasting their time and money. In the end, she realized she couldn't worry about someone being wrong on the Internet. In fact, she found herself becoming a little amused by the crazy spelling errors and madness of these nutjobs. She especially wondered about those people who asked *her* for psychic recommendations! Obviously they didn't read her articles at all, or they assumed that she wasn't skeptical of *all* psychics, only the "fake" psychics, and therefore she must be the best person to recommend a "true" psychic. Occasionally, she found a genuine message among the trash.

Today, she found another email asking for her help.

Hello,

I had a psychic reading with Gil Godsend last week. Something really weird and scary happened to me afterwards. I can't explain it but I'm hoping you can.
Please help me!

Abby Cooper
415-250-6021

What was going on? This was the second cry for help she'd received about Gil in as many weeks! Claudia was very reluctant to get involved, but she was curious to find out about their complaints. What had Gil done to these poor women? After years of laying low, supposedly to devote more time to giving private readings to his fans, Gil was now back in the public eye to promote his new book and seemingly resurrect his career. She wasn't sure what to do about it. But for now, she had an appointment with a suspicious massage therapist. She could only deal with one creep at a time.

Claudia got in her car and set off to Larkspur for her undercover massage. She only reached the entrance to Highway 101 but the afternoon traffic had already come to a grinding halt. To pass the time she switched on the radio and AC/DC's *Thunderstruck* was playing. They played that damn song all... the... time. She punched the scan function, but it seemed that *every* station was playing either AC/DC or Journey. She finally found a station that wasn't so she quickly hit the stop scan button.

"If you were flipping through the radio stations and you stopped here randomly, then you are meant to be listening," said a smooth, sultry voice. "There will be a message just for you…"

It was Gil.

"Oh, for fuck's sake," Claudia sighed.

She preferred AC/DC to this. She couldn't seem to escape Gil Godsend.

"That's right, everyone," said the DJ. You're listening to the Bay Area's KAZZ radio and I'm Johnny Lombard," he said in his most practiced voice. "Our guest this afternoon is psychic medium Gil Godsend and he's going to do some readings for our listeners soon. Gil, I hear the DJs at KNOW in Santa Barbara used to call you… "The Graveyard Guru"."

"That's right, Johnny, although that's somewhat of a misnomer. Contrary to popular belief, the dead aren't hanging out in cemeteries. That's where their earthly bodies were laid to rest but not where their souls exist. Spirits are freed of their bodies and they don't usually have an attachment to their earthly remains. Cemeteries are spooky places, but you won't see spirits there."

"So, where do the spirits go?" Johnny asked.

"This sounds like an answer to a 'Why did the chicken cross the road?' joke, but they're on the other side. The spirits of our loved ones have crossed over to another plane or dimension known as the other side of the veil, a place that some might call heaven."

"You heard him, folks!" said Johnny. "The phone lines are now open so let's take our first caller. We have Stephanie from Oakland. What's your question for Gil?"

"Dump him, Stephanie! He's not good enough for you!" Gil interrupted.

"Wow! You answered my question before I could even ask it!" Stephanie yelped. "Yeah, I'm having relationship troubles."

"I'm sensing that this guy betrayed your trust somehow… My spirit guides are telling me that he cheated on you…"

"That's right, Gil, but he did apologize and promised he'd never to do it again."

"You can't trust him, Stephanie. He'll cheat on you again and again," Gil warned. "This guy is holding you back from your future potential. Your ego has taken a battering. You need to ditch him and develop some confidence and self-love."

"But I don't think I'll *ever* find love again," she sighed melodramatically.

"Hang in there, okay?" said Gil. "You'll meet your soul mate in six months time. Look for a tall man with light blonde hair and grey-colored eyes. His name is Paul. He works in the healthcare industry and does martial arts. Good luck Stephanie."

"Thanks Gil!" she said with sudden positivity.

"Some great advice there from Gil," Johnny said. "The phone lines are going *crazy*! If you have a burning question for psychic medium Gil Godsend, call now..."

How did Gil know that Stephanie was calling to ask about her cheating boyfriend? Claudia didn't believe he was using psychic powers. Was the producer feeding this information to Gil beforehand? And where did he get off interfering in the love lives of complete strangers? In her line of work Claudia was all too familiar with cheaters, dogs, and players, and she was the first person to advise a friend to break up with a philanderer, but Gil was playing with people's lives. His detailed description of Stephanie's "soul mate" sounded impressive on air, but that's all that the public would ever hear about the matter and he'd never be held accountable if he were wrong. Stephanie would waste her time searching for a tall man named Paul with light blonde hair and grey-colored eyes who works in the healthcare industry and does martial arts, instead of looking for Mr. Right, whoever he was.

If anyone was "holding her back from her future potential" it was Gil.

"Now we have Justin from Walnut Creek on the line," said Johnny.

"Hey Johnny. Hi Gil," said Justin.

"I'm sensing that you have a question about your career, Justin," Gil said. "I feel you're unhappy with your current job."

"That's right, Gil," he replied.

"I see money all around you, but none of it is yours... Do you work in finance or banking?" Gil asked.

"Yes! I'm an accountant. I've had the same job for nine years," he complained.

"...You're bored with your work," said Gil. "You don't like your colleagues and you can't stand your boss... he's a jerk. I don't think you're cut out to be just another nine-to-five wage slave. That could never be truly fulfilling for someone like you. You have too much drive and too many good ideas of your own... Does this make sense to you?"

"It sure does, Gil," replied Justin. "That's exactly how I feel."

"You're seeking change in your life..." said Gil. "You want to escape the office... You're considering something completely different...maybe something outdoors, like a park ranger. No, wait...you're interested in landscaping?"

"Yes! I want to be a landscape architect. I want to design gardens and parks."

"But you're concerned about leaving a well-paying, steady job to start a new business in this bad economy. Is this right, Justin?"

"That's right, Gil," he agreed. "I don't know if I'll be able to make as much money as I'm making now."

"I foresee some very good prospects arising from your natural ability to develop opportunities. My advice is that you tell your boss to "take this job and shove it" and pursue your passion," said Gil. "You won't be sorry you did."

"I'm going to do it right now!" Justin decided confidently. "Thanks Gil!"

Claudia thought it was very irresponsible of Gil to advise a stranger to quit his job. What if he had a mortgage or a family to support? He would lose his heath insurance and financial security all because of a stupid psychic hunch.

"More great psychic advice from Gil!" praised Johnny. "Now that we've had the chance to hear a few readings, let's give one away. Be the tenth caller right now to receive a free private reading from world famous psychic Gil Godsend!" he cried with so much excitement he sounded like he was going to piss his pants. "Our next caller is Wendy from Napa."

"Hi, Wendy," said Gil. "I'm getting the strong impression that you have an illness that hasn't been diagnosed yet. What is it about your health that concerns you?" he asked.

"You're right, Gil," Wendy said. "I've put on weight for no reason and I feel sluggish. I'm always sleepy and I have a lack of energy," she said tiredly. "I'm kind of down too. I've lost my zest for life."

"Your symptoms are tied in with an illness your mother suffered," Gil diagnosed. "You harbor a deep resentment towards her because of her sickness, what it did to you, and the fear it left you with. You need to deal with that underlying resentment and fear in order to heal. This is making sense to you, isn't it?" he asked.

"That's true, Gil," she agreed. "My mother did have a chronic illness and I had to take care of her for the final years of her life. I love her, but I feel like I lost so much time."

"Wendy, you need to get in touch with your own body. I sense that meditation and yoga are on the path to wellness for you. Try to find creative or artistic outlets for your stress... I also feel that you may have a chemical sensitivity. Massage is important to rid your body of toxins. Also try an organic, gluten-free diet, and drink lots of green tea. If you don't feel better within three months I suggest you visit a naturopath or an homeopath," he advised. "Remember...natural is *always* better."

"Thanks, Gil!" said Wendy with hope in her voice. "I'll give that a try."

Claudia was angry that Gil was giving medical advice. This woman clearly needed to see a doctor, not some sort of quack. She probably needed medication, not massage and a cup of herbal tea. The longer she put off seeing a doctor, the worse her outcome could be. Gil's advice was useless at best, and potentially dangerous at worst.

"Thanks for that, Dr. Godsend!" Johnny joked. "So...are you a healer too?"

"I don't call myself a healer, Johnny, but others do," Gil replied. "I'm a medical intuitive so I can diagnose people's illnesses. I'm also what some might call an *empath*. This means that I tune into the emotions and feelings of others. I feel what they feel. This ability can be a blessing, or a curse. It means I feel the headaches and colds of people around me. I feel the exhaustion, anxiety and anger vibrations of strangers. But occasionally, I feel the good things that others feel. I feel it when someone's happy, excited, or even drunk or stoned around me. I've had some strange experiences with this ability. Once I was staying in a hotel room and felt the orgasms of the couple in the suite next door!"

What complete and utter bullshit, Claudia thought.

How did Gil know the caller's questions before they asked them? She knew these were all popular questions that people have for psychics. Love, money, and health are the three most common topics clients ask about, so it *was* possible that Gil was just guessing their concerns. But she had learned not to give Gil the benefit of the doubt. He seemed to know too much. She suspected that the producer was taking the callers' questions, pumping them for specific information and then sharing this with Gil so it appeared as if he was reading their minds.

Now it was time to test her theory. Claudia turned off the radio and called the station to get a reading of her own.

The line was so busy that she had to call several times to get through.

"K.A.Z.Z. Do you have a question for Gil?"

"Yes, I do. There's something I need to know urgently!"

"Sure, Miss. What's your name, town, and your question please?"

Aha! She *knew* it! Gil was getting the questions ahead of time!

"Um. I'm... Mary from Moraga."

"And your question for Gil?"

"Was my Uncle Kevin's death really just an accident, or was it...*murder*?"

This was juicy one!

"Whoa! I totally understand why you need to know that! How did he die?" he asked, seemingly pumping her for more information to feed to Gil.

"He...*ahem*...'fell' to his death during a hike," she said dramatically.

The producer was riveted.

"What makes you think it might be murder?" he whispered.

"Well, Uncle Kevin was hiking 'alone' in Colorado when he fell 50 feet off a cliff. He had a lot of enemies," she said mysteriously. "We're still looking for answers."

The producer salivated at the anticipated surge in ratings.

"Don't give Gil any information unless he asks for it," he instructed her. "I'm going to put you on hold until I can connect you."

"Okay."

Claudia laughed at the producer's request that she not give up any information to Gil unless he asked for it. She'd already provided him with *everything* he needed to give a convincing reading. He would believe she didn't know the circumstances surrounding the death, which would allow him to fabricate the details. But this was a set up. If Gil fed back to her the information she gave to the producer then she knew he was cheating. Anyway, someone with real psychic powers should know that she wasn't Mary from Moraga and that she didn't have a dead Uncle named Kevin, but psychics gave numerous excuses for not being able to see through a ruse designed to expose them as frauds.

Claudia had been waiting for her reading for about ten minutes before the producer finally got back to her.

"Hello there, Mary?"

"Am I next?" she asked impatiently.

"No, I'm sorry. We're out of time for today," he announced.

"What?" she cried in surprise.

She was certain that Gil was going to take the bait.

"*But*...I've been asked to give you Gil's personal phone number because he'd like to give you a free private reading instead!" he said in excitement.

"Uh, no thanks," she said, unable to hide her distaste.

The producer was shocked by her sudden disinterest.

"Don't you want to know who killed your Uncle?" he asked.

"Nah. I killed him myself," she said.

Claudia hung up the phone and turned the radio back on to hear the remainder of the show.

"The winner of our competition is Dawn of Daly City!" Johnny announced. "Dawn, you've won a free private reading with psychic medium Gil Godsend!"

"Sounds like she lost to me," Claudia quipped.

So...back to my guest," said Johnny. "Gil, you have fans all over the world but how do you deal with the skeptics?"

Gil chuckled.

"Skeptics are angry people, Johnny. But they're angry at their failings in their lives. My approach is to not return that anger but to show them patience and kindness and hope they see the light some day. But I'm not here to prove to the skeptics that psychics are real. I always invite my audience to make up their own minds. Do psychic powers exist? It's up to *you* to decide..."

Claudia was suspicious that she didn't receive a live reading because they were "out of time for today", but now they'd moved on to the topic of skeptics.

Did Gil somehow guess it was *her* calling into the show?

"Wasn't there some crazy lady who devoted her time to exposing you as a fraud?"

Hmm…

"Ah, you must be talking about Ms. Claudia Cox," Gil said patronizingly. "She means well, but she is very misguided. She once believed that I used tricks in my readings, as many psychic frauds do, but I was able to prove time and time again that this was not the case with my abilities. Ultimately, she was unsuccessful and she disappeared."

"Well…mess with the best…" said Johnny. "Is she flipping burgers somewhere?"

"I hear she works for one of those detective agencies that tries to entrap husbands into cheating so she can destroy happy marriages."

"She's a man hater then?"

"Sadly, yes, although I wish her well…"

Now Gil was talking shit about her in public. This was the final straw for Claudia.

There was someone she needed to call.

She got onto the freeway, put her foot on the pedal and sped off to her appointment. If this massage therapist even looked at her the wrong way, then *he* was going to be the one needing therapy…

Chapter 8

Claudia's massage the day before confirmed the worst suspicions of the spa manager. All seemed fine at first. She was enjoying a relaxing massage from the therapist and he was behaving professionally, until there was an "accidental" slip of the draping sheets that exposed her butt. He apologized for being "clumsy" but then admired her "great body". A few times his hands came too close to her nether regions. Then, in the final few minutes of the session he offered to continue the massage back at his place over a drink or two, where her rubdown could become "a little more intimate". The guy was fired immediately. From now on, he'd have to ply his trade in the personals ads.

Now there was the matter of Gil Godsend and his return.

Taking him on was like playing a game of Whack-A-Mole. Every time she'd slap him down, he'd only pop up again somewhere else. Claudia didn't want to get involved again, but two women had come to her asking for her help.

She decided to call a friend and former colleague for some advice.

From a young age, Steve Shaw was fascinated by Uri Geller's spoon bending and other psychic feats. It soon became clear that Steve was also a psychic superstar who was skilled in prediction, mental telepathy and psychokinesis, that is, the ability to move objects with the power of the mind. In high school he became popular for bending keys and making the school bell go off so the kids could get out of class early. One day he was suspended for bending silverware in the cafeteria so his school changed to plastic tableware until he graduated.

Steve became famous at the age of 18 when he became a test subject for a paranormal research project at Washington University in St. Louis, Missouri. Founded by a generous grant, the McDonnell Laboratory for Psychical Research was established to study psychic phenomena, and they were particularly interested in children with the power of psychokinesis. The researchers began a search to find a true psychic and

Steve was one of two people selected from over 300 applicants, along with 17-year-old Mike Edwards. For four years, scientists closely studied and tested the boys' psychic abilities, and they both demonstrated incredible paranormal abilities. They bent silverware, keys, and coins, and moved paper and pens with their thoughts. They could identify pictures in sealed envelopes, make stopped clocks work again, and cause images to appear on film just by staring into the camera. Steve astounded the scientists who concluded, "It is evident that he has a full spectrum of interrelated psychic abilities."

The laboratory announced to the world that they had found two genuine psychics.

Little did the scientists know that the young men were amateur magicians who were disguised as psychics. Steve and Mike were part of an elaborate hoax code-named "Project Alpha" that was devised by magician and escape artist James Randi, a modern-day Harry Houdini, who was dedicated to exposing frauds in the paranormal community. It was Randi's belief that people such as his arch nemesis Uri Geller are really magicians who present parlor tricks as psychic powers. As he once said, "If Uri Geller bends spoons with divine powers, then he's doing it the hard way."

When the scientists started their research project, Randi urged them to have a magician present in the laboratory who could watch out for deception, either involuntary or deliberate, by the subjects or experimenters. They refused, and it became James Randi that they needed to watch out for because his two plants were using sleight of hand magic tricks to create the illusion that they had paranormal powers.

Randi was later accused of sabotage and trickery, but he believed he was doing good by exposing the flaws in the scientists' research. You see, the experiments weren't performed in a controlled setting. The scientists weren't strict enough with their protocols and that allowed the boys to bend the rules as they were bending metal, but just not with their minds. Also, the scientists weren't open-minded. They went into their research believing in the paranormal and trying to prove that Steve and Mike were psychic. The researchers didn't even check out the backgrounds of their "validated psychics". If they had done so, they would have discovered that they had posed as psychics before. The scientists were too blinded by the fame they thought would follow if they could prove that psychic powers exist.

If they were ever asked point blank, "Are you using magic tricks?" Steve and Mike had been instructed to come clean and admit immediately, "Yes, and we were sent here by James Randi."

But they were never asked.

Instead, the scientists laughed at the rumors circulating that there were spies in their laboratory. When it was finally revealed that the boys were faking their psychic powers, some of the scientists refused to believe the truth, arguing that the young men really were psychics all along and were now lying about being magicians.

Project Alpha fooled the researchers into believing that the boys possessed psychic abilities, and showed that even scientists can have the wool pulled over their eyes. Anyone can be fooled. The researchers had egg on their faces and in the wake of the scandal the laboratory was shut down.

When Project Alpha ended, Steve Shaw adopted the stage name Banachek and went on to become the world's greatest mentalist. He's the real deal that all the fictional TV mentalists are based on. Banachek is a mind reader who can read thoughts that no one could possibly know. He can find hidden objects, predict the headlines of a newspaper, and psychically see a word you've chosen from a book or the serial number on a dollar bill. Mentalism is a category of magic, but Banachek doesn't pull a rabbit out of a hat or perform lame card tricks. He accomplishes the impossible. Banachek catches bullets with his bare hands, drives blindfolded, and has been buried alive…

He has great influence in the magic world. You won't find a magician or mentalist who doesn't use some idea, trick, or routine that has been inspired by Banachek's magic. He is a magician's magician who invents effects for the world's best magicians, including Penn & Teller and Criss Angel. Certain ghost hunting shows have asked him to create seemingly paranormal events to dupe their casts, and their audiences, but he was too ethical to do it. Banachek is honest about his deception.

Like Uri Geller, there are plenty of magicians who insist they are psychic. Banachek doesn't claim to be a psychic, but he is more psychic than any psychic. He takes all five known senses to create the illusion of a sixth sense and simulate what a psychic would actually do. He can replicate all of the psychic powers using psychology and stage magic tricks.

Banachek has said, "So far, there is no scientific evidence for psychic phenomena," and that all psychics seem to be magicians, artists, and entertainers. But he believes that psychic mediums cross the line when they claim they can talk to people who have crossed over.

"They say they help people recover from grief, but grieving is a natural part of death," he says. Lying to people doesn't give them real closure or comfort...

Over the years, Banachek has tested numerous people who claim to have psychic abilities. It's been his job to make sure that the subject wasn't cheating by trying to pass off magic tricks as paranormal powers. Like the old saying goes, it takes a thief to catch a thief; so who better to catch a magician than another magician? He has tested clairvoyants, palm readers, dowsers, people who say they can talk to the dead, and even a woman who believes she can make people urinate on command.

Fortunately, that claim didn't hold water.

Banachek is unfailingly open-minded, kind, and fair, which has earned him the respect of both skeptics and believers alike. Claudia was a big fan. Okay, she used to have a little crush on him. She could never resist a sharp-dressed man; that had been her downfall with Gil, but no one was better dressed than Banachek in the dapper three-piece suits he wore on stage.

Banachek is on the side of the skeptics, but he is one of the rare nice guys in skepticism. He has honesty and integrity, while some other skeptics are as bad as the frauds. Banachek admits that the militant skeptics put others offside and belittle the very people they're trying to convince. As a result, "they don't break down walls, they put up walls."

Skeptics can be closed-minded, and too ready to draw the conclusion that a phenomenon isn't paranormal. They can also be too quick to insist on a natural explanation that may not be correct. There is more than one way to skin a cat, and at least 10 different ways to bend a key. Instead of insisting on explanations for the paranormal, Banachek likes to give people information so they can make a decision for themselves about what to believe in.

He always said, "Don't be afraid to say, 'I don't know, or you know what, I don't have enough information to make a decision. Let me call Banachek'."

So Claudia gave him a call for some advice about the Gil Godsend situation.

"Claudia! How are you, my friend?" he greeted her.

Whenever she called he seemed to be in some exotic or strange location. Today he was doing some filming for a television show in Las Vegas.

"I've only got five minutes to chat right now," he said. "I'm trying to work out how to make three elephants disappear."

Banachek was usually doing something crazy and unexpected. The last time she called him he was searching for a corpse to use in a magic trick.

"That's okay," she replied. "This shouldn't take long."

"You know, I've been thinking about you," he said. "I've seen Gil Godsend in the media a lot of late and wondering if you were going to step up and say something."

"That's *exactly* why I'm calling," she said. "I've been getting complaints about him from some of his female clients. They're asking for my help and I feel like I need to do something…"

"But?"

She sighed.

"It's the last thing I need right now. My business is really taking off, and as you know, in my job I deal with about as many sleazes as I can handle let alone dealing with Gil again. And speaking of sleazes, I've been much happier since I left skepticism. It's been a huge stress reducer to be away from it all and I don't really want to have anything to do with it ever again," she blathered. "Anyway, taking Gil on again feels futile."

"If you've made your mind up then why are you calling?" Banachek reasoned.

"Touché… I'm curious to find out what he did to these women, and I guess I feel a sense of responsibility to them," Claudia said. "But all the years I've tried to expose Gil as a con-artist have come to nothing and he's still hurting people…"

"That's not entirely true," argued Banachek. "These women are coming to *you* for advice *because* of the work you've done all these years."

"Good point."

"You're still helping people through this work," he said. "And remember, you wouldn't be doing this for the skeptics; you'd be doing it for Gil's victims, and to prevent future victims. I think you should get in touch with these ladies and at least hear what they have to say," he advised.

Claudia knew he was right. She had to contact these women and hear them out.

"Thank you, Banachek. I will," she said, thinking she heard an elephant trumpeting in the background.

"You're always welcome," he replied. "Let's keep in touch about this matter. But for now, I'd better get back to these elephants…"

Chapter 9

Claudia sat in the coffee shop in San Anselmo where she'd agreed to meet with Kate Thompson. Her face was aglow with the light from her laptop as she sipped on a cappuccino, nibbled on a blueberry muffin, and revisited old articles she'd written about Gil. For years, she had been preaching to the choir. Her only readers were skeptics who already agreed with her, not those who needed to hear what she had to say.

People only ever seemed to challenge their beliefs if they'd had a negative personal experience with a psychic, not because some skeptic had written a persuasive article debunking a dishonest psychic. Claudia was unenthusiastic about discussing Gil again but this Kate woman seemed desperate to speak with her. She couldn't refuse. And she was pleased that her articles were finally reaching their intended audience.

A pretty woman wearing a bright blue coat raced into the coffee shop. She recognized Claudia from her photographs online and darted towards her.

"Hello, Ms. Cox," she panted. "I'm Kate Thompson. Thank you so much for agreeing to meet with me today."

"I'm very happy to do so," Claudia responded warmly, now feeling guilty that she'd been so reluctant to get involved.

Kate took a seat at Claudia's table.

"I need to talk with someone about my experience with Gil Godsend and you seem to know him very well," she said. "I read all of your articles about him and I think they explain *a lot*," she said with a strained look on her face.

"Let me buy you a coffee and you can tell me what happened," Claudia offered, although Kate was so jittery she didn't really need caffeine.

Cradling a hot cup of coffee in her hands, Kate told Claudia about her session with Gil.

"He knew so much about me and my husband. He almost knew too much. He mentioned specific, intimate details about our lives, and my husband's death. That convinced me, at first. But you've written about how this could be something called a *hot reading*?"

"That's right," Claudia said, flattered that Kate had clearly read her articles. "Hot reading is secretly gathering information about people and presenting it back to them like it's a psychic revelation. It's cheating."

"How is it done?" Kate asked.

"There are many different kinds of hot reading tricks that psychic mediums use," said Claudia. "Some fish for information from audience members before a reading, asking, 'who are you hoping to hear from today?' If someone answers, 'Uncle Arthur', then suspiciously, Uncle Arthur *always* comes through. Others get their audience to fill out family trees or cards sharing personal information that's then used in the readings. They might eavesdrop on conversations in the crowd before a show or they hide microphones in the audience to overhear people talking about the deceased loved ones they hope to communicate with during the reading. These sneaky techniques are so common they call it "pre-show" in the business."

Claudia was on a roll. Once you got her talking about psychics it was hard to shut her up.

"Some psychics give pre-prepared readings to actors or stooges planted in the audience," she continued. "A few psychic mediums have even been caught wearing earpieces and receiving information about audience members from an accomplice. Or they might research their audience using information gleaned from ticket sales. They know where their targets are located in the crowd because of pre-assigned seating. Modern psychics who give private readings often research their clients online in preparation for the appointment. I think this is what happened in your case. Before the days of the internet there were networks of psychics who kept secret files on regular clients and shared this information with other mediums."

After her tirade, Claudia took a deep breath and sat back in her chair.

But Kate looked puzzled.

"This all makes sense, but Gil didn't have much information about me before the reading. I only gave him my name and phone number when I made my appointment."

"That's enough info for a talented con-artist," Claudia assured her.
     "No supernatural powers required."

"But I didn't even tell him *why* I was there to see him," Kate insisted. "How did Gil know that I wanted to contact my husband?"

"People visit psychic mediums expecting to communicate with a deceased loved one," Claudia reasoned. "Most clients hope to hear from a spouse or a parent who has passed."

"Then how did he know my husband's name?" Kate asked as she scratched her head in confusion.

"Well, let's find out, shall we?" Claudia said, feeling certain that she was going to find something damning online.

For a few minutes all that could be heard was the sound of her gentle tapping on the keyboard and the chatter of the other customers in the shop.

Suddenly her eyes grew wide and she looked straight at Kate.

"Your husband's name was Alexander Douglas Thompson..."

Kate's jaw dropped.

"That's him! That's my husband! How did you find that?"

"I did a search for your name and found his obituary in the *San Francisco Chronicle*," Claudia explained. "The notice reads, 'Alexander Douglas Thompson...who is survived by his wife Katherine Jane Thompson'."

Kate's shoulders fell.

"So it's *that* simple to fool somebody?" she sighed. She thought about it for a moment. "Gil initially said my husband's name was Alan *or* Alex. Why did he say this if he knew my husband's name as a fact?"

"He was probably trying to appear mysterious," Claudia said as she waved her hands about in the air like a cheesy magician. "Maybe he was pretending it was difficult to decipher the message from the spirits on the other side. After all, psychics are only actors. They're performance artists."

Kate got herself another cup of coffee and returned to the table where Claudia was still reading.

"You know, there's lots of information in this obituary that Gil could have used in his reading," Claudia said. "It says Alex was born April 15, 1980, and he died February 22, 2013. Gil could determine his age from those dates."

Kate reflected on Gil's words.

"Hmm...He did know that Alex was in his early thirties when he died."

"He could also speculate on the cause of his death," added Claudia. "As the obituary says, 'In lieu of flowers, memorial donations may be made to the Neurovascular Disease and Stroke Center at the University of California, San Francisco'," she read.

"That must be why he guessed that Alex had died of a stroke *or* an aneurysm!" Kate realized. "But how did Gil know that I gave Alex a final kiss on the lips?" she asked.

"What wife wouldn't kiss her husband goodbye?" asked Claudia sympathetically.

Kate had believed in psychics for so long that she was finding it difficult to accept that the reading might just be a scam.

"Gil also knew some things about me that he couldn't possibly have known if he hadn't been told by Alex," she argued. "He called it "validation". He knew that I was wearing diamond earrings that were a gift from Alex for our third wedding anniversary. He also knew that I'd worn them to Alex's funeral. How do you explain *that*?"

"Let me look this up too," said Claudia.

She did an image search using Kate's name. She quickly found a photograph of a smiling Kate wearing a green wrap dress and dangly diamond earrings.

Claudia swung around her laptop and showed it to Kate.

Kate looked crestfallen.

"Oh... I forgot about that photo," she said sheepishly.

It had been uploaded to a social networking site three years ago, around the time of Alex's death. Below the image was a thread of comments in which Kate divulged that Alex had bought her the earrings as a third anniversary gift and that she'd worn them to his funeral. She also revealed that the photo was taken at a work Christmas Party and that her dress was a present Alex gave to her to wear for the occasion. This was all of the information that "Alex" had supposedly told Gil during the reading.

In the photo Kate was wearing the *exact* same outfit and hairstyle that she'd worn to the session that day.

"Gil's psychic connection is Facebook," Claudia quipped. "The internet is a goldmine of personal information that can be exploited by con-artists," she added. "We have no privacy online. People searches and background checks allow complete strangers to find out our age and date of birth, relatives' names, address history, email addresses, phone numbers, marriage and divorce records, criminal records, and much more."

Claudia was on a role again…

"People tend to forget about the trail they leave behind online," she said. "They disclose personal details publicly on blogs, social media and networking sites, forums, shops, news sources, and in obituaries. By the way, Alex's obituary also says he was a resident in San Anselmo, California, at the time of his passing. Using that information, Gil could have done a background search and used an online map to pinpoint *exactly* where you live. He might have even scoped out your house in person so he could make it seem as though he could "see" your house in a psychic vision."

Kate remembered Gil's accurate description of her "big old house".

"Hmm…I suppose that's how he *might* have known that the garden and plum trees need attention, and that I have to clean the leaves out of the gutters", she said, still unconvinced. "But how did he know that I need to get the furnace inspected? Could he have used his psychic powers to see inside of my house?"

"I think that was cold reading, not clairvoyance," said Claudia.

Kate had read that phrase somewhere in Claudia's articles.

"Cold reading is a psychological strategy that is used to give what seems to be a very convincing psychic reading," explained Claudia. "It's a set of techniques that includes making guesses and using generalizations. A convincing psychic has an understanding of human nature, a good grasp of demographical information, and is an expert at flattery."

Kate hadn't forgotten Gil's charisma, confidence, and all of the compliments he paid her.

"As for his comment about your furnace, Gil probably assumed that a single woman living alone in an old home probably wasn't doing any maintenance. This was presented to you as amazing psychic insight, and he got lucky because it happened to be true."

Kate continued to give Gil the benefit of the doubt.

"He also saw that I had a problem with one of the toilets in my home. I had a plumber check them and Gil was right," she argued in his defense. "I had to replace a leaky flush valve in the basement toilet. That was a very specific prediction for Gil to make."

"That's still cold reading," Claudia insisted. "If he didn't specify *which* toilet was faulty, or the actual problem with it. Another cold reading trick is to talk about a trivial thing in the home that seems like a detailed hit, but it's actually common to many people. The psychic might mention some medicine in a cabinet that is years out of date, a box of old photographs that isn't sorted into albums, or a gadget which no longer works, will never be repaired, but hasn't been thrown out."

"I have *all* of those things in my home!" Kate marveled.

"Many people do," said Claudia. "Psychics might also say they "see" a problem with the plumbing or the electricity. Household maintenance issues are common and if the psychic is correct it seems like a hit. If it's a miss they can change course and turn it into a hit by warning, "But I foresee *future* problems". There's nothing mystical about this prediction because all homeowners have these kinds of troubles at some stage. *Either way the psychic can't lose.*"

Kate fetched herself another cup of coffee as she mulled over their conversation. When she sat down again Claudia noticed that her hands were shaking.

"I think I need to find myself a better psychic!" she concluded.

"In my opinion, psychic abilities don't exist," Claudia said. "But there's a big difference between the famous psychics and the little old lady who reads tea leaves as a hobby. There are two kinds of psychics, those who deliberately con people using hot and cold reading techniques, and then there are intuitive people who truly believe they have psychic powers. All they've really done is learned how to do cold reading without realizing it. I'll leave it up to you to decide which category Gil belongs to…"

"You don't believe that *anyone* can talk to the dead?" Kate asked.

"Anyone can talk to the dead," Claudia said with a hollow laugh. "But getting an answer back…that's the hard part…"

The women sat in silence as the whir of the espresso machine could be heard in the background.

"You know, there was something else strange about the reading," Kate said. "I *swear* that I could smell Alex's cologne. It made me feel like he was right there in the room with me."

"What's the name of it?" Claudia asked.

"Acqua d'Estate Essenza by Ermenegildo Zegna," Kate said. "I spray it on my pillow at night to remind me of Alex. It's discontinued now and really hard to find so I have to order it from rare fragrance sites."

"It's possible that Gil wears it too," said Claudia, knowing how much Gil liked expensive cologne. "It's also possible it's another trick."

She tapped away on her laptop and it didn't take her long to find the leak. She swung around her laptop to show Kate what she'd found.

"Here's a public profile showing that the cologne is on your wish list. I guess he bought a bottle of it and sprayed it during your reading to convince you that Alex was in the room."

Kate's eyes were wide with shock.

"Well, that explains why I could smell it on Gil's neck."

Claudia frowned.

"...On Gil's *neck*?"

Kate blushed.

"Yes..."

"What do you mean?" Claudia prodded.

Kate hung her head in shame.

"Um...After my reading we...ended up in bed together. But it's *not* as bad as that sounds. I thought I was having sex with my husband!"

Claudia spat a mouthful of foamy cappuccino across the table.

"He told you *that*?"

"Yes," Kate admitted. "Gil said that he could channel Alex because his spirit wanted to use his body to be able to touch me again. It sounds so... silly... now, but at the time it made sense. I was lonely and desperate. Afterwards he acted like he had no memory of what had happened."

Kate's face was burning red with embarrassment while Claudia's face burned red with anger.

"I feel like such a fool," Kate whispered.

"Don't feel that way," said Claudia firmly. "Gil is a skilled conman. He took advantage of your vulnerability, your loneliness, and your grief."

"I have no excuse," said Kate. "It was obvious when we were having sex that it wasn't my husband. His...technique was different."

The customers at the next table fell silent.

Claudia winced as she tried to find a way to understand Kate's reasoning.

"I suppose what he said made sense in its context," she said.

"And I believed him."

Kate started to cry softly and Claudia placed her hand on the woman's shoulder.

"The desire to believe is a powerful one," she said. "For some people, it's easier to continue believing in psychic powers than to believe that they've been deceived."

Kate shook her head in frustration.

"Gil goes all out to fool his clients," she said.

"He does," agreed Claudia. "He has a good understanding of what his clients want, and giving it to them is worth it to him to get what *he* wants. Psychics tell clients what they want to hear. That keeps them coming back for more."

Kate continued to provide juicy gossip for the customers at the next table.

"I'm sure this is way too much information for you, but the sex was *wonderful*," she said wistfully. Claudia knew this from personal experience, although now the thought made her cringe. "At the time the romance reminded me of our, of my, wedding night, but now my memories are blurred."

A tear sprung up in Claudia's eye.

"I lost my father eight years ago," she said quietly. "So I have great empathy for people who are experiencing loss and grief. When a loved one dies, all that we have left of them are memories. That's why I used to expose these crooks. They're exploiting people's pain and destroying their precious memories."

Kate grabbed yet another refill of coffee. Her hands shook each time she lifted the cup to her mouth for a drink.

"Your explanations makes perfect sense to me, now that I'm in my right mind," she said. "The only part of the reading I can't seem to explain are the names Gil used for me during sex. He called me "Sugarplum" and "Baby" *just* like Alex did…"

"...Which are common pet names for a lover," Claudia interrupted.

"That's true," Kate agreed. "But he also called me *Katherine*. No one *ever* calls me that. Not even my parents when I was a kid and they were angry with me!"

"Did you divulge *anything* about special names you and Alex had for each other?" Claudia asked.

Kate thought about it carefully.

"Yes, I did! I accidentally let slip that I called Alex by his full name, Alexander, when the two of us were intimate."

"Then Gil probably guessed, incorrectly, that Alex also called *you* by your full name when you were intimate," Claudia assumed.

"Hmm… Then that was a clever guess, but wrong," said Kate. "Calling me by a name I never use was the *only* mistake Gil made."

"That's the problem for psychics when they do cold readings," said Claudia. "The rare times that the client also pays attention to the misses…"

The two women stared vacantly out the window at people walking past the coffee shop.

"I think you need to go to the police immediately," Claudia advised.

"Yeah, right," Kate scoffed. "What would I say to them? That I paid Gil for a psychic reading and we ended up having sex because I thought he was my husband? That sounds crazy."

"Kate, he had sex with you under false pretenses and then he duped you out of your money. If you want, I'll go with you to the police station to report the incident," Claudia offered.

"I can't," Kate said. "I'm too embarrassed. I feel like it's partly my fault. No one would believe my story. I just want it to be over. *Please*…" she said with pleading eyes.

Kate was talking like a classic victim of abuse, but Claudia didn't want to push her after her ordeal.

"I won't force you to do anything," Claudia promised.

"Thank you," Kate said with a sigh of relief.

"But… what do you want *me* to do about this?"

Kate looked her dead in the eye.

"I want you to expose him…"

Chapter 10

Claudia scanned the restaurant in Corte Madera looking for a woman with a copy of Gil's latest book. This was the sign for her to identify Abby Cooper. She knew the woman had been a porn star, but she hadn't seen any of her movies.

Not that watching her movies would help me recognize her face, thought Claudia.

She approached a woman who was reading a well-worn copy of *Messages From The Other Side* although Claudia quickly discovered that this wasn't Abby but a devoted fan of Gil's who wanted to talk about how much she loved the psychic medium.

"Oh, for fuck's sake," Claudia said to herself. With the woman's blue hair, crocheted scarf and clip-on earrings she didn't look like an ex-porn star anyway, but you never can tell nowadays.

Claudia spun around and spotted a woman who *did* look like an ex-porn star; her silver ankh earrings jangling, among other things, as she waved her copy of Gil's book in the air. Abby was a Goth girl in her early twenties who wore too much makeup and too few clothes. Claudia wouldn't have otherwise known who she was, but she could see that quite a few men in the restaurant recognized her...

"Thank you for agreeing to meet with me," Abby said with a hint of desperation in her voice. "I need to speak with you about Gil Godsend."

"Not on an empty stomach," replied Claudia as she sat down at the table. "Let's grab something to eat and then we can talk about him."

They scoured the menu. It was the kind of restaurant where the portions are so small you'd have to find somewhere to eat afterwards.

The server came over to take their orders. Abby decided on a kale salad and Claudia chose a quinoa stir-fry.

"Good choices!" praised the server awkwardly, as though she was trained to say this to all of her customers regardless of their order. Then she spied Gil's book on the table. "Oh, my God! I can't wait to read that book! I LOVE Gil Godsend!" she gushed.

"Oh, for fuck's sake," Claudia muttered to herself.

The server's tip had just lowered drastically.

When the food arrived, Abby picked at her kale salad unenthusiastically, as people do, but she drank several glasses of white wine enthusiastically.

Then the conversation turned to Gil.

"So, you had a psychic reading with Gil Godsend?" Claudia asked.

"Yes, it was at his home a few weeks ago," Abby explained. She took a swig of wine, leaned forward and lowered her voice. "Look, I've read your articles about him and I know you're skeptical about psychics, but Gil knew some *very* specific information about me," she said. "He knew that my husband's name was Mark. He described what he looked like precisely. He knew that he had a lip piercing. He knew that he wore a black leather jacket that I sleep in at night. He knew that Mark had a scar from a motorcycle crash and that he died in a similar accident. He even knew some of my... embarrassing secrets. How could he possibly know these things if he wasn't psychic?" she asked.

Abby took another gulp of wine, then sat back in her chair and folded her arms, well, as much as she could. She was convinced that there was no logical answer to her question.

Claudia raised an eyebrow.

"But did Gil *also* know that you're the daughter and only child of Wendy and Scott Nelson?" she asked in her best gypsy voice. "Did he know that your father met your mother at a club where she worked as a stripper? Did Gil know that when you were sixteen you fell in love with your dentist? He promised to leave his wife and three kids for you, but the bastard never did... You had to learn at an early age that abortion is not an appropriate form of birth control... In junior high you feigned stomach cramps to get out of algebra class but the doctors in the emergency ward discovered that your appendix was about to burst... To make extra money you once sold your used panties online... You drive a canary yellow Mazda Mx-5 Miata that a client bought for you during your stint as a BDSM mistress... You drink butterscotch schnapps and after four shots you're anybody's... You were vegetarian for a year until an indiscretion with a lamb shawarma... And you wear a nipple ring and have monthly Brazilian waxes..."

Now it was Claudia's turn to sit back in her chair and fold her arms wearing a smug expression on her face.

Abby's eyes were wide.

"How do *you* know all of those things about me? Are you psychic too?" she asked.

Claudia was completely po-faced.

"I know these things because I read your blog," she answered drily.

Abby had forgotten about her old website, *I Need A Little Discipline*. She hadn't visited it in several years. In fact, she hadn't updated the site since Mark's death. With a sinking feeling she realized that all of the gossip that both Claudia and Gil had on her was available on that blog.

She guzzled down her wine and ordered another glass.

"I think Gil researched you before your appointment," Claudia said. "This is called a hot reading. He cheated. Psychics tell you things that you already know. They never tell you anything you don't know."

"Well, actually, Gil *did* tell me things I didn't know," Abby countered. "He said that Mark had a tattoo of a girl's name on his ankle. The name began with a "P". I told Gil he was wrong but he insisted I ask Mark's relatives about it. I checked with his grandmother and she told me that he'd once had "Paige", the name of his high school girlfriend, tattooed onto his forearm. His parents found out and they were fuming! They forced him to have laser removal. How did Gil know this if he's not psychic?" she demanded.

"Tattoos are common," said Claudia. "If Mark had a body piercing it's likely he had a tattoo too. Gil took a gamble. If he were wrong you'd probably just forget about his miss, but if he was right, then he takes the credit. Anyway, he was wrong about where the tattoo was on Mark's body. You said it was on his forearm, *not* his ankle, but you've ignored Gil's mistake."

Abby thought about this for a while.

"It was just a guess?" she asked. "How could it be that simple?"

"Have you ever seen those TV shows where magicians reveal the secrets behind their tricks?" Claudia asked.

"Yeah," Abby said. "I once saw this amazing trick where a woman in a box was sawn in half. Then the magician showed how he did it. It turns out there were two women in the box, not one," she said with an unimpressed expression on her face. "Suddenly the trick wasn't so amazing."

"*Exactly*," agreed Claudia. "Knowing how the trick is done ruins the magic. The explanations behind magicians' tricks are usually mundane. Gil is really a kind of magician too, but he's less honest about his deception than other magicians are…"

Abby hailed down their server and ordered a bottle of wine.

"What about his biography?" she asked. "Gil's life story is pretty amazing."

Claudia snorted.

"That book is a farce," she said. "*21 Days With Gil Godsend* should have been called "21 Days in Bed With Gil Godsend". The author, Gem Forrest, was a groupie he picked up at one of his live shows. He invited her back to his place on the pretext that he needed an author to write his biography. Instead of talking about the project they fucked each other's brains out. Gem stayed at Gil's house for three entire weeks, which was a record-breaking relationship for him, until he finally got bored of her and booted her out. As she was being ushered out the door she cried out, "What about the book?" Gil said to her, "Write whatever you want to write. Make it good." Then he threatened to sue her if she said anything negative. He silences his critics with lawsuits. He's very litigious. Kind of like the Scientologists."

Abby still wanted to believe.

"Gil *doesn't* have a gift?" she asked as she swilled another glass of wine.

"Oh, he has a gift alright. The gift of bullshit," said Claudia. "Gil Godsend isn't even his real name. Nor is Gil Faulkner. He was born with the plain old name Gilbert James Smith. He doesn't have an Aunt Tillie who schooled him in the occult and became his spirit guide. In fact, he doesn't even have an aunt. He didn't have a twin brother named Will who died of pneumonia at six months of age, but he has an older sister who's very much alive. His parents are divorced and he's not estranged from them, or at least he's not estranged from his mother. I've met Sue Smith and she's a really nice lady. She's *very* well off. I don't know much about his father, but no one does. I think he's a doctor of some kind who lives overseas."

Abby was staring at her, wide-eyed, so Claudia continued.

"Gil never worked as a psychic on the streets of Berkeley," she revealed. "He did live there for a few years, but as a psychology student living on campus at the University of California, Berkeley. He had a substantial slush fund from his mother, which he spent mostly on his cocaine addiction. He wasn't diagnosed with schizophrenia and he was never committed to a mental institution. Instead, he spent eight weeks detoxing in a clinic in Malibu. It was one of those luxury rehabilitation clinics where they do meditation, massage, yoga, and horseback riding. He enjoyed the whole experience so much that he relapsed. Twice. He's a spoiled brat and a momma's boy. That biography was written to create a cult of personality surrounding the fictional character Gil Godsend...and it did."

"*None* of it's true?" Abby asked as she poured herself yet another glass of wine.

"It's mostly fabrication."

Abby looked like someone had just told her that Santa Claus doesn't exist.

But the book was critical of Claudia. Perhaps she just hated Gil.

"Gil *did* host a radio and television show," Abby corrected her.

"That's true," Claudia conceded. "He's also written lots of books. I think he did grow up on a farm although he hates strawberry rhubarb pie. He did work for a psychic fair and he lived with that TV psychic Celeste Stone for a while. She's the one that gave him a taste for fine food, fast cars, and widows."

Abby winced.

"Oh, and he was probably sleeping with his art teacher and the maid," Claudia added.

At least there was *some* truth to the book, Abby thought in relief. She needed Gil's psychic powers to be real. If he wasn't psychic then it meant that she was...

"In your email you said that something weird and scary happened to you after the session. What did you mean by that?" Claudia asked with a frown.

Abby took a slug of wine and leaned in so close that Claudia could smell the booze on her breath as she spoke.

"Gil knew that my husband and I were into... kinky sex," she whispered. "He also knew that I had... a rape fantasy. If you're right then he knew these things because he read about them on my blog..." Abby paused. "He said I need to be careful what I wish for."

It seemed like advice at the time but in hindsight it sounded like a threat. Her eyes welled up with tears and her voice started shaking.

"When I was leaving he predicted that I'd finally get what I've been wanting..."

Claudia turned pale. She knew what was coming.

"...As I opened his door to leave he blocked my exit. He barked at me, "You're not going anywhere," and he slammed the door shut." Abby broke down and cried. "He forced himself on me...twice. At first I thought I was having sex with my husband."

Claudia recalled that Kate had said the same thing.

"I thought he'd taken over Gil's body so we could fulfill our fantasy together. But then he did things my husband would never do, and he didn't respond to our safe word. I begged him to stop but he wouldn't," she sobbed.

Claudia reached over and touched her arm gently.

"In our wrestling we broke his antique lamp and ruined his fancy rug," said Abby.

Now *that* behavior didn't sound like Gil at all, Claudia thought. He loved his antiques.

"Then Gil passed out. When he came to he couldn't remember anything that had happened," Abby said between gulps of wine.

Again, Claudia remembered that Kate had said the same thing.

"Gil thought he'd had a psychic seizure because he'd been possessed," Abby wept. "Maybe it's true. He kissed me and said, "Goodbye, Angel," just like my husband used to do before he went to work every day... I just don't know what to believe anymore..."

A thought struck her and she opened her eyes and mouth wide in horror.

"What if *something else* possessed Gil? Like a *demon*?"

Claudia dropped her forehead into the palm of her hand.

"Abby, let's not look for more ways to excuse his behavior," she said. "You were raped."

The reality of this hit Abby like a smack in the face.

"Why did he do this to me? He could have *any* woman he wants."

"Rape isn't always about sex, it can be about control and power," explained Claudia.

She was horrified. Her ex-fiancé had turned into a monster. She still couldn't believe this was happening. First Kate, and now Abby. Gil was many things but she couldn't imagine him raping anyone. This wasn't the man she once knew.

"It's important that you go to the police immediately," Claudia advised.

Abby panicked.

"I can't! With my background as...an adult entertainer... they wouldn't take me seriously."

"You have as much right to be protected as anyone else..." Claudia insisted.

"But I'd have to tell them that I had...a rape fantasy...and that I'd admitted this to Gil. The cops will think I was asking for it. It's my fault!"

"Rape is *never* the victim's fault," Claudia said firmly.

"But it was what I wanted. Well, I *thought* it was what I wanted... I gave my consent, at first, sort of..."

Abby poured another glass of wine and drank it in a single gulp like she was playing a drinking game at a frat party.

"Rape fantasies are common," said Claudia. "But having a rape fantasy and being raped are two very different things."

Abby pointed a finger at Claudia drunkenly.

"I... want... you...to *get* that son of a bitch..." she said in a garbled voice.

Claudia took a deep breath.

"I will," she promised.

"I hath to go," Abby slurred.

She grabbed her car keys, stood up from her seat and promptly fell down onto the floor.

"You're not driving in that state," Claudia said. "Let me take you home."

She hiked Abby out of the restaurant. They stumbled past Abby's canary yellow Mazda Mx-5 Miata and got to Claudia's car. Abby slunk down into the passenger seat, mumbled her address to Claudia and fell asleep, snoring all the way home. When they arrived at her place, Claudia watched as Abby staggered down the path to her door. She fumbled around in her handbag for her house keys and pushed the wrong key into the lock. Eventually she managed to find the right key and the coordination to unlock her door. Then she disappeared inside.

Claudia sighed.

Gil was out of control. He *had* to be stopped.

Chapter 11

As Dawn Pierce looked around the beautiful living room, her eyes fell on Gil's giant purple amethyst cluster.

"It's shaped just like a penis!" she giggled to herself.

He had such a neat and tidy home. She was certain that these surfaces would stand up to the white glove test. Gil must have a maid, or two, to maintain this mansion because it was difficult enough for her to keep her own modest three-bedroom house clean.

She couldn't believe that here she was in this magnificent house, having won a free reading from radio KAZZ with a world famous psychic! And here he was...*The* Gil Godsend, making a cup of tea for *her*! Her husband David, the poor, helpless dear, couldn't boil an egg, let alone boil the water required for making tea.

Gil emerged from the kitchen with a pot of herbal tea and two cups and sat down at the table with her. Oh boy, was he cute! He poured her a cup of steaming hot tea and the refreshing scent of peppermint filled the air.

"Mrs. Pierce," said Gil. "I sense that you're wanting to hear from your sister today."

How did he know that?

"Yes, Gil," she replied, her eyes wide and hopeful.

Gil closed his eyes, breathed in deeply and breathed out slowly.

He opened his eyes again and looked at her.

"I'm getting an energy of a woman and I sense that she is your younger sister," he said. "I'm going to give you proof to show that she survived the transition that many call "death" and that she is now living in the world of spirit."

"Ooh! Okay," said Dawn.

This was her first time visiting a psychic and it was all exciting and mysterious to her.

"This woman has sandy colored hair, dark brown eyes and olive skin," said Gil. "She looks a lot like you… I'm receiving an "S" name…like Sophia or Sophie."

"Yes! Sophie was her name," Dawn confirmed. "And that description sounds like her too. She looked a lot like me. Some people thought we were twins."

"Sophie tells me that she passed over with cancer a few years ago. This was a women's cancer of some kind…"

Dawn gave a sad sigh.

"It was ovarian cancer," she said, as she remembered the long and painful journey of her sister's death.

"Her illness was a long and painful journey," Gil said as if he'd read her thoughts. "But now she is free of her body and free of her pain… She's saying something about a connection between your mother and the disease…"

Dawn nodded.

"Our mother died of ovarian cancer too. It runs in the family so my daughter and I are screened for it regularly."

"Sophie is your spirit guide and she reminds you to do this," Gil said. "She watches over you and protects you, and she guides you in your decision-making."

Dawn believed this was true.

"I know she's gone but sometimes I feel like she's still here," said Dawn.

"She *is* here," Gil insisted. "Her spirit is here. Her love is here. The two of you share a sister's bond that not even death can break. You see her in yourself everyday, in your appearance and personality. You hear her voice in yours. Sophie is very close to your heart," he said. "I feel you're wearing something that was once hers?"

Dawn pointed to the oval-shaped gold locket that balanced on her ample breasts.

"This was my great-grandmother's locket," she said. "She gave it to my sister who wore it until she died. Now I wear it to keep my sister close to my heart." She approached Gil and bent over him as she opened the locket for him to see what was inside. "Here's a photo of my sister," she said as she showed him the picture and inadvertently showed her cleavage.

"Very nice," he said with a nod of approval. "Did you know that you're wearing a Victorian mourning locket?" he asked. "Memento mori jewelry is worn to commemorate the death of a loved one. The phrase is Latin for "remember that you must die." This style of jewelry has been around for hundreds of years, although it became very fashionable during the reign of Queen Victoria, when her husband Prince Albert crossed over in 1861 and she remained in mourning until her own passing in 1901. Many lockets contained a lock of the departed's hair that was hidden in a glass compartment; such as the one you have on the back of your locket. In the Edwardian period that followed it became popular to store a photograph of the deceased instead, as you're doing today."

Wow, he's cute *and* smart, thought Dawn.

She went back to her chair and sat down as Gil refilled her cup of peppermint tea.

"Sophie says to mention "the shoplifting"," said Gil. "What does that mean to you?"

"Oh my God!" Dawn laughed. "When we were teenagers we were browsing in a department store and I saw a pair of designer jeans that I wanted so badly but couldn't afford. I bullied Sophie into stealing them for me, because her backpack was big enough to hide them. When we got out of the store she admitted she felt so guilty and was so certain that all of the store assistants knew what she'd done, that she put the jeans back on the rack without telling me!"

"Your sister was younger than you, but a wiser soul," said Gil. "She is still your conscience."

Dawn couldn't deny that. Sophie was her baby sister but she was always the more sensible one. Dawn was stubborn, headstrong, and impulsive.

"Sophie's message to you is that she wants you to be happy…but you're *not* completely happy, are you?" Gil asked, his eyes narrowing.

Dawn let out a heavy sigh.

"No…I'm pretty happy…I mean, things aren't perfect, but…"

"Who's David to you?" Gil interrupted.

"He's my husband," she answered.

"I sense he doesn't know you're here."

"That's right, Gil," she admitted. "I didn't tell him that I won the competition to have a psychic reading with you. David's skeptical about psychics and ghosts and that kind of stuff."

This was only one of the many things they didn't see eye to eye about.

"But something else about David worries you," prodded Gil. "...You have a feeling that he's keeping a secret from you, don't you?"

She did.

This hit a raw nerve with Dawn. Her gut had been telling her that something was up with David. He hadn't been himself lately. He started working late nights at the office. He began dressing better. His fashion sense had morphed from wearing sloppy t-shirts with holes in them to wearing business shirts and ties. He even got a new haircut without her having to force him to do so. Was he doing this for someone else? He was always tired too. Most troubling of all was that he didn't want to have sex anymore. And if he wasn't giving it to her, then... he must be giving it to someone else...

Was he having an affair?

"...And all of the little things that irritate you about him are getting bigger, aren't they?"

They were.

Dawn made a mental list of David's annoying habits. He tosses his dirty laundry on the floor. He dumps his dirty dishes in the sink but never washes them. He's rarely ever home, but when he is, he ignores her. He just flops down on the couch to watch television or sits at his computer for hours on end. It's a cliché but he leaves the toilet seat up. He never changes the roll of toilet paper. He drops toenail clippings and beard shavings around the bathroom. He's always chewing loudly, clearing his throat, coughing, snorting, sniffing, burping, and farting. He snores so loudly that many nights she's forced to sleep in the guest room downstairs. Even then she needs to wear earplugs to drown out the infernal noise.

It all drives her nuts!

"These negative feelings are boiling to the surface, aren't they?"

They were.

Dawn found herself getting riled up about David. Here she is, cleaning up after him, washing his dirty underpants, ironing his shirts and cooking his dinner every night, not that he's ever home to eat it anyway, and the ungrateful pig is cheating on her! What did *she* do wrong? He was taking her for granted, after she'd given him two beautiful children and the best years of her life.

She cast a look at Gil in his perfectly pressed shirt and slick business suit. Here was a guy who had it together all on his own. He had a clean smell about him, like fresh soap, that made her want to sidle up to him and sniff his clothes like women do in the television commercials. But he also had an indefinable masculine scent that made her want to nuzzle into his neck.

I bet he doesn't fart in bed, she thought with a huff.

Gil stood up walked around the table towards her. He sat down on the tabletop next to her and looked down into her eyes.

"You're feeling unfulfilled in your relationship, aren't you?"

She was.

Things had fallen flat in their marriage. They didn't share anything together anymore. They had different tastes and interests in everything from food to movies. Not that they ever watched television together anyway. They'd always been different, but now they were drifting apart. Opposites attract...but only for a little while. Forget the seven-year itch, theirs was a twenty-seven year itch!

"You feel he is emotionally withdrawn…"

She did.

David seemed unresponsive and detached. He ignored her. He wasn't giving her what she needed anymore. She wasn't expecting chocolates, flowers, and romantic dinners. Well, yes, she was, but she really needed a man who would pay attention to her.

"You need a man who will pay attention to you," said Gil.

"Exactly!" she replied.

She was still a good-looking woman. Okay, she'd put on a few pounds over the years, but the weight had gone to all of the right places. Gil seemed to appreciate that by the way he looked at her bosom! She needed a man who would treat her better.

"You need a man who'll treat you better."

"Amen!" she cried.

Gil knew what she needed.

"You think about getting even with him, don't you?" Gil said as he bent down closer to her.

She did.

If he was betraying her then she wanted revenge. If he was sleeping around then why couldn't she have a fling too? What's good for the gander is good for the goose. She needed to take the power back and do to him what he was doing to her.

"It seems to me that he should be getting a taste of his own medicine," Gil said as he stared down at her with his piercing blue eyes. "You deserve affection. You deserve to be desired," he said in his low, sultry voice.

He ran his hand gently along the side of her face.

Dawn couldn't believe this hot young guy was coming onto her!

He locked eyes with her and leaned in towards her slowly. Her heart began beating faster. She thought he was going to kiss her.

"I want you to think about what we've talked about here today," he whispered. "I want you to think about what you need to be happy…that's what your sister wants for you."

Gil's eyes wandered to the clock on the wall.

"Unfortunately, our session is over," he said abruptly. "My final client for the day will be coming soon. Allow me to show you out."

He walked her to the door.

After the reading, Dawn felt very close to her sister, but very distant from her husband.

"When can I see you again?" she asked Gil.

He clasped his hands over hers.

"I'm always here for you," he promised. "Goodbye, Mrs. Pierce."

"Goodbye, Gil. Thank you!"

Dawn drove back home to an empty house. She walked into the living room and saw her wedding photo on the mantelpiece. It softened her. She picked up the framed photo and stared at it for a while, her face breaking out into a smile at the memory of the day. They were so deeply in love. David looked so handsome in his suit and bow tie. She looked so beautiful in her ivory mermaid gown. They made a gorgeous couple.

She'd never forget the passion of their wedding night.

"I'm being silly. Everything's fine," she said aloud. "He's not doing anything. He's a good man."

Then she wandered into their bedroom and promptly stubbed her toe on a pair of steel-capped boots that he'd tossed on the floor carelessly. He'd also left a trail of dirty clothes scattered across the carpet. She hobbled into the bathroom and was repulsed to discover that he hadn't flushed the toilet. She could feel her blood pressure rising.

Dawn noticed that it was 5:30pm. It was time to make dinner so she headed into the kitchen. Feeling uninspired, she stared into the fridge, wondering what to make. What did it matter anyway? David never complimented her cooking anymore. He rarely ate at home nowadays. She decided to cook spaghetti with a jar of ready-made sauce for the third night in a row. She filled a pot with water, added a sprinkle of salt and stood over it watching it boil. She added spaghetti to the pot and stirred it mindlessly. Then she remembered that she had switched off her cell phone during the session with Gil but hadn't turned it back on again. Perhaps there was a call from David.

Sure enough, he'd left her a voicemail message.

"Dawn. Look, it's gonna be another late night. I'll probably get in around 10pm. Or later. Don't worry about making dinner for me. I'll just grab something out of the fridge when I get home. Don't wait up...click..."

There was no "Hi honey," "I'm sorry," "I love you," or even a "Goodbye".

He sounded rushed and stressed. Was he really at work still or was he having a romantic dinner with another woman? Maybe he was having sordid sex with his lover in some dirty old hotel. That two-timing son of a bitch! How could he do this to her?

She stood there for a minute, not knowing whether to cry or get angry.

Then she decided to get even.

Dawn turned off the stove and tossed the pot of half-cooked spaghetti into the sink. She raced into her bedroom. She threw on the tightest skirt she could find and a low cut top. She ran a bright coral lipstick over her lips and brushed a peachy-colored blush across her cheeks. She spritzed perfume behind her ears, and up her skirt. She hopped into her car and made a mad dash back to Gil's house.

She rang his doorbell. When he opened the door she threw herself at him, kissing him and pawing at him like a woman who hadn't been touched in many months.

Gil welcomed her lips and hands all over him.

He picked her up with ease and carried her through the house and into the kitchen. If David ever did this it would have been his way of demanding dinner, she thought. But Gil had other uses for her.

What an enormous kitchen he had! Her eyes widened when she saw the craftsmanship of the cupboards and the gleaming stainless steel and marble surfaces. She'd *never* feel uninspired in this kitchen. She'd never dump a half-cooked pot of spaghetti into that sink! Oh God, would she love to bake a cake in that oven! This kitchen would be a joy to keep clean!

Gil lifted her up onto the black marble kitchen tabletop.

He took her hand and placed it firmly on the bulge in his trousers.

"See how much I want you?" he asked in his deep voice.

"Mmm...yes," she moaned. "But..."

Gil placed his finger over her lips.

"Don't feel guilty, Mrs. Pierce," he said as he used his other hand to hike up her skirt. "Your husband has a secret and this...this will just be our little secret. Your husband *isn't* here with us now..."

Chapter 12

The next morning Dawn awoke to a tender kiss from her husband before he left for work.
She didn't kiss him back. Who knew where those lips had been last night?
"I'm sorry I was late last night. Have a good day, honey. I love you," David whispered softly to her, but she pretended to be asleep. As she heard his car drive off she remembered where *her* lips had been the night before.

They'd been all over Gil Godsend.

It was an exciting evening of illicit fucking in crazy places around his home. It started on the kitchen counter top, moved to the dining room table and down to the wine cellar, and ended with soapy wet sex standing in the shower. These were the kind of spontaneous, uninhibited sexual encounters she hadn't had since she got married.

But… it wasn't the passionate lovemaking she shared with her husband. That is, that she *used* to share with him before he changed, she thought wistfully.

Dawn thought about David the whole day.

Perhaps she was being petty about his quirks. Perhaps he had his own complaints about her. Okay, okay, she *knew* that he did. She was aware that she could be nagging and controlling at times. David once complained that she treated him like a project she could "fix". She annoyed him with her spending sprees on clothing, trinkets for the home, and anything on sale. She saved a lot of money spending money on things she wouldn't have otherwise bought.

And, as she proved last night, she could be impulsive.

Apparently, the spirit of her sensible sister *wasn't* guiding her actions then. She gazed at her wedding photo and became sentimental again. David wasn't such a bad husband after all. He did share the household chores. He was her handyman who mowed the lawn, maintained the cars and computers, and prepared the taxes. He was the father of her children. He was a good man, and she loved him. She couldn't let twenty-seven years of marriage go to waste. For better or for worse, that's what she'd agreed to, right?

Dawn felt guilty because of her rash behavior the night before. What she'd done was totally out of character for her. What was she thinking? The rendezvous with Gil was meant to be retaliatory sex, a tit for tat tryst because her husband was cheating on her. Well, she feared David was cheating, and Gil implied he was cheating, and he was psychic. But could Gil have been wrong? Could she be misreading her husband's behavior? Was he really having an affair? Because if he wasn't, then that meant that *she*...

Well, she didn't want to think about that.

Was David a cheater? She *had* to find out for certain. But how could she do that? Should she start reading his emails and text messages? Should she follow him to watch his movements? Should she hire a private investigator to track him? She'd once watched an episode of a talk show about those detective agencies that use sexy undercover agents to tempt husbands to see if they will cheat. Maybe she should hire one of these women to test David and find out if he was cheating on her, or if he could be tempted to cheat.

The thought of testing him this way was titillating but scary at the same time. It was intimidating to think about a younger, more attractive woman flirting with him.

Dawn searched online and the nearest business was an agency in San Francisco called Suspicious Minds. What a clever name, she thought.

Do you suspect that your spouse is cheating on you?
Be the first to know and not the last to find out.
We use surveillance, tracking, computer forensics, and other monitoring methods to find you proof and give you the truth. Our team of licensed private investigators are discreet, confidential, and accurate.
Get the peace of mind you deserve.

Their client reviews were glowing.

I suspected that my husband was two-timing me...and he was! The caring and professional team from Suspicious Minds was able to find solid evidence for me so I could move on with my life, without my cheating husband.

This agency will catch your cheating son of a bitch boyfriend red-handed! I highly recommend them.

Don't sit around wondering if your man is a dog. Find out for sure.

There were dozens of similar reviews and it struck Dawn that in *all* of them the man was guilty of cheating. There weren't any reviews in which the wife or girlfriend was relieved to discover that she was wrong. She did some further research online and found the statistic that 85% of women who suspect their husbands are cheating are correct. Sure, David had never come home smelling of perfume or wearing a shirt collar covered in lipstick kisses, but Dawn discovered that many of his behaviors *were* the tell tale signs of a cheating spouse.

She grabbed her coat and headed straight over to Suspicious Minds.

When she arrived at the agency, Dawn expected that the place would look like something out of an old black and white detective movie. There would be a mysterious private investigator wearing a trench coat and a fedora and smoking a cigarette in a dimly lit office amidst a cluttered library of books. Instead, Suspicious Minds was a bright and airy office with sweeping views of the city. It was furnished with white leather couches and black calf hide accent chairs. There was an aquarium filled with exotic fish and the walls were lined with modern art.

There were no Sherlock Holmes stereotypes here. It was an office full of professional women. A secretary welcomed Dawn, made her a macchiato, and then led her to a room where she was met by a woman who was very attractive and well dressed. She introduced herself as Claudia Cox.

No wonder their success rate was so high for catching cheaters, Dawn thought. What man could resist this stunning woman?

Claudia led Dawn to a chair and the two of them sat down to chat about her concerns.

"What can I do for you today, Mrs. Pierce?"

"I think my husband David is having an affair," she blurted out.

"What makes you think he is?" asked Claudia.

Dawn frowned.

"Well, all the typical warning signs are there. His work habits have changed. He doesn't come home until very late at night. When he is at home he ignores me. He's paying more attention to his appearance. He's buying new clothes and getting his hair cut without me having to remind him! And we're not…intimate anymore…"

Claudia heard these complaints every day. They were all of the supposedly "classic" signs of an affair that people read about in tabloids and women's magazines.

"I'm sorry to hear this," she said sympathetically, "but these behavioral changes don't necessarily mean that he's cheating on you. Do you have any proof?"

"Yes, I do! I was told that he's cheating on me."

It was usually "the other woman" who broke this bad news gleefully to the wife. A malicious mistress who was tired of her lover's promises that he would leave his wife, and wanted to pressure him to take action.

"Who told you that he's cheating on you?" asked Claudia.

"A psychic," Dawn said matter-of-factly.

During her time in this job Claudia had heard just about everything, but she hadn't heard this one before.

"A psychic?" Claudia repeated.

"Yes. He's a really famous psychic too," continued Dawn. "His name is Gil Godsend. Have you heard of him?"

Oh, for fuck's sake, Claudia thought. She should have known.

"Yes. I've heard of him," she said with disdain.

"He's very accurate," gushed Dawn.

"He's a fraud," Claudia muttered under her breath, but obviously loud enough for Dawn to overhear.

"But he knew personal details about my deceased sister that no one else could know!" Dawn argued. "Then he told me that my husband was keeping a secret from me. There's no reason why he wouldn't be right about that too."

"Unless he had an ulterior motive for making you believe that," Claudia replied.

She recalled Kate and Abby's experiences with Gil and shivered.

"You...didn't...um...*do* anything with him, did you?" she asked carefully.

Dawn's face turned bright red in embarrassment.

"Um...Gil made me believe that David's secret was that he was cheating on me. Um...he convinced me that I needed to get revenge by cheating on him. Um...so, he and I... had sex," she admitted.

"Oh, no!" Claudia cried in shock.

This was now the third woman who had been manipulated by Gil in as many weeks, that she knew of...

"But how did you guess that something happened?" Dawn asked.

"Gil Godsend has a reputation with the ladies," said Claudia. "And a penchant for conquering married women."

"Oh."

Dawn felt a little stung. She thought she was special. But that explained why the young and handsome Gil was interested in an older, married woman. Maybe this meant that he was wrong about her husband.

"So, will you take on the case for me?" asked Dawn.

"Yes, and I'm going to handle this one personally," Claudia promised. "I'll track David and see where he goes and what he does. If he's having an affair, or even if he's just capable of cheating, then I'll catch him."

"Thank you."

Dawn sighed in relief. She was still convinced that David was cheating on her. Of course, that belief justified her actions of the night before.

Claudia and Dawn created a detailed profile of David. When they were done, Dawn received a timely call from him letting her know that he would be working late in the office until 10pm that night.

"Typical," hissed Dawn.

"But this is the perfect time for me to start the surveillance," said Claudia.

Dawn was very nervous about what she'd find, or wouldn't find.

It was after business hours so Claudia drove to David's place of work to verify that he was indeed working late.

He had already left for the day.

So far, this wasn't looking good. Where was he and why would he need to lie about what he was doing?

The next morning at 7:00am Claudia sat in her car parked outside the Pierce home. She watched David tumble out of the house into his car and she followed him stealthily. He drove to work directly without any detours. Claudia found a vantage spot outside his building where she could observe David through the tall glass windows of his office. He sat at his desk all day long, stooped over his computer, and only occasionally left his cubicle to grab a cup of coffee or chat with a colleague. There was a framed photograph of him and Dawn at the beach on his desk and Claudia watched him pick it up. She couldn't see his face to find out if he was staring at the image with love or frustration.

At 5:03pm, David left his office and got into his car. He drove to Boon-Nam, a posh Thai restaurant in the Pacific Heights district. Claudia knew the place and was a fan of their mo hor and geng sap nok gradtaa. David parked his car and disappeared into the restaurant. Was this a planned rendezvous with his lover? Minutes later he emerged carrying several brown paper bags and climbed back into his car. Was this food to go that he planned to take back to the office while he worked late? Or was he on his way to a romantic night in with another woman?

Claudia trailed him from a safe distance. David drove to a nearby neighborhood and pulled up at a magnificent home that had amazing views of the San Francisco Bay. He walked along the path, rang the doorbell, and a woman answered wearing nothing but a silken dressing gown and a smile. This must be his mistress! But no, David handed her the bags and was given money in exchange. Clearly, he was working a second job as a deliveryman for the restaurant.

But why was he doing this in secret?

This pattern continued for three more days. Then David changed his routine. He left work on foot at 1pm. Was he meeting with a lover for lunch?

Claudia trailed him and he led her to a jewelry store. She followed him inside and saw him holding an exquisite platinum diamond bracelet. Was this a gift for his mistress? She pretended to browse the bracelet display so she could sidle up to him and strike up a conversation.

"That's a gorgeous piece!" she enthused. "Who's the lucky lady?"

"It's a present for my wife, Dawn," David replied.

"It's beautiful," Claudia said, eyeing the diamonds as they sparkled beneath the store's lights. "What's the special occasion?"

"In one month we'll be celebrating 28 years of marriage," he said fondly.

"You don't look old enough to have been married 28 years!" Claudia flirted gently.

"Thank you," he said, not buying her flattery at all. "We married young."

"I don't know if I could stay married to the same man for 28 whole years," Claudia said with a cheeky grin and a wink. "I'd get too bored. I find it exciting to meet new men," she said suggestively.

He noted her subtle come on. This one must be a gold-digger, he thought.

"I'm a happily married man," he said steadfastly. "I've never been bored with my wife. I think she gets bored with me though. I'm a boring guy," he said a little sadly.

Claudia dropped the matter. Sometimes she felt guilty that she had to lead these guys on, but she also knew that a faithful man couldn't be led on…and this was a faithful man.

"I think you're a sweetheart. Your wife is going to love her gift," she said.

"I sure hope so!" said David. "Dawn saw it in the window of this shop months ago and fell in love with it. Then and there I made the decision to get it for her, no matter what it took. I've been doing overtime at work and holding down a second job to save enough money to buy this bracelet. Sometimes I feel like I'm doing more to destroy my marriage by trying to keep this a surprise," he revealed. "I think my wife suspects that I'm having an affair!" he chuckled as Claudia winced. "But I'm not that kind of guy."

"Well, it was nice to meet you and congratulations on your anniversary," she said sincerely.

Claudia took a look at some jewelry for herself, noting a pair of peacock green Tahitian pearl earrings that she wanted to buy. Then she left the store. She had a report to write.

The next day the two women reconvened at the Suspicious Minds office. Dawn sat across from Claudia, looking tired and stressed. She hadn't been sleeping at night and she'd taken to biting her fingernails.

"Do you want the good news or the bad news?" Claudia asked.

"I'll take the good news first," Dawn said hopefully.

"The good news is that David *has* been keeping a secret from you…but it's a *good* secret! You have a wonderful surprise on the way. He's been working overtime and he took on a second job to buy you a special gift for your upcoming wedding anniversary."

Dawn looked visibly relieved, but very guilty.

"David is a good man," Claudia continued. "So the bad news is that he didn't cheat on you. *You* cheated on *him*."

Dawn was dumbfounded.

"So, he's not an adulterer…but I am," she admitted, staring at the floor in shame. "But Gil *was* right about David keeping a secret from me," she conceded. "I wasn't to know it was a *good* secret."

"Many people keep secrets from their spouses. It was a clever guess, that's all," dismissed Claudia. "The real issue here is that Gil manipulated you into having sex with him. I think you should report him to the police."

Dawn shook her head.

"No way!" she refused, just as Kate and Abby had. "I'd be too embarrassed to admit I did something so stupid. And what would I tell the cops? I saw a psychic who told me my husband was keeping a secret from me, so I had sex with him. They'd just laugh at me."

"You're a victim of his scam, but you're not his only victim. Two other women came to me recently with similar stories of abuse and there could be more if we don't do anything," Claudia urged.

"I just want to move on with my life," Dawn said with tired eyes. "Isn't there anything else you can do?"

"It's ironic that you came to me of all people for help about Gil Godsend," said Claudia. "Before I became a private investigator I spent years exposing his scams to the public. Yet here he is, still scamming people. It just didn't seem to make any difference."

"I can't let this happen to anyone else. Please… try again," Dawn begged.

Claudia gave a reluctant nod.

"I will," she promised.

Dawn was happy with the outcome of the investigation but she was crushed by her own actions.

"How am I going to tell my husband what I've done?" she cried.

"Just be open and honest with him," Claudia advised. "You were tricked by a con artist and it's not your fault, but the two of you might want to see a counselor to sort out your communication problems."

"You're right," agreed Dawn. "This is a terrible misunderstanding. The whole mess shouldn't have happened in the first place."

Dawn went home to repair her marriage; not that David even knew it was broken. She was going to put forth an effort to right her wrongs. She would stop trying to "fix" him and start trying to fix herself. She would quit her nagging and controlling behavior. She wouldn't go on those shopping sprees anymore. And when he kissed her goodbye in the morning, she'd kiss him back. Tonight, she was going to make her husband's favorite meal for dinner, even if he did eat it out of the fridge at 10pm...

Chapter 13

Rainbow Woods and her friend Sally met in a coffee shop in Fairfax. Rainbow ordered an affogato; an espresso shot poured over a scoop of ice cream. Sally studied the menu and changed her mind three times before she finally settled on a cappuccino.

Claudia was sitting at a table nearby and she noticed the two women as they entered the coffee shop. They were typical Bay Area socialites who had too much Botox injected into their foreheads and dermal filler squirted into their cheeks. She eavesdropped their gossip about their sexy new yoga instructor when she heard Sally change the topic.

"That psychic party you threw last week was *fantastic*!" she gushed. "My reading with Gil Godsend was *amazing*!"

"Oh, for fuck's sake," Claudia mumbled under her breath. She couldn't escape Gil wherever she went. "There are *no* coincidences," she said, mocking him.

"Gil knew that I'd sprained my ankle during yoga class!" said Sally.

That was just a clever guess, thought Claudia. Sally had hobbled into the coffee shop wearing yoga clothes.

"He knew that I have a Persian cat!"

Claudia assumed Sally had a pet of some kind because her yoga pants were covered in long white hairs.

"He also knew that I was born in Georgia!"

That's because you still have a Southern accent, thought Claudia.

You didn't have to be Sherlock Holmes to make these observations. They were obvious to anyone who paid attention to their surroundings. It seemed to Claudia that Gil had used psychology in his reading, but not psychic abilities.

"I was surprised when Adam dared to come through in my reading," said Rainbow about her deceased husband. "I didn't think he'd be in heaven. I thought he would have gone straight to hell!"

"You told him to go there enough times!" laughed Sally uncomfortably.

She'd never confess it, but she'd once had sex with Adam in Rainbow's walk-in closet. Rainbow had walked into her bedroom when Sally and Adam were mid-coitus, so they hid naked behind a bulky fur coat. Well, not entirely naked. Sally was wearing a pair of Rainbow's stilettos, and exactly the pair that Rainbow happened to be searching for in her closet. When she couldn't find them she grabbed another pair and finally left the room, none the wiser. Unbeknownst to Rainbow, her husband had slept with several of her friends behind her back.

"Do you remember Gil told me that my aunt was really my sister?" asked Rainbow.

"Don't tell me..."

Rainbow nodded.

"He was right!" she said. "Indigo had a fake birth certificate her whole life and she didn't know it! That night after the party we found her real birth certificate hidden in a book in my mother's old trunk."

To Claudia, this was probably a hot reading because it was too good. Her mind raced with possible explanations. Gil could have researched Rainbow's background before the psychic reading. Perhaps Gil somehow planted the second birth certificate. Yes, it all sounded far-fetched, like a plot from an old spy movie, but any of these theories made more sense to her than Gil talking to the dead.

"Gil was incredible...and such a hunk!" enthused Sally.

She had a crush on Gil and meant to hit on him after the group reading, but he had disappeared.

Rainbow looked around the coffee shop conspiratorially.

"Did I tell you about my tryst with Gil?" she whispered loudly. She wanted people to overhear because she was proud of her conquest with the famous and handsome young man. Gil's good looks reminded Rainbow of her husband when he was younger.

Oh, for fuck's sake, thought Claudia. Not *another* client who'd had sex with Gil.

"No, you didn't tell me!" cried Sally with a touch of jealousy. "Spill!"

"He arrived for the party an hour early. I showed him around my house and then showed him around my...bed."

Come to think of it, Sally noticed that Rainbow looked slightly disheveled that day. She leaned in towards Rainbow.

"What was he like?" she demanded to know.

"He was *big*, if you know what I mean," she said with a sly smile. "And he had stamina." Bitterness crept into her voice suddenly. "He had *so* much stamina I discovered that he'd also slept with my sisters during the party…"

Gil's womanizing *also* reminded Rainbow of her husband.

Sally acted shocked but this was juicy gossip. She would be on the phone telling their friends straight after her coffee date with Rainbow. She was also determined to book a private reading with Gil.

Claudia couldn't stand it any longer. She had to say something but she wouldn't win friends and influence people by interrupting the women's conversation and blurting out, "You're wrong and psychics don't exist." She decided to approach Rainbow and Sally in the only way she thought they would listen to her.

She glided over towards them.

"Hello ladies," she said in a smooth voice. "I was just noticing this beautiful aura around you both. I thought I'd come over and share that with you."

Rainbow and Sally looked at each other like they'd just heard something truly profound.

"Are you a psychic?" Sally asked Claudia.

"I am," she replied as she looked out of the window dreamily.

"We just had a group reading with Gil Godsend and it was such an incredible experience!" said Sally.

"Oh, Gil and I go *way* back," Claudia said casually.

Something in her voice made Rainbow think Claudia had slept with Gil too.

"Can you do a reading for us now?" Sally asked.

"Don't be tacky, Sally!" Rainbow rebuked her. "That's just like asking an off-duty doctor to take a look at your mole."

But Claudia hoped they would ask her for a reading. She had a plan.

"No problem," she said with a wistful smile. "It's my duty to share my abilities whenever I can." She waved her hands in the air mystically. "I can't just turn my ability on and off, but let's see what happens…"

In imitation of Gil, Claudia closed her eyes and breathed in and out deeply. She opened her eyes slowly and fixed them on Sally.

"You have a need for other people to like and admire you, and yet you tend to be critical of yourself," Claudia said.

Sally's eyes widened and she nodded vigorously. She craved acceptance from others. During conversations with her friends she bragged incessantly about her possessions and name-dropped all of the important people she knew. She tended to buy her friendships with expensive gifts. She flattered her friends to their faces, but when they weren't around she gossiped about them and backstabbed them. Sally was just as tough on herself. She was very self-critical and always putting herself down. She was too fat, too old, and too ugly. She often told herself that she wasn't good enough and that she couldn't do anything right.

"You have considerable unused capacity that you have not turned to your advantage," Claudia said.

This was true. Sally had a law degree but she hadn't practiced in decades. Her husband was a wealthy property developer and when they married and moved from Georgia to California she quit her job to become a housewife. She preferred the term "homemaker". When she wasn't shopping, going to yoga class, or homemaking, she spent her time raising money for various charities, but she still reminisced about her days as a criminal lawyer where she grilled witnesses until they broke down and cried. Without her career she felt like she'd lost herself over the years.

"You often have serious doubts as to whether you have made the right decision or you have done the right thing," Claudia said.

Sally always second-guessed herself. She spent too much time churning over everything she said and did. She played scenes out in her mind of how things might have gone if she'd acted differently. She had crippling self-doubts about every single decision she made, big or small, whether it was about her marriage or simply the drink she ordered that morning. She still thought she should have had a latte instead of that cappuccino...or an affogato, just like Rainbow's. She always wanted what other people had.

"At times you are extroverted and sociable, while at other times you are introverted, wary, and reserved," Claudia said.

Sally was known as the life of the party. She was always the loud and obnoxious one in the room, especially when she had a drink in her hand. But this self-assurance was only superficial and masked her lack of confidence. Behind closed doors she was withdrawn and quiet. Sometimes she wouldn't even answer when the doorbell rang. Occasionally, she feigned sickness to avoid going to a party so she could stay at home, drink wine, eat chocolate, and read romance novels instead.

She suspected everyone hated her anyway.

"...And some of your aspirations tend to be rather unrealistic," Claudia said.

When she was browsing in a department store or shopping in a supermarket, Sally often had the feeling that a talent scout would discover her and that suddenly she'd be launched into a new modeling career or land a part on a TV soap.

"I hope my reading gave you some insight into yourself," said Claudia with a flourish of her hand.

"You read me *exactly*!" Sally cried. "Can you read Rainbow too?"

"Oh, you don't have to," said Rainbow shyly, although she was keen to hear what Claudia would say about her. Gil Godsend had given her a remarkably accurate reading, but she was a little wary after her personal experience with him.

"Do you have a possession I can hold for me to connect to your energy?" Claudia asked her.

Rainbow wore a rhinestone brooch that was attached to her scarf. She unpinned it and handed it to Claudia.

"This psychic technique is known as psychometry," said Claudia as she caressed the smooth metal. "I feel that this piece of jewelry has a connection to a female relative."

"Yes!" confirmed Rainbow in surprise.

Men don't usually wear brooches...

"This brooch is very important to you... I feel it belonged to your mother."

"It did! She used to pin it to her scarves, so I wear it that way too."

The odds were that it belonged to her mother. Claudia thought that the piece of costume jewelry must be of great sentimental value because the other jewelry Rainbow wore was made of precious metals and stones.

"Your mother passed long ago."

"That's right. She died in the 1970s."

The brooch looked vintage because of its retro style, while the blue rhinestones and metal had lost their luster suggesting they were decades old.

"I see that this brooch has been kept in a jewelry box or a chest for some time... You found it again recently and have started wearing it in memory of your mother."

"Yes! I just discovered this in my mother's trunk."

The brooch had a musty smell so Claudia supposed it had been stored away and forgotten until recently.

"Your brooch not only tells me about itself, it also tells me about you," Claudia said mysteriously. "I have the impression that you live in a large house with views."

"That's true! I can see the Golden Gate Bridge from my house."

Claudia noticed that Rainbow was dripping in designer labels. She assumed that the woman was wealthy, especially if she could afford a psychic reading with Gil Godsend, and that she probably had a fancy home.

"I see water near your house. I sense that you live near the sea."

"Yes! I live in Tiburon overlooking the Bay."

Claudia guessed that Rainbow lived near the water. Most people in the Bay Area did.

"I feel that travel is in your near future..."

"Wow, yes! I'm about to visit an ashram in India."

On the floor beside Rainbow's feet was a shopping bag from a travel store.

"And you had a recent... encounter... with a man that was less than satisfying, didn't you?"

Rainbow paused.

"Yes..." she said glumly.

Claudia overheard Rainbow talking about her fling with Gil, and noticed how her voice changed when she spoke about his betrayal.

Rainbow was astonished. This girl was almost as good as Gil Godsend.

"How did you know all of that?" she asked.

"You told me."

Rainbow and Sally looked confused.

"What do you mean?" Rainbow asked.

"I didn't use psychic powers, I used my powers of observation," explained Claudia. "The way you dress, your jewelry, and everything around you tells me about you. When I pay attention to these clues I can tell you about you. This is called *cold reading*. It's a way to convince strangers that you know all about them. You don't have to be psychic to be a psychic."

"But my reading was different," said Sally. "How did you know so much about me too?"

"Let me tell you about the Barnum effect," said Claudia. "This is named after P.T. Barnum, the showman who once said, 'There's a sucker born every minute'."

Rainbow realized she was about to become the sucker for this minute.

But this was too much like a lecture for Sally.

"Last century a psychologist named Bertram Forer gave a personality test to his students," Claudia continued. "He ignored their answers and handed them all the same results. Most of the students ranked their analysis as highly accurate although Forer took the profile straight out of an astrology book. He discovered that people interpret vague and general personality descriptions as unique to themselves without realizing that the very same description can apply to most people. For your reading I quoted lines straight out of Forer's original profile," she said with a chuckle. "It works just as well today as it did then."

"So you're *not* psychic?" Rainbow asked.

"I'm not psychic, and neither is Gil Godsend."

Sally liked Claudia better when she believed she was a psychic. She wondered if Claudia really was psychic but was in denial. She still wasn't convinced that Gil Godsend wasn't psychic.

Sally had an appointment with her esthetician to have Botox and dermal filler so she thanked Claudia politely for the reading but rolled her eyes behind her back. She didn't like skeptics. Then she air kissed Rainbow and left the coffee shop. She had phone calls to make.

But a light bulb went on in Rainbow's mind…

She had to shop for a new cashmere pashmina for her pilgrimage to the ashram in Tamil Nadu, but she couldn't stop thinking about everything Claudia had said.

Could Gil have used these techniques too?

She sidled up to Claudia.

"Woman to woman, can I talk to you about Gil?"

"Absolutely."

Claudia hoped this would happen.

Rainbow told her about the psychic party and Gil's highly accurate readings. Claudia explained how hot readings work and suggested that he may have cheated. Then Rainbow admitted she had propositioned Gil before the party. He was resistant at first but then he'd changed his mind suddenly when she remarked that he looked a lot like her deceased husband. Then he'd said something weird about her husband being there with them the whole time. Later that night she discovered he'd also had sex with her sisters at the party. She felt hurt and betrayed.

A few days later she ran into Gil in an antique store in Napa. He was as charming and polite as always but he acted like nothing intimate had happened between them. When she confronted him he denied having had sex with her or her sisters. He said that it would be unethical for him to do so with a client. Then he said something strange about his body being taken over by the spirits of their deceased husbands.

"I couldn't tell if he was insane or if he's had so many women that he simply couldn't remember *me*."

"Or... he could be a fraud," proposed Claudia.

Rainbow considered this possibility silently.

She smiled.

"Well, it was nice to have met you, Miss."

She walked out of the coffee shop a skeptic...

It was time for Claudia to speak with Banachek.

She pulled her phone out of her handbag and gave him a call. He was busy working on a new trick. He was trying to figure out how to convince a man living in New York City that he had time traveled one morning and woken up in a medieval village in England during the Black Plague.

Claudia told Banachek that she had met with the women who'd complained to her about Gil Godsend. In her opinion, Gil was using hot and cold reading techniques during his psychic readings with

Kate and Abby. She believed he was doing extensive background research on his clients that he used in his readings to give the appearance he was psychic. Then he was manipulating these women into having sex with him, if not actually forcing them, but then claiming it wasn't him. He said he was channeling their dead husbands and that he had no recollection of what had happened.

Then Dawn had contacted Claudia as a client. Ironically, she had been a client of Gil Godsend who'd convinced her that her husband was cheating when he wasn't. Gil manipulated Dawn into having sex with him, which almost destroyed her marriage.

"Then, as I was sitting here in a coffee shop this morning I overheard a woman at the next table telling her friend about how Gil did a group reading at her home and had sex with her and her two sisters! Not at the same time though," she added, realizing how that sounded. "To win their trust I pretended to be psychic and gave her and her friend a cold reading to demonstrate the tricks used by psychics. She then confided in me that a few days later she saw Gil again but he denied any memory of having sex with her and her sisters. Then he claimed that his body had been possessed by the spirits of their dead husbands."

Banachek was mortified.

"It's one thing when psychics are fraudulent but it's another when the psychic is a psychopath," he said in disgust. "*You've got to stop this guy.*"

Claudia dropped her head.

"I know," she said reluctantly.

"I'll help in any way I can," he promised.

"I'll need it," she said. "I don't even know where to begin."

"Why don't you start by going to some of his live shows and seeing what he's up to nowadays?" Banachek suggested. "Watch out for any new tricks."

"Will do," she said. "I'll report back what I find."

"Keep gathering evidence," he said. "We'll get him on something. Don't give up…"

Chapter 14

As part of his national tour to promote *Messages From The Other Side*, Gil hit the road for a series of live shows. Tonight he was appearing at an event center in Irvine, California.

The theater seated about 3,000 people and the room was filled to capacity. Gil's audience was mostly made up of young women, with a few cranky husbands dragged along against their will. Many of these women looked like they were going nightclubbing in their snug-fitting dresses and carrying clutch purses that were barely big enough to hold a lipstick. It was well known to them that Gil always gave private readings to a select few fans after the show, and each of them wanted to catch his eye.

With loud music pumping and colored spotlights dancing across the room, Gil's psychic performances had a rock concert vibe. That is, if it wasn't for the floral arrangement laid out on a table that made the stage look like a funeral parlor. Gil's ushers looked like roadies, that is, if they weren't carrying boxes of tissues for the bereaved.

At 8pm the lights dimmed and the crowd cheered. Over a loudspeaker a male voice announced, "Please welcome… *Gil Godsend*!"

Gil bounded out onstage to mass hysteria, looking stylish in a dark brown slim fit suit with a vermilion-colored woven silk tie that blended perfectly into his saffron shirt.

He had the air of a rock star about him.

"Good evening, everyone," he said in his confident and measured voice. "Thank you for joining me here tonight for this special show. I'm Gil Godsend."

This introduction set off the hooting and hollering again, and as the room slowly grew quiet a woman shouted out, "I love you, Gil!"

"I love you too!" he replied to her, but seemingly to everyone. Gil had a way of addressing an entire audience that made it seem as though he was talking directly to each person in the room.

"The living are fearful of death," Gil began. "But we shouldn't be. We were spirits long before we were humans. We're just spiritual beings on a human journey," he explained as he walked back and forth across the stage. "When we die we all have loved ones waiting for us on the other side. These spirits are loving, happy, and kind. There is no more pain. They are now healed and their souls are at peace. It's usually the living who aren't at peace; they're grieving and need closure. And that's what tonight is all about. We'll be bridging the gap between the living and the dead. I'll share messages from your family and friends in spirit to whoever needs a reading the most," Gil said to hopeful faces across the room.

Attending one of these shows was no guarantee you'd hear from your loved ones. In a theater of thousands, only a few lucky people would receive a reading. It was like a psychic lottery, but even if you did score a reading you couldn't be sure who might turn up.

"I know you all have someone in mind you want to hear from, but if you concentrate on hearing from Uncle Peter you may not be paying attention when Grandpa Joe tries to communicate with you. Please keep an open mind and an open heart..."

Gil put on his best cheesy comedian voice.

"Before we jump into some spirit communication, I'd like to tell you about a funny thing that happened to me on the way to the psychic reading," he said to a smattering of chuckles. "I was driving here to the show when a spirit took control of my hands and the wheel. I don't know this area very well, but this spirit had good GPS and knew where he was going. He drove me to a supermarket. In the store I felt compelled to buy eggs, flour, milk, butter, cocoa powder, whipped cream, and cherries. Then the spirit made a detour to the liquor store and forced me to purchase a bottle of port wine, but not any old port. This spirit has fine taste and demanded an expensive 20-year-old tawny port! By this time I was worried that I would be late for the show, but the spirit hadn't finished his shopping spree yet. I was guided to a department store where I was lead to buy a three-pack of XXXL-sized men's underpants."

The audience laughed.

"I feel there's a "G" name attached to this spirit. Does this shopping list make sense to anyone?"

A woman sitting in the fourth row raised her hand and an assistant ran to hand her a microphone. She was sitting arm in arm with a man and another woman, who must have been her siblings. They clung onto each other tightly.

"Yes! Those groceries sound like the ingredients needed to bake a Black Forest cherry cake," she said. "That was our father's favorite. His name was Gus, short for Gustav."

"Gus was born in Germany," said Gil.

"That's right! He was born near the area where the cake originated."

"What about the bottle of tawny port?"

"Each evening dad enjoyed a glass of port as a nightcap. He liked the high-quality brands best. It's now a tradition in my family to bake a Black Forest cherry cake on the anniversary of his birthday. In his memory we each have a slice of the cake with a glass of his favorite port as we sit around the table and reminisce. Tomorrow would have been his 79th birthday and I'm going shopping for these items in the morning."

"What about the underpants?" Gil asked with a smile.

She laughed.

"When we were young, mom bought underpants for dad from us kids as a birthday gift every year. When we grew older, we continued to buy underpants for him every birthday as a private joke. When he died, he had drawers full of unopened underwear that we had to donate to charity."

"Well, this year you won't need to go shopping!" Gil said as he reached behind the curtain wings and emerged with a large gift bag. He came down into the audience and handed it to the woman who began crying. "These are for you," he said as the crowd applauded wildly. "But the woman at the cash register didn't believe me when I told her I was buying the whipped cream for a spirit…"

"Now let's do some readings!" Gil shouted to the crowd's excitement. "How often do we get a song stuck in our heads but we don't know why? This happens to me all the time, and it's happening right now… I have a feeling we're having a shared experience here tonight…"

He walked down the aisle as he quoted song lyrics.

"Don't go trying some new fashion… Don't change the color of your hair… You always have my unspoken passion… Although I might not seem to care…I don't want clever conversation…I never want to work that

hard…I just want someone that I can talk to…I want you just the way you are…"

Gil recited these lyrics to the star struck eyes gazing back at him. Every woman in the room wanted him to love her just the way she was.

"These lyrics are going around and around in my head," he said. "How many people in the audience have been hearing this Billy Joel song too?"

Hands shot up everywhere around the room and people craned their necks to see that they'd definitely shared a group experience.

"It seems we've established a psychic connection across the room," Gil said, "but there's someone right here for whom this song has special meaning. This person lost a spouse with an 'S' name…"

"I think you're talking about me," said a woman nearby.

"Ah! So *you're* the one who put us all on this musical merry-go-round!" Gil joked as he took hold of her hand to strengthen his link to the spirit of her loved one.

"I think so," she said, a little embarrassed that she'd psychically affected the entire room. "*I Love You Just the Way You Are* was our special song. I was thinking about my husband Simon on the way here and the song came on the radio."

"That was a sign from Simon," said Gil. "It was his way of letting you know that he was going to communicate with you here tonight… Now he's saying something about your "blonde hair"…but you're a brunette," he observed.

"Oh, my God!" she cried. "That's the story of how this came to be our song. Years ago I wanted a change so I went to a new hairstylist. I walked into the salon with really long dark hair and I came out with short blonde hair! When Simon saw me he barely recognized me! He sang *I Love You Just the Way You Are* to me and emphasized the line, *don't change the color of your hair.*"

She laughed and the room laughed along with her at this romantic story.

"Simon passed recently, right?"

"Yes. He died six months ago."

"His passing was unexpected."

"That's right."

"I'm getting sharp pains here in my heart." Gil said as he patted the microphone to his chest. "...I'm feeling shooting pains down my arms...I'm out of breathe... My spirit guides tell me that Simon suffered a severe heart attack," he panted.

With a lump in her throat she looked to the floor.

"Yes. It was his first... and his last."

"Your loss was so sudden that sometimes you can't believe he's gone," Gil said with increasing sensitivity in his voice. "In fact, you thought you saw him in public once. You took a photo of the stranger because the resemblance was so strong, right?"

"Yes. Wow! Yes, I did!" she replied in amazement.

"You shouldn't look at the photo so often. You're making Simon jealous!" he said with a wink. "He says he's sorry that he left so abruptly but it was his time to go. You were on his mind until his last moment. His final message to you is, *I said I love you and that's forever. And this I promise from the heart. But I couldn't love you any better. I love you just the way you are.*"

The woman wept softly and others around her dabbed at their eyes with tissues. Gil gave her a hug and walked back into the cheering crowd.

"The spirits like applause," he said. "It lifts the vibrations in the room."

He cocked his head back and looked around. Sniffing the air he started to wander the aisles as if he was being led somewhere.

"I'm sensing the smell of lavender," he said as he wafted the phantom fragrance towards his nose with his hands. "It's like I'm in a field of lavender on a summer's day. The scent is getting stronger in this area here," he said, pointing to a group of ladies who began exchanging knowing glances at each other. "Who loved lavender?" he asked them.

"That was my mom!" answered a woman wearing a lavender-colored sweater.

"I see you're wearing mom's favorite color too," Gil noted. He was partial to a lavender-colored shirt or tie himself. It suited his complexion. "She's here with us now. I'm getting an Elle name, like Elaine or Ellen."

"Her name was Eleanor," the woman replied. "She went by Elle."

"She's saying that some people also called her 'The Lavender Lady'?"

"That's right!" she nodded in excitement.

"Whenever you smell lavender, she is nearby," Gil said. "Elle tells me she adored anything that was lavender-colored or lavender scented, such as soap, perfume, and flowers."

"We had a lavender tribute on her casket. Even the lining was lavender-colored," the woman said.

"She's telling me that she had a beautiful funeral," said Gil. "She says, "Thank you for putting me in that lavender dress and not that ugly pink one!""

The woman laughed.

"I wouldn't have laid her to rest in any other color!"

Gil suddenly clutched his stomach.

"I'm getting sharp pains in my abdomen... I'm feeling nauseous... I sense that part of Elle's stomach was missing... She died of stomach cancer?" he asked.

"Yes, she did," the woman confirmed.

"She wants you to know that she is whole again. She is past her pain," Gil assured her. "My spirit guides are saying something about your daughter, Claire."

"...But I don't have a daughter," the woman said.

"You have another family member by the name of Claire?" Gil asked.

"No," the woman replied with a confused expression on her face.

"Can you think of anyone named Claire in your life?"

"...No..."

"Think hard now..." Gil insisted.

She paused and shrugged her shoulders.

"I'm sorry," she said, wanting so badly to please him. "I can't think of *anyone* by that name."

Gil addressed the audience.

"I'm hearing the name Claire in my head. My spirit guides are never wrong. Who is Claire, please?" he asked as he looked around the room. "I sense this young lady standing to my right side. She has an urgent message..."

A woman sitting right behind him piped up.

"I had a daughter named Claire."

"Ah! Then this next message is for you," he said as a collective sigh of relief traveled across the room. Not that they believed Gil could ever be wrong. "What just happened is known as psychic interference," he explained. "This is when I'm giving a reading but I get my psychic wires crossed and I receive a message that is intended for someone nearby instead. The spirit's energy is so strong that it interrupts the existing reading."

He turned back to the woman.

"Claire is showing me a bowl of cherries. Do you understand that?"

"Um...I don't know."

"Did she like eating cherries?"

"...No. Actually, when she was young a lot of her medicines were cherry-flavored and she developed such an aversion to it that she hated anything that tasted like cherries."

"Well, there's some sort of cherry connection here. Was there something in the house to do with cherries?"

Her expression was blank for a moment. Then she pushed her palm to her forehead.

"How could I forget? When she died we were living on Cherry Lane!" she said, excited that she had remembered.

"Drawing a complete blank during a psychic reading is common," said Gil. "This short term memory lapse is known as psychic amnesia. But sooner or later the light bulb always goes off! Now, years before Claire died she was a happy girl. She enjoyed shopping, surfing, and hanging out with her friends."

"Yes. And then everything changed. She became quiet and withdrawn."

"One minute she was there," Gil snapped his fingers, "and then she was gone..."

"Yes," she said softly.

"She crossed herself over," Gil said. "She took her own life... She says she is sorry." One of Gil's ushers ran towards her with a box of tissues. "You suffer a lot of guilt, but you have to let go of that. If she hadn't died this way, she would have died a year later in a car accident. Part of her knew she was going to die young," he said gently.

He addressed the crowd.

"We can't be expected to understand all of our actions while we're here, but our spirits do have a plan."

Time was running out so Gil darted about the room trying to give as many personalized readings as possible. He dispensed messages and advice from his spirit guides to random people in the audience. Aunt Tillie warned a woman that she needed to quit smoking immediately otherwise she was going to develop emphysema. Will told another woman that her estranged son was willing to reconcile with her. Oleg reminded a man that he needed to return a lawnmower he borrowed over five years ago, which was getting rusty in his tool shed.

Almost two hours into his performance Gil jumped back up onto the stage.

"We're going to close this evening's show with a session of guided meditation," he announced. "I'll be using visualization to ease you into a state of relaxation." Gil's voice began to take on a slow, breathy rhythm. "Everyone can benefit from meditation, and you'll get exactly what you need from it. For some, it will be an opportunity for stress relief and to restore calm to the mind, relax the body, and achieve inner peace. For others, this meditation will facilitate healing, or improve your sense of wellbeing."

He scanned the audience as he spoke, as if he was gazing into each and every person's eyes.

"Meditation also promotes our natural psychic abilities. If you've lost an item, this meditation will reveal to you where it's hiding. If you're sick, this meditation will help guide you to the cure. If you want to make a change in your life, this meditation will show you a path. And if you don't get out of this what you were expecting, don't worry, because you will have gotten something else you needed much more."

Dreamy, ethereal new age music filled the room.

"We're going to turn down the lights, and as they're dimming, I want you to close your eyes slowly," Gil said in a soothing tone. "Relax your muscles. Your body will continue to unwind as you meditate. Now I want you to take in a deep breath. Breathe in slowly…and hold… Now exhale very slowly…Do it again. Breathe in…hold…breathe out… Feel your chest and stomach gently rise and fall with each breath. See how your breath continues to flow…deeply…calmly… Now begin to quiet your mind. Notice any stray thoughts, but don't dwell on them. Simply let them pass.

You won't be distracted by any little noises around you. Focus on the sound of my voice... and my words..."

"...Imagine that it's dusk... Look up into the sky. Become lost staring into the swirling sunset colors... The sky is becoming darker and darker as the moments pass, until finally, the sky is pitch black... As night begins you start to see stars in the sky. First just one star...and then another...and another...until there is a blanket of stars filling the sky. Some are twinkling... See them shine and gleam like tiny diamonds... You notice that they twinkle to their own tempo... They slowly become brighter and brighter... The stars are pure light... Let that light stream into you through the crown of your head... Allow the light to fill your entire being... Feel it flowing through you... This is who you are... Feel yourself in this place... And as I stand next to you in this place in silence, I want you to explore your surroundings..."

As the hypnotic music continued, Gil stood on stage scanning the crowd, almost as if to make sure no one was cheating by having their eyes open. After a few minutes, his gentle voice mixed in with the music.

"Slowly come back down to earth... See yourself in a beautiful garden on a day in spring... It's quiet, safe, and peaceful... Feel the gentle warmth of the sun on your skin... Breathe in the perfumed scent of flowers... You're lying on your back in the soft green grass... Beneath you is the earth... It embraces you... You are now grounded..."

During the guided meditation an assistant walked through the audience. He was careful not to disturb anyone as he approached a woman wearing a scarf wrapped around her head.

"Here's a personal message for you from Gil Godsend," the man whispered in her ear. She took the card he offered and placed it in her purse.

"I'm going to count down from five, and when I do, you'll open your eyes and feel energized, alert, and refreshed. ...5...4...3...2...1..."

Gil snapped his fingers.

"Open your eyes..."

All around the room, eyes popped open and blinked at the bright lights while people stretched and yawned as they awakened from their dreamy state.

"When you go somewhere for the first time, finding your way there can be difficult, but once you've been there, finding the trail back is much easier and faster," said Gil. "The place you just went to is extremely sacred and divine. When you need to go back there it will be waiting for you, and so will I," he promised. "Thank you for joining me tonight," he said. "I hope you found the experience to be inspirational and insightful. I look forward to seeing you all again very soon. Good night!"

Gil left the stage to wild applause.

He received a standing ovation so he returned and gave a grateful bow.

His fans filed out of the hall slowly as they gossiped about how inspiring the show was, how handsome Gil looked, and how powerful it felt just to be in his presence. They shuffled into the lobby to the merchandise table where they snatched up copies of Gil's books, DVDs, and jewelry.

As the woman in the scarf walked quickly through the lobby she reached into her purse and pulled out the card that was given to her. It read:

I understand your pain. The time is right and the connection is strong. Join me backstage after the show for a private one-on-one reading to help you find closure.

Gil Godsend.

Claudia unwound the scarf from her head and went backstage.

Chapter 15

Claudia planned to approach Gil after the show. She was going to try to catch him exiting the backstage door, but this sudden turn of events was much better. She had been given one of the famed "P-Passes" that granted backstage access to a few selected fans and entitled them to a free psychic reading, and usually more, with none other than Gil himself.

During her research over the years she'd only heard rumors about these P-Passes. Until now she wasn't even sure if they really existed or if they were just urban legend. Supposedly, "P" stood for "Premonition", but she'd heard that his crew jokingly referred to them as "Pussy Passes". They were handed out to women handpicked by the crew from the audience, like Gil was some kind of rock star.

Claudia didn't even have to dress like a bimbo to score this pass. Upon entrance to the theater, all attendees were asked to fill out a card "for marketing purposes". It asked for all kinds of personal information; name, address, hobbies, and who you hoped to hear from that night. This was a classic hot reading scam. These cards were collected before the show and Claudia believed the information was used in Gil's act, and for him to procure willing women afterwards. Claudia got lucky pretending to be a young widow hoping to communicate with her deceased husband.

She walked back into the theater and approached the stage. A menacing-looking bodyguard stood at the top of the stairs. She climbed the steps but he blocked her entrance, his muscles rippling as he folded his arms.

"You need to pay the toll if you wanna pass," he said as he leered at her.

"The toll?" she asked. "What do you mean?"

"The TOLL, sweetheart," he boomed as he grabbed his crotch.

"Oh. You're asking me for a blow job?" she asked innocently.

"I'm *telling* you to give me a blow job, sweetheart...that is, if you want to meet Mr. Godsend..."

Was he serious? This was a psychic show, not a 1970s KISS concert.

"I can give you a kick in the balls instead," Claudia said, poker-faced.

"You're a feisty one!" he bellowed as he moved in towards her menacingly. "Let me hear you say that again with my dick in your mouth."

She quickly flashed her P-Pass.

"But I have one of these," she said.

He backed off. Then he inspected the pass carefully because some of these crazy chicks were known to forge these precious cards. This one seemed legit. Then he looked her up and down. She was definitely Gil's type. In fact, she was his type too. On occasion, he was the lucky recipient of a leftover groupie. He didn't even mind a used one. Sometimes he liked them that way. He might get a crack at this chick after Gil was finished with her. Satisfied that the P-Pass was authentic, he handed it back to her with a knowing smile.

She shuddered. He clearly thought that she and Gil were going to...ugh...

"Mr. Godsend is freshening up after his performance. I'll take you back to the green room to wait for him, sweetheart," he sneered. He led her there and slapped her on the backside, which propelled her into the room. "Get yourself a drink," he ordered.

What a misogynistic piece of shit. She still wanted to kick him in the balls.

Claudia was the first person to arrive at the green room. It was tastefully decorated with modern furniture and plush carpet...all in complementary shades of green. Only Gil would insist that his green room actually be *green*.

The food was color-coordinated to match the décor too. Claudia reached for a delicate display of green grapes and tapped them to make sure the perfectly shiny grapes weren't made of glass. They were real, so she grabbed a bunch and nibbled at them. There was enough catered food and drink for him to have invited the entire audience backstage.

She started to feel a little nervous, she hadn't seen Gil in years and she didn't know what to expect, so she snatched a bottle of chardonnay and poured herself a glass of liquid courage. Then she poured herself another one. Soon, the room began filling up with reporters, fans, groupies, and various hangers-on who were there for the after party. She made an attempt to mingle, but she hadn't had enough to drink to deal with this awful crowd of sycophants who only wanted to talk about Gil.

Claudia found a corner of the room and stood watching the spectacle from a safe distance. She jumped when she looked down and noticed a very short man looking up at her. He looked like a smaller clone of Gil.

"Excuse me, Miss. I'm one of Mr. Godsend's assistants. I'm here to take you to meet him," he said in a voice that was a higher-pitched version of Gil's. He reminded her of *Austin Powers'* "Mini-Me" character and "Tattoo" from *Fantasy Island*.

He took her by the arm gently and led her to a private room.

Gil wasn't there yet.

"Can I get you anything? An alcoholic beverage, perhaps?" he asked.

"No, thanks," she replied.

Geez, they were really pushing the booze. Gil clearly liked his clients to be liquored up for their readings.

The Mini-Gil left her alone to wait and she took in her surroundings. In the center of the room was a table with a burning candle that smelled of sandalwood, and the ubiquitous box of tissues. It didn't escape her attention that there was an adjoining room that contained a large bed. Gross.

Claudia took off her trench coat, sat down at the table, and waited...and waited...and waited...This bullshit was typical of Gil's one-upmanship; all of his decadence and flashy displays of wealth, the mystery and secrecy, and then making people wait for him.

Suddenly, the door flung open wide and Gil stood there with his back to her as he signed autographs for a group of fans. She rolled her eyes. More one-upmanship, she thought. His fans eventually left, and then finally, he turned around to face her.

She was annoyed with herself when her heart skipped a beat. She hadn't seen Gil in person for many years. The last time she saw him he'd been a youth, and now he was a man. A very handsome man.

She had to stifle a giggle though when she saw that he was wearing a green shirt and tie to match the green room.

But Gil was caught off guard.

"Hello, Gil," she said.

He stood there, staring at her.

"Gil?"

He was speechless.

"You seem surprised," she said. "Is this where I insert a joke about you being psychic so you should have seen this coming?"

"...*You*..." he whispered.

"Yes, me," she confirmed. "I guess it was synchronicity that I was handed one of your... *ahem*... Pussy Passes. You were right, after all. There are *no* coincidences!"

Gil straightened his tie and regained his composure.

"I've always told you so, Claudia... or should I call you, Mary of Moraga?"

That was the fake name she'd used when she called into Johnny Lombard's radio show the day Gil was being interviewed. She suspected then that he knew who she was.

"How *did* you know that?" she asked.

"I'm psychic," he said with a grin. "And my condolences. I'm so sorry to hear that your Uncle Kevin passed...and your husband too, apparently..."

"Oh yes, my fake husband," she said. "He was still a better choice than you."

"Ouch! That hurt!" he said as he patted his heart. "So, how did you enjoy the show tonight?"

"I'm impressed. You've become a slick act," she complimented him.

She meant it too. She didn't have any respect for his deception, but she couldn't help admiring his showmanship.

"Why, thank you," he said, as he joined her at the table.

"That was a nice touch about the spirit forcing you to buy the groceries and the big underpants," she said. "I've never seen that trick before. Well done. It made me think of the unpopular kid in school who buys lunch for the other children so they'll like him."

"Ah, you can take the girl out of skepticism but you can't take the skepticism out of the girl!" he said with a wink.

"I know that's how you like your women, not questioning anything."

Gil laughed.

He had a warm, infectious laugh and Claudia couldn't help smiling.

"Not the women I care about," he said pointedly. "Claudia, I've missed this banter with you... Isn't this the part of our fight where we make up and go to bed together?"

The smile ran away from her face.

"I'm onto you, Gil Godsend."

"Well, not yet, but you could be," he said with a motion of his hand towards the bed in the next room.

Didn't he *ever* stop thinking about sex?

"No," he replied out loud to her thought.

"How can you joke about this?" she cried in frustration. "I know what you did to those poor women who had private readings at your home," she said, her eyes narrowing. "They came to me asking for my help. You're exploiting the suffering of grieving people!"

"I gave them piece of mind and closure," Gil replied in earnest.

"By fucking them?" She shook her head. "You're a fraud..."

"Keep saying that and I'll sue you for slander," Gil threatened.

"Only the guilty sue for slander", she snapped back. "But there are other names I can call you that'll get around those pesky libel laws, like asshole, motherfucker, and prick!"

"That's not what you *used* to call me," he said with a sly smile.

She looked away as she recalled an uncomfortable memory of the two of them, naked, sweaty, and writhing on the bed together. Her face turned bright red.

Why did she ever have sex with this jerk?

"Because we were in love and engaged to be married," Gil said.

She hated it when he seemed to know what she was thinking, but she believed that he wasn't reading her mind, only her body language. This was just another cold reading trick.

"Don't remind me," she said.

She got out of her chair and stood over him.

"Do you really think I'm here to reminisce about the old times? I'm here to put you on notice. Your unethical behavior will *not* continue. I'm going to expose your scam to the public!"

He raised an eyebrow.

"Oh, really? I think you're trying to take me down because you've always liked my second coming..."

She raised an eyebrow and smiled.

"That's because your first was always too quick."

Gil rose from his seat. Claudia was a tall woman but he still towered over her.

"When will you ever learn, Claudia?" he said in a patronizing tone, making her feel like she was a little girl being rebuked by her father. "Every time the skeptics attack psychics, they attack personal belief systems. Aggressive tactics don't change minds. People only defend their beliefs more passionately. You're telling people they're wrong and stupid but then expecting to persuade them to side with you. *You'll lose every time.*"

He stood there staring down at her with his piercing blue eyes.

It was unnerving.

"Claudia..." he said, his voice softening. "I emailed you a few years ago."

"I know. I ignored you."

"Yes, you did," he said.

She was surprised that he sounded hurt.

"Claudia..."

He still hadn't taken his eyes off her and she felt awkward at this unexpected turn of events.

"Claudia... You're even more beautiful than I remember you."

Did she just batter her eyelids at Gil? Yes, she did. She looked away.

She thought he'd grown even more handsome over the years, but she wasn't going to say so. She had despising him down to an art form, and she just wasn't prepared to give or receive compliments.

"Claudia...I've missed you."

She said nothing.

"I wish..." his voice trailed off.

All of a sudden he was dangerously close to her. He reached out and touched her shoulder cautiously, and then he drew her towards him. He laid his cheek against her head and began stroking her hair. It all felt so familiar to her and she found herself nuzzling into his chest. Her eyes closed for a moment.

What was she doing?

She snapped out of it and pulled away from him.

"Please... don't," she mumbled as she started putting on her trench coat. "I have to go."

"So, you don't want that free psychic reading?"

"I've had enough of psychics for one night," she said in exasperation. "Speaking of which, *I Love You Just The Way You Are* was playing in *my* head during the show too. That's because I heard it on the radio on the way here! I think you did a hot reading on that woman, and then you called in a favor with one of your buddies to play the song because it played on your old radio station, K.N.O.W. Most of your crazy fans would be listening to that new age crap on the way to your show tonight. Shared experience, my ass!"

She opened the door to leave.

"Then again, it could be that I'm truly psychic," he replied. "In fact, I have an urgent message from beyond that you mustn't ignore. Your Aunt Flo says it was a mistake to wear those white silk panties today..."

She looked down at her navy-colored dress. There was no way he could tell if she was on her period, unless he had x-ray vision. How dare he?

"You haven't heard the last of me!" she warned him, her amber eyes flashing angrily.

"I hope not," he said with his annoying grin.

She stormed out the door and slammed it behind her.

Chapter 16

Claudia was at her local shopping mall where she'd just finished a job. Her client wanted her to test her husband who was a sales assistant in a ladies fashion store. Apparently he seemed to think that every woman in the shop was also shopping for a man.

As soon as Claudia walked into the store her target zeroed in on her like a heat-seeking missile. He was full of flattery, but then his job was commission-based. Claudia gave him the benefit of the doubt until he stormed in on her "accidentally" while she was trying on a sweater in the changing room. He was mortified by his indiscretion, but he copped a lustful look at her. Then he had the gall to recommend she try on some of the lingerie they just got in stock. She declined politely; she wasn't about to get caught by him again. The persistent creep then asked for her phone number and invited her out for a coffee before she could finally tear herself away from him.

Now it was time to do a little shopping for herself. Browsing became buying when she spied a designer handbag she'd been stalking for months, which was finally on sale. She even tried on some sweaters in a department store where the assistants didn't barge in on her as she was changing. Then she had a coffee...by herself.

She had just walked into a lingerie shop to buy some black silk panties to replace the white pair she ruined the night before when her phone rang.

"Oh, for fuck's sake," she groaned, thinking it was that creep from the clothing store.

She was relieved to discover that it was Banachek. He was calling from a restaurant in Rio de Janeiro where he was waiting for the bowl of fresh fruit he'd just ordered. He was in Brazil to plan an elaborate illusion in which the Christ the Redeemer statue would dance on top of the Corcovado Mountain during Carnival.

"How did it go at Gil's show last night, my friend?" he asked.

She drew a deep breath.

"It was like a rock concert and Gil was the rock star," said Claudia. "He had the audience in the palm of his hand all night. He's up to his same old tricks, and he's picked up some new ones along the way too," she reported.

Claudia told Banachek about the spirit that forced Gil to buy gifts for an audience member, and the crowd's "shared experience" of hearing a Billy Joel song that had mysteriously played on the radio just before the show. She told him how Gil seemed to know too much, but when he made a mistake he invented creative excuses about "psychic interference" and "psychic amnesia" to explain his misses.

"He knew the names and causes of death of people's loved ones, and he pretended that he suffered their symptoms," she said. "He even knew that the young daughter of one woman had committed suicide."

"That's not something he'd want to be wrong about," said Banachek.

"That's not something he *could* be wrong about," she said. "The audience members were asked to fill out cards with their personal information. Our seats were allocated so he knew exactly who was sitting where in the room..."

"Aha! That old trick!"

"I pretended to be a lonely widow hoping to connect with my deceased husband, and guess what? I received an invitation to go backstage for a private reading and I came face-to-face with Gil himself!"

"He should have seen it coming," said Banachek.

"That's what I said to him!" she laughed.

Claudia told Banachek about the P-Pass she received during the cheesy meditation, her encounter with the sleazy bodyguard, the lavish after party in the green room, and the weird Mini-Gil who led her to a room for a "private reading".

"And there was a *bed* in the room."

"Hmm...that sounds like a few magicians I know," he said. "But were you able to resist Gil's charms?" he asked with a laugh.

Claudia paused.

It was a long, guilty pause. She recalled the look on Gil's face when he saw her again, and that annoying little flutter she felt in her chest when she saw him. She thought about how handsome he looked in his suit and that stupid green tie. She was reminded of their playful taunts, his incessant flirting, and how he enjoyed watching her cringe when he spoke about their past together. But Gil had changed. When she knew him as a young man in his early 20s he was a charming ladies man. Now he was a womanizer.

Then she remembered their passionate embrace, or whatever that was.

That should *never* have happened.

"Claudia? Are you still there?"

"Yes!" she finally answered. "Of course I resisted his charms! Don't be ridiculous!" she said with a nervous little laugh.

"Okay," he said. "I was worried we'd been disconnected."

If Banachek heard the guilt in her voice he was far too much of a gentleman to say so.

"So, what did you say to Gil?" he asked.

"I put him on notice," said Claudia. "I told him that I knew what he was up to and that I'm going to do all I can to expose his scams to the public."

"I bet he didn't take too kindly to that threat."

"He didn't. He said I'm wasting my time attacking people's beliefs because it will only make them defensive."

"He's right," admitted Banachek. "It might sound counterintuitive, but you should take his advice. You catch more flies with honey than with vinegar, as the saying goes. Skeptics have a lot to learn from religious and spiritual groups about how to build community."

"Skeptics think they're right about everything," she said bitterly.

"Both sides should listen to each other more," he said, ever the diplomat.

"You're right," she sighed.

She felt like she was banging her head against a brick wall.

"For years I tried to bring Gil down but nothing ever worked. He always came out smelling like a rose while I ended up looking like a fool. I just don't know where to go from here," she said.

"Then I'm glad I called," said Banachek. "You've confronted Gil privately and now I think it's time that you confront him publicly. I have some contacts. Let me see what I can do to help."

"Thank you," she said in relief.

What would she do without Banachek's support?

At that moment a bowl of unidentifiable meat was delivered to his table. Banachek had accidentally ordered the feijoada instead of the fruit.

"I'd better go now," he said. "I thought I'd asked for the bowl of fresh fruit but I think I see a pig's ear in my bowl. My Portuguese isn't too good."

She laughed.

"Bye, Banachek."

Claudia hung up the phone and took her purchases to the counter. The sales assistant looked disapprovingly at her selection of drab black underpants.

"This design is available in other colors too," she said. "We have some pretty pastels for spring, while white is always a good staple."

Claudia blushed as she remembered Gil's "message" from Aunt Flo. How did he know her period had started? It must have been a guess, or some sort of sick trick.

But every now and then, he did something that made her wonder…

"No thanks," she replied. " I'll stick with these for now…"

Chapter 17

As part of his nationwide tour, Gil made an appearance on *The Julie Davenport Show*, hosted by the former model and actress. She was previously the host of *Jules!*; a daytime tabloid TV show that had its heyday in the 2000s. The line-up was a seemingly endless supply of Ku Klux Klan Grand Dragons, strippers, satanic ritual abuse victims, and people who believed they'd seen Elvis alive.

The show became particularly infamous for its controversial high-rating episodes, *Bigfoot is the Father of my Baby* and *My Wedding Day Became My Exorcism*. Following years of tacky topics, dysfunctional guests, and violent in-studio fights, Julie's audience became jaded, and so did her producers. Her talk show was on the cutting block until it was successfully rebranded as a self-help program, with a fondness for new age gurus and psychic prognosticators, like Gil.

Julie's jaunty theme song began and the host bounced out into the audience, alternatively hugging and high-fiving her excited fans. She wore a tailored black skirt suit with a pop of hot pink to match her lipstick, which was a simple outfit carefully chosen by her personal color analyst and wardrobe team during a meeting disproportionately long for the task.

Julie stood on the set with her signature in pink lights above her head.

"Today I have a special treat for you…our guest is the world renown psychic medium *Gil Godsend*!"

Gil emerged to thunderous applause, gave Julie an overly familiar hug and a kiss, and sank into a leather couch. He adjusted his pose slightly so that the camera could catch the gleam of his sapphire cufflinks. They matched the color of his eyes, and he'd chosen them with no-less care than Julie's image consultants.

"Hello everyone. Thank you for having me, Julie," Gil said suggestively as he threw her a knowing look.

"I...I mean we, always enjoy having you, Gil. I'm lucky enough to be able to call Gil my personal psychic and I've had *many* private readings with him over the years," she said as she shot him back a knowing look. "Gil has just published his latest book *Messages From The Other Side*, and he's agreed to "connect with spirits", as he puts it, for us today. Y'all know a lot about me already, so let's choose someone from the audience for a reading. Who's *dying* to hear from a spirit?"

She laughed excessively and the crowd cheered.

"As I say in my book," said Gil, "there are many deceased family members and friends who are anxious to pass on messages to their loved ones, so it's not up to me to decide who is read."

He stood up and walked to the front of the stage.

"My spirit guides tells me to start here," he said, pointing to the right of the audience. "I'm picking up an "R" name. It could be Rose, Rosie, or Rosemary."

Several hands shot up.

"This lady passed recently," he added, which narrowed the field to a few hopeful faces. Gil raced into the audience towards a woman in the third row. She wore a bright orange sweater and a bad perm that made her look like a poodle. He touched her shoulder gently, "You just lost your mother, dear..."

"Yes," she answered, "My Mom was Rosemary. Her friends called her Rosie."

Gil took her hand.

"I sense that your relationship with Mom wasn't always perfect, and there were times when the two of you clashed. She's saying something about a friend she disapproved of when you were a teenager," he said.

"My best friend Melanie?" she said in surprise.

"That's her. Mom believed that Melanie encouraged you to get into trouble in school and do all kinds of rebellious things."

"That's right!" she said in amazement. "Melanie and I were caught smoking various things, a few times in school. We used to skip classes and go to the mall. We even got matching tattoos on our lower backs. Mom was horrified! She couldn't believe I got a tramp stamp," she chuckled, as the audience laughed along with her.

"But what Mom *didn't* know was that the trouble-maker was often *you*," Gil revealed. "*You* masterminded many of the schemes, but Mom always blamed Melanie."

"Oh my God! That's so true!" she admitted. "*I* was the bad influence. I put my poor mother through a lot..."

"That was a long time ago. You and Mom eventually grew close over the years, to the point that she wasn't only your mother, but also your best friend," Gil said.

"Yes," she agreed with a sad smile as treasured memories of shopping, cooking, and conversations with her mother flashed through her head.

"I feel there's a part of Mom that's physically close to you right now," he said. "You're wearing something she wore. Perhaps a wedding band that belonged to her."

"I am," she confirmed as she twisted the well-worn ring around her finger. "It originally belonged to my grandmother. The very moment Mom died I slipped the ring off her finger and slid it straight onto mine, so it didn't get cold. I've worn it ever since and I *never* take it off," she said as tears trickled down her cheeks.

"That ring will always contain her energy and be a protective amulet for you," Gil added.

Then he looked puzzled.

"Mom says something about a butterfly..."

The woman thought about this for a second.

"Oh yeah! I saw a butterfly in the garden yesterday. A beautiful blue butterfly."

"That butterfly was Mom's spirit trying to get your attention," Gil explained.

"Oh my God!" she gasped. "It fluttered around me in the yard and even landed on my hand. Blue was Mom's favorite color too!"

"Seeing a butterfly will always be a sign that she is around," he said. "Now, Mom has a final message for you. She says she loves you, and that she's always watching over you. Motherhood is a bond that survives even death..."

Gil ended his reading to thunderous applause. He gave a warm hug to the woman, and to her delight, he planted a kiss on her rosy cheek.

She was always a fan of Gil Godsend, but now she was a fanatic.

Julie's show was no longer considered trash TV, but she was not averse to injecting some conflict and confrontation into each episode.

"Thank you for that heartwarming reading, Gil," she raved. "And now we have a little surprise for you," she said with a wicked glint in her eye.

"I sense you're about to introduce someone from my past..." he smiled calmly.

"Oh, you're good," she purred. "Yes! We have your arch nemesis in the audience...Ms. Claudia Cox!"

Gil smiled gleefully.

The camera zoomed in on Claudia who was lost deep within the crowd. She was pissed off that she was relegated to being a member of the audience, while Gil, the supposed "expert", was high up on stage beside the host.

"Claudia is a professional skeptic who has spent many years trying to debunk Gil Godsend and other psychics," Julie said.

The applause for Claudia was far less enthusiastic than it had been for Gil. There were even a few slow claps. Nobody likes a skeptic.

"A bit of healthy skepticism is a good thing, and I used to be a cynic myself...until I met Gil," Julie gushed. "But you, Claudia, have made an entire career out of believing in nothing!"

"Skeptics *aren't* cynics," Claudia corrected her. "Well, they shouldn't be. Good skeptics say, 'Keep an open mind, but not so open that your brain falls out'," she laughed. Alone.

"You just witnessed Gil's incredible psychic reading of a total stranger," Julie enthused. "So, how do you explain *that*?" she challenged her.

"Psychic abilities can be explained as parlor tricks," she replied. "Mr. Godsend just used a technique known as cold reading. This involves reading a person's body language, analyzing the way they dress and the jewelry they wear, and making guesses and vague statements that apply to everybody."

"So you're saying Gil fooled the lady in the audience?" Julie pressed her.

"I think he fished for information which he then fed back to her. This gave the appearance that it was coming from some mysterious source,"

Claudia explained. "But *she* was the one who supplied him with all of the specific details he needed to seem convincing."

Gil sat back in his seat comfortably and allowed his fans to defend him.

The woman in the orange sweater was outraged by the accusations made against the handsome young man onstage that had given her such an accurate reading, and a lovely kiss. Julie darted to her with a microphone in hand.

"Gil is *no* phony!" she cried indignantly. "He knew my mother's name and her nickname. He knew that my best friend from high school was Melanie, and that I have a tattoo! He also knew that I'm wearing my grandmother's wedding ring, and that Mom's favorite color was blue! There's *no way* he could have known these things if he wasn't in contact with my mother!"

"*You* told him these things!" Claudia argued.

"I did not! My mom did!" she insisted with furious tears, to the strenuous applause of the audience.

"Perhaps I can demonstrate one of my other psychic abilities to try and impress Ms. Cox?" Gil offered.

"Whaddaya think, guys?" Julie asked the audience who responded eagerly. "You heard 'em, Gil! Go for it!"

"I'm going to do a demonstration of remote viewing," he said, as he scoped out the audience looking for a subject. "The lady wearing the bright yellow scarf in the second row. Please join me up here."

The woman clamored to get up on stage with him.

"I'm getting that your name has a "c" in it…" Gil said.

"Yes! I'm Christie!" she replied.

"Thank you, Christie. Remote viewing is the ability to see a person, place, object, or event remotely, that is, across distance or time. We all have this ability; mine is just more developed than that of most people. In fact, remote viewing is recognized as a scientific field. The U.S. government even funded a multi-million dollar research program into the phenomenon." He turned to Christie. "What I want you to do is to take me home with you in your mind…"

"I think there are *many* women in the audience doing that right now!" quipped Julie.

Gil and the audience laughed.

"Right now, I want to go home with Christie. I want to see her street, and the inside and outside of her house. I'll describe what I see and she'll verify everything that I'm seeing." He grabbed Christie's hand and held it tightly. "Are you ready?"

"Yes," she said as her hand began to sweat at his touch. She'd had a crush on Gil for many years.

Gil closed his eyes and rubbed his forehead in concentration.

"Christie, I'm going down the street towards your home. Okay, I'm seeing palm trees and a "For Sale" sign in a front yard."

"That's right!" she yelped in excitement. "My street is lined with palm trees and one of my neighbors is selling his house."

"Good. Christie, I'm outside of your home. I see a brown-colored house that's two stories high. There is a garage to one side. I see trees in the front yard."

"Yes, that's my house! It's painted a cream-color and we have a two-car garage. We have several oak trees in the front yard," Christie confirmed.

As Gil remote viewed Claudia busily scribbled notes for her rebuttal.

"Now, Christie, I'm walking up to your house slowly," he said. "There's something strange about the path or lawn leading up to your house…"

"Yes. The roots of one of the oak trees have grown under the path, so the slabs of concrete have cracked. We need to cut down the tree and get the concrete repaved," she said.

Gil held his hand up to his ear.

"Now I'm hearing something as I approach the house. It's a bell or a tinkling noise. I also hearing a dog barking in the distance," he said.

"That's right! We have wind chimes hanging in our backyard that make a tinkling noise in the breeze. And our neighbor's dogs bark and howl all day and night. We've had to file a formal complaint to Animal Care," she added.

"That's good, Christie. I see something else outside… As I approach the front door there's some sort of aquatic animal. It might be a fish or a dolphin," Gil said.

"Wow!" she cried. "I have a dolphin door knocker!"

"Very good. Now, Christie, I want you to open the front door and enter your home… Okay, I'm walking down a short hallway. I see the kitchen to the right. I see a living room to the left with polished wooden floors…and I see stairs ahead."

"We have a hallway leading to the kitchen and living room, which is carpeted. There are stairs ahead leading to the upstairs bedrooms."

"Look around you in the living room." He paused. "I'm seeing a statue. It could be wooden or brass. It seems to have some kind of religious or spiritual significance."

"Yes! I have a jade statue of Buddha on the mantelpiece!" she said excitedly.

Gil gave an exhausted exhale, signaling that he had finished his remote viewing session.

"Thank you so much, Christie," he said. "Can I get a round of applause for her?"

The audience went wild. It was clear whose side they were on.

"Claudia," Julie sniffed. "Are you gonna tell me *that* was cool reading too?"

"*Cold* reading," she corrected the host. "And yes, it was. "For Sale" signs, garages, trees, wind chimes, and barking dogs are all common sights and sounds in *any* neighborhood."

"But Gil even knew her name!"

"He didn't know her name," Claudia argued. "He simply guessed that she had a "c" somewhere in her name. So does my name. So do many people's names."

"Gil was spot on about the dolphin and the statue of Buddha," said Julie.

"He wasn't as specific as you think," said Claudia. "He guessed "a fish *or* a dolphin", and he never actually said the statue was of Buddha. He guessed incorrectly that it was wooden or brass. He saw a "brown-colored" house, not cream-colored, and he said that the living room has polished wooden floors, when it's carpeted. People want psychics to be right, so they overlook these inconsistencies."

"My bedrooms have polished wooden floors!" Christie piped up in defense of Gil.

"But that's not what he said," Claudia insisted. "People tend to only remember the apparent hits, and to forget the misses. Also, there's *no* evidence that remote viewing works. Mr. Godsend forgot to mention that the government experiments into remote viewing totally failed."

Julie turned to Christie.

"Do you believe Gil was able to see inside your home?"

"Absolutely," she answered. "I'm *convinced* of it."

"If Ms. Cox thinks my remote viewing was too vague, then allow me to try something more specific," Gil said. "I'm going to read someone's mind." He peered out into the audience. "The attractive blonde lady wearing the burgundy blouse in the front row. May I have your phone number?" he asked her.

"Yes!" she squealed as she grabbed a pen from her handbag and started scribbling on a notepad.

"Wait...I'm going to read your mind to get it..." Gil said.

"Hang on!" cried Claudia. "That woman could be a plant. Let *me* choose someone instead to prevent him from cheating."

"Okay. That seems fair," agreed Julie.

"But first," interrupted Gil, "I want everyone to concentrate on their phone number. This will increase the psychic energy in the room."

Claudia chose someone in the audience.

"The lady in the green floral dress sitting in the second row," she said, pointing to a heavyset woman who was wearing a muumuu.

Gil pulled out his cell phone. He looked at the keypad and motioned over the numbers like he was about to dial. Then he frowned and shook his head. Finally, he went ahead and dialed a number. Seconds later, a ringtone was heard in the room and the audience gasped. But the phone that rang belonged to a man seated *next* to the woman in the muumuu. He answered his phone.

"Hello?"

"Hey there," Gil said casually as he propped his elbow up over the back of the couch, threw his legs over the couch's arms, and looked up in the air. "How are you enjoying the show?"

"Um...it's amazing! You're amazing Gil!"

"Thanks!" he said. "Can you please pass the phone to your wife?"

The man obediently handed the phone to the lady in the muumuu.

"H-hello?" she stammered in surprise.

"Hi there, Donna. This is Gil. I was going to call you but your phone was switched off. Can you please turn on your phone so I can call you? I don't want to broadcast your phone number on live television," he said.

She fumbled around in her handbag, retrieved her phone and found that Gil was right. Her phone was off. She switched it on and Gil called her.

The performance was a showstopper.

"Are you convinced yet, Claudia?" Julie asked impatiently.

"Not at all," she replied.

"But *you* chose the woman in the audience to prevent cheating."

"It must be a trick of some kind," Claudia argued. "Magicians can saw a person in half, catch a bullet in their teeth, and get buried alive. Why couldn't a magician guess someone's name and phone number too?"

"Then *how* did he do it?" Julie demanded to know.

"I don't know. But just because I don't know how it was done doesn't mean there isn't a logical explanation."

"Claudia, is there a personal reason you don't believe in psychics?" Julie inquired. "Didn't you and Gil once have a pretty hot and heavy relationship..."

A sensationalist "Ooh!" rippled through the room as the audience salivated in anticipation of juicy gossip. This was just like the good old days of the *Jules!* show.

"Mr. Godsend...and I...um...have known each other for a very long time ago," Claudia confessed as her cheeks burned red.

Gil sat on stage with a cocky smile on his face. He enjoyed watching her squirm.

"We were engaged to be married," he added.

"So, you were sleeping with the enemy," said Julie. "Did you put aside your prejudices in bed?"

"It wasn't like that!"

"Did Gil dump you?"

"No! We ended things amicably."

"Then you became a skeptic because you split up?"

"No. I was a skeptic when I met him. In fact, that's how we met."

"*Then what would make you believe?*"

"Proof of psychic abilities shown under stringent test conditions by reputable scientists who can replicate those results," Claudia replied. "That *might* make me believe…"

"It's not my job to *make* anyone believe," Gil interrupted. "My job is to share my psychic abilities with people. It's my responsibility to bring through the words, images, and other messages, the *evidence*, that I receive from the world of spirit."

"We've all seen the evidence here today," Julie said. "I think there's only one person in this room who doesn't believe and never will!"

"For those who believe, no proof is necessary. For those who don't believe, no proof is possible," Gil quoted.

Julie nodded fiercely.

"And on that note, thank you for sharing your incredible psychic insight with us today…Gil Godsend! Be sure to grab a copy of his latest book, *Messages From The Other Side*. That's all for today, but remember…expect miracles!"

Gil received a standing ovation and as the camera caught him he looked straight into the lens with his piercing blue eyes and nudged in one final remark.

"Do psychic powers exist? It's up to *you* to decide…"

The *Julie Davenport Show* theme song began playing and the host left the stage giving more hugs and high fives to her fans. As the credits ran, the camera panned across the audience as they stood cheering for Gil.

The camera zoomed in on Claudia. She was still sitting in her seat, and scowling.

Chapter 18

They say that there's no such thing as bad publicity, but Claudia discovered this wasn't true at all. Her appearance on the *Julie Davenport Show* the day before was a complete disaster. With her good looks and sense of humor she could usually wrap any TV host around her little finger, but Gil could always make her look like a fool. It was just like the old days. He didn't even need to do it himself; he used the audience as human shields against her. He just stepped back and let them defend him with that insipidly innocent look on his face.

Her phone rang. It was Banachek.

"Hello, my friend."

"Hi, Banachek."

He was in a good mood because he'd learned how to order a bowl of fresh fruit in Portuguese. He'd also developed a taste for pig's ear.

"I saw you on the *Julie Davenport Show* yesterday," he said apologetically. "I'm so sorry. Gil is skilled at winning over a crowd and having them defend him."

"Being buried within the audience when Gil was high up on stage made me feel like I was sitting at the kids' table during Thanksgiving," she said bitterly.

She had a burning question on her mind about Gil's performance. She could explain almost everything he did on the show, except for one thing…

"When Gil knew those phone numbers, was that a magic trick?"

"Yes," Banachek confirmed. "That one's a classic."

She *knew* it!

Claudia wasn't going to ask Banachek how the trick was done though. Once she saw him drive blindfolded and she asked him how it was done.

"If I tell you, I'll have to kill you," he replied with a gentle laugh.

Magicians are very protective of their tricks. They like to keep magic magical.

"I've been thinking about your situation," said Banachek. "You shouldn't go head to head with Gil when he has a sympathetic crowd to do battle for him."

"What should I do next?" she asked.

"I made a few calls and you're scheduled to appear on *Night Owl* with Michael Michaels tonight. You'll be interviewed by yourself so you'll get the chance to tell your side of the story."

"Thank you!" she said excitedly.

"The show doesn't have a huge audience but this is a good start."

"I'd better get ready right now," she said, wondering what she was going to wear.

"Good luck!"

"Thanks Banachek!"

Night Owl was a late night talk show that no one seemed to watch. But appearing on there was better than nothing, especially if it was without Gil. It was ironic that Claudia had just been a guest on the *Julie Davenport Show*, while Julie Davenport had been a guest on *Night Owl* the week before.

Claudia had little time to get ready for the show. She blow dried her hair and refreshed her makeup. She wore a heather brown wool skirt suit that was both sophisticated and sexy. Claudia knew that vibrant colors work best on television so she slipped on an orange silk blouse with a tie-neck that complemented her auburn hair. She finished her look with a sweep of a peachy-brown lipstick to match her top. She was ready.

Claudia arrived at the TV station and searched for the studio. As she wandered the maze of halls she passed by Michael Michaels' dressing room. Claudia wondered if the rumors were true that he wore a toupee. She'd also heard that he was a sleaze.

At that moment the door flung open and Michael himself emerged.

"Hello, my dear!" he beamed. "I need to talk with you about our interview. Won't you come into my room?"

Without waiting for Claudia's answer he grabbed her by the arm and dragged her inside.

"Can I offer you a glass of water, a cup of coffee, or perhaps a shot of Irish whiskey?" he asked with the kind of slimy smile that made you think he'd slip a date rape drug into the drink.

"No thank you, Mr. Michaels," she replied politely.

"Please… call me Michael." The words oozed out of his mouth as he ogled her short skirt and long legs. "You know, I've always wanted to have you on my show, my dear. In fact, I've always wanted to have *you*…"

Michael grabbed her by her waist and pulled her towards him as he tried to kiss her. His moist lips puckered as they loomed towards her face. She turned away quickly and his lips hit the side of her jaw instead where they left a sloppy wet mark. She could smell whiskey and stale cigarettes on his breath, and yes, he wore a toupee. She wasn't sure which was worse; his new ill-fitting rug or the comb-over he used to sport. She wondered why he had so much trouble growing hair on his head when his eyebrows and the insides of his ears didn't seem to have any problem at all.

Undeterred by her rejection, Michael ramped things up a notch. He reached up her skirt, grabbed at her crotch and slid his fingers across her panties. It made her skin crawl.

"Please stop!" she begged.

She couldn't believe this was happening.

"I understand," he nodded. "You don't want that "just been fucked" look when you're about to appear on national TV." He pushed her onto a couch and stood over her with his crotch in her face. "This way you won't have bed hair. But your lipstick might need a touch up."

He unzipped his pants and flung out his penis.

"Here's a taste of what you'll get after the show," he said.

He grabbed her hand and ran it over his hardening penis. Then he tried to force open her lips with it. She pursed her lips tight and struggled against him. Finally she managed to push him away.

"What the fuck is wrong with you?" she hissed.

He was truly surprised by her refusal to join him on the casting couch.

"What the fuck is wrong with *you*?" he sniffed. "You're passing up a great opportunity."

"An opportunity for what?" she mumbled as she tried to avoid the stiff penis that dangled dangerously near her mouth.

"To be with me, of course, and to offer you a chance to advance your career on my show. I can *help* you," he said magnanimously.

"I don't need *that* kind of help!" she screamed. "Let go of me!"

She wanted to hit him but if she left a mark then *she'd* be the one seen as the aggressor. It was a fight but Claudia managed to pry herself free from his grasp, and to knee him in the balls. Now she was glad for all of those hours she spent in the gym.

Claudia ran out of the room and down the hall, her whole body shaking with rage and fear. She didn't want to do the interview. She wanted to rush home and take a long, hot shower to scrub his filthy scent off her skin. Then she thought of Kate and Abby and Dawn. She felt she needed to buck up and face the task at hand, for them. Reluctantly, she decided to go ahead with the interview.

She found the *Night Owl* studio and hesitated before entering. How was Michael going to treat her during the interview now that she'd rebuffed him? She took a deep breath and entered the studio. The producer hurried her backstage where she stood in the wings and saw Michael swagger into the studio. He took his seat and glared at her from across the room.

In a rush before show time, stagehands flittered around Claudia. One pinned a microphone to her blazer while another fixed some flyaway hairs. A make-up artist patted down her cheeks with powder and inspected her face.

"Oh! I thought your lipstick would need a touch up!" she exclaimed in surprise.

Hmm…someone had done this before, Claudia realized.

She was so wrapped up in thought that she didn't notice the show had already started and Michael was introducing her.

"Our first guest tonight is…the lovely Claudia Cox!"

She came out on stage to enthusiastic applause. This was a nice change from the cold reception she'd received from the audience at the *Julie Davenport Show*. Michael stood up as she approached and extended his arms to give her a hug. She had to play along and let him hug her, but when he tried to give her a sloppy kiss on the cheek she turned her head, just like she did last time. He still smelled of booze and cigarettes.

"Claudia is an author and a skeptic," Michael continued as she sat down on a lounge chair beside his table. "The magician Harry Houdini devoted his life to debunking psychics and Claudia is a modern-day Houdini who exposes the charlatans."

This was a flattering introduction. Perhaps Michael was going to remain professional during the interview? He turned to face her.

"Claudia, do you believe that people can talk to the dead?"

"I do, Michael, but I don't believe the dead can talk back," she joked.

The audience laughed heartily. This wasn't so bad after all.

"Seriously though Michael, I've been searching for years but I haven't found proof that anyone can communicate with the dead."

She tried to smile sweetly at him but she had a hard time fighting through her scowl.

"Historically, séances have given us our best proof of life after death," Michael said.

"Oh, have they?" she challenged him. "In those early séances the mediums used sleight-of-hand tricks to dupe their clients," explained Claudia. "They produced ectoplasm, but when it was tested it turned out to be made from fabric or even sheep's lungs. Ghosts materialized during the séances, but they were just dolls made from papier-mâché. Musical instruments supposedly played by spirits were really played by assistants. Tables that seemed to levitate were lifted by string or tipped by the mediums using their feet and legs. But these tricks seemed real in a darkened room full of people who wanted to believe."

Michael still wasn't convinced.

"There have been many documented cases of people with psychic medium abilities. Are you saying you don't believe those either?" he asked.

"Many mediums are unscrupulous crooks that prey on grieving people who want to communicate with their dead loved ones," Claudia said. "Let's look at the beginnings of the Spiritualism movement. In Hydesville, New York, in 1848, sisters Kate and Margaret Fox said they were communicating with spirits through mysterious rapping sounds." Her answer was well rehearsed. She'd told this story many times. "They became famous, but towards the end of their lives, the sisters confessed they were faking the phenomena. They cracked their toe joints to make the sounds of the "spirits". The whole thing was a hoax but Spiritualism continued as if their confession never happened."

"You forgot to mention that they retracted their confession," said Michael.

"Only because there was a backlash against them for admitting they were frauds," Claudia insisted.

All of a sudden, Michael turned nasty.

"This doesn't mean that *all* psychic mediums are frauds," he scoffed.

"The whole thing is fake because the very beginnings of spiritualism were fake," she argued. "Since then we still haven't seen any convincing evidence. Today, instead of using parlor tricks with ectoplasm and ghosts, mediums use mentalism tricks instead to make it seem as though they can talk to the dead."

"I'm sure that there are a few charlatans out there," Michael conceded, "but there are also some genuine psychic mediums."

"Like who?" Claudia asked.

"Gil Godsend."

How did she know he was going to say that?

"He's a con-artist," she said.

Michael rushed to his defense.

"Gil Godsend is the world's greatest psychic medium!" he bellowed.

"Gil Godsend is the world's biggest fraud!" she cried.

"He's a good friend of mine," Michael said. "I've witnessed his abilities first hand. He passed on messages to me from my dear mother who is on the other side. Gil knew things about her that *no one else knows*," he said with crocodile tears in his eyes.

Michael took a swig of coffee from his mug. It was emblazoned with the show's logo of an owl perched on the branch of a tree with a moon in the backdrop. Little did his audience know that his mug contained an Irish coffee that was more Irish than coffee.

"You give the impression you're such a goody-two-shoes, but you're not so squeaky clean yourself, are you Claudia?" he said with a devious smile. "We did some digging into your past and it seems that you've been a *very* naughty girl!"

"Huh?" she asked with a frown.

Where was he going with this?

"Let me refresh your memory," he said. "You spent some time in the adult entertainment industry."

"What do you mean?" she asked sincerely.

The interview had taken an unexpected turn.

"You used to work for a phone sex line," he said to a chorus of "Oohs!" in the audience.

This was true.

When she finished high school she tried to find a job as a journalist, but every potential employer wanted her to have a degree. In desperation she took a night job as a phone sex operator. The callers believed they were chatting with sexy chicks wearing slinky lingerie and touching themselves. In reality, there was nothing sexy about the work, or the women. They loathed the men who called. Most of the men were so desperate to hear a female voice they would have had an orgasm listening to Siri. Claudia only worked there for a few weeks until she could scrape together enough money to move to Southern California. She was ashamed of her brief stint as a phone sex worker and she'd never told *anybody* about it.

How did Michael know about this?

"You also posed nude for a girly magazine," he said disapprovingly to more "Oohs!"

This was also true, but there was a lot more to the story.

In her early twenties she dabbled in modeling. One day she was posing for a department store catalogue when the photographer got her liquored up. She'd been wearing a very demure button-up shirt and jeans when he said to her, "Can you undo your top button?" So, she did. Then he wanted her to undo another button. Then another.

"These will be very tasteful shots," he assured her. "No one will ever see these photos. They will just be for your own private collection," he promised her.

She didn't have a memory of the rest of the night but when she woke up the next morning she could tell they'd had sex. That was the last she heard from the photographer.

A few years later she was in Las Vegas when a busload of Japanese businessmen recognized her and started snapping photos, shouting "Oh yes! Oh yes!" She discovered that the images from the photo shoot had been featured in a Japanese porn magazine.

Claudia had signed a model release so there was nothing she could do about it.

"The magazine was called *Oh Yes! Enjoy Your Happy Times*."

How did Michael know about this?

"And now your career involves framing men," he said to "Boos!" from the audience. "You have a detective agency that entraps innocent husbands and breaks up happy families."

"If you want to call catching men who cheat on their wives "entrapment", then *yes*," she replied indignantly.

She'd helped many couples to stay together when wives found out their husbands were honest, but she'd also helped numerous women to make the decision to leave their cheating men. Her job required anonymity. What was this negative publicity going to do to her business?

How did Michael know these things?

Telling these stories about her past, which were only partly true, was nothing but misdirection to put people off the scent of Gil's bad behavior.

"None of this has anything to do with the fact that Gil Godsend is a fraud!" she cried.

"Yes it does, Claudia," he said piously. "This damages your *credibility*."

She tried to respond but he cut her off.

"You may not believe in psychics, but that doesn't mean they don't exist," he said to the camera. "There is so much we don't know about the universe. It's the height of arrogance to think we know everything. We should try to keep an open mind about the paranormal. We'll be back after a break."

Once his microphone was off Michael turned to Claudia with a smug expression on his face.

"Regretting your decision now, my dear?" he asked as he patted down his toupee.

"Fuck you," she replied.

"Yes. Perhaps you should have…" he said. "But it's not *too* late…I can still fix this dreadful mess for you. You scratch my back and I'll scratch yours…"

Claudia tore off her microphone and threw it on her seat. Then she stormed out of the studio. She stepped out of the building into the early morning air. A cooling breeze blew against her burning skin. Claudia was livid. She was disgusted at the way Michael had treated her before, during, and after the interview.

At least no one watched that horrible show.

She decided to walk home to cool off a little. It was actually pleasant walking the empty streets of San Francisco in the early hours of the morning. She was starting to feel a little better when her phone rang. The number was blocked. Who would call her at this hour?

"Hello?"

"Claudia..." said a deep voice that once thrilled and excited her but now made her shudder.

It was Gil.

"Oh, for fuck's sake," she said.

This was just what she needed.

"How did you get my phone number?" she asked. Then she remembered his trick on the show the day before. "Oh, never mind. What do you want?"

"I have a copy of *Oh Yes! Enjoy Your Happy Times* that I'd like you sign," he joked.

Was it Gil who told Michael Michaels about the porn magazine and her brief stint as a phone sex operator? Hang on, she'd never told him about her past. He couldn't be at fault, as much as she wanted to blame him.

"Leave me alone. I've had a bad night," she said meekly.

"I know," he said gently. "I'm sorry Michael Michaels treated you that way."

He didn't know the half of it, but then this kind of behavior was right up his alley.

"Yeah, sure you are."

"I am," he said sincerely. "I don't like seeing you being treated this way. You deserve better.

"Like the way I was treated on the *Julie Davenport Show*?"

"Let's set that aside for a minute," he said. "I need to talk to you. I want you, Claudia, to become my manager."

She almost laughed. She didn't expect this.

"*Are you kidding me?*"

"Not at all," he said. "You're one of the few people I can trust to be honest with me and nobody works as hard as you do."

"You want to be endorsed by your nemesis. That's what," she said.

How good would it look for Gil if his archenemy suddenly defected to his side?

"That's not true," he said. "There are a lot of people out there in mourning who can't move on until they've got some closure. Helping me to help them is the right thing to do…and the pay's not bad either…"

Claudia thought about the things Gil did to give people "piece of mind" and help them get "closure". She shuddered again.

"*Never*," she said.

"Think about it. Please," he urged. "And don't worry about *Night Owl*. No one watches that show…"

"Goodbye, Gil," she said sternly.

Then she hung up on him.

The next morning the news of Claudia's appearance on *Night Owl* and the revelations about her past were splashed across the media.

Chapter 19

The day after her appearance on *Night Owl*, Claudia was walking down the street to work when a group of construction workers started harassing her. That was nothing new. She was used to catcalls and wolf whistles from men in hard hats dangling from buildings, but this time it was different.

"*Oh yes*! *Oh yes*!" they shouted as they pretended to snap photographs of her.

She gave them the finger, held her head up high, and walked on. One of the men yelled out after her, "Hey, sweetheart. How much do you charge for phone sex?"

Clearly, they'd recognized her from the interview.

She thought no one watched that show…

But Claudia had bigger concerns. Over the next few days she churned over the sexual assault. She'd urged Kate and Abby to go to the police with their stories so why wasn't she speaking out herself? Well, she had her reasons. She was embarrassed and didn't want anyone to know about the incident. She didn't want to rock the boat. She wanted to move on with her life and forget it ever happened.

She was also in denial. She was a sophisticated and educated woman; it could never happen to her. But was it her fault somehow? Did she dress too provocatively? Did she flirt with him unintentionally? Did she send him the wrong message? Now she understood how Kate and Abby felt.

She was conflicted in her thoughts. Her anger was mounting over the incident. She was suffering from insomnia. She lay awake at night feeling distressed, while the incident replayed over and over again in her head. She kept thinking about what she should have done, and she imagined different reactions and outcomes. Not saying anything was also weighing on her conscience.

She was shocked that this kind of casting couch behavior still went on and she felt it was her responsibility to others to do something about it. What if it was happening to other guests or to his co-workers? The next woman might get raped. But if she reported him, would anyone believe her anyway? It was just her word against his. Or would they accuse her of being out for revenge for the way Michael had treated her on the show?

After much soul searching, Claudia decided that reporting Michael Michaels to his employer was the right thing to do. She phoned the studio and asked to speak with the producer of *Night Owl*. She had met him before the show that night and he seemed like a reasonable guy. She was amused to learn that his name was Peter Peters. He kept her on hold for almost fifteen minutes before he finally came to the phone. She felt like she was calling the IRS.

"Ms. Cox," Peter said. "…How are you?" He asked hesitantly, expecting to be lambasted for Michael's behavior on the show last week.

"I'm…fine, thanks," she said with equal hesitation. "I was a guest on *Night Owl* last week."

"Yes, I remember. How can I help you?"

"I um…need to tell you something," she began, her voice faltering.

She paused and took a deep breath.

"…Michael…assaulted me that night before the show."

"Oh my God! Tell me what happened," Peter said with what seemed like genuine concern.

Claudia recounted the incident to him in all of its grotesque detail. As she did so she couldn't recognize her own voice. It sounded hollow and timid.

This was a humiliating experience. Peter was silent the whole time.

"I'm going to look into this matter right away and I'll call you back," he said when she'd finished telling her story. "Please don't say anything to anyone else," he begged her.

This was the last thing Peter wanted leaked to the media, hot on the heels of stories of Michael's alcoholism and the news that he was now wearing a toupee.

Peter marched down to Michael's dressing room. He stormed in on Michael who hadn't yet put on his toupee.

"Hey! Don't barge into my dressing room without knocking on my fucking door first!" Michael yelled as he grabbed a baseball cap and slapped it on his head.

"There's no time for vanity," scolded Peter. "Yet another chick has contacted me complaining that you attacked her. What the fuck is going on, Michael?"

"This is ridiculous, Peter. Nothing happened."

"That's what you said last time. And the time before."

"Who's accusing me now?" Michael asked indignantly, but secretly wondering if it was Julie Davenport, or that cute new brunette in accounting he'd cornered in the kitchen last week.

"Claudia Cox."

"Oh, her? We just flirted a little," Michael said calmly as he took a swig from his mug but avoided looking at Peter.

"Flirted? She says you tried to force her to give you a blow job!"

Peter grabbed Michael's mug and took a sniff. The alcohol made his eyes water and he shook his head. Perhaps it was time to book Michael into rehab again.

"Ah...I know what's going on," Michael said in sudden realization. "She's upset because I called her out on national television about what a filthy little slut she is. I had my researchers dig up some dirt on her and I spilled it. That's all."

Peter thought about this for a while.

"Okay. I suppose it's just a matter of 'he said, she said'." That argument might work. "But I have to call her back. What do I say to her?"

"Have her produce some evidence, or tell her to go away."

"Well, alright," said Peter, somewhat unconvinced. "But don't let it happen again..."

He was sick of saying that.

Peter phoned Claudia back that afternoon. She'd been watching her phone nervously all day waiting for his call.

"Hi there," he said.

Claudia thought he sounded cold. This wasn't a good sign.

"I had a talk with Michael and he doesn't know what you're talking about."

"*What*?" she cried in outrage. "He knows exactly what he did to me!"

Then came the argument that she had expected to hear.

"Look, it's just your word against his," he said.

"And my word is the truth!" she cried.

"If that's the case, why didn't you say something during the show?" Peter asked. "It seems strange that you're bringing up this complaint a whole week *after* the show rather than at the time it happened...allegedly happened, that is," he corrected himself.

"I-I don't know," she stammered. "I have many reasons. I didn't think it was appropriate to say anything at the time. I was trying to be professional. I was stressed out. I wanted to pretend that it never happened. Then the more I thought about it I realized I had to speak up."

"I get it," said Peter. "Michael dragged you through the mud on the show and now you're out for revenge," he accused her.

"No. That's *not* how it happened," she argued. "*He* was out for revenge because *I* rejected him!"

"Then... where's your evidence?" he demanded to know.

Claudia paused.

"There isn't always evidence for this sort of thing," she said.

"Oh really? This comes from the woman who doesn't believe in psychics because there's no evidence? That's what you said on the show..."

"Sometimes you just have to believe people and give them the benefit of the doubt, " she said, feeling weak.

"Just the way you believe Gil Godsend and give him the benefit of the doubt? Hypocrite," Peter spat. "So, I should believe a woman who's posed for dirty magazines and worked for a phone sex line? I'm sick of women like you complaining about Michael," he let slip.

"Ah-ha! I'm not surprised that other women have complained about Michael," Claudia scoffed. "Where there's smoke, there's fire. If women keep complaining about him then maybe you'd better start listening to them!"

"I'll listen when someone brings me some proof," Peter said.

"Perhaps the media will listen," Claudia warned him.

Peter sighed.

It was time to bring out the usual threat. He'd had to keep an attorney on speed dial because of Michael's antics.

"Claudia, if you keep running your mouth we'll sue you for slander."

Claudia paused.

She had experience in this game of bullshit. She had been sued before by the Scientologists because of things she'd said and written about them, even though they were true. She had been caught up in expensive and messy litigation for years. As an attorney friend once said to her, "If you're sued. You lose."

He also added, "It's a legal system, not a justice system."

The truth didn't matter. They had tried to silence her and it had worked. So much for freedom of speech.

She didn't know what to say to Peter. For once she was speechless.

"I thought so," he said smugly. "Goodbye, Ms. Cox."

He hung up on her.

For the first time in years, Claudia broke down and cried.

Chapter 20

After her experience with Michael Michaels and Peter Peters, Claudia went through a bout of depression. She moped around her apartment in her pajamas and plowed though tubs of rocky road ice cream and bottles of chardonnay. She binge watched TV soap operas that her mother used to watch when she was a child. Claudia was amazed that after 20 years, the cast members were still the same, and they even looked the same, thanks to plastic surgery.

She used to laugh at the histrionic lives of these characters as they battled affairs, evil twins, and even died only to come back to life; although right now it felt like her own life was as melodramatic as a soap. After sitting around in misery for a few weeks, and putting on a few pounds, Claudia wanted to put the incident behind her and move on with her life. She didn't believe in karma, but she hoped that Michael would eventually bring about his own downfall with his bad behavior.

Right now Claudia had bigger fish to fry than Michael Michaels. She cleaned herself up and went back to work. In the evenings she started researching Gil again. She was preparing to take him down, not that she had a plan yet. She re-watched episodes of *Between Heaven and Earth with Gil Godsend*. She watched videos of his interviews and other television appearances. She took notes and analyzed his techniques. Claudia re-read all of his books, and those written about him, including *21 Days with Gil Godsend*. The bottle of chardonnay came out again for that one. The book was so full of lies it wasn't a biography, it was a work of fiction. She also revisited all of the articles she'd written about him, and mused about how ineffective they were. She had been repeating the same mistakes over and over again but expecting different results.

This time, she had to try something different…

One morning she was sitting at her desk and sipping on her morning latte when she received a call from Banachek.

"Hello, my friend," he said. "I'm stuck in Cairo airport on a four-hour layover. I was bored and thought I'd give you a call."

How could he be bored in Egypt? Images of the pyramids, the Great Sphinx and the River Nile ran through her mind. She needed a vacation.

"Wow! Did you get to see the pyramids?" she asked.

"I'm actually in Cairo, Illinois," he said apologetically. "You know, I just learned that there are 20 Cairos in the U.S alone!" he marveled.

"You really are bored!" she said as he chuckled.

"Look, I've been worried about you," said Banachek. "I haven't heard from you in weeks."

"I didn't mean to worry you," she said. "I've been a hermit since my appearance on *Night Owl*."

"I'm so sorry about that fiasco," he said. "Michael Michaels is a sleazy son-of-a-bitch."

He didn't know the half of it. Claudia was embarrassed that Banachek knew about her past, but he was practical about it.

"Young people do things they later regret," he said. "There are plenty of unscrupulous people waiting to take advantage of others. You know that from your own work. I'm not going to judge you. I'm not a religious man, but let he who is without sin cast the first stone."

Claudia didn't confide in him about the assault. She was too ashamed.

Banachek asked what she'd been up to so she told him about her research but that she wasn't sure what to do next.

"Well, we know Gil's modus operandi," said Banachek. "He does background research on his clients then during the session he convinces her that he can channel her dead husband. Then he manipulates her into having sex with him. Why don't you catch him in the act?"

"How do I do that?"

"Did you ever watch *Possessed Possessions*?" Banachek asked.

"That TV show where ghost hunters track down haunted items in people's homes?"

"That's the one."

On *Possessed Possessions*, a ghost hunting team visited homes that were plagued by paranormal activity. Their theory was that haunted objects in the home were causing the hauntings, and especially objects that had been used in satanic rituals. The team traced the phenomena to the most stereotypically haunted object in the house, usually a creepy-looking doll or a family heirloom. Then they removed the item, to protect the family, of course, and added it to their museum of haunted items in Salem, Massachusetts. Curiously, they removed a lot of "haunted" jewelry and antiques.

"The producer once offered me a substantial amount of money to fake paranormal activity on the show," revealed Banachek. "He wanted to scare the crew."

"I *always* knew that show was a sham!" said Claudia.

"I wouldn't do it," said Banachek. "He later denied that he'd made the offer. I wish I'd recorded his conversation at the time to catch him. Lesson learned. So, why don't you find a decoy, set her up with a fake story, and catch Gil when he tries to take advantage of her?"

"A sting? That's a *great* idea!"

She hadn't done a sting in many years and she missed the thrill of it all. She loved plotting and setting up the target and the big reveal at the end. She could already see the look of shock on Gil's face when she exposed him as a fraud.

It was all so cloak and dagger.

Banachek had to leave. He wanted to find out how many Londons there are in the United States.

Claudia needed someone she could trust for this assignment, so she decided to use one of her colleagues from Suspicious Minds. She went through her books to find a suitable decoy for Gil. Most of the women did spouse surveillance as a second job so they could make some extra money. Some were students working for her as they worked their way through a degree. They were all beautiful women, but they were also accomplished and clever. Gil wasn't an idiot, and she needed someone who could outwit him.

She interviewed a few potential candidates for the project.

Her first interview was with Mary.

Claudia was sitting at her desk when there was a knock at the door. "Come in!"

Mary sashayed into her office. She was a tall, tanned brunette from Brazil who had a Bachelor of Engineering. Mary was intelligent and exotic and just the type of girl Gil liked. He wouldn't be able to resist her.

"What do you want to see me about, Boss?" she asked.

Claudia invited her to sit down and told her about the project. "If you took on this job you'd go undercover as a client to expose a psychic medium. Do you think this is something you'd like to do?"

Mary took a deep breath.

"I don't think we've ever had to discuss religion on the job," she replied. "So I've never told you that I'm a strict Roman Catholic." Mary reached into her green crew neck sweater and pulled out a round gold pendant. "This is a St. Christopher medal. It belonged to my mother and I wear it all the time for protection. I go to church every Sunday morning and receive Holy Communion. I'm even in the church choir."

Claudia realized this was why Mary was never available for jobs on Sundays.

"Conjuring up spirits and evoking the dead is the sin of necromancy. It's strictly forbidden by the Church," she said sternly. "You've been a wonderful boss to me and I'd do almost anything for you, but I can't risk my mortal soul," she said as she made the sign of the cross.

"I understand," said Claudia.

"Thank you," said Mary as she stood up to leave. "And I'll pray for you this Sunday."

Claudia's second interview was with Kim, a student from Korea who was finishing her PhD in agriculture at the University of California, Berkeley. She was a hard scientist. Surely she wouldn't believe in "conjuring up spirits".

There was a knock on Claudia's door.

"Come in!"

Kim walked into the office and took a seat. She was a petite lady with glossy long black hair and porcelain skin. Claudia thought she had the perfect looks to lure Gil.

"You wanted to see me, Boss?" she asked.

"Yes, Kim. But before we begin, do you have any religious leanings that would preclude you from working with a psychic?" asked Claudia.

"Not at all," replied Kim.

Claudia breathed a sigh of relief and told her about the project, without naming names.

"Do you think this is something you'd like to do?"

"Absolutely!" Kim said enthusiastically. "I'd love to bust a fake psychic. They make the *real* ones look bad."

"The real ones?" asked Claudia, dumbfounded.

"Yeah, the psychics with real powers, like Gil Godsend. Have you heard of him? He's amazingly accurate...and cute too!" she gushed.

Oh, for fuck's sake, thought Claudia.

Claudia's third interview was with Ana. She worked in cyber security during the day and at night she worked at *Suspicious Minds* to earn extra cash. She was trying to save enough for a deposit on a house so she could move out of her mother's place. She wanted a home in the Bay Area so it was going to take her a while.

There was a knock on Claudia's door.

"Come in!"

Ana walked into the room and took a seat. Aside from being a talented young woman, she was a Slavic beauty with feline features and a seductive gaze.

"You wanted to talk with me about something, Boss?"

"Yes. I have a special assignment for you."

Claudia asked her if she'd like to go undercover to expose a psychic. Ana was happy to help bust a psychic because she didn't believe in them.

Ana Stanich grew up in a superstitious household. Her mother, Slobodanka, was nicknamed Slob, although she didn't know the meaning of the word in English. She believed that demons and curses lurked everywhere. She lived in fear of everything, especially since Ana's father Dragan died.

Slob was Serbian Orthodox and her home was decorated with gaudy religious art. She was so religious that Ana was named after Saint Anastasija, the family's patron saint. Slob had a wooden icon of Saint Anastasija hanging in the living room that had an oily streak dripping from the Saint's eye. Slob believed her icon was weeping holy tears. Ana confessed that, during a teenage slumber party, a food fight had ensued, resulting in fried chicken being tossed at the icon. Slob refused to believe the oil was from a secular source. The smear had even fooled their priest. It was a miracle, not a grease stain.

But Slob's most prized possession was a First Class holy relic, a piece of wood from the True Cross. She bought it from a peddler when she was on a pilgrimage to Medjugorje, the site where the Virgin Mary supposedly appeared back in the 1980s. The relic was on display in a special reliquary in the living room. Ana didn't have the heart to tell her mother that she'd wasted $1,000 on a fake splinter purchased from a con artist.

Slob also believed in psychics. She saw a psychic regularly, and she read people's fortunes in their coffee cups. Only yesterday she read the pattern of the muddy sediment on the bottom of Ana's cup of Turkish coffee. She predicted that Ana would marry a nice Serbian boy and they would have beautiful Serbian babies. But of course, her mother was trying to marry her off to a nice Serbian boy so they would have beautiful Serbian babies.

Over pizza and a pint of pomegranate cider at a local microbrewery, Claudia briefed Ana on her mission. Now she could finally reveal the name of their target.

Gil Godsend.

"Oh, I fucking HATE Gil Godsend!" Ana cried in disgust. "My father died when I was a little kid and ever since then I've despised these charlatans who take advantage of the bereaved."

This was exactly Claudia's situation.

"But my mother adores him," Ana continued. "She paid big bucks to have a psychic reading with him a few years ago. He knew lots of specific stuff about my family. I suspected he was doing a hot reading."

Claudia beamed. Here was someone she could finally talk to! Ana knew all about hot reading and cold reading. She had even read Carl Sagan's *The Demon-Haunted World: Science as a Candle in the Dark*. She was smart, stunning, and a skeptic.

Claudia had an instant girl crush on her.

After they bitched about Gil over a few more drinks, Claudia got down to business. She had invented a detailed story for Ana's past.

"Your pseudonym is Nina Novakov," said Claudia. "You're the widow of Zoran Novakov. Zoran was 6'4" tall, with curly light brown hair and dark brown eyes. You lived in the city of Kraljevo, nestled between the Kotlenick and Stolovi mountains. Zoran was a pilot with the 98th Brigade in the Serbian Air Force. He died when he was aged 28. The official military explanation was that he suffered a fatal accident during a "training exercise". You suspect that this was a government cover-up and that his plane was shot down during counter terrorism action. After his death, you immigrated to the United States to start a new life with your 4-year-old son, Nikolas."

Now you rent a small house in Novato, California, where the two of you live with Sir Jasper, your pet beagle. You work as a translator and Nikolas is in first grade in school. Your favorite food is sarma, cabbage rolls stuffed with pork, rice and herbs, and you have a blog about Serbian recipes that your grandmother used to make. Your grandmother's name was Zorka."

"My grandmother's name *was* Zorka."

"Then your grandmother's name was Anya," corrected Claudia, making a note about the change on her phone. "Your favorite alcoholic drink is Kruskovac, a liqueur made from pears. Your favorite color is blue and your favorite precious stone is sapphire. Zoran bought you this sapphire necklace for your first wedding anniversary." Claudia handed Ana a sterling silver necklace with a pear-shaped faux sapphire pendant. "Since his death the pear-shaped pendant looks like a tear to you. You wear this necklace *always*."

Ana took off the gold necklace she was wearing and put it in her clutch purse. Then she put the fake sapphire pendant around her neck.

"Oh, and be sure to speak with a Slavic accent and throw in an occasional word in Serbian to make your character seem authentic," advised Claudia.

"I can do that!" said Ana.

"You need to memorize these details carefully," said Claudia. "I've set up fake social media profiles and a blog that contains this information. Your website is called *Nina's Journey*. I suspect that Gil will Google your fake history before your appointment."

Then Claudia asked Ana to stand in front of a white wall in the microbrewery.

"Look sad for the camera," she directed. She took a photograph of Ana. "I'm going to post this photo to your fake blog and say that this was a picture of you at Zoran's funeral."

Ana was wearing a simple brown shift dress and ivory pearl earrings.

"Be sure to wear this same outfit to the appointment, which is tomorrow afternoon at 5pm. I've already paid for your session. Because it's a last minute reading it's classified as an "Urgent Charity Appointment" and it cost $3,000 instead of the usual $1,000."

Ana flinched at this ridiculous cost.

"You mean he charges *extra* for people who are desperate but calls it 'charity'?"

"Of course!" said Claudia. "Gil is a cold, heartless fraud who only cares about ripping people off."

"How are we going to catch him in the act?" asked Ana.

"We're going to record your session with him. You'll call me when you arrive and I'll set my phone to record your conversation," explained Claudia. "I'm no psychic, but I predict he'll start by saying, "Your husband is here with us now..." Then he'll proceed to give you an inaccurate reading based on your fake profile. We're going to catch him in a hot reading and prove that he cheats. Then he'll try to manipulate you into having sex with him."

"Well, we'll just see about that!" said Ana confidently.

Catching Gil wasn't any more dangerous than spouse surveillance, which involved flirting with strangers but avoiding their advances. Some men would get physical, so the women had to be able to protect themselves. All of Claudia's colleagues were trained in self-defense and carried pepper spray or a stun gun for their own safety. Ana carried a pepper spray that looked like a lipstick. She also wore a pair of steel-toed high heels and she wasn't afraid to use them on a man's most tender parts.

"When we have Gil's fake reading and dirty little proposition on record we'll break the story to the media. Hopefully this will be the end of his career," she said gleefully.

"Let's do it!" cried Ana.

They smiled at each other in nervous excitement and drank a toast to a successful sting.

Chapter 21

Ana drove up the steep, winding road leading to Gil's house. Playing the role of Nina Novakov, she wore the pear-shaped faux sapphire pendant that "Zoran" had given to her as a gift to celebrate their first wedding anniversary and the brown shift dress and ivory pearl earrings that she had worn to his "funeral". She stayed up late the night before, memorizing the fake identity Claudia designed for her.

Now she was ready to bust this psychic fraud…

As she walked up the path to Gil's door, Ana dialed Claudia's phone.

"I'm at the target's house, Boss."

"Excellent. Good luck."

Claudia muted her phone and started recording the call. Ana slipped her cell phone into her clutch and rang Gil's doorbell.

Gil answered the door, impeccably dressed in a navy blue suit with a subtle plaid pattern. Ana thought he was very good-looking and imposingly tall.

"Mrs. Novakov. Come in!" he waved her inside. "It's delightful to meet you."

Ana stepped inside his house and smiled charmingly.

"Thanks you wery much for seeing me at shorts notice, Mr. Godsend," she said in broken English. She made sure she transposed her 'v's and 'w's just the way her mom did.

"I have an incredibly tight schedule," Gil replied. "But I have a duty to make time for people who are in desperate need of the help that only I can provide."

He was good-looking, but geez, he was full of himself, she thought.

"May I make you a cup of mugwort tea, Mrs. Novakov?" Gil offered. "I find it enhances my abilities and enables a greater sensitivity."

Was that a double entendre? Gross.

"Da, hvala, Mr. Godsend."

"Although you're not pregnant, are you?" he asked. "Mugwort is very dangerous for pregnant women."

You're the psychic, you tell me!

"Ne, Mr. Godsend," she answered politely.

"I didn't think so."

Nice save, she thought.

"But I sense that your mother desperately wants you to have babies."

Okay, that was true, but weren't most mothers desperate for their daughters to have babies?

"Feel free to look around the reading room and I'll be right back," Gil said.

He disappeared into the kitchen to brew the mugwort tea. Ana had already resolved to not drink it. Who knows what he might put into the tea? Maybe *this* was how he got his clients into bed. Anyway, the drink sounded repulsive. Wasn't mugwort the stuff you use to keep moths away from clothing?

Ana took a look around the room. Gil had a beautiful home that was no doubt built and furnished off the back of his gullible clients. After all, this "Urgent Charity Appointment" had cost $3,000. So much for charity... The reading room was a mix of contemporary designer furniture and antiques. Was that an authentic Fabergé egg on the mantelpiece? Well, that *was* a Porsche Spyder parked in front of his home. For someone so spiritually enlightened he seemed pretty wrapped up in materialistic things.

Then she saw Gil's massive phallic-shaped amethyst crystal.

Someone has a dick substitute, she laughed to herself.

Gil appeared carrying a silver tray with a teapot and two cups sitting on matching saucers. How quaint, thought Ana. Who uses saucers nowadays?

"Did you know that in the Middle Ages mugwort was believed to have magical powers that protected people against illness, wild beasts, and demonic possession?" he said. He placed the tray on the reading table and poured the tea into the cups. Long tendrils of steam rose up into the air. "Today, it is said that a cup of mugwort tea before bedtime will encourage prophetic dreams."

Was he reading this shit straight out of a book? This was weird.

"Many societies use mugwort as a smoking herb," he continued. "Before the introduction of hops, it was used to flavor beer. It is also used as an ingredient in many Asian dishes." He handed her a cup. "Despite its use as a flavoring, mugwort has a slightly bitter taste, so I've added a teaspoon of honey to help it glide down your throat."

And cover up the taste of the date rape drug, Ana thought.

Gil raised his cup into the air.

"Živeli!" he cried in a toast.

Ana looked a little alarmed.

"You *are* Serbian, Mrs. Novakov, aren't you?"

"Yes...um, da!"

"Dobro došla!" he exclaimed excitedly. "Pođite sa mnom!" he said as he touched the small of her back and guided her to a seat at the reading table. "It just so happens that I'm fluent in Serbian. I spent a year living in beautiful Belgrade but I traveled the country extensively. I fondly remember exploring the underground tunnels near the Petrovaradin Fortress in Novi Sad, strolling along the promenade of the Danube in Veliko Gradiste, and trekking the Davolja Varos on the Planina Radan near Leskovac."

Ana tried to look as though she knew what the fuck he was talking about. Both of her parents were Serbian but she was born and raised in the United States. She was an All-American girl. She'd never even been to Serbia. She knew nothing about the country other than the details of the fake story that Claudia has concocted for her.

"Do you want me to conduct the reading in Serbian or English?" asked Gil.

Ana could speak the language, but she was a little rusty. She certainly didn't speak Serbian as fluently as someone who had just emigrated from Serbia to the United States. Her mother always nagged at her about her bad pronunciation.

"English, please. I vant to learn him better."

"Very well," said Gil. "...Now, let's connect to the energy of the spirit world."

He took a seat and lit a tall beige-colored candle sitting in the middle of the reading table. The scent of sandalwood filled the air.

Gil closed his eyes, took several slow, deep breaths and opened his eyes again.

"Your husband is here with us now..."

Claudia had been listening to the entire conversation from her apartment with a huge smile on her face.

"Gotcha!" she cried triumphantly.

Gil was so predictable.

Then the line went dead at her end.

"Oh, for fuck's sake!" she cried. "What happened to the call? It's dropped out!"

She frantically tried to call Ana back but the line was busy.

What was going on?

"Your husband is here with us now…" Gil repeated.

This time his voice was dripping with sarcasm.

What was going on?

"Your husband *isn't* here with us now," he snarled. "But you knew that already, didn't you?" He stood up from his seat, rested his arms on the table and leaned in, glaring at her. "I know you're *not* a widow. In fact, *you've never even been married.*"

The blood drained away from her face.

"Your name *isn't* Nina Novakov. Cut the bullshit. Drop the shitty accent. I know why you're really here…"

Gil came towards her. He loomed over her, and she could see the fury in his piercing blue eyes.

"Claudia sent you here, *didn't she*?"

"Y-y-yes," Ana stammered in fear.

"The two of you thought you'd catch me in a lie and expose me to the media, *didn't you*?"

"Y-y-yes."

"Rest assured. *No one can hear you now.*"

What had she gotten herself into?

He paced around her menacingly.

"Hmm… What shall I do with you?"

She opened her clutch furtively and reached for her pepper spray "lipstick". She would spray him in those creepy blue eyes, kick him in the nuts and get herself out of there as quickly as she could.

"So…Ana… I believe your name is?"

She nodded. How did he know that?

"Now that we've been formally introduced, I'm going to give you a *real* reading," he said. "I'll tell you what you really want to know."

He took his seat again calmly.

She breathed a quiet sigh of relief and closed her clutch purse.

"But I sense that you're a skeptic," he said with a frown. "I need you to keep an open mind, Ana. I can't read someone who has a negative attitude. You *must* be open to the experience."

"I am," she said.

Her cover was blown but this was still a great opportunity to test his psychic abilities. She resolved to answer only "yes" or "no" to his questions to not give him any more information he could use against her.

Gil closed his eyes and took several slow, deep breaths.

He opened his eyes.

"I see an elderly lady standing beside you. Have you a grandmother in spirit?"

"Yes."

It was safe for him to assume that by Ana's age her grandmothers would have passed, she thought.

"This is your maternal grandmother. She is short and plump. She has long salt and pepper-colored hair that she wears piled on top of her head in a bun."

"Yes."

That sounded like a description of everyone's grandmother.

"...I'm getting a name beginning with "Z"... I think it's Zora. No...it's Zorka."

"Yes."

How did he know that? Did Gil see the fake website before Claudia got around to changing "Zorka" to "Anya"?

"Keep an open mind, Ana," Gil scolded her as if he could hear her thoughts. "I'm sensing your negative vibrations. They're blocking my energy."

Skeptics were supposed to keep an open mind, so that's what she would try to do.

"I'm getting that your grandmother wasn't like other grandmothers," Gil continued. "She didn't knit sweaters or bake chocolate chip cookies," he said.

Boy, that was true. She wasn't the kind of grandma who'd make you a peanut butter and jelly sandwich when you came to visit. There was never food in her fridge, only bottles of wine.

Gil sniffed the air.

"I smell alcohol," he said. "I sense that Zorka was... an alcoholic."

"Yes," Ana confirmed in surprise.

Was he really reading her mind?

She could barely remember a time when her grandmother didn't have a glass of wine in one hand and a cigarette in the other, even early in the morning. Her kisses always smelled like alcohol and her clothes reeked of stale cigarette smoke.

"...I'm feeling nauseous," said Gil as he held his stomach. "I feel like I'm going to be sick..."

He breathed deeply until the feeling passed. Ana thought his skin and eyes suddenly looked a little yellow, like he had jaundice.

"...I feel that Zorka developed liver damage...due to alcoholism..."

"Yes."

Zorka started drinking when she lost many friends and family members during the Yugoslav wars. When she became sick, the family tried an intervention to stop her drinking but she was unable to quit. Zorka began to lie about her habit and took to hiding her alcoholism from her family, her friends, and even from herself. When Ana made a surprise visit to her grandmother's house one day she discovered an empty bottle of vodka hidden behind a cushion on the couch.

"Liver disease is what took her from you..."

"That's right," said Ana quietly.

Suddenly she felt like she wanted to burst into tears. The reading reopened an old wound. Her grandmother's alcoholism had destroyed her family, especially her mother. Ana liked an occasional drink, but she hid it from Slob who believed that anyone who drank at all was a raging alcoholic.

Gil looked like he was listening to a voice that Ana couldn't hear.

"Zorka keeps asking a question... Where is my necklace?"

Ana stroked the fake sapphire pendant around her neck.

"She's showing me that you normally wear another pendant," said Gil. "This other necklace is a family heirloom, not a cheap sapphire rip-off."

Ana reached into her clutch and pulled out the necklace she normally wore. It was an onyx Art Deco pendant in the shape of a fan that dangled from a yellow gold chain. She held it up for Gil to see and it swung from side to side like a pendulum.

"This was my great-grandmother's necklace. When she passed, my grandmother wore it until she died. Then mom gave it to me. I wear it *always*."

"Always…except when you're trying to trick me," said Gil with a grin.

Ana blushed. She felt stupid for trying to pull the wool over his eyes.

Gil looked like he was straining to hear something.

"Zorka is fading… She has a final message. She says she loves you…and…*zvini, maca*."

Ana's jaw dropped. *Zvini, maca* means *I'm sorry, kitten*, in Serbian. *Maca* was Zorka's pet name for Ana! To her, this was undeniable proof that Gil had spoken to her dead grandmother.

If Gil could really talk to the dead then there was someone else she needed to hear from desperately, her father, Dragan.

"Mr. Godsend? Could you please… contact my father?"

He shook his head.

"I'm not a DJ. I don't take requests. I talk with whoever *needs* to come through."

Her shoulders fell and she looked at the floor.

Gil's voice softened.

"But let me see if he communicates with us."

He closed his eyes and breathed in and out deeply. Then he opened his eyes.

He looked confused.

"Are you sure he crossed over?"

Ana almost laughed.

"Of course! He died 27 years ago."

Gil frowned.

"I don't feel your father's energy on the other side… But that's because he's *not* on the other side. Your father's still here… My spirit guides are telling me… Dragan *isn't* dead…"

"*What?*" she screamed.

"Your father is *alive*."

"I… can't believe that!"

"It's true," said Gil. "Your mother kicked him out of home long ago. They tell me he's alive and well and living somewhere in southern Florida."

Ana felt like she was going to faint. She must have looked faint too because Gil fetched a glass of water for her. She took a few sips and a few deep breaths.

"How do I verify this?"

"Call your mother and ask her."

Gil left her alone to make the call in private.

Ana took her phone out of her clutch and realized that her connection with Claudia had dropped off. Damn! She'd hoped that Claudia was hearing this conversation. It was proof that Gil was psychic.

Ana called her mother. As the phone rang she took a deep breath.

"Hello?"

She didn't know how to ask this question, so she just blurted it out.

"Mom...is Dad still alive?"

Slob burst into hysterical tears. This was usually her admission of wrongdoing. Ana had to wait for her to calm down.

"Yes," Slob finally admitted. "How did you find out?" she sobbed.

"Gil Godsend told me."

This set off a new wave of sobs.

"I'm wery sorry, Ana," she mumbled.

"Why did you tell me that Dad was *dead* all these years?"

"*He vas dead to me!*" she howled mournfully. "He vas drinking. I kick him out."

Ana had so many questions but now wasn't the time to ask them.

"We'll talk when I get home," she said, and then she hung up.

She was in a state of shock. She didn't remember too many things about her father. He was a handsome man, with kind brown eyes. He had a big belly and he liked to eat. He had a hearty laugh. She was devastated when he died. That is, when she believed he had died. Now that she thought about it, there were little signs here and there that now made sense. There were letters that arrived for her around her birthday that disappeared. She would hear her mother on the phone crying, "Don't call again!" before she hung up. There were times when her mother referred to her father in the present tense, and then corrected herself. Ana always assumed it was Slob's bad grammar.

Her father was *alive*!

Gil came back into the room with two mugs of coffee.

"I believe you prefer this to mugwort tea," he said as he placed a cup in front of her. "I promise there aren't any date rape drugs in this drink," he said with a grin.

Ana smiled. She felt guilty for trying to sting him.

"Thank you," she said as she took the coffee gratefully. "Thank you for everything. If it wasn't for you I would never have known that my father is still… *alive*."

This just didn't feel real to her yet. She started to cry softly.

"Hey, now. This is *good* news," Gil said gently.

He handed her a box of tissues. She took one and dabbed at her eyes.

Gil picked up Ana's necklace.

"We'd better put this back on or your grandmother will be angry," he said.

She swept up her long hair and he unclasped the fake sapphire pendant and put the fan pendant around her neck. His tender touch sent a tiny wave of electricity through her body. At first, Gil seemed like an arrogant prick. Then he'd amazed her with all he knew about her grandmother… and her father.

Her father was alive!

Now, Gil seemed sweet and caring, almost chivalrous, and most definitely psychic! She could really go for a guy like this. He was hot. He was wealthy. He could even speak Serbian. Could she convince her mother that he was Serbian?

She studied Gil's blue eyes, as though by searching them she could understand him.

"You're a very surprising man, Gil Godsend," she said, using her sultry gaze to its full effect. "…You're also a man I'd like to get to know better…"

She touched his hand lightly.

"I'm afraid Claudia has given you the wrong impression about me," he said. "I *never* date my clients."

Ana laughed.

"I don't think 'date' is the word she used!" she said as she drew quotation marks in the air with her fingers. "I hear you…um… sleep with them."

"That isn't me," he said with a frown, but without a trace of irony in his voice. "At any rate, it's not ethical for you and I to do anything," he said firmly. "I must abide by the psychic code of conduct. However…if we'd met under different circumstances…"

His voice trailed off.

"What do you mean, that it wasn't you having sex with those women?" she asked.

"You must go, Ana," he said abruptly. "It's been a pleasure, but please excuse me as I have a business meeting to attend."

"Okay," she said reluctantly.

Ana stood up from her seat and he walked her to the door. She handed him her business card.

"If you ever change your mind, call me."

"Doviđenja, Ana," he said with his grin.

"Goodbye, Gil," she said, shooting him a final sultry glance.

Ana left his house and walked back to her car. She saw Claudia's car parked beside her. Claudia rolled down her window and called out to her.

"Our call dropped as soon as Gil said, "Your husband is here with us now"," she said in exasperation. "He must have used a cell blocker. Are you okay?"

"So you didn't overhear the amazing psychic reading I had with Gil?"

"*What?*"

"As you know, I was very skeptical of Gil, but he's convinced me that he can talk to the dead. He knew personal details about my family that no one else knows."

How could Ana have made a complete turnaround from skeptic to believer?

"Maybe he found this information on the net?" suggested Claudia.

"I work in cyber security," Ana reminded her. "There's *no* trace of me online."

"Okaay." Claudia was unconvinced. "But did Gil proposition you?"

"No. To be fair, *I* came onto *him* but he rejected me because I was a client!"

Claudia was surprised that Gil didn't try to come onto Ana, but he must have known that he was under the microscope...

"I still don't believe in psychics, but I believe in Gil Godsend," Ana said. "Anyway, I need to go home to have a little talk with my mother."

She hopped into her car and drove off.

Claudia sat frozen in her car. She was flabbergasted. How could this sting have gone so horribly wrong? Was Gil bugging her office and phone so he could eavesdrop on her conversations to find out about her plans? Didn't Ana say that her mother had a psychic reading with Gil years ago and that he probably did a hot reading? Perhaps he used the information from that session for his reading today with Ana? Maybe he was keeping files on his clients just like the old-time psychics used to do. The reading clearly hit a raw nerve with Ana and she was far too emotional to think clearly at this time. Claudia would talk with her about it later.

Gil wasn't psychic but he still managed to bewitch people, she thought.

Claudia jumped when she realized that someone was peering into her car window.

It was Gil.

"Hello, Claudia," he said cheerily. His hair was blowing about in the breeze and with his white-toothed grin he looked like a model in a toothpaste commercial.

"Oh, for fuck's sake," she said.

This day couldn't get any worse.

"Ana is a charming lady. Thank you for sending her to me," Gil said with a wink. "Now, have you thought any more about my job offer?" he asked. "We make a better team than we do adversaries."

Claudia scoffed.

"For me to accept I'd have to have my ethics and my integrity surgically removed."

Gil laughed.

"Well, I do have the hands of a surgeon, as you know."

He held up his large, strong hands and she tried not to think of all the times those hands had been all over her body.

"The offer still stands, Claudia. Think about it. Oh, and by the way, say "hi" to Banachek for me," he said with his annoying grin. "I've always been such a big fan of his. That guy would almost make you think that psychic powers exist."

Claudia was furious. She rolled up her window, started up her car and sped away.

Gil watched as her car disappeared down the hill and into the crimson-colored sunset.

Chapter 22

Gil was right. Ana found her father living in Homestead, a town in southern Florida. Dragan had lived there for the past twenty years. When she finally spoke with him, Ana discovered that he had attempted to win back Slob's trust, without success. Dragan liked a drink, after all, he was Serbian, but he was *not* an alcoholic. He tried to contact his daughter many times over the decades, but he couldn't find a trace of her online, and because Ana was still living at home, Slob had been blocking his access to her.

Ana regained her father in her life, and she also gained a younger half-brother that she never knew about.

As soon as he received a call from Ana, Dragan traveled to the Bay Area where father and daughter had a tearful but joyous reunion. There was a lot of relationship rebuilding to do, both between Ana and her father, and between Ana and her mother.

All's well that ends well, but Claudia was still convinced that Ana's session with Gil had been a hot reading. She speculated as to how he knew so much about Ana and her family. Gil could have bugged Claudia's phone and office so he was privy to her conversations with Ana and knew about the sting. On the other hand, Gil could have gathered insider information about Ana's family during his reading with Slob years before. Perhaps Slob used the session as a confessional, as many did, and confessed her guilt that Ana's father was still alive but she was hiding this information from her daughter. Perhaps it was a combination of all of these theories.

Claudia had no proof of anything, but what was more believable, that Gil cheated during the reading, or that he could talk to the dead? In the end, it didn't matter that Claudia could explain away Gil's amazing insights. Ana was convinced that Gil was the world's greatest psychic because he brought her father back from the dead.

Claudia needed a vacation more than ever. She was still reeling from the events of the past few months. Against her better judgment, she'd been dragged back into skepticism by women who needed her help. Now Gil was back in her life. She'd been busting her ass to expose Gil as a fraud but he made her look like a fool at every turn. She opened herself up to public and private humiliation, sexual harassment and assault. This sent her into a bout of depression, and just when she pulled herself out of her blues and summoned the energy to orchestrate what should have been a foolproof sting, the operation had backfired.

She needed to get away from it all.

Claudia made a snap decision to go somewhere for a few weeks. But where should she go? She'd always wanted to visit Easter Island to see the Moai statues. It also happened to be one of the most remote places on earth, where no one would have heard of psychic medium Gil Godsend. But it was too difficult to book a trip there at the last minute.

She thought about how some people choose a destination randomly by spinning a globe and pointing. She didn't have a globe but she had a map of the world on her office wall. She also had a dartboard beside it with a photo of Gil as the target. His face was spotted with numerous tiny holes and it was either by skill or coincidence that his eyes had been obliterated. She dislodged a dart from Gil's jugular vein, closed her eyes and tossed the dart at the map. It landed on Afghanistan. She wanted to go on vacation, not get herself killed. She tried again. This time she struck Somalia. This wasn't going too well. She'd make it the best of three...

The third time she threw the dart it hit an area on the north east coast of Australia with a funny name: Mooloolaba. The town was located on the Sunshine Coast in Queensland. The name alone sounded exciting. She wanted this trip to be impulsive and spontaneous so she booked a flight to leave the very next day. She was usually a methodical packer, but today she packed only a few items of clothing, and a sexy string bikini, her sunglasses, and a tube of sunscreen. Whatever else she needed she'd grab on the go.

It was a long 15-hour flight and it took her a day or two to get over the jet lag but it was worth it. Mooloolaba turned out to be a hidden jewel. She rented a quiet little cottage by the ocean. There were coffee shops, restaurants, and bars dotted along endless beaches. The people were friendly, and the town was full of hot guys who liked a girl with an American accent. This was the perfect place for some sun, sand, and surf.

Her first week was spent at restaurants along the beach where she enjoyed lingering meals and glasses of wine, and she read books in coffee shops. Autobiographies about rock star's wives, girlfriends, and groupies were brain candy to her, like Pamela Des Barres' *I'm With the Band* and Pattie Boyd's *Wonderful Tonight: George Harrison, Eric Clapton, and Me*.

She enjoyed doing nothing, but this gave her too much time to dwell on things.

That Ana discovered her father was still alive stirred up feelings for Claudia about her own father. He wasn't going to come back from the grave. He died of Alzheimer's some ten years ago, but not before he suffered a long and frustrating battle with the degenerative disease. In those early years he became forgetful, but it wasn't like forgetting where you put your keys, he was putting his keys in the fridge. He forgot words, confused people's names, asked the same questions and told the same stories again and again. Once he got lost going for a walk in his own neighborhood.

Before her father developed the disease, Claudia always believed that people with Alzheimer's weren't aware of their condition, but when she got to see the effects first hand, she saw that her father had a keen awareness of his memory loss. His decline was frustrating for him, and it was frightening for her to watch him lose himself.

When she was a little girl, her father gave her a secret code. This was a quote from the poem "Magic" by Shel Silverstein.

But all the magic I've known I've had to make myself.

Yes, she got her skepticism from her father.

The secret code was for her safety, so she wouldn't leave school with a dangerous stranger. In case her father ever sent a friend to pick her up from school, this was the password to let her know that the person was safe. They never needed to use it. But when he became sick, the secret code became a way for them to test his memory and gauge his deterioration. Every time Claudia visited him in the nursing home she asked, "What's the secret code, Dad?" and he recited the quote. Over time, he forgot a word or two. Then, one suitably cold and bleak day, she asked him for their secret code. He looked at her blankly and asked, "What's your name, young lady?"

She was heartbroken. He could no longer recognize her, let alone remember their secret code. Soon he couldn't walk or feed himself. Her father survived another six months but he was already gone.

She still missed him every single day.

Claudia wanted to spend some time by herself and clear her head, but she was lonely. What rubbed it in was that she kept seeing happy couples everywhere. These were gorgeous, laughing women with sun-bleached highlights in their hair who were paired up with men sporting tanned six packs as they carried their surfboards. She had been on more "dates" than just about anyone, but she hadn't been on a real date with someone she actually liked for over a year. Maybe she should have a vacation fling with a tall Aussie lifeguard with freckles sprinkled across his nose.

Claudia went for a stroll along Mooloolaba beach before dinner. She wondered if she should be adventurous and try eating a kangaroo steak that night. She slipped off her shoes and carried them as she walked along the sand and gentle foamy waves lapped at her feet. She breathed in the salty air while she watched golden sunbeams stream through the clouds.

She couldn't help herself. Walking along the beach reminded her of Gil and the old days when they lived together in Santa Barbara. They used to take long walks along Butterfly Beach to catch the sunset over the water. Most of the beaches in Santa Barbara face the south, while Butterfly Beach was one of the few west-facing beaches that caught the sunset. They watched the vibrant streaks of pink and purple stretch out across the sky until the sun drowned in the horizon and darkness fell.

Claudia enjoyed the peace and quiet but she almost wished she had someone to share the moment with her.

"Is this when I'm supposed to look up and see the man of my dreams?" she said out loud.

"Yes, it is," said a deep voice from behind her.

She jumped in shock and spun around. It wasn't a tall, sun-kissed Aussie bloke with freckles across his nose.

It was Gil.

"Oh, for fuck's sake."

She rolled her eyes, but there was unmistakable happiness and softness in his eyes. Gil was dressed so casually she barely recognized him. Instead of his usual suit and tie he wore a pair of navy blue beach shorts and a white linen shirt.

"What are *you* doing here?" she asked him.

"Well, what are *you* doing here?" he asked in reply.

It reminded her of an annoying brother who repeats everything you say.

"I'm here to get away from it all, especially you!" she replied. She shook her head and sighed. "So, how did you and I end up at the same gin joint in all the towns in all the world? This is too amazing to be mere coincidence."

"Some might call it synchronicity," he said with a grin.

"Some might call it *stalking*."

"I came here to see you," he admitted.

Claudia was taken aback by his honesty. He had traveled some 7,000 miles to see her. Was that romantic or creepy? How did he know where she was?

"May I walk with you?" he asked.

"If you must."

They walked in silence for a while.

"This reminds me of the old days when we lived together in Santa Barbara," he said, breaking the silence. "Remember those long walks along Butterfly Beach to catch the sunset over the water?"

"Get out of my head."

Gil fell silent again. He was just glad that he was in her head. They continued walking along the beach together but she felt uncomfortable, like he was going to put his arm around her shoulder or try to hold her hand like they were teenagers on their first date.

As they walked she saw him rubbing his forehead.

"What's wrong? Get some sand in your third eye?"

He laughed with a slightly pained expression on his face.

"No, I've just been getting headaches. My third eye is fine."

As they walked Claudia started thinking about her father again. She'd do anything to hear from him one last time, and here she was with the "world's greatest psychic". In all of these years she'd never had a reading from Gil. Should she test him, here and now?

She stopped walking and looked at him.

"Gil," she said. "Give me a reading of my dad."

He thought about it for so long that she thought he hadn't heard her question.

"Gil?"

He looked straight at her. The softness in his eyes was replaced by sternness.

"That's not a good idea."

"Why not? Would you tell me that my father's still alive too?"

"I only wish that I could," he said plaintively.

"Then you're finally admitting that you're a liar and you *can't* talk to the dead?"

"Not at all... I just know some things that will... upset you."

"*Please...*"

Gil hadn't heard that gentle tone in her voice since they were together. Gone was the stern glare she typically saved for him. As he looked at her the sunlight caught the gold flecks in her eyes and he saw something in them he hadn't seen in years.

He tilted his head as if he was listening to a voice she couldn't hear.

"...Your father has a message for you... He wants you to know that he loves you and that he's whole again. He says, "But all the magic I've known I've had to make myself"."

She froze.

How did Gil know the secret code? Only Claudia and her father knew this.

No one else did.

Her mind searched for a rational explanation. Could she have let it slip to him years ago? Was it a lucky guess? Was he really psychic? No...

All she knew was that she missed her father. Painfully.

When Gil recited the quote she could hear her father's voice like he was right there with her. She dissolved into tears. She felt so weak, so vulnerable, and so alone.

"You're not alone," Gil said.

He took her into his arms. Claudia melted into his body. His familiar embrace felt so comforting, those muscular arms wrapped around her tightly, the smell of his skin, the feel of running her fingers through his thick hair, and the touch of his lips on hers.

Wait... *What was she doing*?

Her body stiffened. This wasn't a scene from a romance novel. This wasn't the man she once knew. This guy was a fraud. He was a smooth-talking con artist. He manipulated vulnerable women to get them into bed. Today, *she* was the vulnerable woman.

She pulled away from him.

"I'm not the man you once knew, but I'm also not the man you think I am," said Gil.

She let his words sink in for a moment. What did he mean? Was she not giving him the chance he deserved to explain himself?

He could tell she was letting down her guard a bit.

"Let's talk about everything over dinner tonight," he said.

From the look she gave him he could see he was going too far, too fast.

"...Or not talk about anything at all... There's this great little Indonesian place right nearby that makes a wonderful gado gado and mie goreng."

He remembered that she loved Indonesian food. She'd forgotten about their romantic trip to Bali to celebrate their engagement.

"You're asking me out on a date?"

"Yes, if you want that. No, if you don't. Then it's just two old friends catching up."

She stared at him for the longest time. What was his motive? Was he trying to get her into bed? Probably. Would he try to push her to become his manager? Then she actually considered his invitation to go out that night. Would it hurt to have dinner with him? She was alone in a strange country. It would be safer for her to have company...but maybe not so safe with him. Although he was an old friend...whose heart she once broke and whose career she was now trying to ruin.

Perhaps she could consider the dinner to be work and she should interrogate him the whole evening? But she was here for pleasure, not business. Didn't she deserve a little happiness and a little fun on her vacation? She wanted this trip to be impulsive and spontaneous.

Gil was always a charming, intelligent, and entertaining dinner companion. He spared no expense during dinner, and didn't bat an eyelid at the cost of champagne and caviar…but then he might expect something in return. She looked into Gil's piercing blue eyes, which seemed to have become more vibrantly blue over time, and she had a flashback of him staring intensely into her eyes while he was on top of her.

Would it hurt to have dinner and have sex with him?

Wait… *What was she thinking*?

Gil was her distant past. He was no longer the man she used to love, the man she was going to marry, and the man she was going to have babies with. There was no white picket fence for the two of them. There was no happy ending with this guy, unless it was one he bought from a seedy late night massage parlor. Too much had happened between them. She could never go back. It was over. It was dead. She heard thunder in the distance and dark clouds started rolling in, as if they agreed with her.

"Goodbye, Gil…"

He looked hurt. She turned around and started to walk away. Instead of making a graceful exit the hot, dry sand sucked her feet down with every step she took. It was like the sand was trying to drag her back to Gil. Then a sudden downpour drenched her. Her hair and clothes were soaked. She walked away for a few minutes and then she looked back. Gil was still standing there in the rain, watching her. *Dammit*. Why did she do that? She turned around and continued walking. This time she didn't look back.

When she woke up the next morning she had a throbbing headache. It almost felt like a hangover, but she didn't have that much to drink last night, did she? She couldn't remember much about the night before, but she could remember her dreams. They seemed so real at the time. She had vivid dreams about Gil all night long. She dreamed they ended up going out to dinner that night. She laughed and had sun-bleached highlights in her hair. His shirt was unbuttoned revealing his tanned six-pack and he was carrying a surfboard. They tried eating kangaroo for the first time, it tasted strong, but not gamey, and they had a few too many drinks. Then she'd taken him back to her place. As soon as they closed the door they fell into each other's arms and fell into bed.

They made love throughout the night.

Then she dreamed that she and Gil got back together. Gil's doctors discovered a tumor on his brain, which was causing his psychic experiences. He had surgery to remove the tumor, and he stopped hearing voices and having psychic premonitions. He quit being a psychic medium and become a clinical psychologist. Claudia sold her business and became a full time author, writing horror novels. Claudia and Gil married and had a beautiful baby boy with piercing blue eyes.

She was angry that her subconscious mind betrayed her with these dreams, or rather nightmares, about Gil. Then she wondered, briefly, in her sleepy, bleary mind, if she should have stayed with Gil all those years ago. She wasn't making magic in her life anymore.

Claudia shook off her dreams, took some painkillers for her headache, and made herself a cup of tea and a slice of raisin toast. She took her breakfast out on the balcony to enjoy the sea breeze. Then she caught up with the news on the net.

She stared in horror when she saw a photograph of her and Gil together on the beach. The photo was taken when he was comforting her, but they were entwined in such a passionate embrace it looked like they were just about to strip each other's clothes off and have sex there and then.

The article was titled, "The Psychic and the Skeptic: We should have seen this coming."

Chapter 23

It must have been a slow news day because the story was splashed across the media.

They said that Claudia and Gil met up in Australia for a secret rendezvous to escape the press. They reported that the pair spent the afternoon cavorting on the beach. That night, they had been spotted together enjoying an intimate dinner at a local restaurant. The couple left the establishment at around 10pm. They were drunk. They laughed and kissed, while Gil had his arm wrapped around Claudia's waist. They went back to a tiny cottage near the beach they were renting. Then Gil emerged about 4am, looking like he'd been kicked out of bed after a "blue", whatever that meant.

They called her a hypocrite for sleeping with the enemy.

Claudia was fuming, but she wasn't sure where to direct her anger. The paparazzi hounded people like Gil, violating the privacy of celebrities wherever they went and telling lies about them. Or did Gil orchestrate this? Did he tip them off about his whereabouts as a publicity stunt? Maybe he was framing her to make her look bad. Perhaps she should be angry with herself for bothering to talk to Gil yesterday.

Claudia still had a headache so she decided to go out for a walk to clear her head and get some coffee. When she went into her bedroom to get changed she sniffed the air and frowned. She swore she could smell Gil's cologne in the room. For years he'd worn Chanel's Allure Homme Sport Eau Extreme. It had a sweet and musky scent. She could even smell it a little on her clothes and in her hair. It must have rubbed onto her when he was comforting her on the beach. That man wore way too much cologne! It wasn't an unpleasant odor, but it smelled of Gil, and that association made it unpleasant for her. She took a long, hot shower and changed the bed sheets to get rid of the overwhelming smell.

Claudia threw on a pair of jeans, a hoodie, a pair of sunglasses and a baseball cap and went out for coffee. As she walked along the beachfront people seemed to recognize her, even though she was dressed incognito. They stared and whispered as she went by.

Thanks a lot Gil, she thought.

She found a hip-looking place that looked like an old garage that had been converted into a coffee shop. She looked at the menu. They had an espresso drink called a flat white and another one called a long black. They both sounded like racial insults.

She ordered a cappuccino and a biscuit, but she was given a cookie.

"Here, a biscuit is a cookie, and what you'd call a biscuit is a scone," the barista explained to her complete confusion.

Australians speak English just like Americans, but sometimes they seem like entirely different languages, she thought.

Her phone rang. It was Gil.

She ignored him.

Claudia sat outside with her cappuccino and watched the waves crashing onto the sand. Soon she found herself people watching and then checking out the men that walked by. I need to get myself one of those, she thought. When was the last time she'd had sex anyway? It must have been at least a year ago when she was seeing that Urologist. She had another week of her vacation left and it was time to have some fun. She was a single woman in a country full of hot guys. She decided to dress up and hit the town that night. She was going to find that lifesaver of her fantasies and get laid.

Claudia didn't pack much in the way of clothing, shoes, and makeup, so this was an excuse for her to go shopping. She found a mall nearby and wandered into a department store. She was searching for sexy underwear and obviously looked lost because a sales assistant approached her.

"Can I help you?"

"Yes, please. Where can I find the thongs?"

"Let me show you," the woman said.

They walked through the store, but to Claudia's bewilderment they went straight past the lingerie section and arrived at the shoe department.

"Um...Where are the thongs?" she asked.

"Here," the woman said in surprise, as she pointed to a wall of flip-flops.

"Those are flip-flops!"

"Oh, did you mean G-strings?" she asked. "Flip-flops are called thongs here and thongs are called G-strings."

Claudia felt like she needed a translator.

After some shopping and lunch, Claudia got her hair done at a salon. Her hairstylist, Misty, had fire engine red hair and wore one of those sleek geometric bobs that no one else but a stylist can carry off. Misty looked at Claudia like she recognized her.

"Haven't I seen you somewhere before?" she asked.

Snip. Snip. Snip.

"I don't think so," said Claudia innocently.

"Hey! I know where I've seen you," Misty said excitedly. "You were in the newspapers this morning!"

Snip. Snip. Snip.

"You were on the beach with that spunky psychic Gil Godsend. Aren't you his girlfriend?"

Claudia sniffed.

"No, I'm not. Well, I was, but that was a *long* time ago."

Snip. Snip. Snip.

"If you're not seeing him can I get his phone number?"

Shut up and do my hair, thought Claudia, otherwise I'm going to seize those scissors and ram them up your ass.

"Sorry, but I don't have his number," she said sweetly.

Snip. Snip. Snip.

"Okay," Misty said, not believing Claudia at all. "So… is he really as, you know…*big*…as he looks?"

Claudia shook her head.

"No. He stuffs a sock down his underpants," she whispered. "It's sad, really."

That night, Claudia stepped out wearing a flesh-colored silk and metallic dress that defied the fashion rule that a woman should accentuate either her tits or legs but not both at the same time. With a plunging neckline, her dress showed her cleavage, while a thigh high slit in the skirt flaunted her long legs. Her hair was styled; she'd had a manicure and pedicure, and she managed to fit in a bikini wax. She was ready to go on the prowl.

As she strolled along the beachfront her phone rang again. It was Gil. She threw her phone into her clutch and decided not to look at it again that night.

She passed coffee shops and restaurants until she came across a pub that always seemed popular. She walked inside and found the place was swarming with football fans watching a game on TV. She stopped to watch it for a minute. It didn't look like American football; these guys weren't wearing helmets or any padding although it was a considerably more violent game than gridiron.

Claudia scanned the pub and immediately she zoomed in on a good-looking guy across the room. He was tall and tanned with curly dark blonde hair. He looked like he might be a lifesaver. And he was looking straight back at her. They locked eyes for a few seconds. He was standing behind a table full of loud-mouthed guys who were wearing football jerseys and drinking beer. They noticed her too and started wolf whistling and cat calling.

"The stripper's here!"

"Give us a lap dance, luv!"

"How much?"

Claudia realized she was overdressed for the pub. Most people there were wearing t-shirts or football jerseys with jeans or shorts. She looked like she was on her way to a nightclub, or a street corner. Feeling self-conscious, she made her way over to the bar where she sat on a stool and pulled down awkwardly on her dress.

"What can I get ya, luv?" the bartender asked.

"I'll have a lemonade, please."

Her headache had only just eased off so she wanted to work her way up to the harder stuff that night.

The bartender brought over a glass filled with a clear, carbonated drink.

She was confused.

"Um, I didn't order a soda, I wanted a lemonade," she said to the bartender.

"That *is* a lemonade, luv," he replied.

Suddenly, the hot guy with the blonde curls was standing right beside her.

"I can translate," he said as he came to her rescue. "Carbonated lemon-lime drinks like Sprite and 7UP are all called "lemonade" here. Also, a soda is called a soft drink."

Claudia barely heard him. She was too busy gazing into his vivid green eyes. They were the color of emeralds, of rice terraces, of a field of grass after rain, of moss growing on rocks and of the iridescent wings on a butterfly.

She shook her head and snapped out of it.

"Two countries divided by a common language!" she said with her sexiest smile. "Thank you."

"No worries," he said with a gorgeous grin. "I can speak American. I spent two years living in New York City working as a hedge fund manager."

Okay, so he wasn't a lifesaver, but he would do. He would do very nicely indeed.

"What's your name?" Claudia asked him.

"I'm Jeremy," he replied, offering his hand. "Jeremy Collins."

"I'm Claudia Cox."

They shook hands. Then a wave of recognition spread across his face.

"Hey! Aren't you that chick who was in the newspapers today? You're the girlfriend of that Yank fella who thinks he's psychic."

Oh, for fuck's sake, she thought.

"He is *not* my boyfriend," she said indignantly. "Well, to be honest, he *was* my fiancé, but that was a lifetime ago. I can assure you that I'm a single woman!"

"Sweet," he said with another one of those irresistible grins, "but dressed like that you won't be single for long."

Dammit, why did his smile remind her of Gil's? She tried to push Gil out of her mind. She looked down at her outfit.

"I think I overdressed tonight."

"I think you look great," he said. "You look just like one of those fancy American actresses on the red carpet at the Oscars."

"Like Nicole Kidman or Naomi Watts?"

He laughed. It was a deep, sexy laugh that made her lick her lips unconsciously.

"If you're feeling uncomfortable," he said, "why don't you cover up with my jumper?"

He took off his football jersey and handed it to her. It was the gesture of a gentleman and it touched her. It also gave her the chance to check out his chiseled chest through his t-shirt. She thanked him as she slipped the jersey over her head and pulled it down over her dress. It smelled good and still felt warm from his body heat.

"Now, that looks better on you than it does on me!" he said.

It would look better crumpled up on the floor next to your bed, she thought.

"Sorry about my mates," Jeremy said with a nod towards his friends. "They carry on like a bunch of yobbos when they're pissed and watching the footy."

"Why are they angry?" Claudia asked. "Is their team losing?"

He laughed good-naturedly.

"Pissed means drunk here. Pissed off means angry."

Claudia blushed. She didn't feel like she was fitting in at all.

"I feel like an idiot," she said.

"You're not an idiot. You just don't know the lingo. Let me shout you a drink and I can teach you some Aussie slang."

"It is loud in here but you don't have to shout," she replied. "I can hear you."

"To shout means to buy someone a drink," he explained.

She blushed again.

"Okay," she said sheepishly.

"What would you like?"

"I'll have something that an Aussie would drink. How about a Foster's?"

He shook his head.

"Foster's is promoted overseas as Australia's favorite beer, but a fair dinkum Aussie wouldn't touch the stuff. Let's get you what I like to drink, a Cooper's Green on tap."

"Okay," she said. "But what's fair dinkum?" she asked.

"Someone or something that's real or true."

"And what's a *blue*?" she asked, thinking about the newspaper articles.

"It's a fight," he explained.

Hmm… So the media thought she'd had a lover's tiff with Gil and booted him out of bed. She laughed silently to herself.

The pub was crowded and noisy. They decided to go outside to the courtyard so they could talk, or have a "chinwag", as Jeremy put it. They had a few drinks and talked about their lives. Jeremy had worked in finance for the past ten years and his job had taken him not only to cities across the United States, but to London, Paris, Frankfurt, Tokyo, and other financial centers. Next week he would be traveling to Hong Kong for two months. His home was on the Sunshine Coast but he was on the road so frequently that it had caused a breakup with his fiancé a few months before.

Claudia pretended that she was sympathetic.

Throughout their conversation she caught herself listening not to what he said, but how he said it. Jeremy's accent was incredibly sexy. She had always had a thing for accents, especially the Aussie accent. Jeremy didn't speak like Steve Irwin or Paul Hogan, instead he sounded a bit more like he was British. She also loved the colorful Australian slang he used, and he taught her a lot of it that night. She learned that fair dinkum Aussies never say, "Put another shrimp on the barbie" because they don't say *shrimp*, they call them *prawns*. When Aussies say they *have the shits* they aren't suffering from a bout of diarrhea, they're angry. When something is *not bad*, it's *good*, and when someone insults you, sometimes it's because they like you.

Jeremy wasn't the lifeguard of her fantasies, but he was a surfer. He was born in the Sydney beachside suburb called Manly, which Claudia thought was very apt. He grew up on the beach and could swim before he could walk. Most days he was in town he woke up at 6am to head down to the beach for a surf, even during wintertime.

Jeremy was smart, funny, and handsome. She hated to admit it, but he reminded her of Gil, although the thing she liked most about Jeremy was that he didn't believe in psychics. He was down to earth, easygoing, and he thought that Gil was full of bullshit.

Jeremy wasn't the lifeguard of her fantasies; he was even better.

Claudia wanted to go home with him that night. A little part of her wanted to have his babies too.

They decided to leave the pub and go for a walk. As they strolled down the beachfront they passed by a convenience store.

"Have you ever eaten a Tim Tam?" Jeremy asked.

"A Tim *what*?"

"A Tim Tam," he said. "It's a biscuit. You'd call it a cookie. You can't visit Australia without trying a Tim Tam."

Jeremy raced into the convenience store and bought a packet of Tim Tams. He tore open the packet and offered her one. She took a bite and her eyes widened. It was a decadent cookie sandwich filled with chocolate cream and coated in chocolate fudge. It melted in her mouth and she immediately wanted another one.

"Well, what do you think?" he asked.

"These are dangerously good. Get them away from me!" she cried. "Those are better than sex."

"Then you're doing it wrong," he joked. "But you only say that because you haven't had sex with *me*."

Yet, she thought.

"There are lots of Aussie treats you need to try while you're here," he said. "Like lamingtons, Cherry Ripes, meat pies, Vegemite, and a true blue Aussie breakfast...I'll make that for you tomorrow morning," he said with a wink.

Claudia knew she would be going home with him that night.

They walked along the beach together. Finally, she was part of one of those happy couples, instead of being alone.

She slipped off her heels and her feet sank into the warm, wet sand. Soon they decided to sit down on the sand to watch the sunset. She realized they were sitting right in the area where she was standing with Gil the day before when the paparazzi took their photographs. She wondered where Gil was and what he was doing. He was probably out on a date right now with some Aussie beauty. Perhaps Misty the hairstylist had tracked him down and figured out that wasn't a sock in his underpants. But why should she care? She *had* to stop thinking about Gil...

She stared out at the golden sun as it disappeared into the dark blue ocean.

"It's so beautiful," she sighed.

"*You* are so beautiful," Jeremy said.

He laid her down gently onto the sand. He leaned in towards her and kissed her. His lips were soft and his stubble tickled her chin. She ran her hands through his thick curls and pulled him closer towards her. His skin smelled just like his jersey, not of pretentious cologne, but a heady natural scent of the ocean and coconut-scented surfboard wax. He lay down on top of her. It felt so good to have a man above her again. She was very turned on, and with his body pressed against hers; she could feel that he was too.

Claudia forgot all about Gil Godsend.

Jeremy pulled back and looked into her eyes.

"Do you want to come back to my place?" he asked her. "I'll try to perform better than the Tim Tams."

She smiled.

"I thought you'd never ask…"

They went back to Jeremy's apartment. Claudia looked around the place while he went to the kitchen to open a bottle of wine. He had a fancy bachelor pad. There was modern art on the walls and some interesting curios on display that he had collected from his travels. There were also signs that he was a beach bum. A wetsuit was strewn over a chair at the kitchen table and a surfboard stood up in a corner of his office. The place was otherwise neat and clean and minimalist. It didn't have that lived in look. Claudia could tell that he didn't spend much time there.

Jeremy came back into the room and gave her a glass of red wine. He took her by the hand and led her outside to a couch on his balcony. They sat down and he put his arm around her. She snuggled into him. His apartment had sweeping views of the beach and they gazed up to look at the stars in the sky. He pointed out to her the Southern Cross, a constellation in the shape of a cross, and told her it was a symbol on the Australian flag. She only knew it as the Crosby, Stills and Nash song.

Claudia finished her glass of wine.

"Do you want another glass?" he asked her.

"No thanks," she said, "but there's something else I want."

She kissed him.

She closed her eyes as she felt his lips trace her neck and shoulders with soft, lingering kisses. One of his hands caressed her thigh while he slipped his other hand under the jersey. He began stroking her breast firmly through her silken dress. He felt her nipple harden and she gave a little moan.

"You need to teach me another Aussie word," she said in a breathy voice.

"What's that?"

"How do you say cunnilingus in Australian?"

He smiled at her.

"How about I show you instead?" he said as he knelt down before her and disappeared under her dress.

The next morning, Jeremy cooked her breakfast, or "brekkie" as he called it. He made a hearty meal of eggs, sausages, bacon, baked beans, grilled tomatoes, and mushrooms with toast and a cup of tea. Claudia noticed that the egg yolks were bright orange instead of yellow. The bacon wasn't thin, streaky and crispy like it was back in the States, it included the meaty loin and it looked and tasted more like ham. She tried Vegemite too and thought it tasted very bitter, but she liked something similar, a salty spread called Promite.

"I have almost a week left on my vacation," Claudia said as she sipped her tea. "What should I see around here?"

"There's lots to see and do," he said. He stared at her with his gorgeous green eyes. "You know, I have this week off before I fly out to Hong Kong. How about I become your tour guide? After all, you need me as your translator."

"You're on!" she cried happily.

They smiled at each other.

And so their one night stand blossomed into a vacation romance.

The following week they were inseparable. Jeremy took her to the beach and tried to teach her how to surf, without much success. They went for walks along the beach, and hikes to see rainforests and waterfalls. They went to a zoo, where she fed kangaroos and she even got to pet a koala. They looked like cuddly teddy bears but they had sharp claws. He took her out to dinner every night to try a different ethnic cuisine, and he cooked breakfast for her every morning. They also spent lots of time in bed.

Claudia hadn't had this much fun in a long time. To her, the Sunshine Coast was paradise.

At the end of the week it was time for them to go back to their lives. Claudia had to return home to the Bay Area and Jeremy had to fly out to Hong Kong. They promised to keep in touch and reconnect if they ever happened to be in the same zip code. They even discussed the possibility of Claudia returning to the Sunshine Coast sometime, or Jeremy visiting her in San Francisco. They just didn't know when their busy schedules would overlap.

Their goodbye kiss at the airport was fraught with sadness and they held each other tightly for the longest time. Claudia fought back tears and even Jeremy's green eyes turned a little red. Sure, they met by chance in a pub one night, but they had grown close over the past week and leaving each other was more difficult than they expected it would be. Claudia knew this had just been a fling, but Jeremy was a guy, a "bloke", that she could really go for.

When the plane took off she couldn't fight her tears any longer, and she cried silently into the sleeve of her hoodie.

The kindly old lady seated next to her reached over and took her hand.

"Aw, darl, did you just say goodbye to someone you love?"

She paused.

"Yes, I did."

Claudia realized she had just admitted she loved Jeremy to a complete stranger before she had admitted it to him, or to herself.

Chapter 24

Claudia had been home for a few weeks after her trip to Australia. She was back to work and everything was back to normal, sort of. She and Jeremy had started something that was quickly becoming a long distance relationship. He was in Hong Kong on business for the next few months and they spoke with each other whenever their time zone difference allowed them to. Claudia also discovered that she was much better at phone sex nowadays…

She prepared for another job that night. Her target was a physics professor at Cal. His wife was worried that he was also teaching biology to some of his female students, because that was what had happened when she was his student. He claimed to be working late in the library every night but in truth he could be found in the college bar. Claudia poured herself a glass of merlot for some liquid courage. She didn't like Coors in a plastic cup. She wanted to look like a graduate student so instead of wearing her usual sexy dresses and high heels she dressed down in a Bears hoodie and distressed jeans. In fact, her jeans were so ripped and torn they were positively distraught. As she piled her hair up in a baseball cap her phone rang.

It was Banachek.

"Hello, my friend."

"Hi, Banachek! What's up?"

"Me," he replied. "I'm chained up and hanging upside down," he said like it was an everyday event.

"Where are you?"

"I'm in my hotel room…only kidding!" he joked. "I'm preparing for a show tonight in Las Vegas. The stagehands are testing the equipment for safety. I can't come down until they're done, so I thought I'd give you a call…"

"Of course," she said. "I would have done the same thing."

He chuckled.

"Well, we have a scoundrel on our hands with Gil Godsend," he said. "Sometimes the best way to predict what a scoundrel will do is to see what other scoundrels have done. Did I ever tell you the story about the Reverend Doctor Jimmy Lee Mercy?"

When Jimmy Lee Mercy was a baby he developed diphtheria. His parents believed he fell sick because he hadn't been baptized yet and he wasn't protected by God, although it probably happened because his parents didn't immunize him against the disease. His case was so severe that he nearly died, and the doctors said his recovery was nothing short of miraculous. As a result, his parents believed he was a miracle child sent from God to save lost souls. They started preparing him for this role from an early age. Jimmy Lee was taught to sing "Hallelujah!" before he could say "Mama" or "Papa".

His parents were members of a Pentecostal Church in Leakesville, Mississippi. One Sunday morning the preacher's wife announced that the preacher wouldn't be giving a sermon that day because he was suffering from food poisoning. 6-year-old Jimmy Lee ran up on stage immediately. He grabbed the microphone and delivered an impassioned sermon that blew away the congregation. It turned out the preacher got food poisoning from a pumpkin pie that Jimmy Lee's mother had baked, but it was never determined if she had poisoned him deliberately, or if she was just a bad cook.

Jimmy Lee was ordained at the age of 7 and he went on to become a famous child preacher. It was said that he received his sermons in his sleep straight from the Lord.

Jimmy Lee was a precocious little boy who preached against the evils of alcoholism and adultery, not that he knew what alcoholism and adultery were, even though his father was an alcoholic and an adulterer. From around the country the faithful flocked to see the miracle child preach the gospel, cast out demons, and heal the sick. The contributions came flooding into the collection plates, which were not plates as such, but more like four-gallon plastic wastebaskets. Elderly ladies donated money for a cuddle and a kiss from the cute boy with a head of chestnut curls who wore a suit that made him look like Little Lord Fauntleroy. Jimmy Lee's mother sewed extra pockets into his outfits so he could stuff money into them, and he did.

His family lived high on the hog until Jimmy Lee hit puberty and his novelty wore off. Nobody wanted to kiss a teen preacher with pimples. Then his father took off with all of the cash. Jimmy Lee never saw a dime of the money he made for his family.

It later came to light that Jimmy Lee's powers weren't divine. In fact, he didn't have any powers at all. His father noticed his knack for mimicry and public speaking and so he trained Jimmy Lee to be a preacher. He was a harsh disciplinarian. Jimmy Lee was forced to memorize his sermons from his dramatic gestures right down to every "Amen!" If he didn't learn his lines correctly his father punished him by sending him to bed without dinner that night, although his mother might sneak him a slice of pie. Sometimes his father pretended to suffocate Jimmy Lee with a pillow in punishment, or he bit him on the head so he wouldn't leave visible cuts and bruises that would mar his public appearances.

In his twenties, gone were the pimples, and Jimmy Lee was now a handsome and charismatic young man. God called him to serve the Church, for real, this time. He became an evangelist. The Reverend Doctor Jimmy Lee Mercy seduced his audience with theatrical sermons as he sang and danced like a rock star. When he strutted across the stage and walked over the backs of seats his followers believed that God was with him. But if they'd seen the same thing at a rock concert they would have thought it was the work of the devil. Jimmy Lee held services across the southern United States where he converted thousands of people and baptized them in the Holy Spirit.

"Unless you are born again you cannot see!" he preached in his thick southern accent.

Jimmy Lee whipped up his followers, and himself, into a frenzy of religious ecstasy. He ranted, wept, and thrust his leather-bound Bible into the air. Filled with the Holy Spirit his followers barked, jumped, twitched, babbled, laughed, rolled, and coughed up cash.

They kept the faith and Jimmy Lee kept the money.

Jimmy Lee and his first wife Bobby Sue left Leakesville, Mississippi, and moved to New Orleans where they founded LOVE Ministries. And Jimmy Lee certainly loved his female congregation. Bobby Sue accused him of knowing church secretary Mary Sue in the biblical sense. Jimmy Lee staunchly denied this accusation. He hired a replacement but then his second wife Mary Sue accused him of having an affair with the new church secretary.

Jimmy Lee preached against "the demon lust" but his Ministry was rocked by sex scandals. One time he was vacationing in Italy when he was photographed by the paparazzi as he came out of a brothel. His excuse was that he asked a taxi driver to take him to a local casino. It just so happens that "casino" also means "brothel" in Italian, although that didn't explain why he was in there for four hours. One journalist gave him the benefit of the doubt that he wanted to visit a casino and not a brothel but asked why a preacher would go to a casino anyway. Jimmy Lee replied that God told him to minister to the gambling addicts in the casino to save their souls from eternal damnation. Then he went to a gambling casino and ministered to the gambling addicts. Then he blew $66,000 on the blackjack table, earning himself the headline *High Roller Holy Roller*.

Jimmy Lee was also the subject of many financial scandals. Most famously, his ministry was involved in a prayer request scam. He appeared on television beseeching his followers to mail in their prayer requests, accompanied by a donation, of course. Jimmy Lee promised to pray over each request personally. In their droves, people mailed their requests to him with cash, or if they didn't have money, they sent in food stamps, or even their wedding rings. Jimmy Lee's staff was instructed to pocket the donations but toss away the prayer requests without reading them. That is, after they'd collected the addresses and personal information to use in future mail outs. An investigative journalist discovered thousands of prayer requests in a dumpster. Jimmy Lee claimed they were planted there in a plot against him. A fraud investigation was launched and Jimmy Lee was indicted on six counts of mail fraud. He was eventually cleared of all charges.

It was an act of God.

Jimmy Lee made constant appeals to his followers, begging them to dig deep for Jesus. He once threatened he would die unless his supporters raised $2 million dollars for his ministry. They did.

"You should have let him die," wrote an atheist journalist.

In response, the ministry raised an extra $3 million dollars.

It seemed that his ministry was always on the brink of financial collapse but he had a net worth of millions of dollars, which was all tax-deductible. Jimmy Lee lived a lavish lifestyle and owned designer clothing, luxury cars, a private jet, a yacht (that he allegedly bought with donations raised for a children's charity), and numerous palatial mansions around the world.

"You'd be surprised how well you can praise God from the back seat of a Cadillac," he once said.

His followers argued in his support that God had blessed Jimmy here on earth. They would get their reward in heaven. And the end of the world was nigh. Jimmy preached from the Book of Revelations and warned of the end times when God would bring judgment on the world. His ministry sold survival kits for the apocalypse, including end of the world burgers, and rapturous hot dogs to sustain the faithful until the Second Coming. Jimmy Lee predicted the end of the world...again and again and again.

Aside from doomsday prophesies, Jimmy Lee made other predictions. He was also believed to be a prophet and mouthpiece for God.

"It's not just anyone who can hear the voice of the Lord," he said.

He predicted earthquakes in countries that always suffer earthquakes, and wars in countries that were always at war. Some of his predictions were vague, like when he predicted that a celebrity would die or a politician would be caught having an extramarital affair. He was less successful when he predicted that God would destroy the homosexual community in America.

During his services, Jimmy Lee preached that his congregation would witness signs, miracles and wonders. When they moved into the glory, the faithful's teeth were filled with gold or supernaturally whitened. Miraculous weight loss was commonplace at his services (although this miracle never seemed to work on Mary Sue). It was said that when bald men were anointed with holy oil they grew hair. Sometimes when Jimmy Lee spoke about his love for Jesus, gold dust appeared on his skin and clothing. Heavenly diamonds and other precious gemstones rained from the ceiling during worship. His followers believed these were blessings, and signs that God was manifesting Himself to them. A skeptical journalist attended one of Jimmy Lee's services and secretly collected samples of the gold and diamonds and took them to a laboratory to be analyzed. The scientists concluded that the "gold" was just glitter and the "diamonds" were cheap plastic baubles.

The journalist remarked that God must shop at the Hobby Lobby.

In the tradition of evangelists, Jimmy Lee was also a faith healer. His healings were miraculous, just like his miraculous recovery from diphtheria when he was a baby. He was a modern-day apostle and people believed that the power of God flowed through him. During his healing crusades the faithful lined up to be healed by his divine surgery. Sometimes the line was around the block. These people were desperate and Jimmy Lee was their last hope. In one case, a man was released from hospital to attend a service. He waited in line so long to receive prayer that he died. That was God's will.

When the faithful approached Jimmy Lee he knew everything about them. He had the "Gift of Knowledge". He laid hands on them, prayed fervently and begged God for their healing. "In the name of Jesus!" he cried out as he struck them on the forehead with his magical right hand. They fell down flat on the floor every time. (Skeptics argued that they were pushed over.) Slain in the spirit, sometimes they stayed on the ground for hours.

People who took medication were ordered to "Break free of the devil" by throwing their pills on stage because they wouldn't need to take them anymore. If they arrived with canes or crutches Jimmy Lee threw them away because they wouldn't need them anymore. In one of his biggest crowd-pleasers, he would heal someone in a wheelchair and order the person to jump out of the chair and push Jimmy Lee down the aisle in it! His followers believed that disease and disability were no match for a prayer and a touch from Jimmy Lee, but if someone wasn't healed it was because their faith wasn't strong enough, or they hadn't donated enough money.

Jimmy Lee was a hypocrite. Whether it was adultery, drugs, lies, or theft, he did all of the very things he condemned from the pulpit. Then he righteously accused his rivals of the same moral transgressions and aggressively orchestrated their downfalls. He didn't like competition. One journalist commented, "There are numerous disgraced evangelists, but Jimmy Lee Mercy is the biggest crook of them all." It was true, but

Jimmy Lee sued the man for defamation in a bogus lawsuit and the journalist's insurance company forced him to settle out of court.

Every time Jimmy Lee was exposed for his exploits he confessed his sins in a tearful and repentant apology to his followers, and to God. Then he preached that to sin is human and to forgive is divine.

"The foundation of Christianity is forgiveness!" he shouted. But he never fell from grace in the eyes of his flock. He could do no wrong because they were true believers. Instead of feeling deceived, they were relieved. Brother Mercy was saved!

"Having forgiveness in your heart brings you closer to God!" he preached.

His flock was very close to God.

Even the non-religious forgave Jimmy Lee because of his abusive childhood. No wonder he was so screwed up, they thought. He was so charismatic and charming that he had a way of winning people over.

Jimmy Lee was an American icon. It seemed that he could do no wrong.

That is, until Banachek and his team investigated Jimmy Lee and found his faith healing to be fraudulent. They discovered many tricks and lies behind Jimmy Lee's shows. The audience members who threw away their crutches and leaped out of their wheelchairs were Jimmy Lee's paid stooges. But they weren't all actors. Jimmy Lee prophesized that a woman with heart disease had many years to live. She died two days later. At one meeting Jimmy Lee prayed for a man with cancer of the spine.

"Get up and walk!" he commanded. "Make the devil mad!"

The man threw away his back brace, hobbled across the stage and claimed his cancer was cured. But it wasn't. He died two months later when his vertebra collapsed because of the strain placed on it during his "healing".

At another service, there was a woman suffering from uterine cancer who wanted to be healed. Jimmy Lee promised to "burn that cancer" right out of her body! But God didn't tell Jimmy Lee that the woman was really a man. In fact, the man had followed Jimmy Lee from show to show and been cured of six different diseases in six different cities, under six different names and two different sexes.

During his healing services, it seemed as though Jimmy Lee was receiving messages from God, but it turned out that God was Jimmy Lee's third wife, Cindy Sue.

"Jiiiii-mmy Lee!" she sang into the microphone. "I love you. I hope you can hear me or this show will be over real fast!"

He was wearing an earpiece and receiving messages from her via a radio transmitter. Personal information about the crowd was collected on prayer request cards before the show and Cindy Sue was feeding names, addresses, and ailments to Jimmy Lee, which he fed back to the audience as though they were divine revelations.

Jimmy Lee wasn't talking to God. He was doing hot readings. His followers were born again, but Jimmy Lee treated them like they were born yesterday.

Jimmy Lee's tricks were exposed on national television. Videotape segments of his healings were played with an audio track of Cindy Sue's voice as she gave him the information she'd gleaned from the audience. The public was outraged at his blatant deception. At first, Jimmy Lee claimed that the videotape was doctored and showed an actor who impersonated him. He said it was an attack by atheists, communists, and Satan-worshippers who were trying to discredit God's work. Then he compared his ministry to a game show. "It's just like *The Price is Right*." Then he finally admitted that he used a radio device, but he said it was to communicate with his television crew. He added,

"My wife *occasionally* tells me the name of a person who needs special prayer."

No one believed him anymore. His ministry soon declared bankruptcy and his career as an evangelical hustler was finally over.

"I remember Jimmy Lee Mercy," said Claudia. "Was that his real name?"

"No," answered Banachek. "It was a stage name. His real name was plain old James Lee Smith. There are many similarities between evangelists and psychic mediums, but there is a reason I'm bringing up the story of Jimmy Lee Mercy and his downfall. I was looking over photographs from Gil's live shows and I think I can see an earpiece in his left ear."

"*What?*" Claudia screamed.

She brought up some photos on her computer, zoomed in on Gil's left ear and saw a small, shiny plastic object wedged inside. She was angry that she didn't spot it herself.

"I see it!" she cried. "That son of a bitch!"

"I was the one who spotted Jimmy Lee's earpiece all those years ago, and I suspect Gil is using a similar trick," said Banachek.

"Hmm… We already know he asks his audience to fill out cards with their personal information," added Claudia.

"He has a show tomorrow night in Walnut Creek."

"I'll be there."

Chapter 25

Claudia sent Ana on the job with the college professor that night so she could prepare to sting Gil instead. She had only one day before attending Gil's show in Walnut Creek and she needed to research the Jimmy Lee Mercy exposé.

How was she going to bust Gil?

Back in the 1980s, Banachek and his team tracked Jimmy Lee for months, attending his shows across the country and uncovering numerous scams. The most damning evidence they discovered was that Jimmy Lee was wearing a hearing aid in his left ear, but this wasn't because he was hearing impaired. It was a high frequency receiver that allowed him to hear messages transmitted from his wife, Cindy Sue, who fed him the personal information about the audience she'd collected by subterfuge. All the while, Jimmy Lee claimed he was listening to God.

It turned out that God's frequency was 39.17 Megahertz.

The technology had changed over the years. Cindy Sue Mercy carried her power source in a large handbag while Banachek and his team used a truckload of equipment to catch Jimmy Lee. They had an electronic surveillance expert who used a complicated computerized scanning system to locate the frequency used by Jimmy Lee. Today, Claudia only needed a frequency scanner app on her cell phone.

The next night, the theater in Walnut Creek was packed with thousands of people who were bursting with excitement that the show was about to begin. But there was one person sitting in the audience who was less enthusiastic about being there. Claudia sat hidden in a balcony seat. She didn't want to be recognized by Gil or his people so she wore a disguise. She dressed down in an oversized black velour tracksuit, which she padded out with extra layers to make it look as if she'd gained a few extra pounds. She wore blue contact lenses and a pair of horn-rimmed glasses with clear lenses. She went without any makeup or jewelry. She covered her hair with a realistic-looking brunette wig that she styled in a bun to cover her earphones. She had an earbud in her left ear only, so she could listen for signals but also hear the show in her other ear.

Her scanner wasn't picking up anything yet.

Was this just a waste of time? She turned down a paying job to attend this stupid show tonight. She could be making money right now instead of chasing Gil. Had she and Banachek made a mistake in thinking Gil was wearing an earpiece? Sure, the photographs looked incriminating at first, but it was hard to tell exactly what, if anything, was in his ear. Could they have been looking at pixilation? Or could Gil have been wearing something totally innocuous in his ear, such as an earplug?

Claudia wished she was wearing earplugs herself when hypnotic inspirational music began pulsing throughout the theater. Then she wished she had a pair of sunglasses when bright colored lights flashed across her face, making her squint. The smell of sandalwood in the air made her sneeze. She hated attending these shows.

Gil arrived fashionably late. At 8:15pm he finally leaped out onto the stage wearing a periwinkle blue three-piece suit. He raised his arms up towards the ceiling.

"Friends, it does my soul good to see so many folks here tonight who have their hearts open to the possibility of communicating with the beyond," he cried.

The audience went wild for Gil.

There were two people on stage although the audience only saw one person.

"My spirit guide Aunt Tillie is here on stage with me tonight," he said.

Then the audience went wild for Aunt Tillie.

"You can't see her with your physical eyes but I see her with my eyes and mind, and I feel her in my heart," said Gil as he patted his chest. "She taught me to have faith in my inner voice so I could become the link between the spirit realms. But I'm just an instrument for the spirits. I'm much like a radio that receives messages from the dead and then transmits them to you, the living."

Claudia thought it was ironic that he used a radio metaphor and she laughed to herself. In her left ear she heard static as the scanner went through the bands trying to find a signal. Still nothing.

"Friends, you were brought here tonight to receive a special message from the spirits," said Gil. "Listen out for that message, but don't be sad if your loved one doesn't appear tonight. Some spirits are louder than others. In their compassion, sometimes your deceased friends and family will stand aside for someone who needs a reading more."

Or they'll stand aside because Gil didn't have insider information about them, thought Claudia.

"Let us do a unity ritual to open the door to the spirit realm," said Gil. "I want y'all to stand up, greet each other, and shake each other's hands."

The audience members duly stood up, introduced themselves, and shook hands with those people around them. Claudia felt like she was at a church service. With Gil's pastel blue suit and his sermon-like introduction, she had to agree with Banachek's comparison between evangelists and psychic mediums.

"Friends, now the link between the worlds is fortified. Let's experience something beautiful together," Gil said to thunderous applause.

There still wasn't a signal on Claudia's phone. She looked at her watch. It was now 8:30pm.

"Why am I still here?" she mumbled to herself as she drummed her fingers on the arms of her seat impatiently.

At that moment she thought she heard a rustling sound through her earphone.

Then a male voice spoke.

"Boss. This is Ted. I hope you can hear me or you're gonna be in some deep shit, dude!"

A bolt of electricity ran through Claudia's entire body.

"There's a hot piece of ass in the first row on your right," said Ted. "She's the blonde wearing a red sweater. Her name is Carla."

Gil walked to the right of the stage.

"My spirit guide has a message for Carla," he said. "Who's Carla? Is there a young lady by that name sitting here in the front row?"

A blonde woman in a red sweater acknowledged Gil by raising her hand. He ran to her with his microphone.

Claudia caught Gil red-handed! Ted was feeding information about the audience members straight to Gil who was repeating it like they were revelations coming to him from the spirit world. This was just like the Jimmy Lee Mercy scam all those years ago!

"I've got you now, you fucking bastard," she said through a sly grin.

"Carla had a bun in the oven but the baby girl was stillborn," Ted informed Gil.

Claudia gasped. This was horrible.

"Sister, I feel that you just suffered a loss," said Gil softly.

"Yes," Carla said in a faint voice.

"You...gave birth to a stillborn baby girl."

"Oh my God," she whispered, her voice cracking with pain.

"The baby died at 38 weeks," added Ted.

"You were 38 weeks pregnant and the doctors...they couldn't find a heartbeat... Your baby girl had...passed."

Carla responded with a flood of tears. Gil placed his hand on her shoulder.

"They induced her," said Ted.

"Throughout your labor you thought... perhaps this is just a terrible mistake.... maybe my baby will come into this world crying tears of life... but there was silence..."

Carla could only nod through her tears.

"She named her dead baby Violet," said Ted.

"My spirit guide tells me that Violet arrived safely on the other side," Gil said. Carla's sobs increased at the mention of her baby's name. "Ma'am, don't give up your faith...I see you cradling a healthy baby boy in your arms within the year...if you just *believe*!"

"I believe! Thank you Gil!" Carla gushed in relief and the audience cheered.

Gil gave her a kiss on the back of her hand but she jumped up and threw her arms around him.

"Grr... Let me hook you up with her for a private reading and you can make that shit happen!" Ted said with an evil laugh.

Claudia felt sickened by what she'd just seen and heard. She was appalled by Ted's crude and callous comments. And how dare Gil promise a woman grieving for her stillborn baby that she'd give birth to a healthy boy within the year?

"There's an ugly chick with big tits in the second row," Ted told Gil. "She's sitting in the center of the room and wearing a pink shirt. Her name is Patricia."

"My spirit guide is bringing me here," said Gil as he moved to the center of the room. "...Who is Patricia?"

"That's me!" a woman in a pink shirt yelled out as Gil rushed over with a microphone. "My name's Patricia!" she said in a thick, nasal New Jersey accent.

"Her husband Ian shot himself in the head five years ago. Bang!" said Ted in imitation of a gunshot sound.

Claudia was shocked by Ted's insensitivity as he talked about such a tragic death.

"Sister, there's a gentleman around you," said Gil. "He tells me his name is Ian... He's your husband...I sense that you lost him about five years ago," said Gil.

"That's right, Gil," she said sadly in her raspy voice.

"He passed unexpectedly...He was here one minute, then gone the next..."

"Yes."

"He... took his own life... with a gun."

"He did," she said with a sniff and a throaty cough.

"They have a ten-year-old son named Anthony," Ted added.

"Ian wants you to know that he's sorry for what he did to you and Anthony."

"Oh, God!" she sobbed as her body was wracked with tears and a smoker's cough.

"I'd fucking kill myself if I was married to her too, with a voice like that, even with those big titties of hers!" joked Ted.

Claudia shook her head in disgust.

"Ma'am, your husband misses you but he doesn't want to see you on the other side just yet," said Gil. "He wants you to quit smoking immediately. Your work on earth is not done. You are here for a purpose. You need to be around to raise your son."

"I will quit, Gil! I promise!" she said as she placed her hand on her heart and the audience cheered.

"Nice cold reading, Boss," said Ted admiringly. "She sounds like a packet-a-day woman," he observed. "Okay! Love 'em and leave 'em. Time to move on."

"Ian is whole again on the other side… He says he loves you…and goodbye, for now…" ended Gil.

"There's a guy nearby. His name is William," said Ted.

"The energy is leading me to a man named William in this same part of the room," said Gil as he waved his hands in that general direction.

Three hands shot up into the air.

"I hate these common fucking names," said Ted. "Let's narrow it down a bit. His friends call him Bill."

"I feel that he goes by the nickname Bill," said Gil.

But only one hand went down.

"When several people believe a message is for them I call it Psychic Confusion. I need to be certain that the message I have goes to the right person."

"The guy you want is the faggot in the fancy clothes," added Ted.

Gil approached a man with his arm raised who was wearing a houndstooth blazer, a scarf and a hat.

"Brother, my spirit guide directed me to you," said Gil.

"His mother kicked the bucket in January," Ted told him.

"I'm sensing a January connection," said Gil. "I feel that you lost someone close to you that month… it was… your mother…"

Bill burst into tears.

"Fucking mama's boy," said Ted unsympathetically. "She died in a car accident."

"I can see a terrible car accident," said Gil. Bill nodded. "I'm getting pains in my chest…I feel suffocated… Your mother… she died in that car crash…"

"Yes," he sobbed.

"He was driving," said Ted. "He killed his own fucking mother, the asshole!"

"She says it wasn't your fault," said Gil. "You are not to blame."

"Oh, thank you, Gil!" Bill cried.

"The little queer is wearing one of her diamond stud earrings."

"You have a memento of your mother with you now…" said Gil. "I feel it's something you're wearing…maybe an earring?"

"I wear one of her diamond earrings," he confirmed between sobs. "My wife wears the other earring." He wrapped his right arm around the attractive young woman sitting beside him.

"That's his wife?" Ted barked. "How did a fucking homo score a hottie like that?" he asked in outrage. "How about I stall him afterwards so you can show her what it's like to get fucked by a real man?"

Claudia was infuriated. Ted had no respect for the audience members.

"His left arm was paralyzed in the accident," added Ted.

"My spirit guide tells me that you suffer from paralysis of your left arm because of the accident," said Gil.

"That's right."

"My spirit guide wants me to lay hands on you," said Gil. "Brother, do you believe that the spirits are able to heal you today?"

"Yes, I do!"

"Then stand up."

The man stood and Gil placed his hands above his head.

"I want you to feel the healing coming through… Feel the healing coming through… Feel the healing…Feel it…Feel it…Feel it…NOW!" Gil shouted as the man fell down flat. Gil helped him back onto his feet. "Raise your left arm!" Gil ordered. The man raised his left arm and the audience gasped. "Open and close your hand." He opened and closed his hand. "Let me shake that hand that used to be paralyzed!" said Gil as the men shook hands.

"Thank you, spirits!" Gil cried.

The audience went hysterical.

"I don't have any more gossip on that pussy so move on to the fatty taking up two seats on his left," said Ted. "She's so fat she could be a contestant on *The Price Is Right*."

Gil turned to the heavy-set woman.

"We have a Spirit Tailgater!" he announced. "This is when a spirit associated with someone nearby takes advantage of the psychic connection and interrupts the reading," he explained. "Sister, my spirit guide led me to you."

"Her name is Claudia," said Ted. "Hey, isn't this your ex-girlfriend?" he chuckled. "The resemblance is amazing!"

Claudia inhaled sharply and felt her face turn red with rage.

"I can't stop thinking about the name… *Claudia*," said Gil. "Is that your name?"

The woman's face lit up.

"Yes, it is!"

"Her father Jim died suddenly of a heart attack two years ago," said Ted.

"I have a message from Jim… He says… he's sorry that he didn't have time to say goodbye… His heart attack took him away from you too soon."

"Oh, my God! You really are talking to my dad!" she said as she wiped her eyes with a tissue.

"She's got all kinds of weight-related health concerns," said Ted. "She's worried she's gonna be pushing up the daisies just like her father."

"The spirits want you to have good health," said Gil. "It's their plan that no believer will ever be sick… But it's up to you…if you confess sickness you get sickness, if you confess good health you get good health…"

"I'm on a diet, Gil!" she said in her defense.

"Yeah, a diet of donuts," said Ted. "She should eat less cookies and more cock."

Claudia felt sick to her stomach. Gil and his crony were going too far.

"She's eating herself out of house and home. Money is tight," revealed Ted.

"The spirits tell me that times have been tough for you," said Gil. "Times are tough for many of us right now…but I want you to know that the spirits see your struggles… They feel your pain… They want you to reap financial blessings… It's their will that you be financially prosperous…. You must give so that you can receive!"

"I have all of your books, Gil! I love you!" she cried out as the audience erupted into applause.

"Do you want me to give a Pussy-Pass to this fat chick, Boss?" Ted asked Gil. "I know you like a little meat on your bones occasionally."

It suddenly dawned on Claudia who this awful Ted guy was. It was that security guard who had challenged her when she tried to go backstage to see Gil after his show in Irvine. He thought she was a groupie and he tried to get a blowjob from her until he realized she had a "P-Pass". She should have known that the sexist pig would have something to do with this! She should also have kicked him in the balls when she had the chance.

Throughout the show Gil had hit after hit after hit, all thanks to the information Ted relayed to him. Ted gave his obscene and offensive commentary and then Gil fed it all back to the audience couched more delicately in new age speak that was laced with quasi-religious phrasing. Claudia spent most of the show with her jaw dropped. If only Gil's fans could hear how their idol spoke about them. Well, she would be the one to tell them!

"Wrap up the show, Boss," said Ted. "It's time for bitches and booze!"

"Friends, I feel a tingling sensation," said Gil. "I'm losing my connection to the spirit world."

Gil finished with a unity ritual to close the door to the spirit realm and then he left the stage to a standing ovation. He came out again and bowed before leaving.

Claudia stayed put in her seat. She was elated. After all of these years she had caught Gil. She finally had him! This was going to be his downfall. She would make sure of that...

But why was Gil dressed like a televangelist? Why was his show so religious in tone? Was this some crazy new phase for him? Some of his comments that night were very ironic, like his radio metaphor and Ted's reference to her being Gil's ex-girlfriend.

Did Gil know she was there?

She heard a rustling sound through her earphone...

"Hello, Claudia," Gil's deep voice crept into her ear. "I know you can hear me...and I see you. I can see all..."

Claudia's heart sank. What was going on? Then she started feeling paranoid. Her hands started shaking. He knew she was there. He knew where she was sitting. Wearing her earphone she couldn't tell if this message was just for her or being broadcast into the entire theater. She looked around and people were leaving. No one was paying attention to her.

"Here is your special message... You thought you had fooled me but I've fooled *you*..."

Then music started playing.

Tell me... what is my life... without your love?

Tell me... who... am I... without you...by my side.

She recognized the song immediately. It was George Harrison's *What is Life*, the song that Claudia and Gil had chosen to play at their would-be wedding.

"You sick bastard," she muttered.

Claudia ripped the earphone out of her ear and stuffed it into her handbag. She got out of her seat and tried to run away but she got caught up in the waves of people spilling out of the theater. She was stuck in the human traffic jam, listening to their praise for Gil's polished performance that night.

Gil Godsend was amazing!
I knew Gil was psychic but I didn't know he was a healer too!
I'm going to book a private reading with Gil.
Gil is so handsome! Is he taken?
I hear he got back together with his ex-girlfriend.
I saw photos of them kissing on the beach during their vacation together in Australia!
Bitch...

Their chatter swam around and around in her head.

Claudia felt like she was going insane.

As soon as she broke free of the crowd and escaped outside Claudia ripped off her wig and glasses and threw them into a trashcan. Then she breathed in the cool night air.

Her phone rang. The caller ID was blocked but she knew who it was. It would be Gil calling to gloat about his set up.

"What do you want?"

"Hello, Claudia."

Yes, it was Gil.

"You dressed down tonight," he said. "I barely recognized you."

"You dressed up tonight," she said. "You looked like that televangelist in *Fletch Lives*."

"Hallelujah!" he hollered. "I'm sorry I tricked you, but you kinda had it coming."

"You're not sorry at all," she spat. "Now I know why you made that comment about being a radio for the dead, and why your show had such evangelical overtones, and why you mentioned my name. It all makes sense. You knew *exactly* what I was doing here tonight."

"I did. You and Banachek spotted the in-ear receiver I wore for you at the last show," he chuckled. "Did you really think I'd use a radio transmitter for my readings? That trick is so… 1980s."

"Being a fake psychic medium is so… 1880s," Claudia quipped.

Gil ignored her insult.

"Did you enjoy the show tonight?" he asked. "I did it just for you."

"That was a really classy way to talk about your loyal fans behind their backs," she said. "I wish they could hear the dreadful things your awful thug said about them."

"They *did*," Gil revealed. "The people I gave fake readings to, and my "awful thug" Ted Ray, were all in on the joke."

"I should have known!" she scoffed. "All your readings are fake anyway."

"Come now, Claudia. It was just a prank."

"It was just a prank at the expense of an audience of thousands of grieving people who paid a lot of money hoping to hear from their dead loved ones tonight," she said in disgust. "Your fans aren't as important to you as your need to make me look like a fool."

"You made *yourself* look like a fool," Gil said. "But I'd rather you work *with* me, instead of against me."

"I'm not interested in playing games," she sighed. "I'm interested in protecting people from frauds."

"You and I can agree on that," he said. "With all the frauds out there the public needs someone like you to help expose them."

"I meant *you*, Gil."

"Whoa! Careful! That sounds like slander. Are you calling me a fraud? No one ever seems to question the deceit and fraud you commit to try and entrap me."

"Asshole," she replied in litigation-safe language. "And to think I almost had…dinner… with you when we were in Australia!"

Claudia hung up on him. Then she tossed her phone into her handbag and stormed off home.

Chapter 26

How did Gil seem to know her every move? He must be watching her, and listening to her.

When Claudia got home she tore apart every room in her apartment as she searched for bugs. She looked in, under and around her lamps, plants, books, furniture, and picture frames. She rummaged through her bedroom closet and dresser. She scoured her kitchen cupboards and drawers. She overturned everything but she found nothing. She hadn't found any eavesdropping devices in her office, phone, or car either when she'd checked after the Nina Novakov fiasco.

When she and Gil were together he always infuriated her by guessing her passwords so nowadays she routinely changed them. She didn't want him to have access to her email, voicemail, text messages, browsing history, and social media, so he could trace her movements. She also kept her eyes open to make sure that Gil or one of his cronies wasn't following her wherever she went.

She felt she was being paranoid but she knew he was out to get her.

When Claudia finished her search it looked like thieves had ransacked the place. The chaotic state of her apartment reflected her emotional state. As she started cleaning up the living room she spied something small and shiny on the floor under a table. Was it a bug? She snatched it up and looked at it. It wasn't a bug. It was the amethyst crystal pendant Gil bought for her at the metaphysical fair on the day they met. What was it doing on the ground? Then she remembered that she cleaned her jewelry recently. She must have dropped it on the floor. Why did she have that old thing anyway? It was time to get rid of it. She threw the pendant in the trashcan.

Claudia was exhausted. She sank down onto the wooden floorboards and stared up at the ceiling. Her mind was racing. She began to have some disdain for the women who were falling for Gil's bullshit. If they were stupid enough to be taken advantage of, then let them! Maybe this would be the only way they would learn. She couldn't spend her life running around trying to save other people from themselves. She needed to start worrying about herself, her career, and her future. She had to think about her budding relationship with Jeremy and where that was going. Gil wasn't worth her time. She had spent too many years chasing after him and trying to bring him down, and for what? In the end, nobody cares that what he's doing is wrong.

"I give up," she whispered to herself.

But it didn't feel like defeat, it felt like freedom.

"I give up," she said boldly. That felt good.

"I give up!" she yelled so loudly that her voice echoed around the room.

She opened up a window and stuck her head outside.

"I GIVE UP!" she shouted into the night. "I GIVE UP! I GIVE UP!"

Dogs started barking in reply.

"Can't you give up QUIETLY?" a faceless male voice screamed back at her from somewhere down the street.

Instead of telling him to fuck off, as she normally would have done, Claudia smiled. She flopped down on her bed, still wearing that velour tracksuit that was surprisingly comfortable, and she slept soundly throughout the night.

The next morning Claudia awoke feeling lighter than she had in months. Gil was out of her life! Today was the first day of the rest of her life, and all that crap. She was walking away from Gil, she was letting go, and she was happy. There was no shame in giving up and moving on with her life. That was the healthy thing to do. This was only holding her back. To continue to hunt him at this point would be obsessive.

Gil was the obsessive type, not her.

Claudia was in such a good mood that she decided to go into work a little later than usual. She was typically a coffee purist who refused flavorings but today she ordered a gingerbread latte with whipped cream and a pumpkin muffin. Life was good.

When she finally arrived at work her receptionist told her there was a woman named Angela waiting to speak with her.

"Show her into my office," said Claudia.

A petite woman with mousy brown hair walked into the room. Exhaustion and worry were etched into her face. Claudia had seen this expression before.

Claudia introduced herself and offered the woman a seat.

"What can I do for you?"

"I'm not sure I should even be here," Angela said, peering around as though someone else might be listening in to their conversation. "It's about my husband. I'm concerned that he might be cheating on me."

"What makes you think that?" asked Claudia.

"Well, we've been happily married for seven years and we have three beautiful children," she said, avoiding the question. "Oliver, Emma, and Chloe…she's only three months old."

"Congratulations!" said Claudia.

No wonder Angela looked so tired.

"Thank you," she said dismissively. "But something happened recently that's made me open my eyes. I was browsing through baby photographs on my husband's phone when I came across some rather…risqué…images." She pulled out her phone. "I emailed them to myself," she said as she showed them to Claudia.

Claudia's eyes nearly popped out of her head.

"Oh!" was all she could muster in reply.

No wonder Angela looked so worried.

"I confronted my husband and he *swears* he didn't take them."

Claudia had heard this excuse before. Angela must have seen the look on her face.

"I know what you're thinking, but my husband has *never* lied to me."

"Everybody lies," Claudia said bluntly. "But if *he* didn't take those photographs, then who did?"

Angela drew a deep breath.

"He says that a colleague snatched his phone and took the photos as a prank."

Bullshit, thought Claudia.

"Um… where does he work?" Claudia tried to ask nonchalantly, thinking he must work at a strip club or a brothel.

"He's an assistant to a celebrity. Beautiful women and groupies surround him constantly. There are always wild backstage parties after a show and it was at one of these that he says the photos were taken...by someone else..."

He must work for a rock star, Claudia thought.

"I've seen possible signs of his cheating before," Angela said. "One night he got home late and I smelled perfume on his clothing. He said a salesgirl sprayed it on him in a department store."

Bullshit, thought Claudia.

"Another time I found a phone number written on a scrap of paper in his shirt pocket. I called the number and a young woman answered the phone. I was too scared to say anything. I confronted him about it and he said the phone number was for his boss from a fan."

Bullshit, thought Claudia.

"I see," she said.

This didn't sound good at all.

"He's a great father," she said in his defense. "The kids adore him. He's also a great provider. We have a nice house and nice cars. The bills are always paid and there's always food on the table. He travels a lot for work and when he's home he works late. I don't know half of the things that go on in his job. He promises me that he's faithful...and I believe him...Well, I believed him...but these photographs have shaken my faith," she said sadly. "I don't know. Maybe I'm being paranoid. I just want to know for sure."

"You have every right to know the truth," said Claudia.

"My mother has never liked him," Angela added. "She never thought he was good enough for me. She doesn't trust him at all. I've spent my whole marriage defending him. She wants me to move back home to Wisconsin with the kids and live with her."

"Every mother worries about her daughter," said Claudia.

"Make no mistake, if he is cheating I'm leaving him and *he'll never see his kids ever again!*" Angela cried with a sudden conviction that surprised even her.

"I would do the same thing," said Claudia sympathetically.

"I need to know what's going on and there's some urgency to my request," Angela said. "He's not around very much but he happens to be in town tonight for an event. Can you go along and...do your thing?"

"Absolutely."

Claudia was determined to catch this guy.

"Thank you," Angela said in nervous relief. "I suppose you need to know what he looks like." She shuffled past the racy photographs on her phone, shaking her head as she did. She found a picture and handed it to Claudia. "Here's a recent photo of him."

Claudia stared at a photograph of Ted Ray, Gil's assistant.

"His name is Ted Ray," Angela said. "He's an assistant to the psychic medium Gil Godsend."

"Leave him!" Claudia wanted to scream at this woman. "Take your children and run back to your mother! Get a divorce! Take that motherfucker for everything he's got!"

She wanted to tell Angela about her husband's demand for a blowjob when he thought Claudia was a groupie trying to see Gil. She wanted to tell her that Ted was an accomplice to a fraud, and that he and Gil had tricked thousands of people at a show the night before, just to get even with her. She wanted to tell Angela about all of the deeply offensive comments Ted made during the show, and his cruel mocking of grief and death. Claudia wanted to tell Angela that she had first hand experience that her husband Ted was a sexist pig, a liar, a creep, a womanizer, and most definitely unfaithful.

Claudia resisted the urge to unleash an angry tirade against Angela's husband. Everything she had to say about Ted was scandalous, but it was all hearsay. She needed some proof to present to Angela. But she should find someone else to do it. She had plenty of capable colleagues who would be willing to tackle this task. She'd get another woman to take this job off her hands, someone who wasn't involved personally.

Besides, she'd just given up, right?

Then it occurred to her.

She finally had an ace up her sleeve.

Chapter 27

The thought dawned on Claudia, was this a setup? Gil seemed to be two steps ahead of her at every point, so was this just another one of his power plays? Was Ted's "wife" yet another stooge? Angela Ray seemed honest and sincere, but she was a connection to Gil, and that was enough to arouse Claudia's suspicion.

Claudia did a thorough background check into Angela and she was who she said she was. But was she really having marital problems? Knowing Ted as Claudia did, Angela's story was highly believable. It was worth the risk for Claudia to try taking on the case. If this was another trap then Claudia would look like a fool, yet again, but if the story was legitimate then the tables had finally turned.

Then Claudia did a background check on Ted. She discovered that this was his second marriage. Clearly, Angela had more patience because Ted's first marriage had only lasted two years. She also discovered that he had current profiles on the dating sites Date with Destiny, One Night Stand, and High Infidelity, a site for people looking to cheat with fellow pot smokers. Ted had some gall as he used his own photographs on his profiles but he had adopted the fake name Simon Tingle.

In her digging, Claudia found out how Gil and Ted met. Six years before, Ted worked as a bouncer in a bar. One night Gil happened to be enjoying a Belgian dark ale in the same establishment. A female patron who'd had too much to drink started flirting with Gil. Things heated up quickly and the two of them decided to leave the bar and go back to Gil's place for a nightcap.

However, the woman's husband wasn't too happy about the decision. He confronted Gil.

"You like messing with other men's wives, do you?" he spluttered. "I'm gonna sheat the bit out of you!"

"I don't foresee that in my future," replied Gil calmly.

The man took a drunken swipe at Gil. He missed.

Ted intervened. He didn't miss.

As the guy nursed his bleeding nose he mumbled something inappropriate about Ted's mother. Ted liked to say a lot of inappropriate things about other people's mothers, but he didn't tolerate such remarks about his own. He responded by breaking the guy's nose. The police were called to the scene and Ted was arrested for aggravated battery. He spent the night in jail, but strangely, no charges were pressed. Claudia wondered if Gil had something to do with that. Ted did lose his job though, but Gil promised, "You'll always have a job with me." He had been Gil's right hand man ever since.

And of course, Gil took the woman back to his place that night...

Claudia started preparing to attend the book signing. She wanted to look a little different that night, but she didn't need to hide because this was more of a reconnaissance mission. She straightened her naturally wavy hair and changed the part. She went with natural make-up, just a few swipes of mascara and a quick sweep of pink lip-gloss. She was going to a book signing, not a cocktail party or a nightclub, so she dressed casually. She wore a white t-shirt and a pair of denim shorts with tan-colored ankle boots. She threw on a black blazer to pull the outfit together.

Claudia didn't think Ted would recognize her anyway. He was the kind of guy who didn't pay much attention to women's faces.

The book signing was held at Read Handed, a bookstore and coffee shop in downtown San Francisco. Gil was doing a reading from his book *Messages From The Other Side* and signing copies. Claudia had seen advertisements for the event over the past few days but she hadn't planned on attending until Angela turned up at her office.

When Claudia arrived at the bookstore she was stunned to see that the line of people waiting to meet Gil was so long that it snaked around the entire building and spilled out onto the street. They looked like die-hard fans lined up to see a rock band. On the inside the line zigzagged throughout the store.

There must have been a thousand people there to see Gil and this was only one book signing of several that had been held across the Bay Area. Claudia was shocked by the staggering popularity of his books. She had several books published too; they debunked UFOs, ghosts, psychics, and other paranormal phenomena, the very stuff that Gil wrote about as a believer. Unlike Gil's books, hers had gone nowhere, even though they had involved painstaking research and took her years to write. Gil's books made it to the *New York Times* best sellers list. Claudia's books barely fell below one million on the Amazon best sellers list. As a publisher once said to her, "Gil's message is inspirational. Yours is...depressing..."

People prefer fiction to fact, she thought to herself.

Claudia could see Gil in the distance. This wasn't one of those book signings where the author sits behind a table, squirming in discomfort because no one knows or cares who he is. Gil was busy interacting with his numerous fans, signing books, giving hugs, and taking photographs with people. There were widows who hoped that while they were getting their books signed their deceased loved ones would stop by with a message for them, and there were fans who were there to flirt with Gil.

He didn't seem to see Claudia. His psychic antenna must have been switched off.

It had been a few months since Claudia had seen Ted, so she checked the photo Angela had sent to her. She scanned the room but she couldn't see him anywhere. Had he lied to Angela about where he'd be that night? Was he out with another woman? Or was he in the stockroom with one of the female employees?

Then there he was. He swaggered as he went up and down the line chatting with the attendees, but mostly flirting with women. He wore a tight black t-shirt that showed off a tattoo of a green dragon that ran down his right arm. It also displayed his hard-earned muscles to maximum effect. Ted spent all of his spare time at the gym, admiring himself in the full-length mirrors and watching other people to see if they were watching him. They often were. He was a good-looking guy and women were attracted to him. He was six foot four and ripped, so they assumed he was well endowed. Mother Nature can be a cruel mistress.

Claudia moved in closer so that she could overhear his conversations.

"You know, I can get you in to see Gil for a private reading tonight," he bragged to one woman. "Give me your phone number."

She duly scribbled her number on a scrap of paper. Now Claudia knew how he got the number that Angela found in his shirt pocket.

"Have you got a book for Gil to sign?" he asked another woman. She nodded. "I can see something else he'd wanna sign," he said as he leered at her cleavage.

Claudia was recording all of this on her phone.

Soon Ted was coming her way.

As he approached, Claudia grabbed the nearest book off the shelf and pretended to be engrossed in reading it, hoping he would walk right past her.

It was too late; he'd already seen her ass.

"That book's an oldie but a goodie," he said to her.

She flipped the book around to look at the title. It was a copy of the *Kama Sutra*.

Oh, for fuck's sake, she thought.

"Sure it's an old book, but the parts are still the same," she replied.

Why did she say that?

Ted laughed uproariously.

"Yes, that's very true," he said as he cast a look at her long legs. "Are you here tonight to see Gil, doll?"

Ted didn't recognize her!

This was her chance to work him…

"That depends. Are you Gil?" she asked with a slow blink of her eyes.

Ted was surprised. He was unaccustomed to this kind of easy flirtation at these events where he usually had to compete with Gil for women. Yet here was a woman who didn't know or care about Gil Godsend!

"I'm not," he admitted. "Gil Godsend is a famous psychic medium. He's here for a book signing. I'm his assistant, Ted."

"It's nice to meet you, Ted. I'm Angela," she said. Claudia thought she saw him flinch a little at the mention of his wife's name. "So that means you're sticking around here for a while?" she said with a glance at the long line.

"I am."

"Me too. I'm just…browsing," she said, as she looked him up and down. As she did she flashed a look at Ted's left hand and noticed he wasn't wearing his wedding ring.

"But I won't be here all night long," he said. "How about you and I grab a drink afterwards?" he asked her breasts.

Gotcha! She thought.

"I'd love to. I'm already building up quite a thirst," she said as she bit her lower lip coyly. She couldn't believe he was buying her corny flirting.

"Great!"

Ted was in, or so he thought. He probably wouldn't even have to get her liquored up first.

"There's a bar nearby on Polk Street called the Sasquatch Shack," he said as he wrote down his number and handed it to her. "It's nice and…intimate. Let's say we meet there about 9pm."

"I'll be there."

"And keep reading the *Kama Sutra*," he said with a nod towards the book. "Later tonight you can show me what you've learned…"

Chapter 28

Claudia arrived at the Sasquatch Shack at about 8:30 pm. The pub had a rustic log cabin theme. It was cozy, with a wood-burning fireplace warming the room, although the decor was tacky. The staff dressed as lumberjacks, including the women who wore midriff-baring flannel shirts, tiny shorts, and knee-high boots. No wonder Ted liked it here. There was a mounted moose head on the wall with a framed sign next to it that said, "Please Don't Touch The Moose". Bronze hurricane lanterns sat on the tables and elk antler chandeliers dangled from the ceiling. An enormous Sasquatch statue took pride of place at the end of the room. The host seated Claudia in a booth right next to it. The Sasquatch seemed to be looking down at her and saying, "You're the one who doesn't believe in me!"

Claudia wondered if Ted would stand her up. In her line of work, married men often talked big but then chickened out. Maybe he was all talk but no action? She swiped on another layer of pink lip-gloss and waited.

Sure enough, Ted arrived just before 9 pm. The San Francisco chill had set in for the night and he wore a khaki jacket that was a size too small so it would show off his biceps.

As Ted walked into the pub he wondered if Angela would stand him up, but there she was, waiting for him. He was mildly surprised that such a classy chick agreed to meet up with him, but on second thought, why the hell wouldn't she? He was a hunk. It unnerved him that she had the same name as his wife, but at least he wouldn't call out the wrong name in bed...

He slid into the seat opposite her.

"Hi, doll. You look lovely tonight," he said with a wink.

Wow, that's original, she thought.

"You don't look so bad yourself," she replied.

"Thanks for meeting me here."

"I wouldn't be anywhere else."

Ted watched her pink-painted lips as she spoke and imagined them wrapped around his shaft. What a little slut, he thought.

"It's getting hot in here," he said as he fanned himself with his hand.

"If you think it's hot in here now, just you wait," she said with a knowing smile.

Claudia needed alcohol fast if she had to be this clichéd. Fortunately, the server came over to their table. When she saw Ted she rolled her eyes.

"I see you're back again so soon, but with another woman."

Ouch! This must be the place where he brings his prey, thought Claudia.

"You must have me mistaken for someone else," Ted replied to the server.

"What can I get you, honey?" she asked Claudia, almost sympathetically.

"I'll have a Long Island Iced Tea, thanks."

Ted grinned to himself. Long Island Iced Tea was the Rohypnol of cocktails. They're so potent that each drink should come with a complimentary condom. He wouldn't have any problems getting into this one's pants.

"And for you, Ted?"

"A brown ale," he grunted.

The server glanced at the sophisticated-looking Claudia and said in a spooky voice, "Ted, I see rejection in your future…"

"And I see your tip getting smaller," he said, smacking her on the ass as she walked away.

The server brought Ted a bottle of Arrogant Bastard ale. How fitting, Claudia thought. All of this flirting was making her feel nauseous, so she looked for a way to get straight to the point.

"Ted, you said that you work for a psychic?" she asked as she sipped on her drink.

"I do. Gil Godsend. He's the world's greatest psychic."

"I don't think I told you that I'm a psychic too," she said.

Ted chuckled.

"Oh, really? Why don't you give me a reading?"

This should be good, he thought, as he took a sip of his drink.

"I'm not the world's greatest psychic, but I'll give it a shot," she said with a charming smile. She closed her eyes and breathed in and out deeply. She opened her eyes and looked at him. "...My spirit guide tells me that your name is... Ted Brown."

He laughed. This one was cute but she was an idiot. Just the way he liked them.

"Nope."

Claudia pretended to be embarrassed.

"Let me try again... My spirit guide tells me your name is...Ted Todd Ray."

Ted nearly choked on his beer.

She continued.

"The spirits say that you're married...even though you're not wearing your wedding ring."

His face started to turn white.

"...I sense that your wife's name is... Angela.... I feel that you've been married for... seven years and that you have three beautiful children... I'm getting the impression that their names are Oliver... Emma... and you have a newborn baby girl named Chloe."

"H-how did you know that?" Ted stammered.

"I'm psychic!"

"Yeah, right," he scoffed. "Who the fuck are you?"

Claudia smiled.

"You don't remember me, do you?"

Ted hated that question. For the first time, he studied her face. Was she an ex-girlfriend? Maybe she was a one-night stand? Did he go to high school with her? Was she one of his wife's friends that he'd slept with? He frowned.

"No...I don't think so."

"You tried to get me to give you a blowjob after the Irvine show when I wanted to go backstage to see Gil..."

This additional information didn't help Ted at all. He tried to force women to give him blowjobs at *every* show. He shook his head.

"No. I don't remember you."

"I'm Gil's ex-fiancé, Claudia Cox."

Realization washed over him like a cold shower.

"It's *you*..." he said like it was an accusation. Ted knew all about her. "What do you want from me?"

"Your wife came to see me because she suspects you're a cheater...and she's right."

Ted thought he'd covered his tracks. He thought he'd been discreet...except for the time she found that phone number in his shirt pocket...and the time she smelled perfume on him.

"Now, I'm going to make a prediction," said Claudia. "You're going to tell me what tricks Gil is using in his show tomorrow night."

Ted sneered.

"How about I go to Gil and tell him what you're up to instead?"

"Then I'll go to your wife and tell her about your exploits and she'll divorce you immediately and move to Wisconsin and you'll never see your children ever again!"

Ted was terrified, for a moment. Then a smug expression crept over his face.

"I'll just tell her you're a disgruntled ex-girlfriend with an axe to grind," he said. He had plenty of those. "You don't have any proof of all the times I've cheated on my wife."

"Don't I?" Claudia asked with an evil smile. She got her phone out of her handbag and pressed play. "I'll just tell her you're a disgruntled ex-girlfriend with an axe to grind. You don't have any proof of all the times I've cheated on my wife."

"And I have this..."

"Keep reading the *Kama Sutra*. Later tonight you can show me what you've learned..."

"Then there's this," she added.

"I'd fucking kill myself if I was married to her too, with a voice like that, even with those big titties of hers!"

"And this..." She handed Ted a screenshot of his profile on the website High Infidelity, that included a photo of him shirtless and smoking a bong.

"Shit, I told her I'd quit," he said.

"Thanks for that extra tidbit," said Claudia as she wrote it down. "And there's more. With all of this evidence your wife will also believe me when I tell her that you tried to get me to give you a blowjob a few months ago. I'm sure the server here will also corroborate that you come to this pub with different women all the time. Now, tell me, how does Gil do his readings?"

Beads of sweat dotted Ted's forehead. He swiped his head with the arm of his jacket.

"It's getting hot in here, isn't it?" Claudia said as she fanned herself with her hand, just like Ted had done minutes ago.

Ted held his forehead in his hands. He didn't know what to do. How was he going to get himself out of this mess? He enjoyed his job and the freedom it gave him. He liked being on the road all the time, having his way with different women in different cities, and then going back home to family life with his wife and kids. He was having his cake and eating it too. Every man would do that if they could, right?

If he spilled the beans he was going to lose his job. If he didn't, he'd lose his wife and kids. He realized he had been more loyal to Gil than to his own wife. He loved her; he just had a funny way of showing it.

It was time for him to be loyal to his wife...

"How does Gil do his readings?" Claudia asked him again.

Ted lifted up his head slowly and looked at her. He pulled out a crystal pendant that he was wearing around his neck.

"He uses *this*."

It was an amethyst crystal pendant. It looked just like the amethyst pendant Gil bought for Claudia at the metaphysical fair on the day they met. The one sitting in her trashcan at home.

Claudia raised her eyebrows at him.

"You're trying to tell me that he uses crystal power?" she asked scornfully. "I've had enough of your bullshit. I'm calling your wife."

She reached for her phone.

"No, wait!" he cried desperately. "It's *not* crystal power. There's something hidden *inside* of this amethyst."

"What do you mean?"

In a dramatic motion he ripped the crystal pendant off his neck and slammed it down on the table.

"What are you doing?" Claudia sighed, thinking this was a stalling tactic.

"I'm trying to break it", he said in frustration as he struck it on the table repeatedly.

"Oh, for fuck's sake."

Claudia shot a withering look at the big, beefy man. She took his beer bottle by the neck and smashed the bottom against the amethyst, breaking it into several pieces. In the middle of the crystal was a shiny piece of metal.

Her eyes grew wide.

"What's *that*?"

"It's some kind of microchip."

"How does it work?"

"These pendants are from Gil's line of jewelry," said Ted. "He sells these things like hot cakes and the microchips somehow pick up information from the people who wear them. I don't know how they work exactly."

"Bullshit," said Claudia impatiently. "I'm going to call your wife right now."

She grabbed her phone and started to dial.

"No, don't!" he pleaded as he placed his hand over hers in an attempt to stop her. "I'm telling you the truth. I don't know how it works. I don't know anything about technology," he confessed. "I'm a dumbass. I didn't even finish high school. Please don't tell my wife about everything! I can't lose her, or my kids…"

Claudia pulled her hand away. She thought she saw tears in Ted's eyes. They reminded her of the tears she'd seen in the eyes of Gil's clients over the years.

Claudia snatched the microchip and pieces of crystal from among the bits of broken bottle and put them in a safe place in her handbag. She still couldn't discount the possibility that this was another one of Gil's setups, but if Ted was telling the truth then she had a little information, and she knew where to go to find out more.

"I've told you what you want to know. You won't tell my wife, will you?" Ted begged.

Claudia looked at him with a deadpan expression.

"That depends on how smoothly this plays out," she said as she took a final swig of her Long Island Iced Tea. "I'll be in touch."

She left the pub.

The server watched Claudia leave. Then she walked over to Ted's table and picked up their empty glasses.

"She didn't stay long! But I knew that one was going to leave," she taunted. "She was too good for you."

She waited for his usual wisecrack response although one wasn't forthcoming. Ted only stared vacantly into the distance. She took pity on him.

"You look like you could do with another drink, Ted."

"Thanks," he said, for the first time ever. "Bring me a whiskey, neat, and keep 'em coming."

Then she saw the shards of broken glass and crystal on the table and floor.

"Hey! What happened here?"

"Not much," said Ted with a resigned shrug of his shoulders. "I just lost my job, my wife, and my kids."

Chapter 29

Claudia turned up to work in a good mood the next morning, despite feeling a little nauseous. It must have been the Long Island Iced Tea she'd had to drink the night before. She was elated. She had the smoking gun! Well, she had the unfired bullet. Now she needed the help of her computer expert, Ana Stanich. Claudia knew that Gil had won over Ana with his smooth talking and tricks, she even suspected that Ana had a crush on him, but she was certain she could bring her around with this new information.

Gil had a show in Oakland that night and Claudia wanted to be there, with Ana in tow. She called Ana into her office. She had just returned from a trip to Florida to visit her father.

"Hi Boss. You wanted to see me?"

"Yes. I want to talk with you about Gil Godsend."

Ana groaned

"Not this again," she said.

"Please… hear me out."

Ana closed her eyes and sighed.

"You need to get over this obsession you have with Gil Godsend so you can move on with your life!"

"I *had* moved on," Claudia said in her own defense. "I know it seems like I'm crying wolf, but some new information has since come to light. It could prove that Gil is a fraud, or it's a chance for you to prove to me that Gil really is psychic."

"Will *any* proof ever be good enough for you?"

"Absolutely. If I'm wrong then I'll give up."

"That's what you said last time."

"Last time I didn't have *this*…"

Claudia opened the drawer of her desk and took out the fragmented pendant. She placed the pieces on the palm of Ana's hand. Ana's eyes widened. Finally, her curiosity was piqued.

"This amethyst pendant is from Gil's line of Celestial Jewelry," said Claudia.

"Hmm...I think my mom has one of these pendants," Ana said, her eyes narrowing in suspicion.

That would explain a lot, thought Claudia.

"This chip was inside of it. What is it?" she asked.

"Let me take a look at it. I think I have my jeweler's loop with me," Ana said as she pulled a small magnifying glass out of her pocket and turned the object around slowly with her fingers like she was a jeweler appraising a diamond ring. "This is a tiny printed circuit board," she said in fascination. "I just came back from a hacker's convention in Vegas and they had this kind of technology there. It's cutting edge stuff. This looks like a skimmer but I've never seen one this small. With the right kind of software these can strip credit card information off a smart phone within three feet."

Claudia's jaw dropped. Just what other kinds of information could it access?

"I had no idea," she said. "Ana, I need your help. Come with me to his show tonight in Oakland. Help me find out the truth."

Ana thought about it. If Gil really was psychic then his innocence needed to be shown, but if it was all just a scam, he needed to be exposed. Gil brought her father back to her, and she was deeply grateful for that, but if her mother did have one of those amethyst pendants, it would explain a lot. Also, she wouldn't admit it to Claudia, but she was a little offended that Gil never called her back when she gave her phone number to him. She suspected that he was still interested in Claudia.

"Okay, I'll do it," she said reluctantly.

"You won't regret it," Claudia promised.

"Famous last words..."

It was another day, another Gil Godsend show.

Claudia and Ana arrived at the theater in Oakland and joined the long line of people waiting to get inside. Claudia suddenly noticed how many people were wearing amethyst pendants, signaling their allegiance to Gil like football fans wearing their team's t-shirt. Claudia was weirded out by these pendants. Did Gil design his amethyst pendants based on the one he gave to her all those years ago?

Claudia and Ana overheard a group of women talking excitedly about the magical powers of their amethyst pendants.

I've started to sleep better since wearing my pendant.
In the first hour of wearing my pendant I found out I'm getting that raise I've been waiting for!
I was wearing my pendant when I bought a lotto ticket and won $20!
I had sinus congestion but when I put on my pendant my nose cleared right up!
Ever since I started wearing my pendant I've been able to vibrate to my soul map in a much clearer way.

After waiting for an hour, the women finally reached the front of the line. When the usher asked for their tickets, Ted appeared out of nowhere.

"I'll take care of these two. They're VIPs," he said. "This way, ladies."

He led Claudia and Ana up a flight of stairs to a cozy box seat. These were perfect seats for the two of them to have the privacy to talk and use their surveillance equipment.

"I hope you'll find these seats to your satisfaction," Ted said politely, and without a trace of sarcasm.

"Thank you," said Claudia.

"You're welcome, Ma'am," he replied with a gallant wave of his hand.

This gentleman was a far cry from the walking penis she had a drink with last night. But she still didn't trust him. For all Claudia knew, Gil might know she was there. Ted could have blabbed to Gil to save his own neck. This might be just another set up, but these were risks she had to take because it could also be her big breakthrough.

Ana was overwhelmed by the event.

"I can't believe how many people attend these shows! It's like a rock concert."

"Yeah, and I could've bought tickets to see the Rolling Stones for the amount these would've cost," said Claudia.

On stage a large bouquet of fresh flowers sat on a table covered with a white silk cloth. Meditation music pumped through the theater while psychedelic imagery played on a video screen in the background.

Excitement built up in the room when a five-minute countdown clock appeared on the screen. When the clock reached ten seconds until the start of the show the audience screamed out the countdown, and then Gil ran out onto the stage, wearing a three-piece hunter green suit with a blue and white polka dot shirt and a navy blue tie.

Claudia thought she heard Ana sigh a little.

Gil leaned against the table like a crooner leaning against a piano.

"A skeptic said to me the other day, 'If you're so goddamn psychic, then what's my name?'

'Asshole', I said. 'By the way, your name is Mitch'."

The audience laughed.

While Gil held court over the theater, Ana used her tablet to scan for wireless signals. Claudia held her breath. She didn't know what they were looking for, but she hoped Ana would find it.

"Whoa!" exclaimed Ana. "This theater is a spider web of signals that are crisscrossing everywhere!" she said as she flailed her arms about. "That's weird… half of these signals are NFC and the other half are Bluetooth."

"Yeah, that's weird," agreed Claudia.

She wasn't sure what Ana meant, but it sounded damning.

"The Bluetooth signals are a class 1 which is kind of rare. The range is as big as a football field," she added. "Wait a minute. The NFC signals are used for extracting information from smart phones while the Bluetooth signal coming from the amethyst pendants is sending that information to a single computer." An evil smile crept across her face. "I'm going to hack into it…"

"Let's start the show!" Gil announced to cheers and applause.

Claudia felt her heart rate speeding up as Ana typed away madly, a manic look in her eyes as she stared at the screen.

"Hmm…that's interesting," Ana said.

"What?" asked Claudia.

"Brandy…"

"What do you mean?"

"I'm being pulled to this section here," said Gil as he motioned to the front row. "I'm sensing a "B" name, like Brenda or Brandy," said Gil. "I want to go to the woman in the green sweater."

Gil raced over to her with his microphone.

"My name is Brandy!" the woman cried.

"Holy shit!" Claudia whispered.

"Max," said Ana.

"Who is Max?" asked Gil.

"He's my father," said Brandy.

"He's here with us now," said Gil.

"He was a firefighter," said Ana.

"Why am I seeing fire?" asked Gil.

"My father was a firefighter."

"He died fighting a house fire," said Ana.

Gil closed his eyes and grimaced.

"The room I'm in is getting very hot… I want to get out of here but I'm trapped… I feel like my skin is being burned… I'm engulfed in flames…" He started coughing. "I can barely breath…I'm choking…" He opened his eyes and looked at Brandy. "I feel that your father died in the line of duty…"

"That's right," Brandy mumbled before she began sobbing into her hands.

"He was a hero," said Gil as he placed his hand gently on her shoulder. "He says he loves you and that he wants you to know he is okay."

Claudia smiled.

This was the beginning of the end for Gil Godsend.

"How are you getting this information?" she asked Ana.

"The circuit board in the pendants is taking information from wearer's smart phones and routing it into a search algorithm that does an instant background check on them and analyzes their social media," explained Ana. "This program extracts this data, categorizes it, and then drops it into a spreadsheet. This lets Gil know where the person is sitting in the room and reveals all different kinds of personal information about them; names, ages, family tree, police records, medical history, obituaries, browser history, purchases, and hobbies." Ana pointed to the spreadsheet on her screen. "See, it says here that Brandy just bought pottery supplies and she has an online store where she sells her handmade items."

"I see bowls, plates and cups… They're handmade…" said Gil. "I see a lump of clay…a pottery wheel…and a kiln…who makes pottery?"

"I do!" Brandy replied excitedly.

"How is Gil getting this information?" asked Claudia.

Ana narrowed her eyes.

"I'm not sure...yet."

Surely he wasn't wearing an earpiece. Claudia had gone down that road before. She zoomed in on Gil with a pair of high-powered mini binoculars.

"I can't see that he's wearing an earpiece, smart watch, glasses, or anything else that would allow him to receive this information," Claudia observed. "He's walking among the crowd so he's not using a teleprompter."

"I bet he's using some sort of new technology," said Ana.

Claudia remembered Gil's comment about the in-ear receiver being outdated. She could hear his voice in her head saying...*that trick is so... 1980s.*

"I think you're right," she said to Ana.

Claudia watched Gil carefully. He was staring off into the distance.

"My spirit guides tell me that someone in this part of the room just had a burglary in their home," he said as he pointed to the right side of the audience. "They're giving me the name Rick."

A man in that part of the room put up his hand.

"My name is Rick and my home was just broken into."

"Then this message is for you." Gil said. He paused and looked up again. "They're telling me that the thieves stole a television and a laptop... They also took some items that had sentimental value to you... I see war memorabilia... and a World War II bayonet that belonged to your grandfather."

"That's right, Gil. Those things meant a lot to me," he said sadly.

Every time Gil received a message from his "spirit guides", he was looking up at the same location on the back wall. Claudia always thought that when he did this he was thinking about what he was going to say; now she wondered if he was *looking* at what he needed to say.

"Whenever Gil talks with his spirit guides he looks up at the left side of the back wall," she told Ana. "Is there something there?"

Ana pulled a gadget out of her handbag.

"I got this from a technology conference," she said. "I've been looking for a reason to use it. It looks like a lens but it's a mini camera and display that I can attach to a camera phone to give it night vision. Cool, huh?"

"Um, yeah..." said Claudia.

Ana attached the lens to her phone and panned around the room. They viewed the audience through the sickly green hue of night vision that they were familiar with from watching ghost hunting shows on television. Then Ana directed the camera towards the area on the wall where Gil kept looking.

"Bingo!" she cried. "The information from the spreadsheet is being projected right onto the wall!"

"But how can he see it with the naked eye?" Claudia asked.

"He can't, unless he's a superhero or something," said Ana. "Gil *must* have some kind of night vision."

Claudia looked at Gil. How was he seeing infrared without using a lens like Ana's or wearing a massive pair of night vision binoculars? She laughed to herself as she imagined the suave Mr. Gil Godsend wearing a stylish suit and a pair of clunky night vision goggles.

She snapped out of it and watched him at work. Now he was doing a reading for a little old lady.

"My spirit guides tell me that you're recovering from hip surgery, but they must be wrong. You're far too young for that," he said with a grin.

The woman was charmed. She stared deep into his eyes through her thick glasses.

"Gil, your eyes are even more vibrantly blue in person!" she flirted.

A memory slid into place suddenly in Claudia's mind. She remembered when she was standing on the beach with Gil in Australia. *She looked into Gil's piercing blue eyes, which seemed to have become more vibrantly blue over time.*

Gil's eyes had always been blue, but now they looked even more vibrant than the days when they were together. Had his eyes changed color with age? Had they changed because of sickness? Was he wearing eye make-up? Was he wearing contact lenses?

Maybe that was it...

"I think he's wearing contacts," Claudia said.

"Hmm... You know, there's a research team that's developing contact lenses with night vision," said Ana. "I know it sounds like science fiction, but such a device would enable Gil to see in the dark with his own eyes. But he'd only want to wear one lens at a time so he could still see true color with his other eye. I'd imagine wearing them would cause some eye strain."

This recalled another memory for Claudia. She and Gil walked on the beach together when he began rubbing his forehead. She joked that he'd gotten sand in his third eye and he replied; *I've just been getting headaches. My third eye is fine.*

Maybe he was getting headaches from wearing the night vision contact lenses?

Claudia was so excited that she felt she was about to faint. She breathed slowly and tried to regain her composure. It was like she was piecing together a massive puzzle, and the picture was forming slowly. It was all starting to make sense. It was still possible that this was a set up, but if it was, it was an elaborate one. That *was* Gil's style, but it was also Gil's style to have the latest gadgets and technology at his fingertips. It was a far-fetched theory, but as always, it made more sense to Claudia than Gil talking to the dead.

A light bulb went on in her mind.

"Ana, can you edit the information before Gil sees it?"

Ana thought about it.

"Yes."

Claudia smiled.

"Then let's do it. He has a show in San Francisco in two days."

"I'm there," said Ana, who was developing a blood lust for catching Gil.

She looked Claudia in the eye.

"You were right," she said. "Gil's a fraud. I owe you an apology."

"No, you don't," Claudia said as she watched Gil darting around the room giving bogus readings to people. "*Gil* owes *you* an apology. Actually, he owes everyone an apology."

Chapter 30

Claudia sat at a table in Exile, a restaurant in San Rafael. She had just finished meeting with a client there, so she decided to stay and prepare for the sting at Gil's show the following night. She was having a pot of Earl Grey tea and she had so much to drink that she needed to visit the restroom. Upon her return there was a bottle of chardonnay and two glasses on her table. She waved a server over.

"Excuse me," she said. "I didn't order this bottle of wine."

"Miss, this is a gift for you from the gentleman sitting over there."

The gentleman sitting over there was Gil.

"Oh, for fuck's sake," she mumbled under her breath.

She knew that by being in San Rafael she was on his turf but she hoped they wouldn't cross paths that evening. She should have learned from her experience in Australia that this world wasn't big enough for the two of them.

After a suitable amount of time, Gil strolled over to her table, wearing a sable grey suit and an olive green shirt and tie, and looking like he'd just stepped off the set of a modeling shoot.

"Ms. Cox," he said with a bow.

"I was just thinking about you, and here you are!" said Claudia with feigned surprise. "Were you reading my mind again?"

"Always," he said with a grin.

She bundled up her notes about Gil and put them away in her attaché case.

"Is that something I shouldn't see?" he asked.

"You're the world's greatest psychic," she said with a knowing smile. "There's *nothing* Gil Godsend can't see!"

"That's true," he said with a nod. He gestured towards her table. "May I have a seat?"

She sighed.

"If you must."

Gil sat down opposite her, leaving a trail of cologne in his wake.

Claudia pinched her nose and fanned her face at the overwhelming smell.

"Phew! You're wearing too much Old Spice there!"

"You have a sensitive nose. I'm only wearing a little," said Gil. "And you know I don't wear Old Spice, I wear Brut 33," he joked.

"Whatever it is it has too much musk in it, but I'm sure you'd smell good to a doe. You know that stuff is extracted from the backside of male deer, don't you?"

"Musk originally came from the secretions derived from the perineal gland of the Tibetan musk deer, but today the creature is endangered and protected," began Gil's lecture. Claudia was sorry she'd asked. "Nowadays the scent is replicated synthetically or plant essences are used instead, although there is a black market for natural musk pods, which are even more valuable than gold. Musk is used as a sedative in traditional Chinese medicine, and to treat conditions of the lungs and heart. It's also believed that musk is a powerful aphrodisiac," he said with a mischievous smile.

Claudia rolled her eyes at the walking encyclopedia.

"You still smell like a buck's butt," she said.

"I'll be your buck anytime."

Gil leaned back in his seat, interlaced his fingers and put his hands behind his head. He looked Claudia up and down approvingly.

"You're looking lovely tonight, as usual."

This was straight out of the book of Ted Ray's original seduction techniques, she thought.

"I didn't peg you as the type of man to use a corny pick up line, Gil."

He hanged his head in mock shame.

"I apologize for using such a worn-out and tired phrase," he said. "Speaking of tired, should I have said instead that you look like you need a solid night's sleep and you have dark circles under your eyes?"

Eyes.

The word pulled her out of the moment and triggered her memory of the night before. She stared into Gil's blue eyes. Were they more vividly blue than they used to be? Was he really using night vision contact lenses at his performances? Was he wearing contacts right now?

Gil noticed her eyes searching his.

"The eyes reveal our secrets," he said. "The windows to the soul, as they say."

She hoped his eyes were about to reveal his secrets.

"Your eyes… they're so very blue," she said absentmindedly.

"Who's the one using corny pick-up lines now?" he joked.

"They seem more blue than they used to be…"

"I age like a fine wine," he said. "Just like this bottle of Bouchard Père & Fils 2007 that you haven't touched yet."

He poured two glasses of chardonnay and handed one to Claudia. She was tempted to try it, this bottle probably cost more than she had earned that day, but she wanted a clear head the night before the sting. Besides, she didn't feel well in the stomach. She put it down to nerves before the big night. She sat the glass down on the table.

"Thank you, but no thank you. I like to keep my wits about me, especially when you're around."

Gil ignored the insult and studied her carefully. She felt uncomfortable under his penetrating gaze. He leaned forward towards her.

"Claudia, did you know that you're pregnant?"

His question totally threw her off guard.

"*What?*"

"You're pregnant."

"That's… impossible!"

"An immaculate conception is it, Mother Claudia?"

She wasn't pregnant! She *knew* that. She and Jeremy had used protection. In fact, they had used two different kinds of birth control. She didn't know why she was even entertaining the possibility. She couldn't be pregnant. But why did Gil think she was? Was he cold reading her? Did he suspect she was pregnant simply because she refused an alcoholic drink? That must be it.

"I'm not pregnant! I can't be!"

"Tell that to the embryo inside of you," Gil said.

The server came over to the table again.

"Can I get you two anything else?" he asked.

"Let's get a snack," suggested Gil. "You're eating for two now, Claudia. What would you like?"

She shot him a foul look although she was feeling hungry. She hadn't eaten all day. She studied the menu. Hmm...what dish would Gil really hate? Ha! She'd order the deep-fried Twinkie. Mmm, the cheese platter looks good though.

"The lady is with child and she has a craving for cheese," Gil said to the server before she could even reply. She hated it when he seemed to read her mind, but she knew he knew that she liked cheese. "We'll have the cheese platter, but without the Camembert, Brie, or feta," he said. He turned to Claudia. "We don't want you contracting listeria from unpasteurized cheese."

"You're being ridiculous, Gil!"

"Then just humor me."

Claudia wanted to humor herself by throwing her drink at him. At that moment, Gil slid her glass across the table and away from her reach.

"No alcohol for you...for drinking or throwing at me."

They sat looking at each other in a silence that was uncomfortable for Claudia, although Gil was having a great time. His eyes fell to her cleavage. She wished she hadn't worn that low-cut blouse that night.

"You do look a little... larger," he said with a swirling hand gesture to indicate her breasts. "You know...down there..."

"If only I could say the same thing about you!" she snapped.

"Ouch!" he cried. "Increased sensitivity to odors, fatigue, cravings, and now moodiness. Your physical symptoms support my psychic evaluation that you're pregnant."

She scowled at him.

"I'm going to the restroom to powder my fucking nose," she said.

"Add frequent urination to the list..."

Claudia stood up so quickly that she felt faint. She was unsteady on her feet. Gil rushed to help her.

"And dizziness," he added as he steadied her. "All the pregnancy signs are there!"

Claudia pulled away from him and stormed off to the restroom. While she was in there she touched up the concealer under her eyes. Damn Gil. She studied her face in the mirror. She admitted to herself that she did look a little tired, but then she was overworked and not getting enough sleep. There were explanations for all of her alleged "pregnancy symptoms". She could smell Gil's cologne because he was wearing so much she thought she would gag. She kept going to the restroom because she was drinking a lot of tea. She felt woozy and hungry because she hadn't eaten anything all day. She was irritable, but that was because Gil was there.

Now that she thought about it, had she missed her period? She was so busy she wasn't paying attention to her menstrual cycle.

She wasn't pregnant. She couldn't be.

As Claudia returned to her table the server brought over a wooden board with a lavish display of fruit and crackers with Edam, Emmenthaler, Smoked Gouda, and other gourmet cheeses.

"Here's the platter with no soft cheeses for the pregnant lady," said the server.

"I'm *not* pregnant!" she cried.

"Oh look, honey. Strawberries!" said Gil. "They're full of folic acid."

"If you call me "honey" again I'll be throwing acid at you," she threatened.

The server backed away from the table and made a hasty retreat.

"Well, this is pleasant, isn't it?" said Gil happily as he carved off a slice of Edam. "It reminds me of our dinner together in Australia."

Claudia's entire face dissolved into confusion.

"*What?*"

"Our night together in Mooloolaba."

"I don't know what you're talking about!"

"Oh, it's like that now, is it?" he said with a wink. "Well, it'll just be our little secret…or maybe not…" he nodded towards her belly.

Claudia didn't know what he meant.

Gil was acting so cocky, which was typical for him, but it probably meant one of two things. Either he knew that she was about to sting him because this was part of his setup, or he didn't know she was about to sting him. After all, he wasn't psychic. She *knew* that now for sure. He was probably just trying to throw her off balance and psyche her out.

She brushed off his comments.

Claudia avoided the strawberries and picked at a few grapes and dry crackers. She tried a little cheese. The thought of cheese had sounded good at the time, but now that it was in front of her it smelled bad. Maybe it was rotten, but she watched as Gil ate the cheese and he didn't seem to notice anything was wrong. The smell of the cheese started to turn her stomach. Her nausea must be psychosomatic because Gil was teasing her.

He noticed her reaction to the cheese.

"Morning sickness?" he asked.

"Gil Godsend sickness," she replied. "Being around you makes me feel sick," she said, with a giggle at her own juvenile humor.

To prove her point that she was fine, she cut off a chunk of Gouda and popped it into her mouth. Then she wished she hadn't. She must have a stomach flu.

"Should I ask the server to bring you a bowl of pickles and ice cream instead?" Gil asked.

"Sure, but if I'm pregnant then I might barf all over you, although that would blend quite nicely with your vomit-green shirt."

"You're color-blind and have no fashion sense," he accused her. "This is an olive green shirt. My vomit green shirt doesn't match *this* suit."

Despite herself, Claudia smiled.

She couldn't deny that she enjoyed sparring with Gil. After all these years they'd slipped right back into their roles. They'd always bonded over insults. He was a worthy adversary. She had to admit that she loved to hate him. What would life be like without him? Did she need to have someone to fight? Without an archenemy, would she lose her sense of purpose? Would she be a hero without a villain?

It was a surprisingly bittersweet moment. Claudia should have been excited that night, she was about to bring down her life-long nemesis, but this meal was mildly depressing, like it was the Last Supper and she was Judas about to betray Jesus. Well, Gil had always had a messiah complex.

Claudia looked at Gil. He was out of gibes for the time being, and was massaging his temples.

"Are you okay?" she asked him.

"Yes. I just have a headache," he replied.

"A headache? Maybe *you're* pregnant!" she joked.

She was ready to trade more insults, but he looked like he was in pain.

"I've been getting these a lot lately," he admitted.

Yeah, headaches from wearing those night vision contact lenses, she thought. Then she remembered the headache he had when they were walking on Mooloolaba beach together. Maybe there *was* something wrong with him. He did look slightly pale. She shouldn't care at all, but Claudia felt a little worried about him.

"It's nice to know that you care about me," Gil said softly. "Because I care about you."

He turned serious all of a sudden.

"Claudia, I have something to ask you," he said as he reached for her hand.

She suspected he was going to try to convince her to work for him.

"I'm *not* going to come work for you, Gil," she said as she pulled her hand away.

"That's *not* what I was going to say," he said. "I'm… going away for a while. Come with me."

This came as a complete shock to her.

"Where are you going?"

"Anywhere *you* want to go," he said. "We can travel to Europe, Africa, Asia, or South America. We can go back to Australia or we can move to a remote island somewhere, just the two of us."

"*Why* are you going?"

"Because it's time," he said mysteriously. "Come with me, Claudia," he said in his hypnotic voice. "We can start over again. We can change our names. We can get married and have kids. You can start writing full time. I know you've always wanted to write horror novels… and I'll…I don't know…I'll become a clinical psychologist or something…or nothing…but we'll never have to work another day in our lives…"

Claudia saw a desperation she'd never seen before in Gil's bulletproof eyes.

Did he know what was about to happen? Was this a ploy to stop her from exposing him? Was he planning to leave the country before she could bust him? Was something else going on? Was he running away from someone or something? Was he sick? And why did he want her to go with him?

She was silent.

"But all the magic I have known I've had to make myself," he said, quoting the secret code between Claudia and her father. "Let's make some magic together, Claudia."

Gil knew how to tug at her heartstrings. She thought about her father. He would want her to follow her heart. For a second she actually considered Gil's offer. The two of them could run away together and start over again. Maybe it could be the way it used to be, or even better. Then she snapped out of her sentimentality. It would *never* work between them. He was a fraud. He was an abuser. He was a womanizer. She was about to crush his career. Gil was showing his weakness. She knew she had him.

"No," she said with a shake of her head.

Gil's shoulders slumped and he looked crushed.

She almost felt sorry for him. Almost.

"I have to go," he said urgently as he stood up to leave. "...And Claudia?"

"Yes, Gil?"

He raised her from her seat and pulled her towards him. He placed his hand in the small of her back and held her tightly as he lifted her chin and she felt his soft, warm lips against hers. There were kisses from his lips, kisses in his eyes, and kisses in his hands. At first, she was so shocked that she let him kiss her, and then she forgot herself long enough that she started kissing him back. It was slow and sensual and achingly tender, but soon it became frantic and desperate.

It was a kiss goodbye.

Gil pulled away from her and looked into her eyes.

"I love you," he said.

Then he turned and walked away.

Claudia stood still as she watched him disappear out of view.

"I loved you," she whispered.

Chapter 31

Claudia lay awake in bed that night wondering about Gil's cryptic conversation.
What was he up to? Why was he leaving? Where would he go? When would he leave? Why did he think she was pregnant? Annoyingly, her musings were continually interrupted by thoughts of that kiss. She replayed the scene in her head again and again. She wavered between thinking, why did I fall for his Svengali bullshit? And, damn, that was a good kiss… Claudia was angry with Gil for daring to kiss her, but also angry with herself for liking it so much.

At 3am she realized she couldn't dwell on these things. She had to stay focused on the prize… exposing Gil Godsend as a fraud.

Then she finally fell asleep.

The next day Claudia still felt a little nauseous but she soldiered on. She let Banachek know what was happening and he gave her some advice on how to tackle the operation. She arranged for the media to be there to witness Gil's downfall. She contacted bloggers, journalists, and reporters and told them that if they wanted to see proof that Gil Godsend was a charlatan, they needed to attend his San Francisco show that night. She promised them a spectacle, and she was determined to give them one.

The first two stings had failed, but third time's the charm.

Gil had made a fool of her time after time. Now it was her chance to finally make a fool of him.

When Claudia and Ana arrived at the theater Ted greeted them at the door.

"Right on time, ladies," he said as he seated them in a box seat again.

Claudia still didn't know if she could trust him or not.

Hypnotic meditation music pumped through the theater as people streamed into the room and took their seats. On stage a white silk cloth was draped across a table. An arrangement of white roses, chrysanthemums, and lilies accented with ferns sat on top. As always, the stage had that funeral parlor look to it and the theater had a rock concert vibe.

At 8pm on the dot, Gil emerged onstage, looking as sharp as ever, wearing a midnight blue suit, a crisp white shirt, and a gold silk cravat with a contrasting vermilion-colored pocket square.

Gil began his monologue to the packed crowd of his adoring fans.

"Life is all about the relationships we have with other people, the moments we share, and the memories we create," he said in his deep, modulated voice. "If you close your eyes you can still taste the spiced apple and flakey pastry of your grandmother's apple pie... You can still feel the touch of your father's sturdy arms wrapped around you tightly in one of his bear hugs... You can still smell the fresh, flowery fragrance worn by your mother that lingered long after she left the room... And you can still hear the sound of your lover's voice gently whispering in your ear, "I love you"."

Claudia froze as the final words she'd heard from him last night now echoed around the room.

"This evening you'll be reunited with those who've passed over," Gil said as he strode across the stage. "Grandparents, mom and dad, aunts and uncles, brothers and sisters, children and friends, are all gathered together... We're here to laugh, cry, and reminisce... This is a family reunion," he said with outstretched arms. "But death leaves us with unanswered questions about our loved ones on the other side. Did they go in peace? How are they doing in the afterlife? What was left unsaid? You want closure.... You want to know the truth... Tonight, there will be answers."

"Oh, yes there will," Claudia whispered to herself.

Ana set up her night vision camera lens and they could see the spreadsheet of information projected onto the wall. The writing was on the wall for Gil.

"Now I just have to hack into the source," Ana said. As she typed away on her laptop the glow of the screen reflected on her face.

Claudia held her breath in suspense.

"I'm in!" Ana announced.

"Excellent!" said Claudia. "Now the fun begins..."

They had created a list of names, diseases, hobbies, and other information so they could change the data in the spreadsheet on the fly, but first, they allowed Gil one accurate reading to give him a false sense of security.

Gil looked up towards the left-hand side of the back wall.

"My spirit guides are leading me to this area here," he said as he pointed to the front middle section of the audience. "I want to go to the man in the blue shirt... The name Luke is coming through very strongly."

"Luke was my father," the man acknowledged. A chill ran down his spine.

Gil walked down into the audience with his microphone in hand. "Your father wants to validate the reading," he said. He closed his eyes. "I'm lying on the cool grass under the dark night sky...I'm gazing up at the twinkling stars... I see a pair of binoculars and a telescope... There's a bookshelf filled with books about astronomy... Your father tells me he was an astronomer... He says that when he died a colleague named an asteroid after him..."

"That's my Dad!" the man confirmed.

The reading was stirring up cherished memories for him.

"You're wearing his watch," said Gil.

"I am!" he said, holding up his arm to show the stainless steel watch on his wrist.

"Your father died recently," said Gil as he closed his eyes. He rubbed his back. "I'm feeling pain and stiffness in my lower back... and numbness in my legs... I feel like I'm having difficulty, how do I say this, going to the restroom... but I feel like I need to go frequently... The sensation wakes me up at night... When I finally go I see blood in the toilet...it terrifies me..." Gil opened his eyes. "I sense that your father died of prostate cancer."

"You're right, Gil," he said, his voice cracking.

"I get the impression that he didn't tell you he was sick," said Gil. "He didn't find out until it was too late for him to be saved... There's nothing his doctors could have done...No one could change the outcome... His destiny in life was set... So he kept the news to himself... He didn't want to worry you... He wanted his final weeks with his family to be happy ones... Not precious time wasted grieving for him while he was still alive."

"Yes," the man whispered.

"He wants you to celebrate the memory of his life... He is now at peace... He watches over you and protects you... And he says he's sorry that he didn't tell you he was dying," said Gil. "He seeks your forgiveness."

"Of course, I forgive you Dad... I love you."

He dissolved into tears.

"Your father loves you too," said Gil as he placed a hand firmly on the man's shoulder. "Hold that love close to you. Love never dies."

The man's voice was thick with emotion.

"Thank you, Gil. *Thank you*. This means so much to me."

The audience burst into applause, while a few people burst into tears along with the son grieving for his father.

You're an evil bastard, Gil, thought Claudia. Enjoy the fame and fortune while it lasts because you're about to fall. She couldn't wait to wipe that smug smile off his face.

Ana started adding false information to the spreadsheet, her fingers typing furiously.

"Let's see how many hits he gets now!" she said.

Gil looked up towards the back wall again.

"My spirit guides are leading me to this lady here in the yellow cardigan," said Gil as he approached the woman. "I feel that your mother passed two years ago."

"...No..." said the woman in surprise. "She's alive and well!"

Gil was equally surprised.

"Gotcha!" cried Claudia.

"That just happened!" cried Ana.

They grinned at each other.

Gil looked up towards the back wall again. He continued calmly.

"That's what they tell me," he replied, like he knew all along. "I feel that someone else around you passed recently."

The woman thought about this.

"Not recently...but my sister Lynne died sixteen years ago," she offered up, trying to help Gil.

"Then this message is for you," he said. "I'm hearing classical music playing... It's a very stirring piece... It sounds like Tchaikovsky... Yes, it's the *Dance of the Sugar Plum Fairy*... Your sister tells me that she was a ballerina... She was a member of the San Francisco Ballet... She played the Sugar Plum Fairy in their performance of The Nutcracker..."

"No!" said the woman in shock. "She was a paraplegic and she spent most of her life in a wheelchair..."

Gil looked confused.

"...But she loved to go to the ballet..."

"No...she was a heavy metal fan."

"Checkmate!" cried Claudia with glee.

Claudia and Ana had to stifle their laughter, but the audience was in disbelief.

Gil Godsend was wrong? How could that possibly be? There were murmurs around the room, but Gil's fans were still on his side as they rationalized his mistakes.

No psychic is always 100% accurate.
He's warming up still.
His chakras are probably out of balance.
I bet Gil was getting those messages for someone nearby who didn't speak up.
There must be lots of psychic interference in here tonight.
When she goes away and thinks about it she'll see that Gil is right.

Gil cut his losses and moved on. He looked up towards the back wall.

"My spirit guides tell me to go to this gentleman here in the grey sweater," he said as he darted towards a man in the fourth row who fit that description. "Your name is Jason."

The man shook his head.

"But you have a relative by the name of Jason..."

The man stared blankly at the ceiling.

"No, I don't think so..."

"Do you know *anyone* named Jason?"

He racked his brains.

"I think my ex-girlfriend's mother's accountant has a son named Jason... No... wait, his name is Jackson."

"I knew there was a 'J' connection here," said Gil, drawing a tenuous link. He cut to the chase. "Who are you wanting to hear from today?"

"My mother, Eve."

"She is here with us now... I see her standing beside you," said Gil. "Your mother was a deeply religious woman... She was a devout Catholic... She once made a pilgrimage to Lourdes where she was cured of a stomach ulcer... The only Sunday she missed church was the day she died... I feel you're wearing one of her religious articles, either a medallion, a cross, or a rosary..."

The man frowned.

"But my mom was an atheist!"

"She made a deathbed conversion," replied Gil without missing a beat.

Gil was grasping at straws with his manipulative comebacks, although this was a face-saving tactic Claudia had seen all psychic mediums resort to, scrambling to force fit their reading after they made a terrible mistake.

"I see her funeral," Gil continued. "There's a wreath with yellow roses and carnations... Her loved ones are standing around in mourning... When she was lowered into the grave you were the first person to shovel dirt onto her casket... She was buried wearing a red satin dress..."

"She was *cremated*..."

The room fell silent.

Claudia could see on the big screen that Gil was starting to sweat. He reminded her of a scared little boy having to give a talk in front of his classmates for the first time. She saw him look backstage for help. Gil was always so cool, calm, and collected. Claudia had *never* seen him this stressed out before. This was better entertainment than any comedy.

"We need some popcorn," she said to Ana.

Gil looked up towards the back wall.

"My spirit guides are leading me to the gentleman over here in the brown jacket," he said as he approached the man. "Your name is Ethan."

"Mason."

"Mason," Gil corrected himself. "You come from a large family with many brothers and sisters."

"Um...I'm an only child."

"But as an only child you always dreamed of having brothers and sisters."

"...Not really..."

"Because you had so many friends," said Gil, trying to bail himself out of that one. He looked up towards the back wall. "I'm sensing there's a shocking secret in your family... Your parents never told you that you were a love child born of an illicit affair..."

"What?" he cried. "I was an IVF baby!"

"That's why you're an only child," said Gil. "Now, I feel there's been a recent death in the family."

Mason thought about it hard.

"I think one of my second cousins just died."

This answer would do for Gil, who was getting desperate.

"I'm supposed to bring up the beach. As a young child, he enjoyed surfing."

"*She* grew up in Utah."

"But her parents took her to the west coast on vacation," said Gil, thinking on his feet. He changed the topic quickly. "She wasn't a very good student. She was sick of studying and couldn't wait to leave school."

"Actually, she was a Professor of Mathematics."

"No wonder she was sick of studying!" Gil replied.

He looked up towards the back wall.

"With this death in the family comes rebirth," Gil said profoundly. "Congratulations are in order. Your wife is pregnant!"

The audience broke out into applause for the expecting couple, although Mason looked worried.

"But I had a vasectomy last year," he said.

"Ah," said Gil. "Then that must be the love child reference!"

There were more rumblings in the audience. People were shaking their heads in disapproval. Gil's fans had finally stopped making excuses for his mistakes, and they had stopped buying his excuses as he tried to recover from his mistakes.

Claudia started to feel bad for the people who were receiving these readings. By making Gil look foolish she was humiliating them too. She felt guilty about dragging these innocent people into her game, but it was for a good cause, wasn't it? She hoped this exposé would make people skeptical about Gil. She also hoped it would make people skeptical about *all* psychics.

"We'd better give Gil a hit or two otherwise he'll stop using the information in the spreadsheet and start relying on cold reading," warned Claudia. "He's good at that and he'll be able to recover from his gaffes and still convince the audience he has psychic powers."

"I'm on it," said Ana.

Gil looked up towards the back wall.

"The spirits have a message for the man wearing the check shirt," he said as he walked towards him with the microphone. "They tell me that your wife passed away three years ago."

"Yes, Gil. That's right," the man confirmed.

Gil relaxed visibly.

"I sense that her name was Victoria, and her friends called her Vickie."

"Yes," he said with a nod.

He was back on track again.

"She was born in England and her family moved to the United States when she was five years old."

"That's true."

The glitch must be fixed.

"And when you met you felt right away that you had a connection... It seemed like you had known her all your life... On a soul level you'd known each other before... You belonged together... It was destined to be..."

"Yes, Gil. You're making my hair stand on end!"

Gil seemed to have his mojo back.

"Okay, I think that's enough confidence," said Claudia.

"Got it," said Ana.

"The spirits tell me that she fell sick quickly, then suddenly she was gone," said Gil with a snap of his fingers.

"But we knew she was dying *for years*," the man replied.

"When someone passes, even if you knew they were dying, you can never be completely prepared," Gil said as he tried to wriggle out of his error. "I feel that you didn't get the chance to say goodbye to her before she passed."

"I was at her bedside holding her hand when she died..."

"She knew you were there," said Gil. "You told her it was okay to let go... She wants to thank you for releasing her soul... And just before she died her final words were... "The light is so bright"."

"...She was *blind*."

Gil took a deep breath and tried to salvage the reading.

"I think she means...she is pure light now... And she can see. Our loved ones don't have disabilities or ailments on the other side; they leave these behind with the physical body. She says she loves you and goodbye, for now."

Gil moved on in a hurry. He looked up towards the back wall.

"Spirit is bringing me here to this lady wearing the green scarf," said Gil as he approached the woman. He paused. "Who is Freckles?"

The lady cupped her hand over her face in shock. Her hand dropped to her lap.

"Oh my God! That was my brother's nickname for me when I was a little girl because I used to have freckles splashed across my nose," she said. "And I called him..."

"Dimples," interrupted Gil. "Because your little brother had a dimple in each cheek."

"Yes, that's right," she whispered in amazement.

Claudia shot Ana a look.

"Don't worry, I'm setting him up for the kill," Ana explained to her with an evil smile.

"But his real name was Robert," said Gil.

She shook her head.

"...It was Rodney."

"No."

"Roger."

"No!"

"Ronald?"

"No...His name was *Gary*."

"That was going to be my next guess," Gil joked. "Not guess! I mean... that was the next message that came through," he said, stumbling over his words. He closed his eyes. "I'm seeing a Golden Retriever... His name was Peabody... He was your brother's childhood pet... The two of them went everywhere together... He slept at the end of your brother's bed..."

"Um, no..." she said. "He had a severe pet allergy. He'd break out in hives if he went anywhere near a dog."

Gil tried to rescue his reading.

"The spirits are now telling me this was a story line from a book that he loved to read as a child."

The woman didn't know if this was true or not, so she said nothing.

Gil looked up to the back wall. Then he looked backstage and Claudia saw Ted giving him the thumbs up. Gil looked up to the back wall again.

This was the big moment.

Whose side was Ted on?

"Your brother shows me handcuffs," said Gil. "He's standing beside me wearing prison clothing... I see bars...I sense that he once got himself into trouble with a younger girl... He spent a few years in the big house, didn't he?"

The woman was stunned.

"My brother was a *Jesuit Priest*," she said indignantly.

"Oh, then I should have said he got himself into trouble with a younger *boy*," said Gil with a laugh.

The woman began sobbing uncontrollably.

There were horrified gasps across the room.

Gil's show was a total disaster. It was like watching a train wreck. Claudia and Ana could hear boos and hisses around the room. People were heckling him. Gil was lucky that the audience didn't have rotten tomatoes and eggs on hand to throw at him. Some wanted refunds. People were even leaving.

Gil decided to quit while he was behind. He cut the show short.

"It's been my honor to be here with you tonight, sharing messages of comfort, joy, and inspiration," he said uncomfortably. "Remember, the conversation with your loved ones doesn't begin or end with a psychic medium. It starts with you, and you can continue the conversation at any time by paying attention to... *messages from the other side...*"

Gil cleared his throat.

"I have an announcement to make," he said, his usually strong voice now sounding raw. "This will be my final show for a while. I need a break to recharge my psychic batteries. I need to turn the voices off... but don't worry, I'll see you all again soon."

Gil stared out into the audience.

Claudia felt as though he was looking right at her.

Then he disappeared off stage. There was no applause, no standing ovation, and no encore.

The audience made their exodus out of the theater. Claudia reveled in their criticisms of his performance.

What was up with Gil tonight?
He was way off.
His first reading was amazing but then it all went downhill from there.
I paid good money to see that?
I felt embarrassed for him.
I felt embarrassed for the people he was reading.
Can psychics lose their powers?
No wonder he needs a break.
So much for world's greatest psychic!
Meh. That was no worse than any other psychic.
Gil Godsend is a fraud...

Claudia was walking on air as she left the show that night. She relished every moment of Gil's failure. It had taken years, but she finally had proof he was a fraud. She couldn't wait to reveal his tricks to the media and watch the ensuing fallout.

Gil Godsend's career as a psychic medium was over...

Chapter 32

Ted stood outside the door to his home. One white-knuckled hand gripped the doorknob and another clutched an enormous bouquet of flowers. He was frozen with anxiety, but he finally forced himself to open the door. When he entered he found his wife cooking dinner in the kitchen and the aroma of chicken soup filled the air. The television was on in the background while the children chased each other around the living room, laughing and screaming. Despite the commotion, the baby was fast asleep in the nursery.

Angela looked up and saw the flowers.

"Uh-oh. What have you done?" she asked with a laugh.

Her smile fell quickly when she saw that Ted didn't share in the joke. This didn't look good. She hadn't heard back from Claudia yet either. In that moment she knew her suspicions and fears about her husband were correct.

Ted took Angela's hands and looked into her eyes.

"Honey, I've... been a bad husband," he said earnestly. "But I want to change all of that, and I'm going to start by being completely honest with you."

"You can't believe a word that comes out of his mouth," said a familiar voice.

They both craned their necks around and saw it was Claudia on the television being interviewed about Gil.

The past few days had been busy ones for Claudia. Since the Gil Godsend scandal broke she had been basking in the limelight of the media. Everyone wanted to hear the story of how disgraced psychic Gil Godsend had been caught cheating, and how she figured it all out. With her beauty, intelligence, and wit, Claudia became an instant media darling. It helped that she was once Gil's fiancé who was now dishing up dirt on him.

Offers came flooding in for television appearances. Even Michael Michaels had the nerve to try to lure her back onto *Night Owl*. She ignored his calls. One producer wanted her to star in a series about busting psychics, while a network wanted to sign a contract with her for a reality TV show about her detective agency. She wasn't interested.

America finally turned on Gil. He was tarred and feathered by the media. There were jokes about him told by late night show hosts in their monologues and merciless parodies of him on comedy shows. Subeditors had a field day penning cheesy headlines.

Gil Godsend's Psychic Scam is Now Crystal Clear.
Psychic Tour Canceled Due To Unforeseen Circumstances.
Psychic Medium Didn't See This Coming.
Gil Godsend Can't See Dead People.
Psychic Medium Dead Wrong.
Second Sight? Wait a Second…
Hitting an Unhappy Medium.
Medium Grows Too Large.
Contact (Lenses) With the Other Side.
Messages From The Other Side…Of The Room.

For once, all the public support was for Claudia. She was finally getting her fifteen minutes of fame, although she didn't want fame, she wanted people to listen to her point of view. She wanted to save bereaved people from being ripped off by these grief vampires, and she wanted to be vindicated for all of the times she told the world Gil was a fraud, but no one believed her. With all of the positive publicity, *skeptic* suddenly wasn't such a dirty word. Claudia was cast as the hero instead of the villain.

She was the good guy, and at last, Gil was the bad guy.

Strangers recognized Claudia in the street and smiled at her. Some gave her the thumbs up or a high five. Others even asked for her autograph. People approached her to share their own experiences with dishonest psychics. One woman came up to her in the checkout line at the supermarket and told Claudia her tragic story.

"My teenage son committed suicide recently and I was just about to spend what little money I have on a psychic medium to communicate with him one last time," she said with tears in her eyes. "Thank you for showing me that this wouldn't bring me closure. Now I can cherish the real memories I have of my son, instead of those made up by a psychic."

Claudia beamed. This made it all worthwhile.

Banachek sent her a text message saying, "Congratulations on a job well done, my friend!"

She also received praise from the skeptical community. Podcasters clamored to interview her about the bust, she was asked to write about her story for magazines, and she was invited to speak at conferences. A publisher approached her to write about her exposé in a tell-all book called *The Truth About Gil Godsend*. People who Claudia disliked over the years, and people who disliked her, were now sucking up to her. Everyone wanted a piece of her.

Other famous psychics seized the opportunity to slam their competitor.

Gil Godsend is a phony but I'm the real thing!
He makes us legitimate psychics look bad.
He was too accurate. That's not how psychic abilities work.
He was far more worried about stardom than cultivating his psychic abilities.
He was a cold reader, not a psychic.
He can call himself a psychic, that doesn't mean he is psychic.
I predicted this was going to happen...

Then there was a hysterical backlash against Gil by his followers. They turned on him with the same fervor they had when they were fans. They attacked him online and some of them started sending him death threats. They stopped buying his books and DVDs, and they cancelled their appointments with him. There were public book burnings and amethyst pendant smashing events that reminded Claudia of fans destroying their records during the 1960s when John Lennon made his comment about The Beatles being more popular than Jesus.

Disgruntled clients came out of the woodwork with their laundry list of complaints against Gil.

His reading was inaccurate.
    His reading was too accurate.

He told me stuff I already knew.
He was too expensive.
I had to wait years to see him.
He was arrogant.
He's a fraud.

There was even talk of criminal and civil actions against him.
But there was no word from Gil. He was laying low.
Claudia had won…or so it seemed…
Within days, the tide turned and Gil's die-hard fans and true believers began to defend their idol. They came out with all kinds of excuses for him.

This is a witch-hunt against Gil led by skeptics.
Gil was framed by rival psychics.
This is a government conspiracy to cover up the fact that psychics exist.
This is a government conspiracy to cover up the fact that psychics exist because they know that aliens exist.
Gil communicated with evil spirits that mislead him during the show.
If you go over the footage of the show you'll see that Gil was still right many times.
Gil had one off night. So what?
He is good at what he does, no matter how he does it.
There were skeptics in the audience and their negativity blocked Gil's psychic energy!

Soon, conspiracy theories arose about the amethyst pendants and the night vision contact lenses.

Gil's enemies planted the skimmers in the pendants.
Gil wasn't cheating; he was using crystal power to do his readings.
Gil was testing the contact lenses for the company that designed the software.
Gil was testing the night vision contact lenses as part of an experiment being conducted by the US military.

I wore a pendant during my reading but Gil said things to me that he could never have found on the Internet.
I smashed my pendant but there wasn't anything inside...
I didn't even wear the amethyst pendant!

Then Gil's fans began attacking Claudia. Again.

She's just a closed-minded skeptic who denies the existence of anything spiritual.
She's been trying to set up Gil for years.
Gil dumped her and she's had a vendetta against him ever since. Hell hath no fury like a woman scorned...
She's a man-hater who makes her living destroying families. Now she's trying to destroy an innocent man's career.
Did you know she was a former porn star? She doesn't have any credibility.

Some of the skeptics turned on Claudia too.

We all knew Gil Godsend was a fraud already. This is old news.
I debunked him years ago myself. She's reinventing the wheel.
Why bother debunking a psychic anyway? Who should we target next, Santa Claus or the tooth fairy?
A set up isn't an ethical thing to do. How is she any better than the psychic? Sure, she exposed Godsend, but she also hurt many innocent people in the process.
We all know she was only doing this so that she could get her own TV show.
Did you know she was a former porn star? She doesn't have any credibility.

It got worse. The women who begged Claudia to expose Gil in the first place got in touch with her again. To her astonishment, this time they criticized her treatment of him and made excuses for his abuse and manipulation.

Dear Ms. Cox,

The more I think back on it the more I know Gil Godsend really was channeling my husband. It was a beautiful way to reconnect with him one last time. I can explain him calling me "Katherine" too – Alex was just trying to prove to me that it was him by saying my full name. Thank you for trying to help, but I think you were a bit harsh on Gil. He was only trying to give me solace and fill the void left by the death of my husband.

Kate Thompson.

Dawn Pierce phoned Claudia and left a message on her voicemail.

Hello Ms. Cox. As you said, the affair was my own fault, not my husband's. It wasn't Gil's fault either. I was caught up in the moment and feeling neglected. I seduced Gil. He made me feel special. Was that so wrong of him? I think that Gil made me believe the worst about my husband so I would be able to see the best in him. Without having my affair I wouldn't have truly appreciated what my husband was doing for me. I now see that all along Gil's plan was to strengthen my marriage.

Rainbow Woods emailed Claudia too.

Ms. Cox,

We met in a coffee shop in Fairfax a while ago and you pretended to be psychic. In hindsight, your sideshow version of a psychic reading wasn't as convincing as Gil Godsend's reading. He knew family secrets and other things about me that he couldn't possibly have Googled! Yes, Gil is a player, but that has nothing to do with whether he's psychic or not, and I believe he is psychic. I hope that one day you too will open your mind to the fact that psychics exist and there is so much we don't know or understand about our beautiful universe.

Rainbow.

Even Abby Cooper emailed Claudia.

Hi Ms. Cox,

I've thought about it a lot and I believe that it was my husband coming through Gil Godsend. It was a safe way for Mark to give me what he thought I wanted. What you said made a lot of sense at the time, but everything Gil predicted has since come true. He told me that my husband had an insurance policy I needed to claim and he was right! I received a payout of $465,000 and now I'm going to college and working in pediatrics. I still believe in the paranormal. Thanks for letting me see the light!

Claudia was appalled. These women had come to her for help and she had done what they'd asked her to do. She had shown them how Gil could have cheated in his readings but they chose to believe instead that his psychic powers were real. Did their beliefs run that deep, or were they in denial? Maybe this was their way of dealing with the trauma. Was it safer for them to believe that Gil was psychic, than to accept that he had mistreated them? Claudia had done the right thing, but now she was the bad guy all over again.

Gil could do no wrong and she could do no right.

Claudia hadn't won. She would never win. She was fighting against Gil's charisma and skills as a con artist. She was fighting against people's hope, belief, and their grief. Death is a potent cocktail of pain, desperation, vulnerability and loneliness, but reason is no cure for the hangover. Death leaves questions, and Gil offered the answers that his fans wanted to hear. He promised to bring back their dead. She threatened to take their dead away all over again.

They needed his powers to be real; otherwise, their loved ones would be gone forever.

"I guess the truth is that psychic powers are as real as you want them to be," Claudia said to no one.

There was no word from Gil. He always knew exactly what to say, and now he knew he didn't need to say anything at all. He didn't need to do anything to salvage his reputation. His fans did it for him.

Claudia busied herself by writing an article that traced her whole history of debunking Gil. She submitted it to *Modern Skeptic* magazine.

To her surprise, a few days later she received a phone call from Martin Phipps, the magazine's editor and publisher.

"That was an excellent article about the Gil Godsend scandal, Claudia," he said in a honeyed voice. "It's current news and I'd like to publish it in the next issue of the magazine."

She was flattered.

"Thank you. That's great news!"

"I've followed your career for a while," he said. "I'm a big fan. Incidentally, I saw your interview with Michael Michaels on *Night Owl*. I never knew that you were a…centerfold."

Why was he bringing this up? It wasn't relevant at all.

"I was exploited by that photographer," she said. "The photographs appeared in that magazine without my permission."

"We all do things we think better of later on," he said with mock wisdom. "But that doesn't mean that it wasn't the right thing to do, and with a body like yours it was *definitely* the right thing to do."

Claudia was caught off guard completely by his sleazy comment.

"I can help your career," he continued. "I'd like to offer you a column in my magazine… *if* you share a copy of the photographs with me."

Claudia was speechless.

How could such a well-known and respected skeptic be skeptical when it comes to ghosts, psychics, and Bigfoot, but not skeptical about himself? How could this guy set himself up as an authority about morals and ethics, but have such a blind spot about his own unethical behavior? Just when Claudia thought she was making a difference, after all her years of hard work, instead of being recognized for her brain this slimy prick was salivating over her body and trying to entice her with a job offer in exchange for a titty shot.

This was quid pro quo harassment.

"I have a better idea," she said. "Why don't you go and fuck yourself? You dirty old man…"

She hung up on him.

In that moment, she hated both believers *and* skeptics.

They almost made Gil look good in comparison.

Claudia started thinking about Gil. She remembered the times he knew personal things about her that he couldn't possibly have researched, and when he made predictions about the future that became true. She could explain them all away, couldn't she? Or did she try to debunk Gil all of these years just to confirm her own biases? Was she only remembering the hits as she saw them, that is, the times when he made mistakes, but ignoring her own misses, when he was right?

Sure, she'd caught him red-handed this time, but he hadn't always used skimmers and night vision contact lenses. This was new technology. Was this scam a calculated move on his behalf? Was it just another prank, like the show where he pretended to be using an earpiece? Did Gil know she was going to expose him all along, and did he just let it happen?

What if Gil really was psychic? What if ghosts actually do exist? What if there is a Bigfoot? What if... Could these things be true? In her search for truth shouldn't she acknowledge that she could be wrong about things she was convinced she was right about? Shouldn't skeptics be skeptical of themselves?

Belief in the paranormal is common, not unusual. As a skeptic, she was in the minority, not the majority. The realization that she could be mistaken threw her into a feeling of vertigo in which she suddenly understood clearly how and why people believe. It all made sense.

...Or was something else going on with Gil? Her mind played devil's advocate.

She could see him walking beside her on the beach in Australia, rubbing his forehead and complaining of headaches. She could see him sitting across from her at the restaurant the night before the final show, massaging his temples and still complaining of headaches. Did he have some sort of condition, a tumor, or a brain injury that was affecting his thinking and behavior? Gil's words at the end of his final show echoed in her head.

I need to turn the voices off.

Was he experiencing hallucinations and delusions? That would explain why he was hearing voices that no one else could hear and seeing things that no one else could see. That might also explain his paranoia and desperation to get away. Kate and Abby both believed that his body was taken over by the spirits of their deceased husbands. They said he'd suffered seizure-like attacks and afterwards he couldn't remember what had happened. Sure it sounded self-serving at the time, and that may be the case still, or did he have a mental illness? Were these voices commanding him to perform these destructive acts? Did he stay in a drug rehabilitation clinic as a youth, or was he really a patient in a psychiatric hospital? When people hear voices they're diagnosed as schizophrenic and put on antipsychotic medication to stop the voices. Was Gil celebrated for this instead?

Was his "gift" really a curse?

Claudia remembered the Gil she knew when they were together. He believed he was psychic, but he hadn't completely lost touch with reality. He wasn't a monster back then. He was a different man. He was sweet and kind and loving. It didn't work out because they had a different outlook on life. But should she have stayed with Gil all those years ago? Perhaps she could have protected him from himself. Or was she looking for a way to absolve Gil in her own mind because she still had feelings for him?

Claudia didn't feel well in the stomach. If anything, the pain was getting worse, so she took some painkillers and hit the sack. As she lay in bed in the darkness she heard her phone ping and the room lit up from the glow of her phone.

It was a text message from Gil.

He said simply, "Claudia, see a doctor immediately. Please."

She stared at the message for a while, and then replied, "I will if you will."

Chapter 33

Claudia woke up feeling sharp cramps on the right side of her stomach. She wondered if she had gastroenteritis or appendicitis. Maybe she was about to get her period, but she'd never had menstrual pains this severe before. When was her last period anyway? It seemed to be late by a few days, if not a few weeks.

Gil's words echoed in her mind.

Did you know that you're pregnant?

She gave a little laugh. That was impossible.

She finally roused herself to get out of bed and get dressed. She wasn't going into work that day, she felt too sick for that, but she made a visit to the pharmacy to buy some medication for her upset stomach. In the store she peeked down the aisle where they kept the pregnancy tests, but she hurried past in search of a hot water bottle. She didn't often listen to her intuition, but a nagging voice inside kept telling her that something wasn't right. She dashed back to the women's health aisle where there was a confusing array of pregnancy tests. One was probably as good as another, she thought, so she grabbed a box and headed towards the checkout.

As soon as she entered the front door of her apartment she ripped open the pregnancy test and read the instructions. She whisked off her jeans and panties and threw them aside. She tried to pee on the stick both sitting down and standing up but her aim wasn't very precise and she made a mess all over the toilet seat and the floor.

Pregnancy tests were designed for men, she thought.

When she was done she closed the toilet lid and sat down on it. She held the test stick and stared at the window in which there was a pink control line.

The idea that she was pregnant was ridiculous. She wore an IUD and she and Jeremy used condoms as a backup. Why was she even bothering to do a pregnancy test? Well, she wanted to prove Gil wrong. Her period was definitely late, but there were lots of possible explanations for that.

She had been under a lot of stress the past few months.

Claudia watched the window and waited for five whole minutes...but no second pink line appeared.

She breathed a sigh of relief and tossed the stick into the trashcan.

Gil was wrong! But of course he was. He certainly wasn't psychic. She must have a stomach bug after all. She would visit a doctor in a day or two if she didn't start to feel better. She popped a few pills and crawled back into bed clutching her hot water bottle.

Her bed was warm and cozy and she fell asleep quickly. Soon she began to dream. She dreamed that she and Gil were together in a Catholic church. It was nighttime and the church was candlelit, giving an eerie glow to the room. They sat on a pew, facing each other as they played a game of Go Fish.

Claudia was annoyed with Gil because he kept predicting her cards.

"Give me that four you've got in your hand," he said with a grin.

Claudia rolled her eyes and threw the card at him.

"I took a pregnancy test, Gil," she said. "Do you want to know the result?"

"The pregnancy test is a modern invention, but for millennia, women have used various methods to try to determine whether they were pregnant or not," he said, ignoring her question. "In ancient Egypt, women believed to be pregnant urinated on wheat and barley seeds. If the wheat grew, she was having a girl. If the barely grew, she was having a boy. If neither plant sprouted, then she wasn't pregnant. In ancient Greece, if a woman suspected she was pregnant she would insert an onion into her vagina and leave it there overnight. If she had onion breath the next morning, she believed she was pregnant... and I'll take that nine you have too..."

Claudia shook her head at his weird little lecture.

"You're good at predicting cards," she said as she flicked the card at him, "but you're bad at predicting the results of pregnancy tests. It was negative. You were *wrong*."

Gil looked at her with his piercing blue eyes and threw down a card.

Claudia looked at it. It was a Queen.

She looked up at Gil quizzically.

"Look again, Claudia," he said, his deep voice echoing around the church.

She looked at the card again. It was a Joker.

Claudia woke up with a start. Wow! That was a bizarre dream... But she didn't assign any significance to it. It was just a brain dump. Besides, she had more pressing matters to which she had to attend. Her stomach still hurt and she needed to go to the toilet. She stumbled into the bathroom and flicked on the light switch. As she sat down on the toilet she saw the test sitting in the trashcan.

Look again, Claudia.

She fished out the stick and stared at it blearily. Wait... was that a second pink line in the test window? She rubbed her eyes and looked again. Yes, there was a second line.

No. It was impossible. No.

She was in denial. It must be a false positive, she thought. Had she done the test the wrong way? Maybe it was an evaporation line or the product was past its expiration date. Maybe she was reading it the wrong way. She read the instructions again. No, she did everything correctly, if messily. Then she held up the stick to the bathroom light. She took it into the living room and held it under a lamp. She looked at it under the kitchen lighting. She shined a flashlight on it. Every time she checked the second pink line was clearly visible. There was no doubt about it, the pregnancy test was positive.

She was pregnant.

Okay, she admitted to herself that she felt nauseous, tired, and a little moody. She was definitely going to the bathroom more often. She did have some food aversions...and maybe her breasts were a little bigger...

Then Claudia remembered Gil's text message from the night before.

Claudia, see a doctor immediately. Please.

That was sensible advice, she thought. She knew that pregnancy symptoms were normal, but surely all of this pain couldn't be a good sign. Perhaps she should see a doctor, just to confirm the pregnancy and make sure everything was okay.

Claudia called her gynecologist, Dr. Fritz, and spoke with a nurse who seemed alarmed by her symptoms and told her to come into the office right away. Within an hour she was sitting on a bed in a treatment room under bright fluorescent lights. She was naked except for a hospital gown and a pair of socks.

"Doctor, you know I wear an IUD," Claudia said. "We also used condoms every time we had sex. How could I possibly be pregnant?"

"No method is foolproof. The only birth control that is 100% effective is abstinence," Dr. Fritz said in a well-rehearsed tone. "Please lie down. I'm going to give you a pelvic exam."

She started pressing down on the right side of Claudia's stomach.

"Ow!" Claudia cried out, wincing at the stabbing pain.

Dr. Fritz looked concerned.

"I'm ordering some blood tests and then we'll know more. I'll be back soon."

A nurse came into the room, took a few vials of blood, and left Claudia alone to wait for the results. She stared around the walls at the diagrams of the female reproductive system, the pregnancy posters, and the racks of parenting magazines. She had always wanted to have kids, but she kept putting it off. Well, having a boyfriend would have been a good start. Many of her friends already had babies, while those who didn't were desperately seeking fertility treatments. They would do anything to be pregnant. She didn't want to leave it too late. Sure, she could hear her biological clock ticking, and loudly at times, but she was always busy doing something. It never seemed to be the right time. Now would have to be the right time to have a baby, whether she was ready or not.

She took a deep breath and made her decision. She would keep this baby!

Claudia thought about all of the changes she needed to make in her life to become a responsible parent. She had to start thinking about prenatal care and childbirth classes. She would begin taking prenatal vitamins immediately, cut back on coffee, and stop drinking alcohol, although she already had an aversion to it. She exercised and had a healthy diet as a rule, but now she needed to avoid raw fish and unpasteurized cheeses. She thought of that night with Gil at the restaurant when he ordered the cheese platter without the soft cheeses. She gave a little laugh.

She couldn't wait to spill the beans to everyone! When would she announce her pregnancy? She heard it was good form to wait until the second trimester to make sure everything was okay, but she needed to tell Jeremy as soon as possible. He was the father. He had a right to know. What was the proper etiquette for having a vacation fling that resulted in pregnancy?

Claudia fantasized about being pregnant. She pictured herself wearing a maternity dress, her hands wrapped protectively around her baby bump. She wondered if she was having a boy or a girl, or should she keep it a surprise until the birth? She didn't think she could wait that long to find out because she needed to start writing a list of baby names. She had always liked Charlotte for a girl, or Aiden for a boy. She imagined herself shopping for baby toys, for rattles and teddy bears, and buying baby clothes and tiny baby shoes. She could see herself celebrating with her friends and family at her baby shower, gushing over their gifts and laughing as they ate cake and played silly games. She daydreamed of being with Jeremy and seeing her baby's heartbeat on an ultrasound. She saw his hands on her stomach and the joy in his vivid green eyes as they felt the baby kick for the first time. She could see herself lying in a hospital bed after her labor with Jeremy's arms around her. She looked tired and sweaty yet deliriously happy as she held and kissed her precious newborn.

Her heart skipped a beat. She could do this. She wanted this.

"I'm pregnant," she said nervously, an excited smile spreading across her face.

It *was* the right time to have a baby.

Finally, Dr. Fritz came back into the room with her results.

"You're pregnant," she confirmed.

But there were no congratulations. Claudia could tell that something was wrong.

"Based on the date of your last period you're about 8 weeks along, but your HCG levels are low for where they should be," said Dr. Fritz. "I'm going to do an ultrasound."

She disappeared and returned wheeling a portable ultrasound machine into the room. Claudia was afraid but she tried to keep calm. Everything would be fine. She lifted up her hospital gown, bracing herself for cold gel to be squirted across her stomach.

"It's too early for an abdominal ultrasound," Dr. Fritz said apologetically as she slid a condom over a probe. "I need you to put your feet into the stirrups."

Claudia shuffled down into place and stared at the monitor. She could see a black circle. Was that her uterus? An ovary? She could never decipher those shadowy images.

Dr. Fritz was silent for the longest time and it made Claudia more nervous.

"It's just as I'd feared," the doctor said. "There's no gestational sac in your uterus, but I can see a mass near your right fallopian tube."

Claudia didn't know what was going on, but judging by the tone of the doctor's voice, it didn't sound good.

"What does this mean?"

"I'm sorry," Dr. Fritz said softly. "You have an ectopic pregnancy. This is when a fertilized egg attaches outside of the uterus. Pregnancy when using an IUD is rare, but when it happens it's more likely to be ectopic. Unfortunately, it's not a viable pregnancy."

Claudia felt tears welling up in her eyes.

"What happens next?" she asked.

Her voice sounded strange to her.

"Often we can use medication to terminate an ectopic pregnancy, but this is an advanced case. You're probably going to need emergency surgery. It looks like the embryo has implanted in your fallopian tube and you're experiencing a lot of pain. The tube might rupture and you could… well, let's just say that I'm glad you came in to see me when you did."

Claudia was in a state of shock.

Now *wasn't* the right time to have a baby.

Claudia was rushed to hospital. The next few hours were a whirlwind of cold hospital rooms and a barrage of tests, while kind doctors and nurses hovered over her in a panic. She was feeling worse. She had developed a fever, her blood pressure was very low and she was light headed. She started having pains in her shoulder and back.

Everything was happening too fast. She wished Jeremy was there with her.

She felt sad, scared, and alone.

As she sat there in a daze her phone pinged. It was a text message from Gil.

"You're not alone. I'm with you."

Did he know what was happening? How did he know? She didn't have time to think about it any further. She was wheeled off to the operating room and prepped for surgery. She stared up at the ceiling with tears in her eyes until she went under the anesthetic.

Hours later Claudia woke up in the recovery room feeling sore and disoriented. A doctor pulled back the curtain railing of her cubicle and explained what had happened during the surgery. She had been given an emergency laparotomy. Dr. Fritz's diagnosis was correct; Claudia had an embryo that had implanted in her right fallopian tube instead of her womb. When they opened her up they found that the tube had ruptured and she was bleeding internally, which explained why she had been in so much pain. The tube and ovary were so damaged they had to be removed.

She was lucky to be alive.

Claudia was transferred to a private room where she lay in bed, deep in thought. Now that her ordeal was over should she confide in anyone about this? She'd told her receptionist, but did anyone else need to know? Should she tell Jeremy? He had been the father. Didn't he have a right to know? What was the proper etiquette for having a vacation fling that resulted in an ectopic pregnancy and emergency termination surgery?

Before she told anyone else she needed to come to terms with the situation herself. She barely had time to process what had just happened to her. That morning she didn't even know she was pregnant. Then she suddenly was, but now she wasn't. Not only had she lost her baby, she had also lost half of her reproductive organs. She blamed herself. She should have paid better attention to her body. Maybe she could have prevented this from happening. Claudia felt empty and lost. Nothing could have prepared her for this and it was going to take her some time to get over the experience.

Her body ached, but her heart was aching more.

Her nurse, Nicole, brought her a meal on a tray and Claudia asked her for some painkillers and a sedative. She nibbled on a piece of dry toast and sipped a cup of tea. She watched some television and flicked through a trashy magazine until she finally felt sleepy. It had been a long day and she tried not to think anymore, but she had one final thought before she drifted off into sleep.

How did Gil know that she was pregnant?

When Claudia awoke from a short nap she was startled to find Gil sitting on the bed and holding her hand.

"What are you doing here?" she asked as she tried to sit up.

"I'm here to see you."

The genuine concern in his eyes reminded her of the days when they were in love. All of a sudden she felt overwhelmed by her emotions and on the verge of tears.

"I… lost my baby."

She burst into tears. He took her in his arms and cradled her gently as she cried into his shoulder. She let him. She needed someone.

"I'm so sorry," he said softly. "But it's okay, we'll have more children."

She pulled back from him. Her eyes could barely stay focused and she was cloudy from the medication.

"How did I know that you were pregnant?" she slurred. "How did I know that you were sick? How did I know that you were in the hospital? And what do you mean, "*We'll* have more children"?" she demanded drowsily.

He brushed the hair out of her eyes and caressed her cheek.

"Don't worry about anything, Claudia," he comforted her. "Everything will be okay, I promise. For now, you need to get some more rest."

He kissed her on her forehead and she fell asleep again.

When she woke up later Gil was gone. Her memory was such a blur that she wondered if he really had been in her room or not. Maybe it was just another whacky dream.

Chapter 34

Claudia awoke from a night of restless sleep. At first, it seemed she was waking up from a bad dream, but then she remembered the events of the day before and her heart sank. She had lost her baby.

She felt dazed and weak and her vision was blurry. She fought to open her eyes and as she did she could see the silhouette of a man sitting beside her. Oh, for fuck's sake. What was Gil doing here again? Couldn't he just leave her alone? She was recuperating from surgery and she wanted to be by herself for a while.

"Why are you here again?" she asked in frustration.

There was a pause. She'd offended him. Good.

"But I thought you'd be glad to see your Australian translator!"

Her heart skipped a beat.

"Jeremy?"

"You're supposed to say, "G'day mate"!"

Hearing his cheerful, laid-back voice was soothing to her, like sinking into a warm bath.

Her eyes focused and she could see him. He gave her a tired smile and ran his hand through his unruly curls. He wore a crumpled pin-stripe suit. The top button of his shirt was undone and his tie was loosened. His suitcase and laptop bag were on the floor beside him. She was relieved and excited that it was Jeremy, and not Gil. She had missed him so much, and especially now.

"Jeremy!"

"Hi, sweetheart," he said as he kissed her gently on the forehead. Today he didn't smell like the ocean or coconut surfboard wax, he smelled fresh and earthy, like the air after a light rain.

"What are you doing here?"

"I just finished my contract in Hong Kong and I'm on a 5-hour layover in SFO before I head on to Chicago for a week," he explained. "I wanted to surprise you with a visit. When you weren't at home or answering your phone I was worried. I went to your office and your receptionist told me what had happened. I was...devastated," he said with tears in his eyes.

"I'm sorry I didn't tell you," she said sadly. "I wanted to, but it all happened so fast. I did a home pregnancy test yesterday morning and it was positive. I was in shock. I was also in a lot of pain so I went to the doctor and before I knew it I was in surgery."

He squeezed her hand.

"I'm sorry you went through this alone."

"That's okay," she said. "I can handle it. I've been alone a long time."

This made him feel sad. He'd been alone a long time too.

"I want to talk to you about that," he said. "But first, are you okay?"

"I'm okay, but I'm not at my best," she said apologetically.

Claudia looked around her. She was a mess. She was hooked up to various machines and there was a bedpan sitting on a side table. An untouched cup of tea and a slice of toast with a bite taken out of it sat on a tray beside her. She was wearing a pink hospital gown with nothing underneath and she wore a pair of beige slipper socks. She hadn't showered for two days or brushed her teeth, and she wasn't wearing any makeup. She was very embarrassed by her appearance. The first time she saw Jeremy she was totally overdressed and today she was completely underdressed.

He didn't notice any of that. Her natural beauty held him captivated. He gazed at her clear, bare skin and flushed cheeks. Her hazel eyes seemed honey-colored against her untamed auburn hair. She looked raw, natural, and flawless.

"This is the first time I've seen you without makeup," he said, "and you've never looked more beautiful to me than you do now."

Claudia didn't believe him but she didn't want to spoil the moment so she accepted his compliment. Then she noticed a massive bunch of red roses on the table beside her bed.

"Those roses are beautiful!" she shrieked. "Thank you! You shouldn't have..."

He looked down at the floor.

"I didn't," he admitted sheepishly. "They're not from me."

Claudia should have known. It was an ostentatious gesture that smacked of Gil Godsend. Clearly Gil *had* been there in her room. It wasn't just another whacky dream.

"But I did bring you this," he said as he reached into his suitcase and pulled out a plush stuffed koala. "I saw it at the airport the day we said goodbye, and it reminded me of how much you loved petting the koalas at the zoo. I bought it for you and I've carried it around with me since then, waiting for the day I could give it to you in person."

She was moved. This meant far more to her than an expensive bunch of roses. It was thoughtful and genuine.

"That's very sweet of you," she said as she took the toy from him and cuddled it. "Thank you."

Jeremy took a deep breath and loosened his tie some more.

"Claudia, you thought I was someone else when you woke up, and here's this enormous bunch of red roses. I'm guessing they're from that Gil Gottfried bloke."

His joke came out sounding more bitter than he had intended.

"Look, if you guys have something going on then I can step aside," he said. "I'll understand. Just let me know."

This did look bad. Gil had been pursuing her and if she was honest with herself, she'd had fleeting moments when she had wondered, what if? Gil was trying to reel her back in again, but she was resisting him. She felt guilty that she'd mistaken Jeremy for Gil when she woke up, but didn't he notice that she had sounded irritable, not happy, when she thought Gil was there? Also, she had mistakenly thought that the roses were from Jeremy, not Gil. Surely these things showed her true feelings.

Gil was her past.

"Gil was here just to say goodbye," she explained. "He's leaving the country, he didn't even tell me where he's traveling to. Believe me, there's *nothing* going on between him and me."

She was adamant.

Jeremy looked relieved. He cleared his throat.

"Claudia," he said cautiously, "When we said goodbye I realized that my feelings for you were very strong. I thought, don't be a mug, this is just a holiday romance, but I haven't been able to stop thinking about you. The time we spent together gave me some of the best memories of my life and I'd... I'd like to make more memories with you."

He paused. She stiffened. Was he going to ask her to marry him? Surely this was too soon…

"I… want to find a way for us to be together," he said. "I want to give a relationship with you a fair go. I want to see what happens."

Claudia's heart soared. This was exactly what she wanted.

"I feel the same way too," she said.

A smile spread across his face.

"But…"

His smile fell.

"…But I'm concerned because our lives are so complicated," she continued. "Long distance relationships are difficult. We live in different countries and you're always traveling."

This was the reason his last relationship failed, she thought warily.

"I'm tired of being on the road all the time. I'm bloody sick of living out of suitcases in hotel rooms," he said with a nod towards his bags on the floor. "I'm home so rarely that my own apartment looks like a hotel room. I want a home… I want a family."

That stung them both a little, knowing what they'd just lost.

"I'm prepared for the effort it'll take to make this work," said Claudia. "Are you?"

"I am," he replied. "I'll take some time off from work so we can be together, or I'll get a transfer to our San Francisco office. I'll do whatever it takes. I don't want to lose you," he said. His eye contact was steady but soft. "What's just happened to you…to *us*…has only proven to me that life is too short and I need to follow my heart."

That's exactly what her father would have said.

Jeremy was right. Life was too short. She had been wasting time trying to help people who didn't want her help. In her job she had been experiencing the heartbreak of relationships without getting to experience the joy that relationships can bring. She needed to take happiness where she could find it, and her happiness was with him.

Gil was her past.

Jeremy was her future.

"Okay," she answered, lost in thought. Then she realized how half-hearted that sounded. "I mean *yes*," she said with certainty. "Yes!"

Jeremy's vivid green eyes lit up. He wanted to pick her up and dance with her around the room, but she was too fragile for that right now. Instead he kissed her cheek and hugged her.

He checked his watch.

"Shit! If I don't leave for the airport right now I'm going to miss my flight," he said. "But you have no idea how much I want to stay here and take care of you."

Claudia wanted him to stay too. She didn't want to go back to an empty apartment. She pictured herself going home with Jeremy. She saw herself snuggling up to him on the couch as they watched a movie together. She felt his warm body up against hers in bed at night. She smelled the delicious breakfasts he would cook for them every morning. He seemed to be thinking the same things.

"Just say the word and I'll stay," he said.

Please stay, she thought.

But she wanted to be strong. She didn't want to be a burden to him. She also didn't want to be the reason he lost his job. They would sort it all out in time.

"Go catch your flight," she said regretfully. "I'm just going to be laid up in bed all week."

He hesitated.

"Are you sure?"

"...Yes..."

"Okay," he said reluctantly. "But I'll call you when I land in Chicago."

Jeremy kissed Claudia goodbye, but only goodbye for now, and he left.

Her body still ached, but her heart wasn't aching as much anymore.

Then Claudia was alone again. She sighed, clutched her toy koala, and looked around the room. She saw the huge bunch of red roses. It would have been a kind and loving gesture if they had been from Jeremy, but because they were from Gil it felt like an attempt at manipulation. What did Gil want from her? Well, she knew what he wanted.

He wanted her.

She spied a small card among the flowers. She reached over to get it, and hurt her side as she did so. Damn you, Gil. She opened up the card but there were no words inside, just a long telephone number written in Gil's handwriting.

    She googled the prefix and traced the number to Belize.

Chapter 35

Claudia sat on the edge of her hospital bed. She was finally going home today!

She had taken a shower, brushed her teeth, and changed out of her hospital gown back into her own clothes. Her appetite had returned and she was eager to get out of hospital and have a latte and a blueberry muffin. She almost felt human again.

Her doctor paid her a final visit and he was pleased with her progress. She was ready to be discharged. Despite the ectopic pregnancy, and losing a tube and an ovary, he told her that she would likely be able to have a healthy pregnancy in future, if she decided to ditch the birth control.

Maybe I'll be leaving the hospital with a baby in my arms next time, she hoped.

As she waited for nurse Nicole to discharge her, Claudia flicked through the morning's newspaper. One headline in particular caught her eye.

Night Owl Host Charged with Sexual Assault.

According to the article, veteran talk show host Michael Michaels had been arrested and charged with multiple counts of sexual assault. But this was just the tip of the iceberg. The news emboldened a parade of other women to come forward with their stories of harassment and assault at his hands. They were celebrities, interns, and even his dry cleaner. Where there is one there are usually others, and there is strength in numbers. The police urged other victims to speak up.

Claudia wondered if she should speak up too.

His Modus Operandi was to make inappropriate sexual advances towards his female guests before their appearance on his show, with the promise that he would further their careers if they would go on a date with him. He did research and background checks on all of them and if a woman refused to go out with him, he revealed her dark secrets, and some lies, during her interview and damaged her reputation publicly. This story sounded familiar to Claudia. If the woman agreed to go out with him, he gave her good publicity on the show. Afterwards, he took her out for a drink, got her liquored up, and then dragged her back to his place where he sexually assaulted her.

It seemed that Claudia dodged a bullet.

One victim was fellow talk show host Julie Davenport who appeared on *Night Owl* the week before Claudia did. Julie took up his offer and went on a date with him after the show. When they got back to his place he pressed her up against a wall, choked her, slapped her across the face several times and then had sex with her.

Claudia didn't like Julie at all, but she believed that no woman should have to go through that.

Of course, Michaels denied the allegations, saying that all of these women had consensual "rough sex" with him, of the kind found in erotic romance novels. He became the victim. He complained that he was the target of disgruntled and jealous ex-lovers who were angry because they could never "win" him.

The reporter investigated Michaels and dug up a lot of dirt on him.

He had a 20-year-old criminal record for frotteurism. As a teenager he had been caught rubbing his genitalia against women's thighs and bottoms on a crowded BART train. When he was imprisoned overnight he tried to do it to a fellow prisoner. He was put on probation for a year and ordered to undergo psychiatric counseling. A year later he was caught doing it again at a shopping mall in the food court.

His ex-wife also revealed his fetish for domination and sadism that supported the victims' claims. She wasn't interested in that sort of thing herself, not that it stopped him from doing it to her, and so she divorced him. With no outlet for his obsession he started seeing prostitutes and dominatrices around the Bay Area. That is, until he had enough celebrity power that he could abuse it. According to his wife, he had a large collection of clothes pegs too, although she didn't know what he did with them. It was just another weird thing about him.

When media reports of the scandal first emerged, the television network fired Michaels from his job. They also dismissed his long-term producer Peter Peters, for covering up for him all of these years. With Michaels gone, Julie Davenport was offered the role of hosting

Night Owl although her response was, "No thanks. Nobody watches that show!"

Michaels' lawyer said his client would be pleading not guilty and that he planned to launch a lawsuit for defamation against the network and his victims. Michaels was granted bail, set at $100,000, on the condition that he surrender his passport and live with his mother while the case was heard. He was forced to wear an electronic tag around his ankle while he was under house arrest at his mommy's house.

Whose credibility was damaged now?

Claudia smiled to herself. She didn't believe in karma or the Law of Cause and Effect. Poetic justice is for fiction. People don't always reap what they sow, and what goes around doesn't always come around, but occasionally, when bad people keep doing bad things, they eventually get caught…

After she was discharged, Claudia presented the enormous bunch of red roses to nurse Nicole.

"These are for you from that sharp-dressed guy who was here the other day," she said.

"You mean Gil Godsend?" Nicole cried, patting her chest in surprise.

"That's him!"

"They're beautiful! So… you're not with him?" she asked carefully.

"Absolutely not."

"Oh my," she said as she checked the card and saw the telephone number written inside.

Then Claudia left the hospital and went home.

Chapter 36

It had been three months since her surgery and things were going well for Claudia. Her business was flourishing and so was her bank account. Jeremy was in her life. He had already made three trips to visit her in San Francisco. Gil was finally out of her life. She hadn't heard from him since he visited her in the hospital. Everything was great, although she felt like something was missing. She couldn't put her finger on what that was.

One morning, Claudia was making herself a breakfast burrito when she received a call from Banachek. He had been away on tour so she hadn't heard from him in months.

"Hello, my friend."

"Hi Banachek!" she said excitedly. "Long time, no hear. What crazy place are you in today? Kathmandu? Timbuktu?"

"I'm in the craziest place I've ever been!" he replied.

'Where's that?"

"San Francisco!" he said with a laugh. "How about we meet up for dinner tonight?"

That night, Claudia and Banachek met at Cha Cha Cha, a South American restaurant in the Haight-Ashbury district of San Francisco. The place was decked out like it was carnival time, with masks, beads, paper lanterns, and string lights. The brightly painted walls were lined with Santeria shrines decorated with offerings to the saints. The room was packed with people enjoying seafood paella and pitchers of sangria while they talked loudly to compete with the pulse of salsa music.

Claudia hadn't seen her friend in years and it was a happy reunion.

They toasted Gil's downfall with glasses of sangria.

"First of all, nice job busting Gil Godsend!" Banachek praised her, as their server brought over a plate of plantains with black beans and sour cream. "I'm very proud of you. I couldn't have done a better job myself."

"Thank you," she blushed. She was flattered to hear this from her hero. "Your support was far more valuable than you'll ever know. It really got me through this."

"I was happy to help," he said. "I only wish I could have seen the look on Gil's face when he realized he was busted."

"I imagine it was similar to Jimmy Lee Mercy's expression when you busted him!" Claudia said with a smile. Then the smile disappeared from her face. "You know, it was really strange. At first I had a lot of public support for what I did but within a few days people turned on a dime. They went from attacking Gil and praising me to attacking me and defending him."

"That's what I wanted to talk with you about," Banachek said grimly.

The salsa song ended and the din in the room died down. He looked to the floor and shook his head. The atmosphere suddenly turned dark and ominous. Claudia looked around the room and whereas before she noticed the upbeat colors and bright lights, now the macabre décor leaped out at her instead, the evil eyes, black candles, and skulls.

She felt uneasy.

"Okay..." she said hesitantly.

"When I told you about the Reverend Doctor Jimmy Lee Mercy I never got to finish the story," he said. "After Jimmy Lee was exposed as a fraud, he made a comeback." Banachek leaned back into his chair and sighed heavily. The music started again, but now it was more somber. "Well, he never really made a comeback because he never really left..."

Banachek and his team had uncovered a shocking tale of trickery and deceit on the part of the Reverend Doctor Jimmy Lee Mercy who had used his religious authority to mislead millions of people. His followers believed that he received divine revelations from God during his faith healing services. It turned out that he wasn't hearing the voice of God; he was hearing the voice of his wife who passed on personal information about members of the audience. Jimmy Lee was exposed as a con artist on national television and his ministry went bankrupt.

After Jimmy Lee was revealed to be a charlatan he fled the country. He lay low for a year or so, but he was eventually tracked down to South America like he was a Nazi criminal in hiding at the end of World War II. He settled down in Noiva do Cordeiro, a remote farming village in the south-east of Brazil that was known for its sweet tangerines, banana plantations, and bougainvillea plants. Soon the village also became known for healing. It was God's will that Jimmy Lee begin faith healing again.

He grew his hair long, he grew a beard, and he donned a linen suit in white, the color of spirituality, truth, and purity. Jimmy Lee Mercy transformed into Diego de Deus, or James of God, and he founded the Casa de Amor, a spiritual healing sanctuary.

His fame spread quickly.

James of God was believed to be a modern day Jesus who could cure everything from cancer to blindness, although he was very humble about his gift.

"I do not cure anybody," he said. "I am merely an instrument in God's divine hands," he said with a slight southern accent.

From around the world, thousands of people made pilgrimages to the Casa de Amor every week to be healed. The steady stream of visitors also dressed in white clothing as they waited for hours or even days to be received by James of God. During the healing session, he prayed as he stroked his hands down the person's body, casting out the evil spirits causing the disease. He became known as The Stroker for this healing technique.

James of God was said to heal a million people every year. He didn't charge a fee for his services, although he welcomed donations. He also prescribed an obscure herb to every person he saw. Fortunately, this herbal remedy was available from his sanctuary.

James of God's time in Brazil wasn't without scrutiny. He was ordered to stop his activities by the Roman Catholic Church, but he argued they had no authority over him, only God did. On several occasions he was arrested for practicing without a medical license, but he argued that he wasn't a medical doctor, he was a spiritual healer, and they had no authority over him, only God did.

Following the deaths of several of his acolytes, the herbal remedy was tested and found to contain *Psilocybe Mexicana*, the hallucinogenic mushroom.

Then James of God was accused of molesting one of his patients. He performed spiritual surgery on a woman's breasts although she suffered from a brain tumor. It seemed as though he always stroked the breasts of his female patients regardless of what ailed them.

Noiva do Cordeiro was infamous for having a disproportionate population of women, and they all needed healing. Mercy fathered four children during his time in the village, and each child to a different mother. It was here that he met his fifth wife, Maria Susana, who was thirty years his junior.

Ten years later, Jimmy Lee Mercy left Brazil. He had been the subject of too many scandals during his time there, and besides, he couldn't watch *The Young and the Restless* and Brazilian supermarkets didn't stock cheese in a can. He resurfaced in the United States and founded Mercy Ministries in Sebastopol, California. He ditched the bumpkin-sounding Jimmy Lee in favor of the more sophisticated Reverend Doctor James Mercy. He cut his hair short, shaved off his beard, dumped his white clothes and started wearing fine suits. He was a little greyer although he was still as handsome and charismatic as ever.

He was born again.

Then he began to resurrect his career.

Mercy was soon back to his old tricks, but with a new twist. He began peddling "miracle spring water" during early morning and late night broadcasts on popular cable TV programs. He claimed the miracle water was drawn from a spring in Japan, near the site of the Fukushima Daiichi nuclear disaster. Miraculously, animals and people who drank from the spring were spared radiation sickness. He told his audience that drinking the water would provide miraculous protection from sickness for them too, and also eliminate their debts, repel curses, and attract blessings from God.

"This miracle spring water is a spiritual detox for your soul," he promised.

In their droves, people sent in their hard-earned money and gave testimonials of the water's power, even though it was tested independently and shown to be tap water.

With his success in merchandizing god, Mercy branched out into holy relics. He began selling blessed coins, holy crosses, hallowed anointing oil, miraculous rings, sacred shoe liners, divine Dead Sea salt, and prayer handkerchiefs impregnated with Mercy's sanctified sweat. He said that he mopped his brow personally with each piece.

"I give these gifts free to anyone seeking the love of Christ!" he said.

Sure, they were free to receive, but to unlock their miraculous powers you had to donate money to Mercy first.

"Give, and it will be given to you (Luke 6:38)," he added.

Once people donated money they didn't receive their miracles, but they did receive numerous solicitation letters requesting more money.

The divine Dead Sea salt was tested independently and proven to be table salt instead, but this didn't affect sales because you can't test scientifically for God's glory.

Then Mercy Ministries turned commercial and produced a line of holy grocery items.

"Jesus should be in your heart! Jesus should be in your mind and your thoughts! And now, with my line of food products, Jesus can be in your stomach too," he said.

He sold a selection of breads, bagels, pastries, and tortillas under the label Our Daily Bread. There was a range of breakfast foods and cereals, catering to different denominations, including Pope Tarts, Lord Loops, Second Coming Crunch, Cruci-Chex, Raisin' the Dead Bran, Special †, Pro Life, and Prayer Puffs. They manufactured laundry detergent, dishwashing liquid, soap and other cleaning supplies to wash away your stains, and your sins. They even had a line of personal care items, such as deodorant, feminine products, and Blood of Christ-flavored toothpaste. His foray into groceries ended when it was discovered that Khrist Krispies contained *Psilocybe Mexicana*, the hallucinogenic mushroom.

With the advent of the Internet, Mercy decided he would corner the online religious market. His new mission, Virtually God Ministries, was the first to offer live interactive prayer, chat room confessionals and on demand sermons.

"Now you can sleep in on Sunday mornings and praise the Lord in your pajamas!" he said.

Doing away with the prayer request box, Mercy Ministries accepted online prayer requests, promising that a virtual congregation of millions would pray for each request until it was fulfilled, for a small fee. Mercy Ministries was also the first organization to offer instant ordination. This became so popular that they began to sell other titles, including exorcist, archbishop, cardinal, and even sainthoods for people who were dead or alive.

"Because you deserve a sainthood," he said.

Mercy preached that if you believe in God, you have to believe in Satan too.

"Not believing in the devil won't protect you from him," he warned.

He believed that the devil was actively at work in the world. For Mercy, there was a demon lurking around every corner. Sickness, poverty, relationship problems, and bad luck were all curses caused by demons.

"Everyone is possessed by the devil!" he cried.

Everybody was possessed by the devil, except Mercy, of course. He claimed to be the world's leading exorcist and that he had dealt with more demons than anyone on the planet. To cast out the demons that attack and destroy Christians, Mercy offered exorcisms in person, on the phone, or online. He also starred in *Devil of a Job*, a reality TV series about his work. The number one spiritual enemy that Mercy encountered was Jezebel, the evil spirit responsible for lust, sexual addiction, and pornography. He made it his personal mission to save people working in the sex industry.

"God's desire is that we stay pure and use our bodies as tools for His use and glory," he said.

He started XXX Ministries, a Christian outreach program based in Las Vegas, to give sex workers the opportunity to receive salvation and eternal life. Mercy encouraged them to turn away from their sinful lifestyles and turn to God. He taught that Jesus loved them, despite their morally depraved and disgraceful lifestyle. He also founded the Bibles for Bimbos scheme, in which Mercy personally distributed Bibles to sex workers on the streets, and in strip clubs and brothels across the country.

This is how he met his sixth wife, Sue.

Jimmy Lee Mercy went from one scam to the next.

If there was anything miraculous about him it was his ability to reinvent himself.

"In the end, our exposé of Jimmy Lee Mercy was nothing but a temporary setback to his career," said Banachek.

"But you destroyed him at the time!" Claudia cried.

"Only for a little while," he said. "You see, Jimmy Lee was never a faith healer. He was always a con artist. He's very good at being a con artist too, so naturally he was going to go back to it. What else would he do? He wasn't going to turn over a new leaf and suddenly become a firefighter or a volunteer with the Red Cross."

Claudia was so outraged that she had to order a coconut flan for dessert.

"How did Jimmy Lee develop a cult of personality all over again?" she asked. "How did his followers get past his crooked past?"

Banachek poured them both another glass of sangria.

"There's no one answer," he said. "Jimmy Lee fled to a different part of the world where no one knew about his history and he reinvented himself there. By the time he returned to the States many people had forgotten about him and what he did, while the media has a short attention span. The true believers had their fingers in their ears the whole time. They never believed he did anything wrong in the first place. Other people simply forgave him. He's a man of God, they thought. He's trying to redeem himself. Some of his followers were isolated from the story in the first place. They watch *The 700 Club* but not the news or late night talk shows and so they never heard about his downfall. Then Jimmy Lee also acquired a whole new generation of followers who didn't know he had a shady past."

"Surely this story isn't typical," Claudia said. "He just got lucky, right?"

Banachek shook his head.

"Unfortunately, Jimmy Lee Mercy isn't the only one," he said. "Dishonest evangelists, healers, and psychic mediums; all of these charlatans follow a formula. They make their fortunes deceiving their followers. Sooner or later, they're exposed for being frauds. They lay low for a while and then they rise again like phoenix from the ashes. They can't lose. When we knock down their walls they rebuild them. No matter how badly they're exposed, they always bounce back and usually bigger than before. Decades later, Jimmy Lee Mercy is *still* going strong. He's worth more than ever. If anything, his fall helped to boost his career. He once said, "You can't make a comeback without taking a fall"."

Claudia was silent as she thought about all of this for a while.

"Are you warning me that this is what will happen with Gil too?" she asked.

Banachek nodded. "Psychics are predictable."

Claudia could already see signs of this happening, without Gil having to do anything. Had he planned his own fall? That would be just like him. It seemed as though he was going to lay low for a time and make a comeback, just like Jimmy Lee Mercy.

Gil Godsend seemed infallible.

She signed in frustration.

"When will this end?" she asked.

"This *is* an end," said Banachek. "But the moment that something ends, something else begins."

"So, should I just get off the merry-go-round right now? Should I quit while I'm behind?"

"Not at all," he said. "Your work is very important. You've helped many people over the years. You change minds with what you do, but you'll never be able to change *everyone's* mind."

Claudia ordered another coconut flan and Banachek poured them both another glass of sangria.

Chapter 37

Claudia arrived at work, made herself a cup of coffee and sat down in her office to catch up on the news. The story of the day was that popular TV psychic Celeste Stone, Gil's former sugar mama, was facing criminal charges for defrauding the wife of a politician who had come to her seeking spiritual advice. Stone convinced the woman that her husband's affair with his intern was caused by a 200-year-old curse that required an expensive cleansing ritual, and then another one, and then another one. Stone told her victim that harm would come to her and her family if she didn't keep paying up. She bilked the woman of almost a million dollars.

This was the third famous psychic who had been exposed by the media in as many months. Since Claudia busted Gil Godsend it seemed the tables were finally turning on psychics. Maybe Banachek was wrong this time?

When Claudia got home from work that evening she was too tired to cook dinner so she made herself a bowl of Raisin Bran.

"Raisin' the Dead Bran," she said to herself with a laugh, thinking of Jimmy Lee Mercy's line of breakfast cereals. She was about to take a mouthful when her phone rang. It was obviously an overseas number and it looked somewhat familiar, but she couldn't place it. She was going to let the call go to voicemail but her curiosity got the better of her.

"Hello?"

"Hello, Claudia," said a deep voice that sent a bolt of electricity through her body.

It was Gil.

"Well, if it isn't Gil Godsend," she said through a little smile that she tried to hide. "Why are you calling me?"

"Is that any way to greet your former fiancé?" he said with mock surprise. "It's been six months since I last saw you and I've been waiting patiently for your call."

"A real psychic would know that I was *never* going to call."

"Oh, I predicted I was going to receive a call," he said. "I just didn't know it would be from Nurse Nicole thanking me for the bunch of roses."

Claudia chuckled.

"Where are you?" she asked.

"I'm calling from beneath a coconut tree on a beach in Caye Caulker. I'm laying on the sparkling white sand, staring at the emerald waters, and feeling the warmth of the sun on my skin," he teased, knowing that it was the rainy season in the San Francisco Bay Area.

Claudia remembered the phone number Gil wrote on the card with the flowers. She had traced it to Belize.

"So...that's in Belize?" she asked.

Okay, he wasn't in South America like Jimmy Lee Mercy, he was in Central America, but that was close enough.

"It's an island off the coast of Belize in the Caribbean Sea," he said precisely. "It was formerly known as British Honduras until 1973. Belize remained a British colony until September 21, 1981 when it gained independence. Then..."

"...Skip the history lecture," she said with a yawn. "What do you want?"

"I want you to move here to live with me," he said frankly. "But I'll settle for a visit from you."

"A coconut must have fallen on your head," she said with a shake of her head. "I can't visit you. I'm seeing someone."

"Oh, I know all about your boyfriend, Steve Irwin," he said dismissively. "But do *you*? Do you know that he once received a fine for possession of cannabis?"

"Um...No, I didn't. So what? Anyway, *you* can't talk. You had a cocaine addiction!"

"Yes, but I didn't get caught."

"Not getting caught doesn't mean you're not guilty."

"My point is that you don't know Jeremy very well."

"Why, Gil, you sound jealous!"

"Of course I'm jealous," he said matter-of-factly. "But that's not why I'm saying this. I'm worried about you and I want what's best for you. Before Jeremy makes that transfer to his San Francisco office and the two of you move in together, you need to ask yourself, how well do you really know him?"

Things had been blissful for Jeremy and Claudia. Despite his busy schedule, Jeremy visited her at least once a month. They spent most of that time in bed, and she could still see his vivid green eyes staring down into hers. Every day they were apart they held marathon telephone conversations that lasted deep into the night. They laughed and cried as they talked about everything from their childhoods to their hopes for the future. Jeremy was going to transfer to his company's San Francisco office as soon as he could and they were going to move in together. They didn't want to wait any longer; they wanted to start a family immediately. She was given the go ahead from her doctor and so she ditched her birth control.

They were in love.

Then things turned strangely quiet. Jeremy's calls became less frequent and then his visits stopped altogether. She barely heard from him at all nowadays, except for a few short emails and the occasional voicemail message. She knew that he was in Zurich. He had been working there for the past two months. That is, if he hadn't already dashed off somewhere else. His former fiancé had split with him because of his constant travel for work. Claudia feared she would break up with him for this reason too. Was the silent treatment his chickenshit way of breaking it off with her? Why had Jeremy cooled off so suddenly? He might just be busy, although the thought that he was seeing another woman had crossed her mind. Maybe Gil was right. How well did she really know Jeremy? Perhaps it was only a vacation romance after all and she was waiting for something that was never going to happen.

She felt like her life was on hold.

"Don't put your life on hold any longer," said Gil.

She still hated it when he got into her head.

"Come and see me," he said. "I can have you on the beach here with me within hours."

Claudia looked out the window at the gloomy grey skies and endless rain. She imagined herself wearing a bikini and sipping on a cocktail as she lay on the sand soaking up the sun without a care in the world, except for the fact that Gil would be there too.

Wait... how did Gil know that Jeremy was planning to move to San Francisco to live with her? How did Gil know her boyfriend's name was Jeremy?

How did he do that?

Gil was obviously trying to plant a seed of doubt in her mind about Jeremy, but the doubt was already there. She had to admit, she wasn't sure how well she really knew Jeremy, but how well did she really know Gil anymore? He was a different person nowadays. The man she was once engaged to was sensitive, kind, honest, and loyal. She would have stayed with him, if only he'd been a firefighter or a teacher instead of a psychic medium. The man she found years later was egotistical, unscrupulous, greedy, and manipulative. He was a womanizer who took advantage of Kate, Abby, Rainbow, and Dawn, and probably countless other women over the years. He was a charlatan who preyed on vulnerable people who desperately wanted to make contact with their dead loved ones. He led a risk-filled, thrill-seeking, hedonistic lifestyle. He was a far cry from the nice young man she once knew.

Who was the real Gil Godsend?

Then there were moments when Claudia caught glimpses of the old Gil. He was still quick-witted and intelligent, even if he was a walking, talking encyclopedia sometimes. She had never bantered with anyone the way she did with Gil. It had always been a weird kind of foreplay for them. He was charming and charismatic, and she couldn't deny that he was handsome. He made her feel angry and gave her butterflies in her stomach at the same time. She remembered the way he used to gaze at her with his piercing blue eyes, as if there was no other woman in the world. He looked at her that way still.

She also couldn't forget that Gil had told her she was pregnant and then warned her when her life was in danger. If she'd continued thinking her ectopic pregnancy was a stomach bug she could sleep off, she could have died. She didn't know how he did it, but he saved her life.

For some time she had felt as though something was missing in her life.

Was that Gil?

"When you broke up with me all those years ago I was devastated," he admitted, the pain in his voice still sounding fresh. "I tried to distract myself with other women, and with drugs, possessions, and power. I felt empty. I became bitter and hardened. It took years, but I thought I was finally over you… Then I saw you again…" he said, the flatness lifting from his voice. "In that moment, it felt like my heart started beating again."

Claudia remembered her heart skipping a beat when she saw him.

"I haven't been able to stop thinking about you ever since," he said. "Claudia, you're the *only* woman who's ever challenged me. I've met my match in you." He paused. "For many years I've felt like something was missing in my life. That something turned out to be someone, and that someone is you. It's always been you."

Gil's voice was deep and low, clear and confident, smooth and sexy. It was hypnotic. His voice reminded Claudia of *The Hypnotist*, a poem by Leonard Cohen that she read back in high school.

I heard of a man
Who says words so beautifully
That if he only speaks their name
Women give themselves to him.
If I am dumb beside your body
While silence blossoms like tumors on our lips
It is because I hear a man climb stairs
And clear his throat outside the door.

When Claudia met Gil she realized that *he* was that man.

Gil Godsend was the hypnotist.

"Claudia," said the man who says words so beautifully that if he only speaks their name women give themselves to him. "Come and see me."

Her resolve was weakening.

"I haven't been with another woman since I saw you again," he said. "You're the only woman I ever want in my bed."

Maybe he was a bad boy who would be a nice guy… for her.

"We need to talk about everything," he added.

She closed her eyes. She breathed in deeply and breathed out slowly. Who was she kidding? Despite her better judgment, despite everything that had happened, she still had unresolved feelings for him.

Claudia was always fascinated by people's blind spots. These gaps in people's logic allowed them to think rationally about some things, but to ignore their irrational thinking about other things that served their own biases. It's hard to look inwardly and see your own prejudices. One of her best friends believed in ghosts but thought the idea of Bigfoot was stupid. Her uncle used to think that acupuncture was hogwash, but he made his own colloidal silver. That is, he did until he developed a condition called argyria from drinking the stuff and his skin turned as blue as a Smurf.

Yet here was Claudia, a "professional skeptic" who was drawn to the world's most famous psychic. She had feelings for the man she had tried to ruin for years. This was a man whose whole belief system was completely at odds with hers. Gil was her blind spot. She was no smarter or better than anyone else. She was biased. She was a hypocrite. She was human.

She realized that people only think rationally with their minds, but not with their hearts.

Gil wasn't the nice young man she once knew; although Claudia wasn't the young girl he once knew either. They had changed in the years that had passed. Gil's fans worshipped him, and their unwavering adoration had warped his thinking. Claudia thought that she was skeptical, but she had grown closed-minded, cynical, and jaded over the years. They came from different sides of the fence but they saw themselves as infallible. Yet neither of them was perfect. Both of them had baggage. But perhaps they could leave the past behind and start afresh, especially if he gave up being a psychic.

"Why do you want to see me?" she asked. "I ruined your life."

"No, you didn't," he said gently. "You *saved* my life. It's been good to lie low and get away from everything for a while. I needed a break from the voices. It's very laid back here and I wanted to take some time out to relax, do nothing, and… I don't know…grow a beard."

Gil was lying low and growing a beard? That was *just* like Jimmy Lee Mercy! Next he was going to wear a white linen suit and change his name to Gil of God…

"Are you going to establish a spiritual healing sanctuary and father four children to different women too?" she asked.

He laughed.

"If that's what it'll take for you to be with me," he joked. "Although there's only one woman I want to have children with."

Claudia was glad that Gil couldn't see her biting her lip.

"We're meant to be together," he said. "Remember I once told you that we were married in a previous life? Remember I told you that Aunt Tillie said you were crucial to my success and happiness?"

"Do you *really* believe that crazy shit?" she asked him.

"Claudia, I don't believe it. I *know* it."

That's kinda nuts, she thought.

Hmm…he said that he needed a break from the voices…

"So, are you still getting those headaches?" she asked him.

"…Yes, but everybody gets headaches," he said, shrugging it off.

"Did you ever see a doctor like I asked you to?"

"Yes, and I was supposed to have some tests, but I never got around to it."

Maybe he was sick and whatever was wrong with him was the cause of his behavioral changes. What kind of person would she be if she didn't try to help him?

"I'll visit if you promise to see a doctor again," she heard herself say.

"Done," he said. "I hear there's a wonderful healer in Brazil by the name of James of God."

Claudia gasped. Banachek was right all along! Gil was laying low for a while after his fall until he could reinvent himself overseas and eventually make a comeback in the United States because he missed television soaps and cheese in a can.

"You motherfucker!" she cried. "I can't believe I was almost taken in by you. I know exactly what your game is… Well, you can have your gullible fans and slutty groupies. You can have your misguided fame and fortune. You can have your comeback where you push miracle spring water and religious breakfast cereals and then rise from the ashes to become even bigger than before!"

Gil paused.

"I was only joking along with you," he said calmly, puzzled by her outburst. "You're the one who mentioned Jimmy Lee Mercy."

She tried to calm down.

"But it looks like you're planning to do what he did."

"I'm not," he said firmly. "I don't want any of that bullshit anymore…Claudia…I just want *you*."

She wanted to hang up on him, but she wanted to stay on the phone with him forever. She never wanted to see him ever again, but she wanted to be wrapped up in his arms. Why did Gil have to come back into her life? She was elated that Gil was back in her life. What was going on inside of her head? She felt so confused and conflicted.

"Come and see me," Gil repeated.

Things were clearly over between her and Jeremy, she thought.

"I'll explain everything to you," Gil promised.

She wondered what it would feel like to kiss Gil with his beard.

"I need you in my life," he said in his hypnotic voice.

Of course, if she visited Gil she would probably end up in bed with him.

"Think about it and I'll call you again tomorrow night," he said.

Should she run in the other direction, or should she run with the devil?

"Okay," she said.

Okay she would think about it, or okay she would go?

"Goodnight, Gil."

"Goodnight, Claudia…and… I love you…"

She hung up the phone. Her cereal was too soggy to eat so she poured herself a glass of chardonnay and flopped down on the couch. She looked outside and it was still raining hard. In her mind she found herself packing a bag with a bikini, a pair of sunglasses, a bottle of sunscreen, and little else.

As she sat on the couch she spied the trashcan. She thought about the amethyst pendant sitting in there, waiting to be thrown out for good. She fished it out, rolled it around between her fingers and held it up to the light. She peered into it to make sure there wasn't anything inside. There wasn't, and that technology wasn't around in those days anyway. Why did Gil copy this design for the amethyst pendants in his line of jewelry? Was it some weird kind of tribute to her? She had friends who ceremoniously burned letters from their ex-boyfriends and destroyed their old gifts that only reminded them of love gone wrong. Why did she keep Gil's pendant all these years? Why didn't she throw it away? She had to admit to herself that it still meant something to her.

What should she do?

To go and see Gil would be a mistake.

What would people think?

She didn't know if it was the wine talking, but suddenly she didn't care any longer. To hell with everyone else. There was still something between her and Gil and she needed to explore it. She wanted to make some magic in her life again.

"Fuck it. I'll go."

At that moment Claudia heard her phone ping. Someone had called a while ago and left her a voicemail message.

It was Jeremy.

"Hi, sweetheart," he said, sounding tired but happy. "I'm so sorry I've been out of touch. I've been flat out like a lizard drinking, as my old grandfather would say. In Aussie slang that means I've been *really* busy. They've had me working 12-hour days on this project for weeks on end. To make matters worse, the time difference between San Francisco and Zurich is brutal. When you're awake I'm asleep and when I'm awake you're asleep. The times I've called I've missed you. Hell, I've just missed you, sweetheart, but I have fantastic news for you… for *us*. I finally got that transfer to our San Francisco office that I've been begging for… starting immediately! I've packed my bags and they're putting me on the next flight out to the Bay Area. I'll have you in my arms again very soon. I can't wait to begin my life with you… G'night, Claudia…and… I love you…"

Chapter 38

In his dressing room, Gil stood in front of the mirror wearing only a pair of blue boxer shorts that were embroidered with his initials. His carefully selected outfit lay folded across a chair and his shoes sat on the floor. He held a crystal flute of champagne, which he drank and then smashed into the fireplace. Mozart's Requiem in D minor played softly in the background and he waved his hands in the air as though he was conducting the orchestra. A candle burned in the middle of the room, releasing the faint scent of sandalwood into the air.

Gil was ritualistic about dressing before an important event.

"I don't know why you spend so much money having your underwear monogrammed when your mother could just write your name on them instead," said a voice in the background.

Gil shook his head.

"I'm *so* thrilled to have you back in my life," he replied.

He put on an ash grey-colored French-cuff shirt and a burgundy silk tie, both by Charvet, the tailoring family that had once dressed Napoleon Bonaparte. Gil wrapped a platinum Blancpain watch around his wrist and fastened the clasp. Then he opened a tiny red velvet box and took out a pair of white gold diamond cufflinks, which he inserted through the cuffs of his shirt.

"Nice cufflinks."

"Thank you. They're antique Cartier cufflinks that I bought from auction at Christies," Gil said proudly. "They once belonged to Sir Winston Churchill."

"I see…they're second-hand. You spent too much money getting your underwear monogrammed to be able to afford a new pair. You know, you can get cufflinks from the thrift store if you're hard up for cash…"

"Oh, so *that's* where you found those shoes!"

It was a special occasion, so Gil wore his favorite bespoke suit made by Ferdinando Caraceni of Milan, a tailor so famous that Yves Saint

Laurent used to have his suits made by them. Gil flew to Italy six times to be fitted for the charcoal grey suit, which was hand cut and sewn to his personal requirements. He slid on a braided Brunello Cucinelli belt, slipped on a pair of grey cashmere argyle socks and his burgundy Berluti Oxford shoes. Then he spritzed his neck with Chanel's Égoïste, his new signature scent. He didn't wear fragrances with musk anymore.

He was ready.

"You look like a gentleman in that stylish suit."

"Thank you," replied Gil, who was slightly shocked by the genuine compliment among all of the sarcastic barbs.

"Now all you need is a top hat, mutton chops, a handlebar mustache, and an ear trumpet."

Gil raised his eyebrow as he fixed his tie in front of the mirror.

"I can have you removed by security in seven seconds flat," he said.

A laugh echoed around the room.

The Reverend Doctor Jimmy Lee Mercy appeared behind Gil in the mirror.

He placed his hand firmly on Gil's shoulder.

"I'm only joking," he said with a hint of a southern accent. "I'm proud of you, son."

Gil smiled.

"Thanks dad."

When they stood next to each other the family resemblance between Jimmy Lee and Gil was striking. They were both tall with the same muscular build and strong jawline, piercing blue eyes, and luxuriant hair. Jimmy Lee's hair was now salt and pepper and Gil's chestnut brown locks were flecked with grey although both men were still as handsome and charismatic as ever.

They left the dressing room and walked side-by-side down the hall to the backstage area where they could hear the enthusiastic crowd cheering for Gil. Jimmy Lee peeked out through the stage curtain. His eyes widened.

"Look at that huge audience out there!" he said in awe. "Are you nervous?"

"No," replied Gil without hesitation. "I belong on the stage."

"Like father, like son," Jimmy Lee nodded approvingly. "What an extraordinary resurrection you're about to make. It reminds me of the return I made after that disaster with Banachek. That sonofabitch didn't even know he was doing me a favor. As I told you, you can't make a comeback without taking a fall."

"This is just as I predicted," Gil said with a grin.

The theater was packed full of people who were buzzing with anticipation.

Gil's fans hadn't forgotten him.

All of a sudden the lights went out in the auditorium. The excitement in the room increased. After a few moments the room quieted down enough that the audience could hear a piano gently playing a ballad. They grew quieter as they listened. After a few minutes the music stopped dead and the audience became excited again, but still nothing happened. There was an uncomfortable silence as people looked around the room wondering if Gil would emerge at all. Suddenly, a small blue spotlight appeared on stage. The spotlight swelled gradually until Gil could be seen standing there with his head bowed. He raised his head slowly and looked up into the audience.

"Good evening, ladies and gentlemen… I'm Gil Godsend…"

The crowd went wild. Some people ran up to the stage while others burst into tears.

"It's good to see you all again…" he said with outstretched arms.

Claudia shook her head and sighed as she sat watching everything from a box seat.

She hated attending these shows. She disliked his rabid fans with their unquestioning commitment to Gil and their creepy swarm behavior. She'd heard that the police had to protect Gil from his adoring crowd when he arrived at the theater that night. She also loathed the groupies who dressed like they were going to a nightclub in their hope that they would get to meet their idol. The smell of sandalwood in the air always made her sneeze and she couldn't believe that some people were still wearing their amethyst crystal pendants. Some things never change.

She was amazed that Gil could sell out these arenas as easily as a motivational speaker as he could when he was a psychic medium.

Claudia was feeling curious. Gil surprised her that night by revealing that his father would be attending the show and that she would finally get to meet him for the first time at dinner afterwards. She had a surprise for Gil too. Banachek was in town and would be joining them for dinner too.

Claudia felt embarrassed when she told Banachek that she and Gil were back together again, but as always, he was understanding and supportive.

"We can't chose who we fall in love with," he said.

Claudia hoped Gil had taken his medication that day and that he'd be on his best behavior at the restaurant. She dressed nicely for the occasion because she wanted to make a good first impression. She had met his mother Sue on a few occasions and she liked the woman, but Gil had always been evasive about his father. All Claudia knew was that he was a doctor of some kind. Apparently he'd been working overseas for the past few years and Gil hadn't seen him for a long time. Gil seemed uncharacteristically nervous about the meeting between Claudia and his father. In fact, she'd never seen him so anxious before.

Anyone would think his father was Adolf Hitler, or Jimmy Lee Mercy, she thought to herself.

Claudia shifted uncomfortably in her seat. These chairs weren't designed for pregnant women. As she squirmed about she could feel her baby moving too. It felt like butterflies fluttering in her belly.

"Hello, little one," she said softly as she rubbed her growing stomach.

Gil predicted she was having a boy, a fact that was confirmed by the sonographer during an ultrasound, but Claudia thought it was just a good guess because Gil had a 50% chance of being right. After much disagreement they finally decided on the name Aiden. This was Claudia's choice because Gil wanted to go with the considerably more conservative James. In a fair compromise they agreed that James would be the boy's middle name, just like it was Gil's.

To this day, Gil still said things that made her wonder if he really was psychic. But there must be some things that Gil couldn't predict. Like, what kind of man would her baby become? What would he believe in and what would he stand for? She hoped he would become a firefighter, a teacher, or something else honorable, but that he wouldn't become a psychic medium. She imagined that her son would be intelligent, just like his father. He would be tall and handsome, just like his father. And there *was* one thing that Gil hadn't seemed to predict…that her baby's eyes might be vivid green instead of a piercing blue…

About the Author

Karen Stollznow is the author of *God Bless America, Language Myths, Mysteries and Magic,* and *Haunting America.* A co-host of the popular Monster Talk podcast, she has spent many years investigating psychics, ghosts, Bigfoot and other anomalous claims. A Doctor of Linguistics, she has taught at several universities in the United States and Australia, and was a Researcher at the University of California, Berkeley. Karen was born in Sydney, Australia, and she currently lives in Denver, Colorado, with her husband Matthew and their son Blade.

www.karenstollznow.com

Made in the USA
San Bernardino, CA
06 December 2016